WICKED LITTLE Secrets

SUSANNA IVES

sourcebooks
casablanca

MAR 2014

Published by Sourcebooks Casablanca, an imprint of Sourcebooks,
Inc.
P.O. Box 4410, Naperville, Illinois 60567-4410
(630) 961-3900
Fax: (630) 961-2168
www.sourcebooks.com

Printed and bound in the United States of America.
VP 10 9 8 7 6 5 4 3 2 1

To my husband

One

VIVIENNE TAYLOR REPRESSED A MISCHIEVOUS SMILE AS she gazed at the female members of the Wesley Congregational. The way the ladies sat in three neat rows, with their earnest faces poking out from their morning caps, resembled a gardening bed of black and white lacy flowers. They gathered for the weekly Bible lessons held in the parlor of Gertrude Bertis's home on Wickerly Square.

Aunt Gertrude banged her cane on the floor, signaling the beginning of the lessons and scaring Garth, her pug dog, who had been snoozing at her feet. "Sisters, today we shall have a special reading in celebration." Her mouth hiked slightly around the edges… the closest she came to smiling. For though she had a plump, flushed face—the kind made for grins and laughter—she kept her mouth and brow in tense, severe lines, making her appear decades older than her forty-one years. She wore her hair in a snug bun, but a few rebellious strands of silver and brown escaped and curled about her face. Her corset was laced tight, constraining her expansive, round form into rigid feminine contours. Yet when she gazed at her niece, a tender glow melted all the hardness in her eyes.

"My little Vivvie is engaged." Aunt Gertrude reached over and patted the top of Vivienne's hand. A wave of warmth flowed through Vivienne's body.

The ladies cooed *"How lovely,"* and *"Won't you be a beautiful bride?"*—not the sort of disapproving words Vivienne had heard most of her twenty-two years, words such as *"Proper young ladies do not bring up the marriage customs of the ancient Spartans at dinner parties,"* and *"Proper young ladies do not ask the circulating library for books by the Marquis de Sade,"* and the one that embarrassed her father the most, *"Proper young ladies are not asked to leave the ladies' seminary."*

Vivienne had done something right, even if for the first time in her life, as her sisters Hannah and Fiona had claimed. Just when her family was a few pounds from debtor's prison, Vivienne managed to catch John Vandergrift, the son of the manager for South Birmingham Railroad. With a flourish of his pen, the elder Mr. Vandergrift could fill her father's machinery factory with orders.

"Vivvie has come up from Birmingham to be near her fiancé," her aunt continued. "I met him just yesterday, such a fine, considerate young man. I know Mr. Bertis would have approved." She turned her head and gazed up at the portrait of the honorable Judge Jeremiah Bertis, posed in his court robes and wavy wig. He held his jutting, Romanesque nose high, as his heavy-lidded, dark eyes looked disapprovingly on everything below him.

"Mr. Vandergrift is wonderful, isn't he?" Vivienne gushed. "I have to continually pinch myself. I can't believe that he proposed."

"Well, it's little wonder," said Mrs. Lacey in her honey-sweet voice. She resembled an elf with her small stature, frizzy white hair, and bright smile. "You're ravishing with those green eyes and black curls. And your breasts are so ample. You know how gentlemen just love breasts."

"Breasts!" Aunt Gertrude cried. "Mrs. Lacey, pray restrain yourself!" She squeezed the bulbous head of her cane as she fumbled about the medicine bottles on the side table, finding a blue square one that Vivienne recognized to be *Dr. Philpot's Wonderful Nerve Tonic for Ailing and Suffering Ladies. Soothing Menses, Hysteria, and Other Female Complaints*. She popped the cork, took a discreet swig, and then sniffed, dabbing the edge of her mouth. "A lady's virtue is far more desirous than her physical beauty. There is many a lady suffering in the flames of hell for her vanity." She let her words fall as heavily as the sentences her husband handed down to the poor women brought before the London courts. "Now, for your own benefit and Vivienne's, you shall read from Proverbs, Chapter 31, verses 10–31."

"I just need to get my spectacles." Mrs. Lacey reached for her reticule, still smiling despite the warning of her soul's incineration in hell. She rooted through her personal effects, handing her neighbor various embroidered linens, perfume bottles, and a dried, crumpled flower to hold. "Isn't that the prettiest little chrysanthemum? I hope that gentleman didn't mind when I plucked it from his coat. Ah, here are my spectacles. Now, what was I supposed to read?"

"Proverbs, Chapter 31, verse 10. Proverbs is after Psalms." Vivienne rose, took the lady's Bible, turned it upright, and flipped to the correct page. "It was written by King Solomon. He was forever writing proverbs and songs, you know. He had over five hundred wives."

"Good heavens," Mrs. Lacey exclaimed, taking the Bible. "How many times a day do you think he—"

Aunt Gertrude cleared her throat. "The verse, if you will."

Mrs. Lacey held the Bible to the tip of her nose and squinted behind her spectacles. "'Who can find a virtuous woman? For her price is far above boobies.'"

"It does not say 'boobies'!" her aunt barked. "'Her price is far above rubies.' Rubies!"

"I just love rubies," Mrs. Lacey exclaimed. "I am always telling Mr. Lacey that—"

Aunt Gertrude banged her cane. "Please refrain from any personal digression."

Thirty minutes later, Mrs. Lacey had progressed exactly six verses. Garth, now asleep again, made little snorts at his owner's feet. Vivienne tried not to fidget. She forced herself to sit up straight even though her back ached from the hard chair. Could the future wife of John Vandergrift excuse herself to the privy and escape? Would that be the action of a Biblically virtuous wife? As Vivienne contemplated the moral dilemma, she noticed, through the window, the wild, untamed gray hair and spry body of her aunt's neighbor, the Earl of Baswiche. He stood in her aunt's tiny box garden, wearing only a beige banyan that reached to the calves of his bare legs. His eyes sparkled with a devious light.

"Pardon me," Vivienne interrupted, "but Lord Baswiche is in the garden."

"What?" Her aunt whipped her head around to the window.

The earl's mouth cracked into a wide grin. "Hello, ladies!"

He spread his arms and his banyan opened. Between his slightly bowed legs, his male parts dangled like meat strung in a butcher's window.

Vivienne put her hand to her mouth to hide her giggles.

Mrs. Lacey gasped. "What a big—"

"Get out of my garden, you dirty sinner!" Aunt Gertrude shot up, almost stumbling over Garth, as she yanked the curtains over the window. "Miss Banks!" she shouted for the housekeeper. "Go next door and tell that wicked Lord Dashiell that his grandfather is in my garden again."

Lord Dashiell was home! Vivienne's blood surged with excitement.

"My poor nerves." Her aunt beat her palm against her bosom. "I feel an attack coming on." She grabbed *Dr. Philpot's* and gulped down the contents. "Where is Banks? Banks!" she cried, violently shaking the bottle, trying to get out one last drop.

"She is down in the kitchen getting the cakes ready," Vivienne said. "I'll tell Lord Dashiell." She started for the door.

Aunt Gertrude's eyes widened. "Don't you dare go to that house of ill repute next door—a shameful Babylon. What would your father think of me for allowing you to be corrupted? Now let us sit down." She eased back in her chair, and her nostrils flared with her rapid breath. She gripped her cane, running her fingers up and down the shaft. "Mrs. Lacey, read the next verse," she said in a controlled calm. "You were saying, 'She girdeth her loins with strength.'"

"I'll just tell his butler," Vivienne assured her. "I won't be a minute. How could I possibly get corrupted in that short a time?" She scooted off before she could be stopped. She hadn't seen Lord Dashiell since he left for Rome over a year ago and, who knew, he might be heading to Russia the next day. Typically, he stayed in London long enough to land into a scandal and then he was off again.

Outside, she scanned Wickerly Square, adjusting her eyes to the light. Built a few decades after the Great Fire, the houses were not nearly as fashionable as those in Cavendish and Grosvenor Square to the west. Dull stacks of gray stone with dark windows edged the square—the homes of middling families. Dashiell's domicile stood at the corner and towered over its neighbors, giving the square a lopsided appearance, as if his were the manor house and all the other homes mere tenant outbuildings. In the center of the square, protected by a block iron fence, was a grass-covered park. In each corner grew spreading oak trees with low branches, perfect for a young girl to climb.

One afternoon, a little over ten years before, she

had been daydreaming in the tree growing nearest Lord Dashiell's home when she first spied on the famed scoundrel. She had been sent outside after inventing a fantastic game she called "Keep Out of the Ocean," which required shoving all the parlor furniture together and pretending it was a cluster of islands in the South Seas. Then she leaped from chair to table to harpsichord without falling into the ocean and being devoured by hungry sharks while singing at the top of her lungs. Her uncle had thundered out of his library, his face creased with rage. "Bad seed!" he boomed. He never called her by her name or *my little Vivvie* like her aunt, just *bad seed*. "Why are you intent on destroying my home? Do you know what happens to little girls who don't respect other people's property?"

"You put them in the gaol?" she ventured.

"Precisely," he answered. "And wipe that insolence from your face when you speak to me. Mark my words, you are rotten in the soul and will come to ruin."

So she had been sent to the square with a copy of *Institutes of the Laws of England* to learn the legal process by which wicked little girls came to ruin. She had scampered up the tree and set the book on a high branch in hopes a bird might drop on it. There, hidden in the thick foliage, she felt safe. With the exception of Aunt Gertrude, every adult in her life just scolded her. Now that his wife had died, her father was forever losing his patience with Vivienne, who was as excitable as her sisters were calm. Every few months, she drove the poor man to such distractions that he would claim that he couldn't do anything else with her and would send her to Uncle Jeremiah's so she could "learn how to behave herself."

The way she saw the situation, she would just continue to let down her father and uncle, and there was only one sensible solution to the problem: to stow away on a boat to Egypt and raid tombs. She was thinking of the specifics of her plan, which included dressing like a boy, eating hard tack, perhaps even bugs, when she heard a rich, resonant male voice say, "What a fine climbing tree you have."

She had gazed down through the leaves at Lord Dashiell and gasped. He could have stepped straight out of her imagination, filled as it was with blood-thirsty pirates, fierce Mongols, and courageous Templar knights. He was about twenty-one years old then. His dark hair flowed loose over his collar in disheveled curls, and his bronze skin was so tanned that he could have been Marco Polo himself. With his high cheek-bones, strong chin, and blue shadows under his eyes, he appeared quite Gothic, like the heroes in those books her older sister was always reading. Though the ironic twist to his full lips and sparkle in his chocolate-colored eyes belied any dark, stormy thoughts of the Gothic variety.

"I'm Dashiell," he had said, in a kindly voice meant for children, as he pointed to his home. "I just moved there. Our home in Berkeley Square burned down."

"Oh, I've heard of you," she said. "My uncle told my aunt that you're a heathen, whoremonger, and adven-turer, and that we're not supposed to talk to you." But looking at this striking species of heathen, her uncle's orders flew from her head. "What's a whoremonger?"

He blinked and his smile tightened from easy to nervous and he started to edge away. "Er, maybe you should ask your uncle."

"Why do adults always answer my questions by saying I should ask another adult?"

He stopped, tossed his head back, and laughed—a welcoming, musical sound. She turned on the branch until she was hanging by her knees and gazing at him from upside down. "I wish I could be an adventurer. I would go to Egypt."

"Well, I just got back from Egypt."

"Really!" She spun down from the tree and landed with a soft thud on her feet. "Did you dig for a Pharaoh's lost treasure? Have you ever found a mummy?"

He knelt down, putting himself at her level. "I have, but most everything of value had already been stolen. It's extremely difficult to find a fresh grave." He dug into his pocket and drew out what looked to be a pale rock. "I did find this in the Valley of the Kings." He turned the curious rock over. It was sanded flat and carved with tiny pictures.

She squealed. "Is that a real hieroglyph?"

"Made over three thousand years ago. Perhaps during the reign of Ramesses the Great."

"Do you know what it says?" she asked.

"Two pots and a goat, I think."

She scrunched her eyebrows. "No, that can't be right. These things were supposed to be about Pharaohs, Isis, and cobras."

"I'm sorry if I procure boring relics." He would have her believe that he was terribly offended, but the quiver on his lips gave him away. "You might as well take it, as no one will want dull hieroglyphs." He took her by the wrist and dropped the stone into her palm. Then he winked.

Her young heart swelled with love. For the first time in her lonely life, she had met a kindred spirit. Except he got to live out all the adventures she could only dream about.

For the next few weeks, she told her uncle that she still wasn't sure what happened to wayward girls who didn't mend their wild ways, and that she should continue reading his law book to find out. Then she would secretly wait in the tree in hopes that Dashiell would come out with another ancient treasure or another fabulous tale of his journeys. Only later did she realize that she was getting the child's versions of these stories—missing all the exotic details that titillated society such as concubines, mysterious lovers, and duels.

A month after she met her hero, she came outside to find his carriage being loaded down with trunks and him dressed in somber gray wool. Traveling clothes.

"Good-bye, my secret little sister," he told her. "I'm heading to Cypress. I've gotten into too much trouble again."

Tears burst from her eyes. "You can't leave me." Her father had written and said she shouldn't come home for another month. And although she loved her aunt with all her heart, she couldn't bear any more of Uncle Bertis's constant scolding and calling her a bad seed.

Dashiell knelt, withdrew a handkerchief from his coat, and wiped her eyes. "Ah, my little Vivienne, don't cry. All I do is make women cry."

"Take me with you. I'll run away. I can help you dig, and we can explore wonderful places together."

"You know that's impossible," he said gently.

"No, it isn't!" she screamed and stamped her foot.

He sighed and raised her fingers to his lips. For a moment she thought he might kiss them, and she felt a strange, almost scary, quickening of her heart. Instead, he gently nipped at her pinky finger.

"W-what are you doing?"

He flashed a mischievous grin. "Performing the sacred ritual of the cannibalistic Bazulo tribe in Africa."

She wanted to be angry with him, but giggled in spite of herself. "There is no Bazulo tribe in Africa."

"Are you quite sure?"

"No."

"Well then," he chuckled. His features grew grave and he placed his hand over his heart. "When you make the sacred Bazulo vow, you swear that you will always keep the other in your heart and be there should that friend ever need you. So even if I am hundreds of miles away, I promise that I shall always come back to my secret little sister."

Since that time, Dashiell had popped in and out of her life, exciting her imagination and then leaving again. They would never again be as close as they had been that summer. Although her family might attest otherwise, Vivienne had grown up. And Dashiell continued to be, well, Dashiell. The Bazulo vow was forgotten; it was just something silly he made up to comfort a distraught child. She knew she could never run off with him, being a heathen, whoremonger, and adventurer, and perhaps that was why he still filled her imagination like a bad-behaving, handsome Dionysus—an untouchable Greek god. Of course, her aunt never learned about her niece's secret kinship with the notorious rake, else she might have an apoplexy, and if her father found out, he would truly disown her once and for all.

She knocked on Dashiell's white front door, quite an unassuming entrance for the so-called Babylon. Rivers, the earl's reed-thin, graying butler, answered and looked down at her with weary eyes, like an old man who had seen too much. Behind him was a museum of antiquity and curiosities. Japanese warrior masks, Viking helmets, and various armor from around the globe ran up the stairwell. In the hall stood an upright wooden Egyptian coffin painted with an image of the poor bloke once entombed within it.

"You lying, cruel-hearted scoundrel!" a woman screamed out from an opened door on the first-floor balcony. "You can go back to hell and crawl up the Devil's arse where you belong!"

Vivienne's veins pulsed with excitement. *Oh no, what has Dashiell done now?*

The butler didn't react, his face as blank as ever, as if this were just another ordinary day in the Earl of Baswiche's household.

"Good morning, Mr. Rivers." She smiled, pretending not to hear the violent stream of curses ringing out in the high ceiling. "It's been several months since I've last seen you, but I must say, you look to be in good health."

"Thank you, Miss," he answered in a deep monotone. "I'm afraid Lord Dashiell is engaged at the moment."

"Why the hell did I come back for this?" Dashiell muttered between gritted teeth. He had been in England only a few weeks and already he was embroiled in an ugly romantic entanglement—one that might have flustered a more proper gentleman. However, after having survived being kidnapped, ransomed, robbed, drugged, and held at the point of knives, guns, and other weaponry in stinking bum holes around the globe, two cracked women on the verge of killing him or each other was just an annoyance.

"I think we all need to calm down." He held up the palm of one hand and gripped his falling trousers with the other.

"Mad lady need to calm down," spat his lovely French ballerina, pointing an ornate medieval executioner's sword at the other woman's creamy throat. Her lithe dancer's body was clad in Dashiell's coat, which she had snatched off the floor when Mrs. Lily Harmon rushed into his chamber—an angry flurry of gold silk and red hair—and interrupted their lovemaking.

Dashiell wasn't concerned with Lily's threatened throat, but the bust of his precious gray-eyed goddess Athena that Lily held over her head. "Lily, take several deep breaths and think about what you are doing. Three thousand years ago, some craftsman put his soul into creating that Athena. The soil of Greece has preserved her all this time. Her history is far greater than this tiny misunderstanding."

"How philosophical of you," Lily said, a wicked grin spreading over her mouth, and she dropped Athena, letting the goddess of wisdom shatter on the floor.

Dashiell emitted a gut-wrenching groan akin to the cry of a wounded wolf. "What the hell is wrong with you?"

"Oh, I'll tell you what is *wrong* with me!" Lily screamed. "I waited for you all night. And the whole time, you were with… with… that dancing whore!"

"You ugly dog woman!" The ballerina threw the sword. The blade made a limp arc in the air, missing Mrs. Harmon entirely and slamming into the Roman frieze of Minerva that Dashiell had dug up in Bath. Crumbling stone showered the floor.

"Everyone just stop!" Dashiell thundered, holding up his hands, causing his trousers to fall. "Dammit!" He quickly snatched them up again.

"You assured me your husband was in Manchester with his mistress," he told Mrs. Harmon, fumbling with the buttons on his trousers. "So I showed up at your house last night like you asked. And do you know who greeted me? Your ten-year-old son."

"No, he wouldn't." Fear and uncertainty began to shade Mrs. Harmon's eyes.

"He thought I was Sir Harry and then asked if you were going to leave his papa and run away with me."

And it was at that moment—having to reassure a weeping son that his papa and mama would love him no matter what might happen—that what Lily had promised him would only be a "fun" flirtation turned sour. He had fled her house, running down Drury Lane, feeling as if his skin was on fire. He dove into a theater and disappeared into the crowd on the ground floor. As the ballerinas whirled on the stage in flowing white skirts, he got lost in remembrances of his parents' famed dalliances, and then his own sordid affairs with women. From there, he continued to emotionally spiral downward, which explained the beautiful French ballerina in his bed.

"You're lying." Mrs. Harmon shook her head, her curls flapping about her cheeks. "My son knows nothing about you. About anyone."

"I think you would be shocked to learn what a child knows about his parents' infidelities." Dashiell took a deep breath, bracing himself for the impending violence. "You said it would be an uncomplicated affair. No emotions involved. But I think you were wrong, and we shouldn't continue this… whatever *this* is."

She was silent for a beat, the shock setting in. Then hurt and rage contorted her face. "You hateful duddering rake!" She snatched up a vase and scurried out the door.

"Bloody hell!" He chased after her. "That's a canopic jar with Pharaoh Cheops's liver in it. I paid twenty camels for that!"

Lily gave a bark of hysterical laughter and tossed the relic over the banister as she rushed down the stairs. Shattering pottery rang in the air.

"Noooo!" screamed a new female voice.

Dear God, not another one! Priesthood in some remote monastery in the Swiss Alps seemed very appealing at the moment. He jolted to a halt on the top stair.

Vivienne Taylor stood by the door, cradling a clay tablet in her arms like a jealous mama. Her shiny black hair had grown longer since last he had seen her and curled in tame spirals by her cheeks. Her high cheekbones were flushed a beautiful pink and her eyes glittered like pale emeralds in firelight. His heart felt like it dove out of his skin. He kept forgetting she wasn't a roly-poly, mischievous, innocent girl any more, but this ravishing, mischievous, innocent lady.

"Not this one," Vivienne told Mrs. Harmon, clutching the tablet to her breasts. "It's Persian and very, very old. Why don't you throw something else, like that frie—" She stopped mid-word. He saw her eyes light on his naked torso and a dark erotic wave of heat rushed over his skin.

Dammit, she's your little sister. Get a hold of yourself.

He snatched a black and white spotted Zulu shield from the stairwell and covered himself. "I… I didn't know you were coming." He tried to sound casual.

Meanwhile, Lily had seized a porcelain clock from the Chinese writing desk and hurled it at his temple. He raised his shield, and the timepiece bounced off cowhide and smashed on the railing, raining tiny metal parts onto the floor.

"I hope one day someone breaks your heart into as many pieces," the lady spat.

"No one will be able to break my heart if you kill me first," he pointed out. "I'm terribly sorry, Miss Taylor, but would you mind returning at another time? I'm being murdered at the present."

"Let her stay," he heard his little French dancer say. "Be good lesson for her." She stood at the top of the balcony, his coat barely covering her female regions.

He peeked at Vivienne. What must she be thinking?

Vivienne's bright gaze darted from him, to the ballerina, to Lily, and she burst out in laughter.

"Do you find watching someone have their heart broken amusing?" Lily cried, approaching Vivienne with a rather deadly swagger in her hips, ready to unleash her fury.

"Lily, leave her alone." Dashiell leaped over the stairwell, and his foot landed on a shard of broken glass. "Damnation!" He grabbed his toe and yelped in pain, but no one paid him any attention.

"You are quite an exquisite creature," Lily purred, running her finger down Vivienne's cheek. "I wager you think that your beautiful face will hold some sway on this scoundrel. But let me save you some grief, my love. This rogue cares more about that precious Persian clay tablet in your arms than his own mother. Soon he will destroy your heart and bring tears to your pretty little eyes, just as he did all the countless ladies before you."

Vivienne regarded Lily for a moment. Then she tilted her head and said, "I'm so sorry, but I don't think Lord Dashiell can break my heart. For I am engaged."

"Engaged?" Dashiell echoed sharply.

A lovely, joyous smile graced her lips that made her dimples come out of hiding. His heart dropped like a dead bird from a branch.

"Yes," she gushed.

He had never seen her gush. He didn't like it. He wanted little Vivienne back—the one who idolized him.

"I know, you feel sorry for the poor gentleman, don't you?" she said.

"No. It's just… just…" He swallowed. He always knew he would lose his little sister to another. She deserved to fall in love with someone who would be faithful and bring her a lifetime of happiness. The kind of man Dashiell could never be. But instead of congratulating her, he stood swaying on his bloody feet, clutching his Zulu shield to his heart, bereft, while Lily laughed at him from deep in her throat.

"Best wishes for you and the lucky gentleman," he finally managed.

"Thank you." She swept forward and handed him his treasured Persian tablet. "I came to tell you that your grandfather is in my aunt's garden and insists on disturbing our Bible lessons on being a virtuous wife. Did you know such a wife is expected to rise before dawn, go out to the merchant ships to buy foods from afar, purchase fields, and plant crops? And if that isn't enough, she must also sew tapestries, spin linen, flax, and wool, and then sell them. I think that is a bit excessive. You would wonder what her virtuous husband is doing, wouldn't you?"

The room fell silent as the other ladies stared at Vivienne, baffled. But Dashiell, who always found her odd observations endearing, struggled to keep a straight face.

"Anyway, I should go. My Aunt Gertrude thinks I'll get corrupted here." Vivienne performed an abrupt bob of a curtsy and turned to leave. At the door jamb, she glanced over her shoulder, a devilish spark rallied in her eyes. "Oh, I should mention that your grandfather has no clothes on."

"What?" Dashiell yelled. The precious clay tablet slipped from his grasp. He dropped the shield and caught the relic at the same moment the shield slammed his already injured toe. His howling curse was concealed by the raucous laughter ringing through the hall.

The earl sauntered upon the scene, his robe loose, his percy hanging free.

"You should have seen old Trudie." He cackled. "I thought her eyes were going to pop out of her head. You can tell she ain't seen a man in a long time."

Dashiell slicked his hand down his face and wondered if the morning could get any worse.

❧

Vivienne quickly closed the door, but not before hearing another colorful snatch of Dashiell's profanity. She put her palm over her mouth, trying to stem the flow of laughter that gurgled up. Her nerves still crackled from the sight of Dashiell's bare chest, stripped all the way down his torso. He put to shame all those illustrations of naked men she had found in the medical journals at the library.

"Miss Taylor! What in God's name are you doing coming out of Lord Dashiell's home?"

Vivienne's laughter disappeared with a gasp. John Vandergrift waited by her aunt's front step, holding a package that was tied with large looping pink ribbons. Under his neat mustache, his mouth dropped open in shock and his chiseled features pinched in disapproval. In contrast to Dashiell's tousled appearance—even when completely clothed—John was fastidious in his dress and manner. His sage coat molded to his well-formed shoulders without a single wrinkle. His reddish-blond hair curled neatly below the brim of his high hat. "Come away this instant before anyone sees you!" he hissed.

"Oh God," Vivienne muttered. She had made another stupid mistake, and after she promised her father she wouldn't.

Just three weeks before, two men in coats with the seams straining around their bulging muscles had arrived at their door in Birmingham. Their blank reptilian eyes had raked over the house and then Vivienne and her sisters, twin smirks cutting the corners of their lips.

"Nice place 'ere, wouldn't be thinking this bloke don't have a tanner," one of them had said and then jerked his head toward Vivienne. "Tell you wat, if he don't pay, we kin share this pretty 'un. But he can have them ugly girls with 'im in debtor's prison."

Papa had no choice but to welcome the filthy scoundrels into his library. Outside the door, Vivienne could hear the crash of chairs being toppled over and ugly threats from the men about how they were going to hurt him. After they left, she found him slumped over his desk, his bruised face buried in his hands.

"When you go to the Vandergrifts' party... you remember to give his son some pretty smiles," he had said in a weak voice.

Vivienne went to the party. Her lips hurt from smiling for so long, but a week later, a miracle occurred on the magnitude of burning bushes and parting seas. John proposed. That night, her father made her kneel before him. He clutched her hands in his and the perspiration on his red forehead glistened in the lamplight.

"Vivienne, promise me you'll make him a perfect wife, that you won't cause any more trouble."

She kissed his fingers. "I promise, Papa."

"And for God's sake, don't tell him about our financial troubles. Understand? I just need enough work to make a payment. Then we can get on our feet."

She searched her father's face, crinkled with lines of worry. "H-have I made you proud, Papa?"

His lips twitched. "Yes," he conceded for the first time in her life.

Well, he certainly wouldn't be proud of her at this moment. She rushed down the walk to John. "I can explain. You see, Lord Dashiell's grandfather was in Aunt Gertrude's garden. He had no clo—I mean, he was acting most peculiar. I hurried over and spoke to their butler regarding the matter. Lord Dashiell had guests, so I really didn't converse with him, except to exchange a few words like 'Hello,' 'How are you,' 'What a fascinating mummy tomb.' The usual things." She gave a hollow, false laugh, trying to make a joke of the moment.

John didn't laugh. His eyes were like hot blue flames. "Did he touch you?" He spoke in the same stern tone her father used when he wasn't pleased with something she had done… which until recently covered all her activities aside from breathing, eating, and sleeping.

"Of course not," she said feebly, even as she remembered touching Dashiell's fingers when she gave him back the Persian tablet and how the feel of his skin sent a current of hot electricity through her body.

"Vivienne, you're going to be the wife of a consequential man. Your behavior reflects on me. You can't just pop harem-scarem into bachelors' homes… and certainly *not* Lord Dashiell's. What were you thinking?"

She couldn't say she was dying to see her old friend whom she had been secretly meeting for the last ten years.

"I-I made a mistake," she said, and latched onto his free arm. "That is all."

He studied her face. "You are a most beautiful creature. Tell me my father isn't right, that I haven't acted rashly by asking for your hand."

Oh, Lord! If John jilted her, well, she wouldn't be able to go home. She couldn't tell her father that she had ruined him. "I said I made a mistake!" she cried. "I-I love you!"

A smile broke across his handsome face. "Say those last words again."

She let out a long breath. "I love you."

He peeked at either side of the street, checking to make sure the square was empty, and then brushed her cheek with his lips, a pleasant tickling sensation that caused her to giggle.

"I brought you something, my pet." He handed her the package.

In their few weeks together, she had learned that he didn't hesitate to lay down large sums at tailors, carriage makers, or wine merchants. "Only buy the finest," he had told her with a sparkle in his eyes, as if his words were a compliment to her. Vivienne's belly squirmed in the knowledge that she had to conceal from him for her family's sake—she wasn't the finest; in fact, she was a desperate bargain.

"You are too good to me," she said. She pulled the pink ribbon loose and the paper unfolded around a beautiful leather volume. *The Ethereal Graces of the*

Delicate Sex: Being a handbook on the proper conduct of young ladies upon entering society and consequentially marriage, by Mrs. Beatrice Smith-Figgle.

"Oh no…" she muttered, before she could stop herself.

John's brows creased.

"I mean, oh yes!" she cried. "Oh yes! What a lovely gift!"

"I thought of you when I saw it." He took the book from her hands and opened it. There were small pieces of paper with his handwriting in the creases. "I've even marked the sections to which you should pay special attention."

She swallowed the sour taste in her throat. "Thank you. I shall endeavor to memorize every word." In truth, she already knew it by heart. Her former headmistress had made her stand before the class and recite long passages from the book after she had sewed hieroglyphs into her sampler and turned in her French assignment in the misshapen Greek that she had tried to teach herself.

"Now, let's go inside. Maybe your aunt will give us a moment alone."

"I should warn you that Aunt Gertrude is conducting her Bible lesson." She gave him a gentle nudge in his ribs. "Those ladies are going to fawn all over you."

A teasing smile played on his lips. "I have no objection to ladies fawning over me."

She gave a soft laugh as she wrapped a proprietary hand around his elbow and led him to her aunt's door. In the corner of her eye, she saw the red-headed woman rush out from Dashiell's house, clutching a yellow and black Greek vase. Blood rushed to her face.

She yanked John inside and slammed the door just as the lady threw the ancient vase on the pavement and screamed, "You lying blackguard!"

Two

After the ladies had sufficiently fawned over John ("What a fine man." "Our Vivienne is indeed lucky." "You know she was tossed from ladies semin—" "Be quiet, Mrs. Lacey!") and the vanilla cakes and fruit jellies were consumed, the ladies dispersed to their homes.

John rose from the sofa, withdrew his pocket watch from his striped waistcoat and checked the time. "I must be off as well," he said, snapping the lid shut. "I have a pressing engagement this afternoon with Mr. Montag." He spoke the man's name in reverent tones, for Mr. Montag was the owner of South Birmingham Railroad and a regular sun god to John. "His family has taken up residence in their Grosvenor Square home."

He headed for the door. Garth leaped from his owner's lap and chased him, barking and spitting. "What the devil," John exclaimed.

Vivienne grabbed Garth by his collar, pulling him free of her fiancé's cuff.

"You naughty, naughty puppy," Aunt Gertrude

cried. "How dare you be so rude to Mr. Vandergrift. Stop immediately."

Vivienne shut the excited hound in the parlor. From the hall, she could hear him snorting about the threshold.

"Dearest, do remember to read the book before you meet Mr. Montag," John said. "I want you to be perfect."

"I will be," Vivienne said and stole a quick peck on his cheek. "For you. I promise."

After seeing John off with another small kiss, Vivienne returned to her aunt in the parlor.

"I'm so happy for you, little Vivvie," her aunt said. "He will take such good care of you. Such a fine man."

Vivienne put her arms around her aunt's neck. "My heart is full from knowing I have brought happiness to you and Papa."

"There now," her aunt said, gently pushing Vivienne away, always uncomfortable with emotional displays. "I think we shall have a quiet afternoon after the excitement of the morning. Garth, come away from that window immediately," she ordered her dog, who was barking at John through the glass as he stepped into his brougham. "You should be ashamed."

With the incentive to achieve perfection, Vivienne picked up *The Ethereal Graces of the Delicate Sex* with a new motivation to learn Mrs. Beatrice Smith-Figgle's teachings. The binding was smooth leather without the words "banal, insipid, vapid" that were etched over the title on Vivienne's copy back home. She lay back on a sofa pillow and opened to Chapter One:

The softly murmured word, the downcast gaze, and gentle blush of rose. These qualities are the perfection of the proper female...

Already Vivienne's mind began to drift, and she forced herself to focus again. *I must be perfect.*

A lady's true nature is to please her helpmate. Her beauty must appease his sight, her gentle words must calm his woes, her shy smile must convey the pleasure of his presence...

Vivienne yawned, her eyes veering off the page to a spider building a web above the wall crowning.

Be perfect! she muttered and returned to the book.

Finally, after twenty minutes of this game, she temporarily gave up, closed the tome, and opened the *London Times* she had found discarded on the train up from Birmingham. She was halfway through an article about an English expedition into the jungles of South America when she saw the advertisement for the Royal Academy.

The works of the late Lawrence James will be displayed in the Gold Room. Author Mrs. Beatrice Smith-Figgle will be presenting the first in a series of lectures to educate ladies of gentle breeding on the great masters of art. The ladies will only study appropriate works.

The lecture was scheduled for today at two in the Blue Room. Perhaps this was what she needed for proper motivation, to meet the famed author in person. She checked the clock on the mantel. The lecture began in forty-five minutes.

"Aunt Gertrude, the author of the book Mr. Vandergrift has given me is lecturing today," Vivienne said. "It's for ladies of gentle breeding and at the Royal Academy. May I go?"

Her aunt fingered the edge of the Bible she was reading. She rarely left the house except to go to church, and she was always hesitant about letting Vivienne anywhere beyond the environs of the square. "Very well," she finally said. "If Mr. Vandergrift would approve. But you know it will tax my poor nerves until you are safely returned under my roof. Harold will take you in the carriage. Now, mind you are to wait inside for him after the lecture and not wander off into the street. London has become a regular Sodom and Gomorrah, I tell you."

⌘

When Vivienne arrived at the Royal Academy, she had to think she was safer out in the lawless streets of Sodom and Gomorrah. The building was packed with men—only men—and not the usual stately patrons or oddly dressed artists whom Vivienne would have expected to find, but boisterous, wild-eyed men who looked as if they'd just stumbled in from a chop house or gaming hall. The stairs were so clogged it took five minutes to reach the correct floor. The whole time, she clutched her overstuffed reticule and copy of *The Ethereal Graces of the Delicate Sex* close to her chest, giving sharp elbow jabs to several men who "accidentally" bumped into her.

Finally, she found the source of the male attraction: the Lawrence James exhibit. The men who waited to get in formed a disorderly line outside double doors. A gentleman dressed in dull gray livery and sporting a curled wig guarded the entrance, letting only a few men pass at a time. Across the hall was the Blue Room, but the door was locked.

As she turned to ask the guard for help, the door to the Lawrence James exhibit swung open, and two men with large, lustrous eyes ambled out as if drunk. On the wall above them was a massive painting of a lady with moonlit skin and honey-colored hair reposing on the gentle waves of a blue silk sheet. One hand rested behind her head, while the dainty fingers of her other hand entwined the fine curls of her most feminine area. Her breasts were round and more than a little generous. Yet to Vivienne, the most scandalous detail of this painting wasn't the tantalizing breasts or the slight parting of the lady's limbs, but the enticing smile on her lips as she gazed boldly at the viewer.

A thick heat burned in Vivienne's female parts. She stood mesmerized. In her imagination, she lay on those same sheets, her breasts exposed, all these men gazing upon her.

"Pardon miss, may I help you?" she heard a man say. The guard was looking at her with raised, expectant brows.

She jumped backward, falling into the lap of a man sitting on a bench behind her. She leapt up and tightened her book to her chest, trying to appear prim and proper. "I-I am here for the lecture on art masters for *ladies of gentle breeding*," she announced loudly, as if to assure every man in the room that she was such a lady. There were several snickers from the queue.

"Aye," the guard said. "Mrs. Smith-Figgle sent a note this morning saying no gentle ladies would attend on account of the Lawrence James paintings."

"Well, I think she could have decided in enough time to put a retraction in the paper." Vivienne fumed at the inference that she wasn't a gentle lady.

"This here James exhibit was supposed to be over by now," the guard explained. "But thems downstairs pushed back the opening while the police searched for them stolen paintings. But then they gives up and put the exhibit on anyway, without them masterpieces. So Smith-Figgle didn't know what's what."

"Umph," Vivienne said. Now she had to wait an hour before Harold came around with the carriage. She wasn't ready to fight off the elbows and roaming hands on the staircase just yet. So she edged down the bench, putting several feet between herself and the man whose lap she'd had the misfortune to acquaint herself with.

The owner of the lap had a gin blossom nose and smelled like the Thames on a hot summer's day. He smiled at her and leaned in. "I like pretty ladies of gentle breedin'."

"Thank you," she said weakly, then pulled her bonnet lower and raised the book to her face, but she couldn't read a single word. The moonlit nude filled her mind, so vivid and detailed it was as if this Mr. James had painted it on her brain. She squirmed in her seat, trying to stop that dark pulse between her limbs.

The door opened again, and she tried to keep her eyes focused on the pages, but she couldn't. Her gaze strayed to the beautiful painted siren who seemed to stare at Vivienne and silently whisper, "You want to be me, don't you?"

No! No! These thoughts are wrong.

She raised Mrs. Beatrice Smith-Figgle's book to block the seductress's image as four well-dressed young men strolled out. They shared a deep, throaty laugh.

"Let's get out of here," one said. "I've got an itch that needs some scratching. What say you, John?"

John! Vivienne peeked over the edge of the pages. Surely, not her John.

One of the gentlemen had turned so that Vivienne could see the side of his face. Her lungs went flat. Her fiancé!

"I think Seven Heavens is in order," he announced, slapping his friend on the shoulder, unaware of his fiancée not four feet away. "I've got an early wedding present tucked away for my pleasure," he said rather loudly, as if he were bragging to all the men in the room.

"Your personal James painting in the flesh, heh?" one of his friends asked.

"A darling little thing," John replied, the reckless sneer on his lips lifting the side of his mustache.

Vivienne bolted up, ready to throw the stupid delicate sex book at John. But he had folded into the crowd around the stairs. She wanted to chase after him. Yell at him. Drag her nails down his face. She kept swallowing, thinking she might cry, but all she felt was the emptiness of shock in her heart.

She shouldn't expect her husband to be completely faithful. Mrs. Hudson, the family housekeeper and the closest thing Vivienne and her sisters had to a mother, told her that a husband's wandering was the "sad cross married ladies had to bear." But she didn't want that kind of marriage. She wanted… she wanted to be some man's only love. All her life she felt she had been competing for the attention of her father or trying to please her uncle. For once, she wanted to be the loved one, the praised one.

Then she remembered her father's bruised face after the duns had finished with him and his plea for her to behave. Just what had she agreed to?

She let go of the book, and it thudded on the floor.

"Careful there, gentle lady," the red-nosed man said.

❧

The old landau lumbered through packed streets. Vivienne rested her head against the cool glass window of the carriage. Her stomach hurt, and she felt a headache blooming in the area just behind her temples. The city appeared to be painted in pale gold as the late afternoon sun drooped just below the rooftops. People were going home, their heads down, collars turned up. Merchants were sweeping their steps and bringing their signs inside. As the carriage rolled into Wickerly Square, she spied a dirty street boy wearing a bright blue coat over his slender shoulders standing before her aunt's door. The boy's limbs had grown out of his clothes like an insect bursting through its old skin. His coat sleeves barely came to his wrists. Dirt stains streaked his trousers, and the heels of his scratched boots were worn down.

As the landau approached her aunt's mounting block, the youth's head whipped around and Vivienne saw that he wasn't a boy at all, but a diminutive young man, about her own age, with brownish-blond hair brushed forward in oily strands. His nose was bent as if it had been broken. He took off across the street, jumping the fences in the center of the square and then disappearing.

Just how much separated Vivienne from this poor ragged street pauper probably begging for an odd job so he could eat? If it weren't for the money lent by creditors and an offer of marriage, she and her sisters might have the same fate. She felt guilty for being so angry at her fiancé.

You probably misunderstood John, she told herself. She shouldn't be so quick to jump to such unsavory conclusions. She must strive to be better. She hugged her book to her chest. "Perfect wife," she murmured as the carriage came to a stop.

❧

When Vivienne opened Aunt Gertrude's front door, the house seemed on fire with activity.

"Oh, my nerves!" Her aunt's wail echoed down the stairwell. "No, not *Dr. Gideon's Pills of Fine Humor*. I need *Milner's Coca Tonic Wine* at once."

Milner's Coca Tonic Wine! Her aunt only took that for the most dire of nerve spasms. All thoughts of her fiancé and being a perfect wife flew from her mind as Vivienne rushed up the stairs and into her aunt's chamber.

Aunt Gertrude was sprawled on her bed, her pointy lace boots hanging over the edge and her expansive belly forming a mound atop the covers of her white bedspread. A handkerchief was unfolded over her face, its center rising and falling with her breath, and her Bible was clutched to her chest.

"Jesus, come for me!" she cried. "I am ready."

The housekeeper's nervous fat fingers were knocking about the small apothecary on Aunt Gertrude's commode. "Aye, I can't find the blessed tonic."

At the foot of the bed, distraught Garth was turning in circles, barking at the ceiling as if making his own beckonings to the Lord.

Vivienne snatched up the green square bottle, sat on the side of the bed, and removed the handkerchief from her aunt's face. Perspiration slicked the little hairs about Aunt Gertrude's forehead; her cheeks were flushed and her eyes large and wild.

"What is the matter?" Vivienne cried and shoved two pillows beneath her aunt's back. Her aunt was so stiffly laced she couldn't bend but slanted her body instead.

Vivienne tilted the bottle back, giving her aunt the tiniest sip, but the woman grabbed the medicine and took a rather sailoresque swig. "Oh, love, it's the plagues of Egypt!" she cried and gulped down more.

"Now stop talking like that," Vivienne said soothingly. "The Thames hasn't turned to blood, and I don't see any flies or frogs or other pestilence about. What has put you in such a state?"

Aunt Gertrude seized her niece's hand. "My dear Vivvie, promise me that you'll be a pious wife. That you will always stay above the price of rubies."

Vivienne paused. John's arrogant smirk when he spoke of his early wedding present filled her mind. What was the price of a virtuous husband? Above diamonds? Or perhaps a gentleman's worth didn't fluctuate with his lapses of virtue?

"Promise me, dear Vivvie, that you'll be a virtuous lady," her aunt insisted. "This is the most important thing in all the world." Her eyes narrowed. "No matter how the devil may tempt you… with… with ripe luscious apples and golden calves and silken chemises."

"Wait, silk chemises aren't in the Bible. Biblical women wore—"

"But they are in the black soul of the devil, I tell you! Chemises, lacy drawers, and stockings are all in there. He waits for a lady to slip, he whispers to her, enticing her, tingling her… tingling her nether regions."

"Nether regions?"

"Lady parts! The devil dwells in a lady's parts," her aunt cried. Vivienne thought of all the paintings lining the walls at the Royal Academy, those ladies with their devil-filled parts exposed.

Her aunt released an anguished whimper and reached again for her bottle, but Vivienne held it tight. "I'm not quite sure coca tonic wine is what you need. Perhaps *Dr. Gilliam's Elixir for Clear Thinking*—"

"You must remain steadfast in your faith," Aunt Gertrude continued. "Pious in your actions. Promise me that you'll never give in to the wicked desires of your body."

"But if I'm married, shouldn't I…"

"Promise me!" her aunt screamed and squeezed Vivienne's fingers.

Vivienne bit her lip to stifle her cry of pain. For a woman prostrate on the bed, begging Jesus to take her from this world, she was remarkably strong.

"Say it!"

"I promise," Vivienne conceded, although she wasn't quite clear about what exactly she was vowing.

Surely it wasn't wicked for a man and wife to do things that begat children? Her aunt was so distraught as to not make sense. Married couples were being fruitful and multiplying all the time in the Bible, and based on Vivienne's very limited education in these matters, begetting involved the tingling and mingling of the wicked parts. A husband's and wife's parts, that is, not those of a fiancé and his early wedding present.

"Now tell me, what is the matter?" Vivienne said in a forced calm voice and kissed her aunt's cheek. "Let me help you."

"You can't." Her aunt raised her eyes to the heavens. "Only the Lord can."

"Well, perhaps I can be of assistance to the Lord," Vivienne suggested. "What has happened to upset you so?"

"I shan't speak of such things."

"Come now. I'm your little Vivvie. You can tell me."

Her aunt shook her head. "'Tis too horrible."

Garth had stopped spinning and now crawled to his owner and licked her chin. "My little doggie," Aunt Gertrude cooed and clutched her Bible tighter to her bosom. "I want to be alone with my Savior and my doggie." She covered her face with her handkerchief again and sniffed. "And do leave the tonic."

Miss Banks cleared her throat and jerked her head toward the corridor. Vivienne trailed her into the hall.

"What has happened?" she asked in a low voice.

The housekeeper was a thick Irish woman with a

blubbery face and stubby neck on her wide shoulders. Her hair was still a lush red with only a few silvery threads running from her temples.

"Oh, I mustn't say anything," she said loudly, her eyes drifting toward her employer. "Don't you be a'frettin' and a'worryin' when you need to be gettin' married." The woman started to the room at the end of the hall, looking over her shoulder to make sure Vivienne followed.

Vivienne almost said, *No! That's Uncle Jeremiah's study!* But then she remembered that he was dead. All these years later and his words, "Stay out of my library, bad seed," still held power. It was a relic of a room, seemingly unchanged since the early 1700s when Aunt Gertrude's great-great-grandfather moved in. The walls were decorated with panels covered with a heavy fern-colored print resembling a medieval tapestry. The same pattern of flower gardens and weeping willows was repeated in both the upper and lower panels. Between the windows hung another painting of Jeremiah Bertis, again in his black robes, his face as grim as ever. Against the wall stood a huge mahogany bureau like the one her father had in his study.

Vivienne pulled off her gloves and tossed her bonnet back. "What is this plague of Egypt?"

"Aye, it is indeed a plague. A plague of vile rats."

Vivienne released a long breath. She thought something truly terrible had happened. "Just have Harold put out some traps."

"No, miss, the human kind of rat: a wee man in a blue coat. But, like I said, you don't need to distress yourself about him. Or worry that he brings an envelope, just for the missus's eyes. Then she starts to cryin' for her coca wine and shuts herself in her chamber, talkin' to no one, not even to me. Then a day or two later, the man would come again, and the missus would give the envelope back and that would be that. But you need to be thinkin' about your wedding dress and what flowers you're going to wear in your pretty hair."

"And you don't know what was in the envelope?"

"The missus said she would let me or Harold go if we were to have anything to do with the man." She edged closer, lowering her bushy brows. "I just thinks it curious that some of missus's jewelry is goin' a'missin'. But perhaps I don't know what I'm talkin' about. I'm getting old and my mind is slipping," she said, though her green eyes were sharp as cat's claws.

"Good Lord. Do you think it's extortion?"

"I don't know, Miss," the housekeeper said, shaking her head. "But the missus had been givin' all her money to your father on account of the workshop. Now all those funds her husband had are fair near gone. But don't you fret. We'll manage, even if we have to go to the workhouse. Harold says he knows how to trap and skin a rabbit if we run out of food."

Vivienne chewed the edge of her nail. *So that's why she sent that letter saying she couldn't help Papa anymore.*

Was her entire family on the brink of ruin and she the only person who could save them? Hard resolve formed in Vivienne's heart. If she couldn't keep John from wandering, she could at least stop a vile man from taking advantage of her aunt. "Well, she can't let go of me! I'm blood."

"You're the missus's favorite niece. Loves you like her own daughter, she does. She be always a'sayin', 'That little Vivvie is so clever.' I never believed Mr. Bertis when he said you were a bad seed and would come to ruin." The housekeeper's face soured. "But you know how he was." She remained silent, her words still lingering like a frightening organ chord in play when the villain enters. "But Lord, I shouldn't speak ill of the dead. Now don't you agonize that your aunt will lose all her money on account of an ugly rat in a blue coat and have to die in a cold workhouse. You're young and need to be enjoyin' yourself."

But between John's early wedding present and the rodent in blue, the last thing on Vivienne's mind was enjoying herself. Just what was in those envelopes that the tiny man delivered?

Three

THAT MORNING, DASHIELL CONFINED HIMSELF TO HIS dining-room table—the only clean surface he could find in the house—with a pot of black tea, a plate of beefsteak and mustard sandwiches, and the cracked stump of his beloved Athena's neck, all he had managed to piece together of the goddess in the last two hours. His fingers ached from holding the tiny tweezers, his eyes burned from gazing through a magnifying glass, and his head still throbbed from last evening's overindulgence.

Yesterday, after Lily had finished destroying his prized possessions, his ballerina friend had gone back to the theater, and he had expressed his intentions not to speak to his grandfather for another ten years, he strolled down St. James, found a dark corner in a dark club, and began pouring from a bottle of brandy. He leaned back in the leather chair, extended his legs, and watched the burning coals reflected on his glass—a hypnotic, soothing pattern. He marveled how he always felt more at home when he wasn't at home.

He thought of his first residence, that pile of

mildewing bricks outside of Oxford where he was essentially "stored" as a boy while his parents dashed about England and into the arms of lovers. He had been a quiet runt of a child. The physician said he had a delicate constitution and should stay indoors and away from crowds. So he was always walking about the quiet corridors with a fat history book hugged to his chest like literary armor, asking when his parents were coming back and if perchance one of the boys from the village could come and play with him. No one ever came. One day when he was seven, the maid brought him breakfast on a tray, and on the side of the china was what looked like a tiny painted rock. He rolled it in his palm.

"The gardener said to give that to you," the maid had said. "He found it in the garden. He thinks it's from a Roman mosaic."

"Roman!" Dashiell cried and whipped his head around to the heavy glass window where the gardener was tearing blighted shrubs from the lawn.

After the maid left, he cast aside his tray, snuck downstairs, out the front door, and onto the lawn. From that moment, no physician's order, pleading tutor, or housekeeper could keep him confined inside. By summer's end, he had uncovered an entire mosaic and the foundations of a Roman home by himself. One afternoon, as he was breaking off cake-like soil from a Roman brick, several local boys, older than he, studied him through the leaves.

"Little Lord Dashiell, is it true about your mama?" a brave one with severe buckteeth asked while the others giggled.

He set down his shovel. "What about my mama?"

"That she ran off to Holland with another man," the boy said, causing another round of giggles.

"That's a lie!" Dashiell threw his shovel at them. "She would have told me."

But she hadn't. And in Holland she took up with a Frenchman and resided in Paris for a few years, before heading off to India with another fellow. Young Dashiell learned of her scandalous rambles like everyone else, from the society columns, for she only sent him a letter once a year after his birthday. The lines were littered with trite endearments, how much she missed him, and other such lies. Even now, the only times he heard from her were when she needed money.

And his father hadn't been any better. He died in a courtesan's bed, having been shot by the woman's former lover. The memory of that night took another glass of brandy to forget and then another two for the memory of his own affairs. When he was in his late teens, there were the jaded matrons who seduced him and used him for sport, and as he got older, there were the grasping actresses who bled him for money, the bored cheating wives like Lily who thought he held the answer to their misery, and the exotic women in foreign lands who all blended together in his mind. His affairs were a nasty cycle of degradation for all participants. So he made it a practice to keep his emotions safe from the claws of women.

He poured the last of the brandy into his glass. But then Vivienne turned up again, all grown up and dangerous. That precocious, lonely child he had befriended had turned into a beautiful lady possessing a magnificent spirit. He should have left that little girl in the tree, never felt sorry for her, never let her wiggle her way into his feelings. He felt that old restlessness in his heart, as he did whenever things became emotionally dangerous. He needed to leave.

After opening another bottle, he set his new destination: Hong Kong. A few more sips of brandy later, he decided to stand on the chair and state his intention to the club by giving an impromptu lecture on the Silk Road. An appreciative crowd, those drunken men.

Now, his head and body hated him. He picked up another shard of his broken goddess with the tweezers and held it to the window light. *Where the hell does this piece go?*

At that moment, the very object of last night's obsession passed the window, with Garth on a leash. A soft shiver came upon him like an unexpected pleasant breeze and his headache lifted. She was wearing a straw bonnet decorated with delicate ivy leaves that matched her rather worn cloak. The wind flushed her cheeks a lovely crimson and tossed her black curls around her face.

The hound sniffed Dashiell's fence, raised his hind leg, and squirted a little doggy calling card on the railing. "Stop that, Garth," he saw her say as she tugged on the leash. A playful smile drew on his lips, and he instinctively rose to join her, just like years ago. Then he stopped and sat down. He couldn't encourage her anymore or allow her to share in his hobbies. She was an engaged woman and he was a rake, a blackguard, a rogue, and all those other names ladies called him before they picked up a three-thousand-year-old relic and threw it at him.

Yet as he gazed at her, he realized something was wrong. Her brows were drawn, causing those little lines above her nose, and she bit down on the edge of her lip. Perhaps he should go to her after all.

The door swung open and crashed against the sideboard. The left side of the Athena's neck split apart and broke into pieces. *Dammit to hell!*

"I heard from the boys that you're leaving for China," the earl yelled. He wore a high-collared coat, padded so as to restore his chest and shoulders to their approximate build of forty years ago, and tight trousers on his thinning legs. His hair flowed as wild as his addled mind. "Now, the boys and I have been discussing your problems. They believe that what is wrong with you is that you keep running away. That you think you're going to find happiness in some old thing in the sand. What else did we say... oh yes... that you refuse to grow up."

The "boys" were a bunch of graying men who, along with his grandfather, had been terrorizing the clubs and gaming hells of Mayfair for the last forty years.

"I would appreciate it if you would not discuss my so-called problems with your friends," he said, trying not to choke on the earl's powerful cologne. "And I'm glad to see you finally got dressed."

"You're a fine one to speak. Vivienne came over here yesterday, and you're wandering about with your trousers loose and no shirt. Now what kind of impression is that going to make?"

"Funny, if you hadn't had your piece hanging out, she wouldn't have come over at all! You should apologize."

"Apologize? Last time I darkened Gertrude's door

on account of those actresses getting our addresses confused, she hit me with her cane. I found it a bit exciting, I must say." The earl picked up Dashiell's cup and took a long sip. He nodded out the window to Vivienne. "Just look at her. Pretty as they come. I was thinking—"

"Please don't," Dashiell inserted, yanking his cup back.

"—that you should marry Vivvie. Such a saucy little thing. She is perfect for you."

"And you thought showing her your naked body would entice her to join the family?" he said drolly.

His uncle shrugged, seeing nothing amiss. "Well, you didn't seem too inclined to show her the family gift."

"She's happily engaged to someone else," Dashiell said with finality, hoping to put an end to the subject both in conversation and in his heart.

"So?"

"Naturally, you don't perceive a moral conflict here, do you?"

The earl tried to run his hand through his thick, wild hair, but got stuck on a tangle and gave up. "It's in the Bible that they are constantly reading over there: Love thy neighbor as you would have them love you, and such."

Dashiell rose with a long, put-upon sigh. "As usual, you have gotten the meaning turned around. But for the sake of argument, let us follow your logic." He held up a finger like some Cambridge don. "I *love* Vivienne like a friend. So as a friend, I want her to be happy, loved, and wanted. Things, to be honest, that I don't think she has had much of in her life." He paused. "Now, you don't want your friend near someone who would hurt her, do you? A man who would break her heart, her spirit, and leave her to cry."

He envisioned tears in those pale emerald eyes of hers, pain he would cause by infidelity or abandonment. Just the idea was a knife filleting his insides, but he knew he would do it—all that desire turning to disgust and restlessness as it did every time he got close to a woman. "You want someone to give her love, devotion, and happiness. Everything you are…" he swallowed, "incapable of providing."

"What? I thought she loved those little curiosities you were always giving her."

"I was speaking in emotional terms." Dashiell picked up a shard of Athena's ear and rolled it in his palm. "If I really loved Vivienne, I wouldn't *love* Vivienne. She is the one female I care about whom I haven't hurt, and I'm keeping it that way."

"Good God, I get a headache just talking to you," the earl said. He banged his knuckles on the table. "Why don't you join me and the boys? We're going to that artist's exhibit at the Royal Academy." A bright, childish light sparked in his eyes. "You know, the one with all the naked women."

Truly, his grandfather should live in a bathhouse for how much he loved nudity both in himself and others. "Thank you, but no. I understand Lawrence James's few masterpieces were stolen, so I have little interest in the rest."

"But they're *naked*." He stared at Dashiell for a moment before shaking his head and quitting the room. "I just don't understand you."

"That could only be a good sign," Dashiell muttered to himself.

He sank into his seat and stared at the fragments of Athena scattered across the table. "This is impossible." Nonetheless, he picked up his tweezers and, piece by piece, began to rebuild the goddess again. He was plucking a section of her ear lobe from the wreckage when, out of the corner of his eye, he spied his grandfather conversing with Vivienne in the square.

Dammit! No telling what that lunatic was out there saying.

Vivienne was nodding at the earl's words with a patient yet strained smile. Then his grandfather pointed straight at Dashiell and waved for him to come outside.

That did it. Dashiell was leaving for Hong Kong tomorrow.

He sighed and grabbed the plate of sandwiches. By the time he got outside, his grandfather was gone, no doubt in his disarrayed mind thinking he was leaving the two love birds alone.

Up close, Vivienne's eyes were large and her eyelids droopy, as if she hadn't slept. Still, the fatigue lent a beautiful fragility to her face. She had fashioned an Egyptian scarab he had given her long ago into a necklace. It lay on the pale, soft skin above the rise of her breasts. His senses quickened and he wanted to touch her, as if this small distance between them was as big and void as the Dead Sea.

"I-I thought you both might be hungry from so much exercise," he said, trying to sound casual. He squatted down and put a sandwich on the ground for

Garth. The pug smashed his face in it, making strange gurgling and grunting noises. Dashiell ruffled the hound's wrinkled neck and stood.

"And one for you," he said to her. He swirled the sandwich under her nose, letting the aroma tempt her. "They're my favorite: beefsteak and mustard."

Vivienne giggled, and her tense features relaxed. She took a bite and began to chew, gazing up at him from under her lashes. Dear God, he wanted to kiss that porcelain jaw, trail up to her ear, and get lost in her luscious hair.

Then something in the square attracted her attention and her eyes widened. "Blah hann nnaann koof!" she cried.

"What?"

She made two big chews and swallowed down the sandwich in a big inelegant gulp. "It's the man in the blue coat," she said with breathy urgency. "Quick, go back inside."

She yanked on the leash. Garth, his face still deep in beefsteak, growled as he dug in his paws between the pavers, refusing to leave his sandwich.

"Not now, Garth!" She bodily scooped up the growling hound and dashed into the alley on the side of Dashiell's house that led to the back gardens and mews.

Dashiell, confused, stood on his step holding the plate of sandwiches, as a tiny man in a bright blue coat sauntered into the square.

Using his thumb and forefinger, Dashiell did something he wouldn't have done for any other lady; he picked up Garth's half-eaten, smashed sandwich and slipped into the alley. "What is going on?"

Vivienne grabbed him by his coat lapels and yanked him to her. "Don't let him see us," she said in a tense whisper.

"Who?"

"The man in the blue coat." She peered around Dashiell's shoulder and bit down on the edge of her thumbnail, her eyes tensed with concentration.

"Is he an unwanted admirer?" Dashiell's hands balled into fists around the platter of sandwiches. "Do you want me to take care of him?"

"No!" she hissed. "Just stay here!" She put her back against the brick wall and tiptoed down to the mouth of the alley, keeping Garth's leash clutched so tight her knuckles were white. She turned her head, putting her cheek against the brick, and peered along the walk running before their homes.

Garth pawed Dashiell's trousers, giving him a pathetic look. Dashiell dropped the dog's sandwich on the ground with a splat and Garth plunged his wrinkled face into the bread.

"What the hell is going on?" Dashiell demanded.

Her hand sliced through the air, silencing him. She stepped closer to the edge to get a better view. "There, he is leaving now," she whispered and tugged on Garth's leash. "Come on."

The dog lay down on his prized sandwich, refusing to budge.

Vivienne stomped her foot. "Ughh!" She stared at the dog and then at Dashiell. She flashed him a sweet, beguiling smile and held out the leash. "Do keep him. I hope I shan't be gone long."

"*Hope*," he echoed. "Who is this man?"

She didn't answer, but lowered the brim of her bonnet and set out into the square, making a fast beeline toward the man in the blue coat as he turned the corner out of the square. In his hand, he held a fat envelope he hadn't had a few minutes before.

Dashiell scooped up Garth with one hand and tucked him under the arm holding the plate of sandwiches, then scrambled after Vivienne.

She turned her head when he caught up with her, her eyes fired with anger. "What on earth are you doing?"

"Funny, I was going to ask you the same question."

"I'm following the man with the blue coat," she explained, as if it were completely rational behavior. "Now stay at home, please. This doesn't concern you."

"What? You are deranged if you think I'm letting you loose in London by yourself."

She gave a frustrated snort and flicked her wrist. "Fine then, just get far behind me in case someone recognizes you." She raised the hem of her gown and ran ahead, leaving him in her wake.

What is happening here?

The tiny man strutted, carefree, shoulders swinging, as if it were the fashionable hour in Hyde Park, unperturbed by the crowds of people crushing against him.

Vivienne tracked him like an excited bloodhound. Behind her flapping hem, Dashiell followed, hatless, holding Garth and a plate of beefsteak sandwiches. The hound's curled tongue strained for the sandwiches. Dashiell felt as idiotic as he ever had in his life. But he couldn't leave Vivienne alone, not as men's gazes boldly raked over her as she passed, too intent was she on the tiny man to notice their smirks of appreciation.

"Keep your damn eyes to yourself," Dashiell growled as he slammed his shoulder against one gentleman who had the audacity to turn and whistle at her figure.

Vivienne didn't hear. She veered right, heading for the slums of St. Giles.

Bloody hell! He rushed to catch up with her, grabbing her elbow with his free hand. "Enough of this game. You need to turn around. It's dangerous now."

"No," she said, a gritty determination in her eyes a Spartan soldier would have admired. Then she surged ahead and disappeared in the human congestion.

"Damn that lady," Dashiell spat, turning the corner after her onto a narrow street. The houses were streaked with soot and collapsing on their rotting beams. Clothes fluttered from windows and lines strung between the buildings. The reek of animal waste and sour perspiration assaulted his nose. Mothers clad in stained, faded dresses clustered on the stoops outside their doors, holding their crying babies. Barefoot children whose faces were smudged with dirt chased each other up and down the walk, avoiding the open gutter and the drunks who stumbled about with shiny, vacant eyes. Above the general roar of chatter rose the cries of the muffin and pie vendors singing out their goods.

Garth cowered in Dashiell's arm, afraid for his little doggy life. Dashiell was beginning to believe the hound had more damn sense than Vivienne.

Vivienne! Where is Vivienne? In a split second, at

least a dozen images of Vivienne hurt, crying, bleeding rushed through his head. Then, in the tangle of people, he spied that damn blue coat stopping before a dirty building and then disappearing inside… and Vivienne not ten seconds behind. She paused at the door, looked about her, then walked on and stopped a few feet away, turning back to study the grim residence.

Dashiell pushed through the inebriates and vendors to where she stood. "I don't know what you're doing. But you need to go home," he ordered. "Right now."

His words seemed to bounce off her hard head, unheeded. "Wait here," she said slowly. "I'm going to knock on the door. I need to find out his name."

He grabbed her arm, causing Garth to yelp. "Now you just stop. You are not safe. I'll get the house number as we pass and ask around about it."

"That is far too complicated," she replied. "I'm simply going to knock on the door and say that I am looking for Mrs. Highgate—she was my former school mistress, the one who tossed me out. A witch of a woman. Anyway, he will say she isn't there, and I will say something like 'This was the name and address I was given,' and hopefully he will tell me his name."

For a second, he couldn't respond. Although Vivienne had grown into this ravishing lady, her sense of fear and self-preservation was still clearly that of the twelve-year-old girl in the tree who wanted to run away with him. "I'm beginning to believe you've been lying to me all these years. That you actually live in Bedlam and every once in a while they let you out to visit your aunt. Now why is knowing this man's name worth risking your life?"

"He is, um, a business associate of my father," Vivienne replied coolly.

Dashiell scrutinized her face with his hot eyes. "You are lying," he said. "I know when you're lying."

Fine, so he guessed her deception, but she was losing her patience. "I told you to stay back at Wickerly Square."

"What? You are very lucky I followed you. My dear lady, this is St. Giles. You know, sometimes referred to as the most dangerous place in all of England. You're lucky you haven't been knocked to the ground and had that little scarab ripped from your neck, or worse. Now why are you risking your life for this man in the blue coat?"

Vivienne studied his face. Angry lines formed around his mouth, and his eyes shone almost black. She couldn't possibly explain that her aunt was potentially being blackmailed. She swallowed and considered turning back and going home, but she didn't know if she would get another moment to come back. If this were indeed the most dangerous place in all of England, at least she had Dashiell with her as an unwitting aid.

As she debated, a swarm of pie and trinket vendors descended on them. As Dashiell shouted that in no uncertain terms would he buy a stolen pocket watch or eat meat pies fit for vultures, she nimbly slipped between the vendors' carts. She just needed a few seconds, that was all! Dashiell might become angry, but she had greater concerns than her neighbor's wrath.

A pair of dirty doves nesting in the timbers above her looked down with tiny black eyes as she knocked on the wooden door held by rusty hinges. The little man answered the door. Up close, she could see his features for the first time. Ginger-colored freckles dotted his delicate face. He possessed large, thickly lashed blue eyes and a rather feminine pink mouth. His gaze traveled up and down Vivienne's body and he began shaking like an excited squirrel. "'Ere to see Mrs. Jenkinson, are ya? Come in, come in."

He took off his hat and violently waved it, beckoning her inside. She hesitated. This wasn't a very good idea, but who was Mrs. Jenkinson? She looked beyond the man to a tiny entrance hall painted a pale azure with splotches of white, as if to recreate clouds in a sky. A broad young lady came down the stairs, dressed in cascades of pink ruffles. Blond ringlets fell about her plump face and squinting eyes. She didn't look too frightening, Vivienne thought.

She peeked over her shoulder at Dashiell. His angry face glowered at her from above the shoulders of the muffin and pie men who held him hostage. His lips formed a vicious slew of profanity, probably with her name inserted between obscenities, but she couldn't hear him from the noise of the crowd.

At least he knew where to find her if she didn't come out.

"Why, thank ya, dearie," she said, trying to adopt the brash accent of the peasant women who sold fish in the market in Birmingham. "And wot be your name?"

"Willie," he said, fingering his hat. "This 'ere is my ma and me's place." He jerked his head toward the stairs as if he were proud of the hovel.

Vivienne took a tentative step into the hall, intending to go no further. But Willie closed the door behind her and then clasped her elbow, pulling her into the adjoining room. The pink-ruffled lady now sat on a sagging burgundy sofa beside a bony companion clad in a matching gown. In the corner, another woman wearing the same pink uniform plucked one of the three strings on a harp that looked as if it had fallen off the back of a wagon more than a few times.

The ladies regarded Vivienne with dull eyes and gaping mouths. Was this some sort of strange boarding house for witless ladies?

"Now don't you pay attention to these old things," Willie said. "You ain't like them. These 'ere are just a few weeks away from the streets."

The streets?

She gasped as the realization blossomed in her head. This was a brothel! A mixture of shock, fear, and curiosity hit her at once.

She stared at the ladies. Physically, they looked no different than the ladies seen shopping for poultry and thread at the markets. There was no special distinction about them, no overflowing breasts or faces stained with makeup or gaudy clothes. Yet these women lay with several men a night. Well, perhaps, she thought. Vivienne really wasn't knowledgeable about the specifics of the prostitution trade. There was something about these women that was both repulsive and fascinating at the same time.

Willie let go of her arm to knock on a door along the back wall.

Vivienne began to back up, ready to bolt. "You know, really, I think I have the wrong add—"

"Ma! We 'ave a new girl. You 'ave to see 'er!" Willie shouted. Again he grabbed Vivienne's arm and pulled her forward, his face beaming as if Vivienne were some wrapped present he was giving his mother.

The doorknob shook as if jiggled by a key. When the door opened, a petite lady with a pert, upturned nose peered out. Her pale blond curls and vivid blue eyes contrasted against her tanned, dry skin. Wrinkles cut deep valleys under her eyes and around her mouth. Ugly brown splotches marred her cheeks. Mrs. Highgate's words, "A lady always wears a bonnet," echoed in Vivienne's mind.

Behind Jenkinson was a miniscule study only big enough to hold a slim, scratched oak desk and a chair. On the desktop sat a lit lamp, a cut-glass decanter of some dark spirits, and a familiar-looking open envelope, but Vivienne couldn't see its contents because the woman stood in the way.

Jenkinson cocked her head and eyed Vivienne. Her lips were parted, and Vivienne could see her teeth, all black stumps. "Wot are you doin' 'ere?" she demanded.

Vivienne took a step to her right, trying to see over the woman's shoulder. "I was given this address." She could just make out a gold chain peeking out of the envelope when the madam stepped forward and grabbed Vivienne's chin.

"Who gave ya?" The woman blasted Vivienne with a breath of acrid liquor.

"My… um… former mistress, but I was asked to leave," Vivienne said, straining to look around the woman's head.

"I think Mrs. Fontaine could use 'er," Willie said. "We could sell 'er to Fontaine to get 'er off our backs."

Jenkinson dropped her hold on Vivienne and turned her head to look at her son. Vivienne saw the flash of a gold chain dotted with tiny sapphires spilling out of the envelope. She remembered the Sunday her aunt let her wear that very necklace to church for her fifteenth birthday. This foul madam was blackmailing her aunt.

"You don't know nothin' 'bout business," the madam barked at her son.

"I'm very sorry," Vivienne said. "I didn't hears your name?"

For several long seconds, the woman scrutinized Vivienne with narrowed eyes. Hers were surprisingly beautiful eyes, the color of blue marbles. Vivienne had to believe that at one time, this monster of a woman had been very attractive.

"Adele Jenkinson," she said finally. "The girls 'ere call me Mama Dellie. I suppose you can too and all."

"Mama Dellie, I'm afraid there might be a tiny mistake." Vivienne just needed to slip quietly away without making a scene, and then she could think about what to do next.

"See, she has 'em nice manners," Willie said.

"You want to work for Mrs. Fontaine, don't you?" his mother asked. "She would set up a girl like you right nicely."

"I…"

The front door slammed with a hard thud, and Dashiell stomped into the parlor. His brows slanted down like an angry hawk and his left cheek quivered with fury. In his hand, he still held the plate with the one remaining sandwich, while a terrified Garth hid his head under Dashiell's armpit, his leash wrapped about his shivering hind legs. "I am taking you home now!" Dashiell hissed through clenched teeth. "Do you understand?"

"Just what the 'ell is going on 'ere?" Jenkinson yanked Vivienne behind her and screamed, "Sidney!"

On the floor above, there was the sound of scraping, like a chair being pushed back, and then the whole house shook with the pounding of footfalls. For a second, Vivienne felt she had fallen into the "Jack and the Beanstalk" fable and was about to urge Dashiell to cut the beanstalk to keep the giant from descending from the sky when the largest, most perfectly square man she had ever seen took up the entire entrance to the parlor. His shoulders were about as wide as his torso and legs combined, and he held his head at an angle to keep it from grazing the ceiling.

Dashiell groaned. "Oh, bloody hell."

"Darlin', find out wot this gentleman wants," Jenkinson ordered.

Sidney snorted through his nose like an angry bull and gave Dashiell a hard, mean eye.

"Don't hurt him!" Vivienne freed herself from Jenkinson's grasp and threw her body between Dashiell and the giant. "This 'ere is my—my 'usband," she cried. "You see, we 'ad a fight 'cause he don't make no money. We 'ave six children and—and that dog— all hungry. And he don't do nothin' but sit around all day, drinkin' and good for nothin'. I says to him, if you don't get money, I will."

Dashiell wore the most incredulous, yet horrified expression on his taut face. When he spoke, his voice came out high and stiff as if the words hurt to utter. "That's what I was comin' to tells you, my sweet sugar muffin. I found work." He held out the platter. "Look, I have food here."

"Oy, you mean it?" she wailed, trying to get all teary-eyed for realism.

"I sure do, my little butter biscuit." He looked like he could slap her. "Now you can get the hell home and raise our six children proper."

"Honestly, I should'a known!" Jenkinson barked. Her eyes squeezed to slits and she looked hard at Vivienne. "I was right bein' suspicious of you. I don't know what game you're playin', but you don't have six starvin' children. If you did, you'd sell that purty li'l necklace around your neck to feed 'em." She jerked her head toward Dashiell. "And this man 'asn't worked a day in his life, not wearin' 'em fine clothes. And look at his hands! Sidney, take her necklace for the trouble she's caused me."

The bull of a man lurched forward, and the floor shook on impact. She could smell the metallic scent of hard gin wafting off him. His eyes were shiny and dilated with intoxication. He put his enormous hand on her necklace.

"Don't you dare touch my scarab!" Vivienne kicked the man's shin. He didn't move, solid as the cliffs of Dover, but emitted a low laugh that sounded like rumbling thunder. He pushed her backward, and she stumbled against the harp.

She heard the ringing sound of the platter hitting

the floor and Garth's startled yelp. Then something
flashed across her face. It was Dashiell's fist ramming
into Sidney's face. "Don't you goddamn touch her!"
he shouted. "Vivienne! Get out!"

She ducked under his arm, fell to her knees, and
grabbed Garth's leash as he attempted to hide under
the sofa. The ladies shrieked and leapt up, stepping on
her hand as they fled. *Ouch!*

As she came up with a scared and whimpering
Garth in her arms, Dashiell's head slammed onto the
sofa cushion beside her. "Oh my God!"

He had that stupefied look as if he had just suffered
a hard blow. She turned and gazed up. Sidney stood,
swaying on his feet, a lopsided smile hanging on his lips.
He had his fist pulled back, ready to deliver Dashiell
another punch. Rage rushed through her. With one
hand, she ripped an ugly lamp from the side table and
swung it at the giant's face, missing him entirely, instead
slamming Dashiell's collarbone. "You are not helping,"
he howled. "Go outside before you kill me."

"I won't leave you," Vivienne cried.

Sidney grabbed Dashiell by the collar, yanked him
up, then wrapped his arm around Dashiell's neck,
choking him like a python.

"Now, you just let him alone," she shouted at the
terrible Sidney. "Or… or I'll set this dog on you."
She held up Garth, who tried to hide his bulging eyes
under his paws. "He is vicious, really he is."

Sidney laughed through his big yellow teeth, and
with the hand what wasn't around Dashiell's neck,
pushed her and Garth onto the floor.

"You bloody puff guts," Dashiell growled and

rammed his elbows into the giant's ribs. He fell back, stumbling in his drunken state, giving Dashiell time to extract himself and land two lightning quick jabs to the man's fleshy jaws.

"I said, get out," Dashiell ordered Vivienne in the hardest, most malevolent voice she had ever heard, at the same time dodging Sidney's fists.

Still, she wouldn't budge. "But—"

"Now!" he yelled.

She rushed for the door with Garth hugged to her chest. Over her shoulder, she took one last peek just as Dashiell slammed Sidney's gut. The man groaned, listed sideways, and smashed against the wall.

"You touch my wife again, and I'll kill you, you goddamn rump splitter," Dashiell growled.

Vivienne waited on the walk, chewing on three fingernails. She didn't feel much safer outside as a crowd of sharp-eyed street urchins, drunks, and women in garish rags had begun to gather, all curious about the goings-on at Jenkinson's place.

❦

From outside the brothel, Vivienne could hear the shrieks of women, the banging of metal, then a heavy thud and the musical reverberation of the harp's strings. Dashiell shouted a terrible curse word that started with "f." Then glass shattered, and the sand-wich plate was thrown out of the window, breaking into pieces on the street. The throng of spectators whistled and cheered like this was a sporting game.

Garth leapt from her arms, sniffed the fragments of the plate, and began to growl menacingly at the brothel.

"Oh capital, Garth," Vivienne yelled. "Couldn't you have gotten angry a few seconds ago when it mattered?"

Why was she upset with Garth when this was entirely her fault? She couldn't let an innocent man—well, somewhat innocent man—perish on account of her reckless actions.

"Wait here," she ordered Garth as she wrapped his leash around a lamp pole. Then she swung open the brothel door. Dashiell stood at the threshold. He had a red circle on his jaw and three parallel scrapes that looked as if fingernails had been slashed across his cheek. Rose-scented white powder covered his clothes. Behind him, all was silent inside the brothel.

The crowd broke out in applause, as if Dashiell were a champion pugilist.

"I'm so, so, so sorry," Vivienne cried.

He ran his hands down his chest, straightening his coat, and then stretched his neck to the left, then the right. "Don't talk to me," he growled.

Four

DASHIELL STALKED THROUGH THE STREETS BACK TO Wickerly Square, keeping his hand tight on Vivienne's wrist to keep her from scurrying to some other squalid rookery and getting him killed. She hurried alongside, trying to keep up with his stride, as she held traumatized Garth. The hound pleaded to Dashiell with his round buggy eyes as if to say, "Don't leave me with this mad lady!"

Dashiell found a narrow alley running beside a wine merchant's shop and pulled her inside. The lane was empty except for a bony black cat pawing at something small and dead in the gutter. Garth leapt from Vivienne's arms and the cat shot off, disappearing into a small opening at the bottom of a rotting door, leaving Garth to sniff and then roll on the deceased creature.

"You're going to tell me what the hell is going on," Dashiell ordered.

"I'm sorry. I didn't realize it was… was… a brothel. You should have told me."

He flung up his arms. "And how was I supposed to know that?"

Her head jerked back, confused. "But... but y-you're a rake."

He let out an exasperated sigh and clamped his hands on her shoulders, drawing her so close to him that her subtle vanilla and jasmine scent filled his nose. "My dear Miss Taylor, I would have trembled to say this before, but clearly you are no longer a little girl." He leaned down until his lips just touched her little shell-shaped ear. "I do not have to pay for pleasure, my little sugar muffin," he whispered.

She was all too much. Her smell, her feel clouded his brain. His pulse, still wild from the fight, surged even higher and he took a small nibble of her lobe, letting his tongue glide along its edge. He heard her gasp, and her breasts brushed against his chest, unleashing a low animal desire in his body. In his mind flashed an image of her against the alley wall, her legs around him, as he took her in a wild frenzy of pent-up desire. His secret little sister. Oh God, she had become so dangerous to him. He let out a long, ragged breath and withdrew.

The pink edge of her tongue showed through her parted lips. Her green eyes were large and lush, like a Scottish landscape after rain.

"Why did you follow this man with the blue coat?"

She leaned against the brick and rubbed her lips together. "I shouldn't tell you."

He took a curl of her hair and wound it on his finger. "But you *want* to tell me," he said. "You can trust me. Remember the Bazulo vow."

A smile flickered momentarily on her lips, and then her features tensed back to that tight worried expression. "You can't tell anyone."

"Of course I won't. You know that."

She related a story about coming home from the Royal Academy to see the man in the blue coat leaving her house, her aunt in hysterics, and her suspicions of blackmail. "So I followed him to see where he went," she concluded.

"Why didn't you go to your fiancé for help—or to me, for that matter?"

"I couldn't tell John. He would…" She gazed down. "He wouldn't approve."

"Hell, I don't approve. You could have gotten really hurt."

She flashed him a hot eye. "Don't patronize me. I knew what I was doing. I had all I needed to know and was about to leave, without busting out the windows, mind you. But you stormed in, acting like some overgrown Ajax."

"Ajax?" he echoed incredulously. "This is what I get for saving your life? Oh, and that six children act was quite convincing. I should warn this John fellow that he has his hands full with you, cracked lady."

"You can just go to… to…" She tried hard to repress the expletive, but it burst forth. "*Hell!* I told you not to follow me, anyway." She turned with a frustrated cry and stomped off.

Garth, left shivering by Dashiell's leg, looked up at him with frightened bulbous eyes and whimpered. "Wait!" Dashiell called. "You forgot your dog. He's scared." In fact, Dashiell was scared too. *What has Vivienne gotten into?*

She spun around so fast that her cloak and gown formed an ellipse about her body. She stalked back and scooped up Garth, squeezing him to her bodice. Tears were spilling out of her eyes, running down her cheeks.

The pain in his chest hurt more than any blow Sidney could give. "Good God. What did I say?" he whispered, hearing the deep quiver in his own voice. "I-I didn't mean to call you cracked. I'm the cracked one. Everyone knows that. Please say that you will forgive me?"

"It's not that," she choked. Unable to wipe her tears, she ran her face over Garth's wrinkled head. "My father is in terrible financial straits. His workshop burned down, and the insurance company claimed he started the fire intentionally. They called him a criminal so they wouldn't have to pay. So he had to borrow funds, but by the time the workshop was rebuilt, he'd lost his customers. Now these vile men are threatening him, but he can't pay his debts, certainly not at the interest the money lender is charging. We could lose everything."

"Oh, Vivienne, why didn't you say something?" He'd had no idea that Vivienne's family was going through such hard times. That she had been suffering so while he was off playing around the globe. "Let me lend you some money. Let me do something. Anything."

She shook her head. "No, it's all better now. I'm marrying John. His father is the manager at South Birmingham Railroad and he can give Papa enough work to begin paying down his debt." She tried to smile but failed. Garth licked a stray tear that was rolling off her chin. "It's just been hard watching Papa get hurt. Please don't tell anyone. It's just… I didn't have anyone to talk to."

"Of course." Dashiell took Garth from her arms and set him on the ground. Then he wrapped her in his embrace. "Don't worry," he said, wishing that damn bonnet wasn't there so he could kiss her soft hair. "We'll figure this out together. I promise."

Vivienne closed her eyes and felt the muscles of his chest contract beneath her cheek, hard and powerful, making a protective wall around her. She didn't feel secure and safe in John's arms, where she was constantly trying to make him like her, trying to be what he wanted. But with Dashiell, a man reviled by her family and all of polite society, she drifted in easy, drowsy peace. She snuggled closer, wishing she never had to go back. Just she and he, together, her head resting on his heart, the feel of his thigh gently rubbing against her as their bodies swayed together. She wished the tender quivers in her heart could continue, unabated, for the remainder of her life.

What are you thinking?

She leapt away and stared at him. His chest rose with fast, shallow breaths like hers. His eyes were dark with fear and another scary emotion that she couldn't name but tingled down to her bones. How did what was meant to be a kind embrace turn so dangerous?

"You called me your wife at the brothel." Her voice was tense and brittle. "In olden days, we would be as good as married for that statement," she said, trying hard to make it sound as if marrying him was as absurd as her becoming the Queen of Denmark. "I'm afraid John will be quite put out."

He laughed nervously. "Sorry to beg off, but that's what we rotten, no-good scoundrels do. I think you are better off with this John fellow in marriage. But I'm great at solving mysteries and setting blackmailers straight."

Vivienne exhaled, feeling safe again, yet disappointed. Both knew a line had been crossed, waking dangerous emotions best kept dormant. Still, she wouldn't easily forget the powerful sensation of his embrace and how it stirred her heart and senses in ways John's touch never had.

"Come on, Garth, it's time to go home," she said.

❧

They strode out of the main shopping streets and into the narrow lanes of residences. Garth zigzagged about their feet, sniffing the street lamps and doorways. The morning's frantic tempo had eased, and the walks were clear but for a few servants sweeping the steps and nurses pushing baby carriages.

"So if we are to begin this investigation of the man in blue, we should start with what we know," Dashiell said, sounding more like his old self.

"No. This is not your problem."

"Clearly, you don't remember the section of the Bazulo vow that claims if one party is hereto in some way connected to or the target of blackmail, it is the responsibility of the other party to make it their problem," he said in comic severity.

She chuckled nervously, still feeling her insides prickly and excited. "I missed that section."

"You really should know all the terms and conditions before you make such an important vow," he said, still serious. "Now, what of your aunt? Can you think of anything that might tie her to a brothel's madam? Any scandals in your aunt's past that are blackmail-worthy?"

"Aunt Gertrude?" Vivienne laughed that a sentence could contain both the words "scandal" and "your aunt." "The only scandal in her life floats over from your house."

"What about your uncle's death? Anything that would signal foul play?"

She thought for a moment and then shrugged. "No, after years of claiming I would send him to his grave, he ate a pigeon pie, crossed Holton Street, and promptly had a heart attack. I had nothing to do with it."

"Any affairs that you know of? Any by-blows?"

Vivienne cringed with embarrassment just thinking of her uncle in these terms, but Dashiell didn't seem the least bit fazed, as if it were the natural order of things that men had affairs outside their marriages. Again, she thought of John at the Royal Academy, and her belly tightened.

"I-I don't think so," she stammered.

"Perhaps his hand was padded to give a certain verdict," Dashiell speculated. "Can you go through his personal effects and see what you find?"

"Of course," she mumbled absently, for her mind was still focused on John and his early wedding present.

"Meanwhile, I'll discreetly ask around town. Married men tend to live different lives outside their homes."

Vivienne's gaze shot to Dashiell's face.

He raised a brow, anticipating a question. "Yes?"

She opened her mouth, but couldn't form the words. How do you ask if it is acceptable for a man to keep a mistress outside of his wife or fiancée? But then, who else but Dashiell, a man who never bothered with the trivial niceties of society, would give her a straight answer. This was her chance. But she just couldn't ask something so monstrous, so personal. "N-never mind."

Vivienne fell quiet, and that little crease of worry appeared again between her brows. Dashiell could feel anxiety radiating from her, causing his nerves to tense. Some worrisome thought was circling in her head like wasps around their nest. He knew she wasn't going to leave this mystery alone; she was too much like him. But unlike him, she was naïve and innocent. He couldn't very well tie her down while he looked into the matter, although this option had its appeal in his illicit imagination. So he was going to force his way into her problems. Be vigilant that nothing happened to her until that blissful wedding day when he gave his beautiful friend to someone else.

Overhead, he could see the smoky chimney tops of his home rising above the roofs as they entered the street running behind their square, where the ivy grew pell-mell over the walls. They continued around the corner into the shadows of the narrow alley beside Dashiell's home.

"Well, good-bye," she said and then reached up and gingerly brushed his bruise. "I'm sorry I caused you such trouble." Even over the tender skin, her touch felt like a feather and sent some tingles of pleasure through him.

"It's nothing." He gave a nervous chuckle. "What else was I going to do today, anyway?"

She didn't leave but stood there, biting down on the edge of her lip.

"Out with it, Vivienne. I can feel your brain buzzing away in there."

She took a deep breath. "Yesterday at the Royal Academy, I stumbled upon the Lawrence James exhibit."

He smiled to himself, thinking he knew where this conversation was heading. Poor innocent and infinitely curious Vivienne. "Did you enjoy it?"

She flashed him a hot look, and he stifled his laugh. "I overheard some gentlemen—*married* gentlemen—talking about having women tucked away at a place called Seven Heavens? Is it a brothel?"

Maybe he didn't know where this was going, after all. "Yes," he said, slowly and carefully. Seven Heavens was a flashy bordello that had moved into Mayfair five years ago and had threatened the upscale conservative brothels that had long served the upper echelons of British society. The place was a gaudy circus, taking in beautiful ladies from around the globe. The services had themes like African Safari, Japanese Tea, or Wild American Frontiers.

"Have you been there?"

"Of course not!" Which wasn't exactly true. God, she had such a trusting face; he couldn't lie to her. He slicked his hands down his face. "Fine, once, a year or two ago, but not to… you know. My grandfather hurt his back there. Look, I told you I don't pay for pleasure. I'm not—"

"Is it like that brothel we just saw?" she swallowed. "Because Willie—that's the little man's name—said that I didn't belong there. That they could sell me to a

Mrs. Fontaine. That it would be a great honor or such. Do you know this woman?"

What was Vivienne not telling him? Something about Judge Bertis? "She is the madam of Seven Heavens," he said, gazing at Vivienne's angst-ridden eyes. "Look, it's entirely possible that your uncle had a little—"

"It was my fiancé John I overheard talking about Seven Heavens." Her words burst forth. "Do most married men have mistresses? Please tell me, I don't know—"

"Jilt this John right now." Dashiell felt his fists ball as black anger gripped him. He was going to kill John. And not the modern way of a quick painless bullet, but a slow, torturous medieval disembowelment. Granted, most every married man of means in London kept a hidden mistress or visited brothels. But Vivienne's husband sure as hell wouldn't. "I'll lend you money, whatever you need."

She shook her head. "I don't think you understand the extent of my father's debt. Besides, how could I explain it to Papa? He despises you as much as my aunt does."

He opened his mouth to say something vile about John, but her distraught face arrested the nasty words. "Do you love John?" he asked softly.

"Yes," she said, then looked down to where Garth's leash was wrapped around her hand. "I suppose."

"You suppose?"

"I shouldn't have said anything." She blew a sharp, frustrated breath, lifting the tiny wisps of hair about her forehead, and tugged Garth. "Let's go."

She took a step onto the square. The dog released a low, teeth-baring growl. She suddenly whirled around and pressed her palms on Dashiell's chest, pushing him back into the alley.

"What the hell?" he cried, slamming the wall. "Is the man in the *yellow* coat here now?"

"It's John!" she cried, her face turning porcelain white. "He's come for a call."

Five

VIVIENNE CLUTCHED THE SQUIRMING GARTH TO HER bosom and pressed her back against the alley wall. "If John sees us together, he'll be so upset." She could hear the quiver of panic in her whisper. "I'm supposed to be... well... perfect."

"What? You *are* perfect. You know who isn't perfect? That John arse. But I'm about to change that. Tell me, do you have any reservations about adopting children?"

"Stop, Dashiell, I probably just misunderstood him, and it's all nothing. Now just wait here until we are inside."

He tilted his head at a rakish angle. "Perhaps," was his cool response.

Why did she feel like she was asking the ravenous lion not to eat the lost and injured gazelle?

She set down Garth, smoothed her cloak, and again stepped out onto the square with a bright, stiff smile on her face.

"Why, John, when did you arrive?" she said in a cheery voice, as if nothing were out of the ordinary—just a casual, relaxed stroll with Garth, whose eyes were bulging as he growled and pulled on his leash to get at her fiancé.

John did not answer her in kind. In fact, he was quite angry. "Where have you been? The servant has been combing the streets, looking for you. Your aunt is so upset. She had to take a special elixir. I came out here to search for you."

Oh Lord!

"I–I was just walking Garth." She tried to sound innocent. Garth leaped for John's cuff. Vivienne yanked him back and trapped him under her skirt.

"For two hours!"

"Has it been that long?" A hot flush crawled up her neck. Garth hissed and flailed in the layers of her petticoats. "I guess I lost track of the time, thinking about our wedding and planning my trousseau."

"I was worried to death about you. You're far too trusting and naïve of worldly ways. When we are married, I shall employ a proper companion to watch over you. Not all men are gentlemen."

"Haaalllllo, Miss Taylor," Dashiell's voice echoed in the square. He rounded the corner, weaving about, unstable, as if he'd managed to get wildly drunk in the last two minutes. *What the hell is he doing?*

"Who is that?" John asked.

"Probably just some vagrant." She grabbed John's arm and tried wheeling him toward the door without tripping over Garth. "Let's go inside."

"Don't hurry off!" Dashiell called out. "It's me. Your neighbor."

He ambled up the walk with a lopsided grin on his battered face.

He performed a low bow, nearly falling over and then righting himself on the iron railing that ran in front of the houses. "I'm Lord Dashiell. And you must be—"

"This is my fiancé, Mr. John Vandergrift," Vivienne intervened. Her smile felt as rigid as steel.

"You look pretty bad there, your lordship," John remarked.

Dashiell leaned close to her fiancé. "Got in a fight at a bawdy house," he confided with a wicked glitter in his eyes.

Vivienne gasped. She dug her nails into her palms to keep herself from putting matching nail marks on the other side of the blackguard's face.

"My lord, that is hardly appropriate for Miss Taylor's ears," John admonished him.

Dashiell burped. "I do apologize. I realize Miss Taylor is the *perfect* proper lady and all." He stumbled closer to her fiancé, putting his face barely an inch from John's. "You, sir, are a lucky man. Remember that." He lost his drunken slur, enunciating his next words with crystalline precision. "With a lady like Miss Taylor, I doubt you would even consider taking a glimpse at another lady. Good day to you." He stepped forward and slammed into John's shoulder, sending him against the iron railing. Garth poked his head from underneath Vivienne's skirt and barked.

John grabbed his shoulder in pain.

"A thousand apologies, my good man," Dashiell said. "I'm rather dangerous"—he paused, his eyes turning black and vicious, the edge of his teeth glinting below his snarled lip—"when I've had too much to drink."

He let out a maniacal laugh, worthy of a maddened, bloodthirsty Nero or Caligula. It echoed behind him as he sauntered to his door. There he glanced back, his gaze catching hers for the briefest second. He winked.

‿⁀

Fifteen minutes later, Vivienne sat beside her aunt on the parlor sofa. Her nerves were edgy, as if she had drunk a bucketful of black tea. Meanwhile, her aunt was oddly calm given the recent events. A small, uncharacteristic Mona Lisa smile curved her mouth as if da Vinci had painted it there, and she slowly swayed like a tree in the breeze.

At her feet, Garth sat at attention, his lips back, teeth bared, round eyes keen on John's every movement.

"Dashiell is lucky I'm a gentleman, else I would have darkened his daylights," John said as he paced before the marble fireplace, grinding his fist into his palm. "Had you not been there, Vivienne, he would be flat on the ground for his impudence."

Her aunt lifted the small brown bottle of *Dr. Melvin's Brain Restorative for the Special Disturbances of the Female Nervous System* on the table beside her chair. "You are a fine gentleman not to stoop to that blackguard's d-despicable level. *Whosoever shall smite thee on thy right cheek…* wait, or is the left cheek the one? Oh, dear. Well, he should turn whichever cheek hadn't been smitten before." She took a sip and made a discreet hiccup.

"I did not turn the other cheek!" he cried, indignant, then reddened to have been so ill-bred as to contradict his hostess. "I am above making a spectacle of myself in public, which is more than I can say about that miscreant."

All you care about is appearances, Vivienne thought as she studied his immaculate blue coat with the fresh white carnation in his lapel.

"I never want you to speak to that scoundrel again," John ordered her. "Not even a simple 'hello.' If you see him on the street, don't even look at him."

"But what if…" She bit down on the inside of her lower lip. *What if you share a sacred Bazulo vow to keep said scoundrel as your bosom confidant regarding a potential terrible family secret?*

"I said, never speak to him again." John came to kneel before her and took her hands in his. "Dearest, you have no idea the depth of depravity of that man. I'm here to protect you and keep you safe. You must obey me, because I know what is best for you."

She looked into his cobalt eyes and felt a jab of guilt. If he knew where she had been today and with whom, he would rescind his proposal on the spot, leaving her father at the mercy of the debt collectors and her aunt to a vile St. Giles madam. She had to choose between John—and her family's security—or her dear old friend, the depraved blackguard. The correct choice was obvious. Angry fiancé trumps secret scoundrel friend every time. "I-I won't speak to him again," Vivienne whispered. Her chest felt heavy and hollow, like those months after her mother died. "I promise."

"Good girl," John said, rising to his feet. "I'm sorry, but I must take leave of you. Naturally, I had not intended to stay so long. Vivienne, in the future, you must stay in the square when walking Garth, for propriety's sake and your own safety."

❧

Dashiell gazed up. The sky had turned a deep indigo color with the coming of night. He stood outside the door of the one place in England more dangerous to him than St. Giles: Christie's. Just last week, his man of business had warned Dashiell that he was down to seventy-five pounds in the bank, and that he shouldn't waste any more money on antiquities until his quarterly dividends arrived. "No more relics unless you dig them up from the London streets yourself," were the man's exact words.

Dashiell drew a long breath and braced himself. *You will buy nothing, Dash. Rien. Nullus. Niente.* Not even that bust of Queen Hatshepsut he had been lusting after. He was here only to see Robert Teakesbury, the famed solicitor, secretary of the Imperial Society for History, Cartography, Exploration, and Related Matters, and the man who annoyed Dashiell most in the world.

Yet up for auction that evening was an irresistible gem of a painting titled *A Venetian Woman* by Lawrence James. On the canvas, a luscious, olive-skinned beauty reclined on a bed of green velvet. Her loose dark hair curled about the gentle mounds of her breasts and then down the taper of her waist. In the arched window just above her right shoulder, the lights from the Rialto Bridge burned like hazy globes in the night, casting a slant of light across her golden-bronze eyes, making them appear to gleam like a wild tiger's in the bush.

Vivienne, he thought when he first saw the creation, but he couldn't figure out why. The image didn't look a thing like her except for something about the model's eyes: a mysterious invitation—seductive, yet innocent, eliciting that same primal gut hunger he felt whenever he was around Vivienne.

He tried to ignore the painting, but those alluring eyes followed him as he edged about the auction room, teasing, taunting, daring him to look again at her luscious body. "Buy me, big boy," she seemed to whisper. "You want me." No weeping Greek theater masks or noseless busts of Roman generals could silence her siren call. Finally, Dashiell did what he always did when temptation beckoned: succumb to it. He planted himself firmly before the canvas, letting the Italian Vivienne's seductive power wash over him and pool in his loins. In his mind, he pulled her down onto her lush velvet bed, blew the air of life into her lungs, and made love to her in a wild burst of released sexual frustration. And then again—slowly, calmly, tenderly—when the passionate storm had abated.

Good God, what is Vivienne doing to me?

Dashiell shook his head and found a seat in the empty back row of the mostly empty auction room. He slumped down in his chair, his legs extended, arms crossed at his chest. Being auctioned was a catalog of sermons that was being fought over by a foursome of

uptight antiquarians. Bored, Dashiell's mind drifted
back to fantasies of the Italian Vivienne. This time,
they made slow, gentle love in a gondola as it floated
under the arched bridges of Venice. Her mouth open
with ecstasy, her hair splayed about her head as the
tiny boat rocked with their rhythm.

A warm, strong hand clamped onto his shoulder,
and a large diamond flashed in his eyes. "Lord Dashiell,
I'm surprised to see you."

Dashiell jumped. He turned and found himself
staring into the bright dry glitter of Teakesbury's
hazel-gold eyes and his omnipresent bemused smile.
The scent of starch and sweet cigar smoke wafted from
his immaculate black coat and deep gray cravat. His
dark hair swept across his forehead in a silken wave,
and he wore a trim mustache that drew into fine
points on the sides.

He gripped a cane topped with the gold head of
what many mistook for an odd cat but which was
actually an Indian mongoose. "I heard you had gotten
yourself in a bit of trouble, old chap, and were headed
off to Hong Kong after you promised you would
speak at the Society."

Several heads turned in the rows in front of them.
Teakesbury nodded his greeting.

"I don't know what trouble you're talking about,"
Dashiell said, trying to sound both casual and innocent.

"Oh, the usual Lord Dashiell variety—cheating
wife, ambitious courtesan or actress, crying, vows of
revenge, a ship bound for the East." Teakesbury drew
a cigar out of his coat and beckoned a footman for a
light with a mere bend of his finger. "You're rather

predictable, my boy. Maybe you should try something new. Perhaps growing up."

Dashiell clenched and unclenched his fist. The solicitor was always just a few words away from having Dashiell land him a facer. And the man knew it.

Teakesbury took delight in being an antagonistic arse because he possessed a valuable gift that made him the most sought after solicitor in London: he knew everything about anyone of consequence. He was the human mongoose who could sniff out information from the very air and dirt. Dashiell first met Teakesbury when the solicitor helped put away his father's murderer. Over the years, Dashiell developed a grudging respect for the man despite the ever-present urge to darken his daylights.

"I need to talk to you later," Dashiell said through his tight jaw.

"Of course you do, good man." Despite the dozen or so empty chairs around them, Teakesbury took the one beside Dashiell, sat, and crossed his legs. "Need some legal counsel?"

"Nothing of the sort," Dashiell said, turning back to the auction and pretending to be interested in the prints of King George III that were on the block. But the smoke from Teakesbury's cigar seemed to curl around his face like ghostly fingers, tickling his nose and coating his throat. The glass eye of the mongoose appeared to wink at him. Even when the solicitor was doing nothing, he still managed to grate on Dashiell's nerves.

An ugly garnet brooch fashioned in the shape of a hedgehog and a deceased vicar's library of books detailing the weather patterns of Scotland were auctioned before the James painting was presented. A hush fell over the crowd as the Italian Vivienne lay unabashedly naked before them. Her painted eyes seemed alive and staring straight at Dashiell.

"I want you," she whispered to him from her easel. His blood started to flow south to his loins.

"The bidding starts at five pounds," the auctioneer said.

"Put me in your bed chamber, big man," she cooed. *No, Dash, don't do it...*

But his sex had taken over his brain, and his hand shot up with the alacrity of a love-fevered adolescent's penis. Teakesbury gave a low rumble of a laugh. "You don't want her," he quipped. "She's a bad bargain."

Go to hell! Dashiell kept raising his hand until fifteen pounds later, the tiger-eyed Italian Vivienne was his.

❧

As Teakesbury was oiling his way about the patrons at Christie's, Dashiell and his treasure stood outside the auction house. He couldn't wait until he got home to look at her stunning body again and ripped back the paper wrapping, letting the gaslight bathe her naked skin in golden light. He released a long, low ahhh, feeling a pleasant tingling in his percy.

Teakesbury strolled through the doors, smile intact, cigar in mouth, cane in hand, the coveted Queen Hatshepsut under his arm The warm happiness in Dashiell's loins drained away.

"Lord Dashiell, even in art you manage to choose the wrong women." The solicitor shook his head, his annoying smile in full beam. "I was interested in this beautiful lady myself when I first ran across her. You see, I represent Mrs. Lawrence James, and I was instrumental in putting together the exhibit at the Royal Academy. This one simply wasn't good enough for such a prestigious venue."

Irrational anger ripped through Dashiell that the solicitor would dare suggest that his stunning Italian Vivienne wasn't "good enough."

"The painting has sentimental value to me," Dashiell said through his gritted molars. Conversations with Teakesbury were hard on his jaw.

"The technique is poor, probably one of James's early works." The solicitor pointed at the canvas with the bejeweled hand holding the cigar, delighting in pointing out Dashiell's foolishness. "The perspective is off in the background, and the colors are muddled. But you can see the man's potential in the detail of her body. I estimated it to be worth five pounds and you paid twenty."

"Thank you for the art lecture. But I said I bought it for sentimental reasons."

"And my client thanks you. No doubt you've heard that times have been hard on the poor widow and her infant." Teakesbury's eyes grew large like a sad puppy's, but the cynical glitter remained.

"And I don't suppose you are offering her free legal counsel from the kindness of your black heart?"

"You amuse me," Teakesbury said with a low chuckle that caused the ash to fall off his cigar. "By God, I think you are my favorite gentleman in London." He threw the nub of his cigar down and ground it under his cane. "What did you want to speak to me about? Has it something to do with that scratch on your face? In a bit of a scrape, lad?"

Dashiell lowered his voice so the people streaming from Christie's couldn't hear. "What do you know about Judge Jeremiah Bertis?"

Teakesbury arched a brow. "Are you asking for free legal counsel from the kindness of my black heart?"

Dashiell's fingers itched to blacken the twinkle in Teakesbury's eyes.

The solicitor laughed, an expansive magnanimous sound from deep in his belly. He patted Dashiell on the back. "Let's talk in Rupert's Club."

Dashiell cleared his throat. "I was thinking we should go to Brooks's." A respectable place, devoid of the usual riffraff that Dashiell attracted.

"Come now, what's wrong with Rupert's? It's just around the corner."

Teakesbury didn't wait for him to answer, but began to stroll toward St. James Street, his cane clicking on the pavers.

❦

The pub was crowded with bleary-eyed lords and sirs, exhausted from a day spent gambling in the nearby hells. Drunken parliament members and civil servants debated each other around the bar. Meanwhile, lightskirts flitted about on the catch for a wealthy customer. The crystal chandeliers and elaborate plaster friezes were blurred in the haze of smoke, drifting like a stratus cloud just above his head.

Dashiell had not been in the establishment more than a minute when he was accosted by some of the more colorful ladybirds. Welcoming, come-hither smiles curled on their red-stained lips. "What happened to your face, love?" "Was a lady mean to you?" "Oh, let me comfort you."

Teakesbury chortled. "Why do I bother with the theater when your company is far more amusing?"

Dashiell bit back his curse and tightened his grip on the Italian Vivienne, pushing through the crush to a table by the marble fireplace where the coals burned a deep luminous orange. He set the painting in the leather chair beside his.

The naked Italian Vivienne brazenly gazed at the club with her lusty, tigress eyes as if she could consume every man there. He felt embarrassed by her lack of modesty, and quickly arranged the paper wrappings to conceal her bare breasts and thighs.

A comely barmaid in a yellow gown, laced so tight she looked like a champagne cork about to pop, traipsed over. "I say, Lord Dashiell, I haven't seen you for a few months. I feared you had died in some faraway place. Would you like the usual crank?" She leaned down, exposing the valley between her breasts. "Or something different?" She ran her tongue over her upper lip.

"J-just the usual will be fine," Dashiell stammered.

The barmaid's mouth thinned in disappointment. She directed her attention at Teakesbury. "And you, sir?"

The solicitor ordered a cherry brandy and watched the barmaid sashay off.

Dashiell cleared his throat. "I've just come here a few times," he assured the solicitor. "Just for crank. Not for… for… you know."

Teakesbury didn't respond but arched a brow, content to let Dashiell stew in his discomfort.

"How's your family?" Dashiell finally managed, struggling for respectable conversation.

"Robert Jr. is in his third term at Eton," he said. "Mrs. Teakesbury is embroidering a fire screen for my office. It's a dear thing, a bird on a branch." The solicitor leaned back in his chair and put his elbows on the armrest, steepling his fingers over his lap. "Now, why do you want to know about Bertis? Has this to do with one of your women?"

"Dammit, Teakesbury, I'm on the board of St. Joseph's Charity School for Boys and some other charity… which I can't remember at the moment… but I've traveled the world. I have a huge collection of antiquities from all periods. And, let us not forget, I'm a contributing member of the Imperial Society for History, Cartography, Exploration, and Related Matters. Despite what you may like to think, not every aspect of my life is about women." This particular aspect was very much about a woman, but the solicitor didn't need to know that.

"Relax, my good man, I'm ribbing you." Teakesbury patted Dashiell's shoulder. "Bertis was a little before my time. He was a puisne judge of the Queen's Bench. But he must have taken everyone's turn at Old Bailey. In his eyes, if a man had been brought to court, he was probably guilty, and if he wasn't, a few years in Newgate would teach him never to argue his grievances to court again."

"What of his personal life? Any connection to a madam down in St. Giles named Adele Jenkinson?"

"A St. Giles abbess?" The human mongoose lit up. "Tell me more of this Adele Jenkinson." He reached into his pocket and drew out a cigar without taking his eyes off Dashiell except to light it on the candle in the middle of the table.

"She might have been a beauty in his day, but now her skin is leathery and all her teeth are rotted. She lives in a regular stop hole with a lobcock named Sidney and her son, Willie, an annoying squirrel of a man. I think she may do business with Angelica Fontaine."

The solicitor smoothed the fine corner of his mustache with his thumb and index finger as he thought. "That's not unusual. Every flesh peddler in the city is trying to supply a rare gem to Fontaine. From what I understand, a new girl at Fontaine's gets a debut party where the top bid wins her for the evening, or if she is lucky, a man takes her as his mistress. Either way, she can make more in one night there than in two years on the street. Fontaine cuts the profit, so it's a good business all around."

Dashiell paused for a moment and drew a line on the table with his finger. "You just said Lawrence James's widow was your client. I think I remember hearing that Fontaine was once his mistress, or should I say James was Fontaine's, as he seemed to be the kept one. What happened to that affair?"

"What you would expect. Once James finally achieved some success, he decided he wanted to marry some young, beautiful thing, and not the dried-up woman who had supported him during all those years he struggled."

"That's rather harsh," Dashiell said. "I think I might

be a little angry if I were Fontaine. In fact, I think I might feel entitled to some of his masterpieces."

"You think she stole those paintings?"

"Perhaps."

The solicitor blew out a plume of smoke and gazed at Dashiell through the haze. "I truly loathe to admit that you and I think alike. It frightens me. I went to Scotland Yard with my suspicions. Yet, she is innocent according to the police and every inquiry made into the theft. But come, my good man, what official is going to go after her? She's got secrets on the whole city." He studied the fiery tip of his cigar. "So you say this Jenkinson woman ran a stop hole abbey. Did you see any masterpieces of art lying about, by chance?"

"Just cheap jewelry, watches, fobs—a small operation. She didn't strike me as too intelligent."

"Nonetheless, I'll have one of my clerks check on her."

The barmaid returned and set two glasses on the table. She jerked her head toward the door. "Your grandfather is here."

"What!" Dashiell's head whipped around to the door.

Several piercing whoops rose above the chatter of the club. People began to crowd about the edges of the room, parting the seas for the Earl of Baswiche and "the boys."

"Oh God," Dashiell groaned.

"Teakesbury," his grandfather said as he nodded to the solicitor, then fixed his wild gaze on the painting. "What are you doing with that portrait of Vivienne?"

"What?" Dashiell bolted from his seat and regathered the fallen wrapping around his painted seductress.

"Good God, this is not Vivienne! It doesn't look a thing like her. Vivienne has pale skin and dimples in her cheeks, and she doesn't have brown eyes."

His grandfather squinted at the painting. "Can't really say I've noticed her eyes before."

How could he not notice her eyes! "They're pale green, like ivy covered in icy snow."

His grandfather's friends exchanged infuriatingly knowing glances.

"My boy's in love." The old man beamed, like some proud society mama announcing her daughter's engagement.

"Bloody hell, I am not!"

"He's got it bad, I can tell," said the earl's friend, Sir Milton. "Never seen a man so much in love as to have to carry around her portrait and all. Who's the lady?"

It seemed like every head in the room turned toward Dashiell. The chatter of conversation and the clatter of utensils and glasses ceased.

"Vivienne Taylor," his grandfather said, oblivious to his audience or the twitching of his grandson's hands, itching to go around his scrawny neck and squeeze his vocal chords permanently shut. "She's Gertrude Bertis's niece, you know, ol' Judge Bertis's wife. A saucy beauty, Vivienne is."

It probably wasn't prudent to take a table knife and murder his grandfather *à la* Thomas Becket in front of a solicitor and a room full of witnesses, no matter how much satisfaction Dashiell would derive from the act.

"Vivienne is *not* in any way attached to me," Dashiell explained with a controlled coolness. "She is an honorable and proper young lady who happens to be engaged to another man, and she is certainly not the model in this painting."

"What's the matter with your boy?" Sir Milton ribbed the earl. "He can seduce every lady in London except the one he's in love with?"

"Remember we discussed his problems with commitments," his grandfather reminded his friends. "How he gets scared."

"Oh," the sympathetic old men said in unison, as if Dashiell suffered from some heinous medical condition such that, upon hearing the word "commitment," his penis would shrink to the size of an acorn.

He slid his hands down his face. "Good God."

"Please excuse me." Teakesbury rose, stubbed out his cigar, and then reached for Hatshepsut. "While I would love to sit here and be amused by your little amorous exploits, Dashiell, I've serious work to do."

"I'm going too." Dashiell shot his grandfather a lethal glare, but it didn't make the slightest dent in the old man's happy, addled expression.

"Hell, Dash, it's just seven!" he cried. "There's a special party at 67 Knightsbridge. Invitation only, and clothes are unnecessary."

The old men giggled, as if giddy to expose their flabby, aging bodies to some poor ladies. Dashiell had to believe a thousand torturous deaths at the hands of the Spanish Inquisition would be a more pleasant way to pass the evening than hanging about with his naked grandfather and his exhibitionist friends. "No, thank you." He tossed a tanner on the table and picked up Italian Vivienne. Hugging her protectively to his body, he hurried after Teakesbury, finding him in the alley.

"So this conversation was really about Judge Bertis's niece?" Teakesbury said.

"Pay no attention to my grandfather. He—"

In a flash, the solicitor raised his cane, holding its butt like a blade point between Dashiell's eyes. "Now listen to me. Judge Bertis was not my favorite judge; nonetheless, I consider him a colleague. You're a faithless scoundrel, Lord Dashiell. All you do is cause hurt and pain. You stay the hell away from Bertis's niece. Understand?" He thumped the cane against Dashiell's cheekbone.

"Ouch! Dammit. Why did you have to do that?"

Teakesbury retracted his staff and began walking into the fog. Then he spun around, swirling the mist about the edge of his coat. "Oh, and one more thing. Don't forget you are lecturing at the Imperial Society next week. I have you slated to speak after Newberry."

⤜⤝

During supper, Vivienne toyed with her mushy potato croquettes drowned in brown sauce as she made elaborate plans to sneak into her uncle's study. Although she realized she couldn't talk to Dashiell anymore, he was right that she should check her uncle's personal effects for incriminating evidence. She wished John hadn't seen her and Dashiell together or that Dashiell hadn't behaved so much like an obnoxious drunk, for now she had to promise never to talk to him again. She had to forget him once and for all, say good-bye to those girlish fantasies about running away to exotic lands with him to dig up mummies and ancient villages. She had clung to those stupid dreams for too long. She poured another cup of black tea. Assuming her little visit to her uncle's study would be a clandestine, midnight mission, she needed to stay awake.

Down the table, Aunt Gertrude was cutting her mutton into tiny pieces and dropping them on Garth's china plate on the floor. "Who's my little puppy? Who's my own sweet sugar? It's you!" she would say as the dog smashed his face into the plate, eating in his noisy spitting manner. Once all the mutton was gone, the merry game was over. Her aunt pushed away her uneaten mounds of croquettes.

"I'm quite fatigued and desire to sleep." She rose from the table. "I trust you will read the Lord's word in my absence."

So after Miss Banks had put her mistress in bed and then gone to the basement to wash the dishes, Vivienne retired to her room. Following her aunt's instructions, she opened her Bible and cursorily read two dull verses from Samuel: *Now there was a certain man of Ramathaimzophim, of mount Ephraim, and his name was Elkanah, the son of Jeroham, the son of Elihu, the son of Tohu, the son of Zuph, an Ephrathite: And he had two wives; the name of the one was Hannah, and the name of the other Peninnah: and Peninnah had children, but Hannah had no children.*

Vivienne closed the book. She picked up the rose glass oil lamp from the side table and padded down to Uncle Jeremiah's study.

She cautiously approached his great, mahogany bureau as if his ghost might rise up and slap her wrists for trying to delve into his secrets. She knew what to do. Her father had inherited a matching bureau upon his wedding to Vivienne's mother. Inside was a secret compartment where her father hid the sparse family jewelry—hideous antique stuff that she would dress up the cat in when her father was working.

She set the lamp on the floor and then dragged a ladder-back chair over. Standing on the chair's seat, she patted about the top of the cabinet until she found the small skeleton key. Then she set to work. She opened the desktop with the key, removed the top drawer, and ran her fingertip along the back recess. She stopped on what felt like the tip of a tiny protruding nail and pushed. There was the slightest click and the bank of drawers shifted down, allowing her to ease them out. In the very back was a little U-shaped pigeonhole. She wedged the tip of her fingernail in it and eased the wood forward until a thin, rectangular wooden box fell out.

Then she saw something different from her father's desk. Uncle Jeremiah's secret compartment had a lock on it.

"Dammit!" she whispered, then pressed her hand to her mouth. She had been around Dashiell too much. He was a bad influence on her vocabulary.

Holding the slim box close to the light, she examined the tiny lock. *Hmmm… a rather primitive mechanism. My father made more complex locks in his factory.*

She plucked a pin from her hair, causing a wavy strand to flop into her eyes. She tried to twine the wayward curls around another pin, but that only caused an avalanche of hair to fall. Frustrated, she pulled every pin from her head, until all of her tresses were loose and flowing about her shoulders.

She bent the edge of a hairpin, stuck the tip in the

lock, and ran her fingernail along the crack in the seam, catching the latch. *Open Sesame.* The box's lid flew back.

Inside was a brown leather book about the size of her hand, so old and well-used its bindings had turned to shreds. Tucked beside its spine was something thin and dark. At first, she thought it was a sentimental lock of hair. But when she picked it up, she found it wasn't a braid of hair, but a tiny sack like the ones used for sausage casing. A curious thing to hide, unless it was saved from a sentimental meal. However, saving the casing was quite unromantic, if not bordering on disgusting.

She set it aside and carefully opened the fragile book.

She read the words, blinked, and read them again, just to make sure she wasn't delusional.

Dec. 2, 1825: It has been a month since Barbara let me peek at her succulent, dimpled cheeks. Oh, my fingers itched to spank each one.

Vivienne touched her own dimpled cheek. Who was Barbara and why did her uncle slap her in the face?

March 12, 1826: Deborah Nixson was a very wicked lady's maid indeed for stealing her mistress's perfume. How she led me on a merry chase around her parlor. What delicious delight I took in administering the back of a hairbrush to her impertinent plump buttocks.

Vivienne's jaw dropped. What kind of person takes delicious delight in spanking?

November 14, 1826: Lovely meeting with Molly O'Brien this morning. I pulled up her petticoats and spanked her jiggly, bouncing bottom as she squealed with pleasure.

Pleasure? Vivienne had been spanked for breaking objects in the house and accidently saying "fudge" when she tore her stocking in church, and it was hardly pleasurable. Was this something all gentlemen did? Was it part of the intimate act? She knew the rudimentary basics of life, thanks to her friend Lavinia Sizemore. She had taken Vivienne and her sisters into the shrubs behind the factories and explained that where babies came out was where they were put in. She pointed to the workers sitting on the walk between shifts, eating muffins. "Every one of those men can't wait to get his part in a lady's private place and make a baby. My sister says that's all they think about, even in church."

Since Lavinia was prone to exaggeration, Vivienne made their housekeeper, Mrs. Hudson, confirm her friend's outrageous assertions. "You're not supposed to be knowin' those things," Mrs. Hudson had said, and then held up a long, thick cucumber she intended to slice. "Look here, if you are talking to a man, and you look down at his trousers, and it looks like this here cucumber is in there—sticking up, big and hard-like—then run And never, never touch a man's thing, no matter how much he begs, unlessin' of course you are married to him. Even then you don't have to touch it unlessin' you want him to get off his lazy arse and do something for ya!"

Her sisters were revolted. Vivienne was intrigued.
She had tried to imagine a man's private part the size
of a cucumber. Secretly, she looked at illustrations
of naked men in the medicine books in the circula-
tion library, but none of their privates looked like a
cucumber, more like carrots and shriveled mushrooms.

However, Mrs. Hudson and Lavinia didn't say
anything about spanking. Surely John didn't do these
things. She hoped.

She stared at the vile book, waiting like a slimy
leech on the desk. Taking a deep, fortifying, be-strong-
Vivienne breath, she sat again and opened to the first
page of the book with the very tips of her fingers as if
she might contract some scarring, poxlike disease from
it. She quickly scanned the entries, stopping on one
dated April 23, 1827.

> *Adele Jenkinson's pert little tail has caused a public
> disturbance. How she flaunted her sweet bum before
> me, just begging for a smart spankie.*

Vivienne's breath quickened.
On April 29, he wrote:

> *Naughty, naughty Adele performed a wicked
> minuet, waggling her rosebud rump before me. Oh,
> how she did squirm over my knee.*

For the next four months, Jeremiah pined for
Adele's sweet broadside in rather Byronesque poetic
elegance. However, by September, there was no more
mention of Adele or her anatomy. Her rosebud had

bloomed, withered, and then fallen off the vine, being replaced by another's more cozy backside for the wintry months.

Vivienne closed the book and retied the string around the worn leather cover. She put everything back in the wooden box, set it on the desk, and stared at it, waiting for tentacles or grotesque gargoyle-like heads to grow. She felt numb. She grappled with the facts, trying to tack down her disarrayed thoughts. *Adele Jenkinson is blackmailing Aunt Gertrude. Adele Jenkinson knew Uncle Jeremiah. Uncle Jeremiah spanked women who weren't his wife.*

Did he spank Aunt Gertrude? Did John spank his early wedding present?

She quivered with revulsion.

She hated being a virgin. She didn't know what she was doing or how gentlemen were supposed to behave. And the one person she was supposed to talk to about these matters, her fiancé, might be so scandalized as to call off the wedding.

Outside the window, she heard the clomp and rattle of a carriage approaching. The groom called "whoa" to his horses and pulled to a stop next door.

Dashiell! She could ask him. He was impervious to scandal. *No, Vivienne, don't do it. You promised John…*

Yet her mind felt full to the point of overflowing with murky vileness. She couldn't go about with these spanking thoughts circling in her head with no one to help her sort them out. And she had made the sacred Bazulo vow with Dashiell… and she should at least tell him that she couldn't keep her word… and he always made everything better… and John need not find out… and, after all, she would never speak to Dashiell again. Never, ever, after this one last time.

She crossed to the window and shoved open the stubborn pane. Dashiell was stepping down from his carriage. He held what looked like a painting wrapped in brown paper. Waving off his groom, he started up his walk.

"Lord Dashiell," she called in a whisper.

He didn't hear his name above the rattle of the departing carriage.

"Lord Dashiell."

He continued toward his front steps, unaware of her. She grabbed one of her uncle's fat law books from the nearby bookshelf and hurled it, intending to hit the ground near Dashiell's feet. Instead, the heavy volume slammed him on the shoulder.

"Dammit!" he shouted and grabbed his arm, nearly dropping his painting. "What the hell?"

His gaze shot up to where she stood at the window. The night breeze batted the curtains about her and blew her hair into her face. She swept back the stray locks with her hand. "I need to talk to you. Urgently," she said softly, yet loud enough to be audible. "Can you meet me there in the alley?"

His body jerked, like a soldier coming to attention. "Just let me put you, I mean, this painting inside."

Six

WITH THE WOODEN BOX CONTAINING THE VILE, filthy, disgusting diary tucked under her arm, Vivienne carefully checked the stairwells and corridors, sneaking through the house and out into the dark alley like an unseen thief.

Dashiell leaned against the brick wall, a black shadow in the residual gaslight flowing in from the square. She could see the lines of his biceps straining against the fabric of his sleeves, the flat hard plane of his belly, and the line of strong muscles running down his thighs and calves.

John was a fool if he thought he could knock Dashiell to the pavement, she thought.

Dashiell was a panther of a man. Sleek, dark, and honed.

He lifted the edge of his hat. His brown eyes sparkled in the darkness, feral, almost dangerous, though she felt no fear, just the quickening of her blood with anticipation. That most private place inside her, that place where supposedly all men wanted to put their cucumber, pulsed.

"What do you want with me?" His voice was a husky whisper.

She intended to say something rational, about the diary and Jenkinson and that he probably shouldn't look at her that way, but all that came out was some strange string of vowels. She swallowed and tried again, "You mean something illicit, don't you?"

He leaned down until his face was near hers. She could feel the heat of his body on her skin. "That's mostly why I meet ladies in an alley, my little butter biscuit."

Oh Lord, she could kiss him, she had just to lean a little closer and those lips, oh those lips would be on hers, tasting her, teasing her, sating this madness and—

What are you doing? You are engaged to John! Remember him?

She took a big step backward. "Uncle Jeremiah could be the foulest, most disgusting, and vilest of men. But I'm not sure!" The words burst out of her.

"Really? I just learned he was an irreproachable stiff-rump."

"Oh, please don't say that word 'rump' or I think I will be positively sick. I found his diary in a secret locked compartment in his desk." She pulled the volume from the wooden box. The sausage casing was stuck on the cover. "And I found this other thing. It was hidden with his diary. Maybe it means something." She held up the casing to the dim gaslight. .

"Vivienne, that's armor."

"Armor?" She shook her head, confused. "Like a man wears to war?"

"No, like a man wears on his… you know… when he is doing… things."

"You are making no sense. What kind of things? Murder things? Blackmail things?"

"Lovemaking things."

The meaning exploded in her mind. "Are you saying my Uncle Jeremiah wore this on his… his… his…" She dropped the armor and screamed. Dashiell's lips were on hers in a twinkle of a second.

Oh!!

Oh.

Ohhhh.

The warm softness of his lips sent a hot, heady wave through her that silenced her thoughts. Everything was him. The hard contours of his chest and the tingle of her nipples as they rubbed against him, the taste of his tongue as it caressed the tip of hers, while his thigh pushed between her limbs, invading her, seeking that place inside her that throbbed, deep and wet. She was free-falling, all her muscles giving way to his touch. His hand rose up her back, pushing her against him. He filled her with his musky pine and cardamom scent mingled with brandy, cigar smoke, and something sweet, like ladies' perfume.

Ladies' perfume! It felt like the sun burned in her head, incinerating her brain. What was she doing?

She pushed his chest, slamming him against the wall. Her throat was so tight it hurt to breathe. "John says I'm not supposed to speak to you anymore," she cried.

"What? You were the one who wanted to meet in the alley. Maybe I'm wrong, but I assumed that would entail speaking." Then he laughed—that rake had the gall to laugh, a thick vicious sound. "Or maybe that wasn't your intention. After all, you were the one with the armor."

The roar of rushing blood filled her ears. He had said just a few words too many. Something broke inside her; some wall crashed to the ground. "Aren't you clever? Standing there, reeking of perfume. No doubt you were in some brothel like Seven Heavens before you came here. Who knows, maybe you ran into John? Maybe you two had a little orgy of prostitutes."

"Can you keep your voice down? I really don't want to be arrested."

"I think it would be an interesting little experiment to go door-to-door in the square and see how many men are actually at home with their wives—their perfect wives—and how many are with some woman under a dark bush in Hyde Park with thingies on their things."

He pulled her back to him, wrapping his arms tightly around her, as if to subdue her. "Hush, love."

"Don't touch me! Don't call me love! Don't… don't…" In all decency she should pull away, but his arms felt so safe and gentle, like being tucked under a layer of warm blankets as the early morning rain pattered on the window.

"Now tell me what is the matter," he whispered, running his palm soothingly down her loose curls.

"I found an Adele Jenkinson in Uncle Jeremiah's diary. They knew each other." She pressed the diary into his chest, but couldn't bring herself to describe what she found there.

"I can't read it out here. Follow me." He took her hand, squeezed it, and led her around to the back gate of his mews. "Wait," he said and slipped inside.

The horses stared at him as he took a brass lantern

from the wall. Outside, Vivienne waited, her arms wrapped tight around her. The beautiful golden light spilled into the courtyard, illuminating her face. He had the urge to draw her to him again; he wanted to feel the exhilaration of her touch, disappear in her scent and lips again.

But she must have sensed the danger, for when he stepped closer, she edged away from him and held the diary out, pinched between her two fingers, like it was fouled baby cloth, careful that her fingers did not accidentally touch his.

He opened the diary and read aloud. "Pauline was a naughty *jeune fille* and needed a smart spanking. I gave each cheek a good—" He burst into laughter. "Hi ho, old Bertis was a spanker! This is fine, indeed."

"Is this normal?" Vivienne asked, her face a tense ball of angst and confusion. "Is this how men behave? Do you go around spanking women?"

"No!" That wasn't entirely correct. "I mean, not unless they want me to."

She shook her head. "I'm so stupid, so ignorant of a man's world."

"You might be shocked how very little there is to it."

She studied him. "Why do you smell like ladies' perfume and spirits? Where were you before you came here?"

"Do you really want to know the vile, revolting truth?"

"Yes," she whispered.

"Let's see," he said, rubbing his chin, pretending to be serious. "I went to Christie's and bought a painting." He left off irrelevant details such as it was a nude by Lawrence James and the model's eyes glittered all seductive and beautiful just like Vivienne's in the dancing lantern light. "Then I went to a club with a solicitor where several ladies, reeking of perfume, came up to greet me. I ordered some crank and asked the solicitor about Jeremiah Bertis. Then I—and this is where it really gets depraved, you may want to cover your ears—I came home and kissed a hysterical lady in an alley to keep her quiet."

Vivienne's shoulders drooped. "I'm bad, aren't I?"

"Not as bad as your uncle."

"I'm just so confused about everything, Uncle Bertis… and… and… John." He brushed her cheek. The feel of his skin on hers felt so lovely, yet she had to turn away. "I shouldn't let you do that. I belong to another and you know it."

A breeze blew down the alley. She shivered. The night was suddenly somber and colder, though nothing had radically changed in the weather.

"I'm sorry," he whispered.

She nodded. For a few seconds, they said nothing, just listened to the sounds of London at night: distant curses, the clomp and rattle of traffic, and an occasional nightingale.

"Is spanking normal in relations between a man and a lady?" Vivienne asked again.

"Maybe a fun pat or as a little lovemaking game, but not to the extent your uncle did. This is quite perverse and, frankly, embarrassing."

"Do you suppose Mrs. Jenkinson has letters from him with accounts of how he spanked her? I know I would pay most dearly to keep that silent."

"The problem is that we don't know because we

haven't seen what is in the envelopes that your aunt receives. We can't go to Mrs. Jenkinson and say that we know Jeremiah spanked women. Because that might have nothing to do with the blackmail—or if it even is blackmail. Then we would be giving her more material to use against your aunt and no evidence for us to prosecute her."

"I have to get in Aunt Gertrude's room and find the letters, which is almost impossible since she never leaves home except to go to church."

"And if she had any sense she would burn them." He paused. "Did you say you found this diary in a secret compartment?"

"Yes, I knew to look there because his desk is like my father's at home."

"So, Bertis hid his perversion, because if he were found out, he would be ridiculed in society and lose his stature as a judge. No doubt he didn't expect to drop dead on Holborn eating a pigeon pie. He probably always assumed he had time to destroy the diary." Dashiell slapped the book against his palm, "How many women do you think are in this book? Fifteen? How come none of them came forward before?"

"Because he held something over them!"

"Most likely. Did Jeremiah keep copies of *The Proceedings* for the years he was a judge?"

"I don't think so."

"Dammit, I'll have to go down to Old Bailey and check the records."

"No, no, not you. You have done enough. This is not your problem."

"Vivienne, you can't go to Old Bailey alone,"

he said in a weary voice. "It's a dangerous place for an unescorted lady. The trials are on, people milling about drunk and bloodthirsty to see hangings."

"But I'm not supposed to sp—"

"—speak to me," Dashiell finished. "Yes, I know. So why don't you ask John to escort you?" He asked it innocently, yet sarcasm boiled beneath his words. "Perhaps he would like to beat up a ruffian for you too?"

"You know I can't," she cried. "You-you saw what he is like."

Dashiell opened his hands, palms up. "I'm your Charon between the worlds, love. You want to put yourself in the most dangerous places in London, then you're going have to get on my boat and let me carry you or, preferably, let me handle it *alone*."

She groaned and flung up her arm. "I'll tell Aunt Gertrude I'm going to a lecture or something. But after that, we can never meet again. This time, I mean it."

❧

The next morning, Dashiell's eyes shot open, his heart racing. The dim, coal-laden light of early morning peeked through the tops of his windows.

Vivienne had left him last evening after making him agree to "accidently" run into her at two in the afternoon by the gates of Old Bailey. After they parted, Dashiell's emotions were crumpled in a tight wad and his nerves were jumpy with pent-up energy. He downed two glasses of brandy but couldn't quench his thirst. Her kiss, her taste, her smell had unleashed a primal hunger and now he couldn't get her out of his mind… or his sex.

He had resolved to go out and find some green-eyed, raven-haired beauty to relieve him of his frustration, so that when he met Vivienne today, every ounce of that pesky desire would be drained from his body. Yet the hearth coals in his chamber had wafted their drowsy lulling heat, and his down mattress felt so comforting, and the Italian Vivienne had stared seductively at him from where he had temporarily propped her by his bed. He shut his eyes, determined to nap for a few minutes, but the soothing tide of excellent brandy swept him back to the feel of Vivienne's lips, and he sank into dream land, where his rational mind couldn't venture and stop him from feeling her bare, silky smooth skin below his as he moved inside her. How she shut those glittery eyes, and her thighs trembled as she cried out in pleasure.

Then somewhere in the early morning, the sensual dream had turned to nightmare, and he had woken up with a start, his heart pounding, his body bathed in sweat. *Oh god, I've bedded her!* Terror like the twenty-four hours he'd spent as a hostage down in a dried well in Persia assailed him. He had to run, to get away from here. Then he saw Italian Vivienne still staring at him at her place by his bed. It was a dream, he realized, gasping air as if he had just finished running a race. A dream.

He fumbled for the pocket watch he left on the table and squinted, trying to make out the hands.

Six twenty. Bloody hell. He was usually just wandering home at this ungodly hour.

He groaned, kicked off the covers, and sat on the edge of his bed. "This is your fault," he accused the

Italian Vivienne. He pulled his banyan off an obliging stone goddess in the corner and headed down to the water closet.

It was after nine when his grandfather sauntered home. Dashiell, now barbered and wearing a somber gray coat and trousers, was preoccupied with hanging Italian Vivienne. Not an easy project, as it meant finding space on his already cluttered wall, and he didn't trust his servants to move his precious archeological babies. He stood high on a ladder, holding a brass picture hook, the painting dangling from a wire. Below, Rivers and two footmen were debating how much more to the left the painting needed to move.

"Wouldn't it be easier just to marry Vivienne and put her in your bed?" his grandfather quipped, surveying the slabs of hieroglyphics, broken pieces of frescoes and friezes, and various paintings set about the floor awaiting new homes.

The footmen's lips trembled with repressed laughter.

"Pardon us," Dashiell barked at the servants, then regretted it. Vivienne was fraying his nerves. The men scurried out, their faces tensed with worry. After all, if Dashiell let them go, they would have to find work in a "normal" home, which might actually keep account of the amount of wine they drank, insist on no relations with female servants, and demand that they serve meals other than breakfast.

"This does not look at all like Vivienne," Dashiell said, stepping down from the ladder. "Stop talking like that. And don't go about telling everyone that I love her."

"Love isn't something to be ashamed of," the earl stated. "It's the subject of art and poetry and all those damn plays Shakespeare foisted on us. How is it the French get that amusing Molière chap and we get Shakespeare?"

"This is not a contemplation of art or theater," Dashiell said. "If you say that I love her again, I'm not reading any more parliamentary bills or writing speeches for you. Nor will I talk sense into the next jealous lover who wants to put a bullet through your head. Have I made myself clear?"

The earl shrugged, showing no indication of concern. Instead, he walked over to the commode, poured a brandy, and swished it around in his mouth. "So why were you talking with Teakesbury last night?" he asked. "I didn't think you two were friends."

"We're not." Dashiell hesitated, choosing his next words carefully, as his grandfather had a propensity to hear things that Dashiell had never uttered. "We were just talking about Teakesbury's law business. I didn't know he had such an extensive career. He even worked on some cases that were brought before Judge Bertis." Dashiell tried to sound humdrum, as if he could have as easily talked about the Queen's Cabinet appointments or the price of wheat.

"Is that so?" his grandfather asked, not taking his grandson's bait.

So Dashiell needed to be more direct. "What do you remember about Bertis?"

"Is this because you're in love with his niece?"

"Look, I warned you. The next man who wants to fight you, I will just give him my gun."

The earl examined the refraction of sunlight on his glass. "He was an arse. The day we moved in, I passed him in the square. I bowed and introduced myself, being the neighborly sort. I told him about the fire at our Berkeley Square home, and how we were going to live here for a while until we could rebuild. He just said, 'I'm glad it's of a temporary nature.' No 'Welcome to the square,' or 'Have you met my wife?' Hell, it was a least a month after I arrived that I first saw Gertrude. The poor girl looked nearly as worn out and broken as she does today."

"Did you ever hear of Judge Bertis being involved with other women in some perhaps deviant manner—say, like spanking."

The earl's eyes widened. "Jeremiah was a spanker?"

Dashiell held up his palm. "I didn't say that. I just asked if you knew of him involved in suspect behavior with perhaps equally suspect women."

The earl began to pace, his hands clasped behind his back. His nostrils flared with his hard breathing. "I *knew* something wasn't right with him by the way he treated Trudie."

"What do you mean? Did he abuse her? Beat her?"

"I would say he didn't touch her. I felt sorry for her. She was unhappy in bed."

Dashiell studied his grandfather. In his pale gray eyes, he saw something, a tender emotion. "Tell me, why didn't you move back to Berkeley Square after you rebuilt our home there? Have you and Gertrude—"

"I've never touched Gertrude!" his grandfather shouted, as if Dashiell had questioned his honor as a gentleman. "It's nice here, you know." The earl tugged at his cravat, his eyes averted from his grandson's. "Quiet. Look, there is something you need to know," the earl said finally, with a deep reverence in his voice.

For a moment, Dashiell thought he was going to impart some terrible family secret involving Gertrude. That she was his lost sister or something. Dashiell wouldn't be surprised. He always suspected he was related to half of England.

"Son, I'm a seer into the feminine soul."

"A what?" Dashiell should have known his grandfather was incapable of a serious discussion. He could gain greater insight conversing with a hyena about the reasons for the collapse of the Roman Empire.

"It's a family gift," his grandfather admitted. "You've got it too."

Dashiell rubbed his forehead. "Well then, I should make myself a little sign and go sell my clairvoyant powers in Covent Garden. I'm sure my man of business will be thrilled with the additional income."

"Wait," the earl said. "What makes you think Jeremiah was a spanker?"

"I just heard a rumor, that is all." Dashiell shrugged, trying to appear casual. "If you didn't know, it probably can't be true. In any case, I wouldn't go about saying anything."

"What kind of gentleman do you think I am? Trudie's a damn good woman, better than Jeremiah ever deserved. I wouldn't dream of embarrassing her."

Dashiell's mouth hung open. He waited, thinking that perhaps his grandfather might see something a tad ironic in his proclamation. After several seconds, Dashiell gave up and asked the obvious. "Then why do you expose yourself in front of her and her Bible friends?"

His grandfather jerked his head and blinked. "That's not embarrassing."

"Dear God," Dashiell muttered, hoping that either his grandmother or mother had lied about the paternity of their firstborn son.

❧

After breakfast, Vivienne asked Harold to go out and buy a copy of *The Times* as she was unable to leave the square. The man must have traveled to Portsmouth to buy the newspaper, for he didn't return until after lunch. She took the paper to her chamber, spread out the pages on her bedcovers, and searched for any lecture within the vicinity of Old Bailey that her aunt would allow her to attend. At one-thirty, the Royal Academy had a discussion concerning the composition in da Vinci's works.

She opened her trunk and sorted through all her books and notebooks until she located the booklet she wanted: "A Tour of Roman and Medieval London." Guilt weighted her belly as she used the sparse visitors' map to trace a route from the Royal Academy to Old Bailey. She had promised John she wouldn't talk to Dashiell again, and already she had kissed the scoundrel, and now she was planning a clandestine meeting.

She touched her lips, letting her mind drift back to the memory of his kiss. John's kisses were pleasant, but Dashiell's touch was like velvet on fire. Soft, sensual, and burning all the way to her feminine core. She had turned and turned through the night, burrowing her head under the pillow and the covers, but the memory of the feel of his body, the taste of brandy on his tongue, and the way her breasts tingled when he pressed his chest against her kept sneaking into her brain, refusing to go away.

This is the very last time, she promised herself, stifling a yawn. She couldn't let Dashiell delve deeper into her family's problems… or her heart.

She heard a quiet tap on the door and quickly shoved the pamphlet back into her trunk. "Yes?" she called.

Miss Banks slipped into the chamber. "Pardon me, Miss, but Mr. Vandergrift has come."

Shame knotted her insides. "P-please tell him I'll be right there." She took a deep breath. *Oh God, give me strength*, she prayed and then realized God probably wasn't too happy with her.

❧

From the stairwell, Vivienne could hear Garth growling and her aunt saying, "Come here, you naughty, naughty dog. Let go of Mr. Vandergrift's cuff this instant." She entered the parlor to find Garth being reined in by Aunt Gertrude's chair. "Just you behave yourself!" her aunt admonished him. Unfazed, the hound peeked his wrinkled face around the upholstery and snarled at John.

"I just had these trousers tailored," her fiancé muttered, brushing fur from his legs. When he saw Vivienne, he stopped what he was doing, rushed forward, and squeezed her hands. "Mr. Montag has invited us to attend the opera in their box tonight," he said. "They desire to meet you."

Tonight? Why tonight? "How wonderful," she mustered and forced a smile. As if she didn't have enough to worry about without the addition of meeting the man who had the power to make or destroy her father with a flourish of his pen.

"Wear your hair up with those curls falling from the top," he said, lifting a strand of her hair. "Just like the first night I saw you. I had never seen a more lovely vision. My fiancée must be the most beautiful lady there tonight."

"And she will be," her aunt said. "But even more lovely is Vivienne's kind heart and virtuous nature." She placed her hand on her Bible and closed her eyes. "As it says in Peter, *Whose adorning let it not be that outward adorning of plaiting the hair, and of wearing of gold, or of putting on of apparel; But let it be the hidden man of the heart, in that which is not corruptible, even the ornament of a meek and quiet spirit.*"

Vivienne wished she could shrink into a little ball and disappear under the carpet. In her mind, she saw herself pressed against Dashiell, wantonly kissing his lips in an alley, and now she was planning a secret meeting. A fine example of her meek spirit and virtuous nature.

Then, as if to add more stones to the already crushing weight of her shame, Aunt Gertrude continued, "Little Vivvie has been so good. You would be very proud of her. She hasn't gone into the square near that terrible Lord Dashiell, but stays at home improving her mind with the book you kindly gave her."

"Very good." John gave Vivienne an approving look. "I am quite pleased to hear that it is making a favorable impression. My future wife should be above reproof."

"Don't you mean *reproach*?" Vivienne said.

John arched an eyebrow. "Pardon?"

Vivienne blinked. "I thought… that is… Caesar's wife Calpurnia had to be above *reproach*. Well, at least that is how the phrase is usually translated. Of course, the Roman leader made this decree and then gallivanted off to Cleopatra's arms."

Her aunt gasped. "My dear, you mustn't correct your husband," she said. "Why, he is the head of your home, your heart, your mind. You must submit to him in all matters."

"But-but I am… am…" Vivienne swallowed the word *right* and said "sorry" instead. Studying John's handsome, rigid face, her married life stretched out before her in a flash, a diet of a thousand unspoken words, sentences, paragraphs burning in her stomach.

"Don't worry, she'll learn just the way I did when I married Mr. Bertis," her aunt told John. "How patient he was, and he taught me the true duties of a wife." Her thinned lips began to twitch and she reached for the bottle of *Dr. Philpot's Wonderful Nerve Tonic* beside her Bible, taking a quick swig. "Now perhaps you two would enjoy a walk together. The Lord has made a lovely day."

"Actually," Vivienne began, trying to sound casual as her heart raced. "I… I thought I might attend a lecture—a ladies' lecture at the Royal Academy—"

"Certainly not!" John thundered, his face turning red and severe, like her father's when Vivienne had upset him.

"But it's just a lecture—"

"I will not be swayed." John held up his palm.

"There is a particularly offensive exhibit at the Royal Academy. For your own sake, you must not attend. I'm shocked that the Academy would allow such obscene nude art to be publicly displayed."

Vivienne's mouth fell open. *You didn't look so shocked the other day,* she wanted to fire back.

"Nudity!" Aunt Gertrude fanned her flushing face with her fingers. "I almost let my little Vivvie be exposed to... to... naked limbs and ankles and... and nether regions! Vivienne, you may not go!" She reached for her tonic again and took a large gulp. "London is overcome with pestilence and lewdness, I tell you. What are decent God-fearing people to do? That God in his mercy should destroy it like he did Sodom. Oh, Mr. Vandergrift, I am so glad you are here to guide my little Vivvie. You do so remind me of my dear, dear husband."

Vivienne made a tiny, choked squeak.

Her aunt gazed up at her husband's portrait. "He was such a fine man."

A fine man, indeed! Vivienne thought. A fine lecherous old spanker whose secrets could destroy her family and her future marriage. Now how was she going to get to Old Bailey to meet Dashiell? She needed time to think.

From under the chair, Garth growled.

Vivienne pasted a simpering smile on her lips. "Thank you for protecting me," she told John. "When will you be returning this evening, so that I might properly prepare my hair to fall in curls as you desire? I do so want to make a good impression on the Montags. I must be perfect for you," she said, swirling around in her tide pool of guilt and lies. But, she reminded herself, some of her words were quite true. She desperately needed to make a good impression on the Montags. In fact, she truly had to be perfect.

Yet first she had to find a way to hush up the man in the blue coat and his horrible mother, or all the beautiful curls falling on her face couldn't get John to the altar or keep her father from debtor's prison.

God, after today, I'm not talking to Dashiell ever again. And this time I truly mean it. Then I'm going to be virtuous and meek and quiet for the rest of my life.

⅋

Where is she?

Dashiell drew out his silver watch: 2:49. One minute had elapsed since he last checked the time. She was now nineteen minutes late. He ran his hand across his chin.

What if something has happened to her?

He peered out onto the street from where he was concealed on a footpath two blocks from Old Bailey. The entire block reeked of unwashed bodies and alcohol. The crowd, a curious assortment of Londoners—from well-dressed clerks to vagrant men in tattered rags—pressed the round brick walls of the court and prison, waiting for word from the trials inside. Everyone's eyes were wide and shiny, drunk with the anticipation of death. The scene made Dashiell think of the human sacrifice rituals of certain indigenous peoples, when the great sky gods came down and filled the bodies of the natives, making them sing and dance about fires.

What was his thinking last night? Kissing Vivienne had turned his brain to mush. He should have never agreed to let her come along. He began to pace, berating himself and letting his overactive imagination run wild with the worst scenarios. *If anything happened to her…* His hands balled into hard rocks, ready to beat to death some would-be assaulter of his little sister.

"Dashiell," he heard her call. The sound of her voice washed like clean rain over him.

She rushed down the path, her old green cloak flapping behind her. She stopped and pulled back the net concealing her face, over the brim of her straw bonnet. Her cheeks were red and eyes bright from exercise.

"I'm sorry I'm late." She pressed her palm to her chest, her words tumbling out between great gasps of breath. "I told my aunt and John that I wanted to attend a ladies' lecture so I could slip away to meet you. John wouldn't let me go to a lecture at the Royal Academy on account of the Lawrence James exhibit. So that left 'The Proper Irrigation for Herb Gardens' at the London Ladies Flower and Garden Society. It started fifteen minutes ago, and then I had to sneak out the back of the building so my aunt's groom wouldn't see me leave. I ran all the way here. I only have forty-five minutes."

"Why didn't you let me just go by myself?"

"What if you found out some terrible family secret?"

"First of all, if we find something in the written records, by definition, it's not a secret. And second, your family's secrets would only be cute cuddly kittens compared to my family's secrets."

She surveyed the rowdy throng clotting the street and ran her tongue across her upper lip, thinking. "I'll go first, and then you come in as if you didn't know I was there. 'What a pleasant surprise to see you,' 'Imagine meeting you here' and so forth."

"Meeting someone in court is hardly a pleasant surprise. It's more a question of 'what have you done?'"

She let out a huff of breath and rolled her eyes. "Just don't make it look like we planned to meet."

She replaced the net over her face and hurried out onto the street, wedging herself into the crowd. He followed her, immediately ignoring their agreement to accidentally meet in order to swat several roving male hands from her skirt.

Vivienne pushed her way to the gate, where two young guards stood just inside the bars. She raised her net and gave the gentlemen a wide smile. "Pardon me," she shouted above the commotion. "I desire to read the court records. I'm trying to determine what happened to my dear, lost Uncle Lionel."

The guard on the right leaned against the gate. His eyes drifted from her face to her bosom. "Sorry luv, we can't let anyone in 'less they 'ave business wiv the court."

She forced herself to keep smiling. "As I told you, I do have business."

"Well then, we will be down to the pub in an hour," the other guard informed her. "Maybe we could arrange a li'l something special."

She felt a strong hand squeeze her shoulder. "How about getting your sad arses sent to Calcutta? Is that something she can do for you? I'm Lord Dashiell, and you *will* let in my cousin." He sounded so cold-blooded he could have said he had business in the court as the murderer. "Now."

The guards bolted to attention.

"Yes, m'lord."

As they passed through the tiny courtyard, Vivienne glanced up at Dashiell from the corners of her eyes.

"Imagine meeting you here!" she said in a syrupy voice, her ruse now in shambles. "What a pleasant surprise!" She flashed him hot eyes. "If John learns of this, I'm going to make you find me another husband. Consider it your cousinly duty."

"Now there's a real threat. It would be hard to find some poor chap willing to put up with a lady as ramshackle as yourself."

"Might I remind you that this was *your* idea."

"Just the part about checking records, not you tagging along and upsetting the guards."

The entrance hall was clogged with people. The air was humid with pungent human sweat. The place smelled no better than the adjacent Newgate prison. Dashiell held onto her, pulling her through the crush. Inch by inch, they pushed through the crowded entrance hall, coming to a set of stairs where another guard waited.

Vivienne started to politely explain. "Pardon me, I would like to see *The Pro*—"

"I'm Lord Dashiell."

The guard bowed. "Very good, m'lord," he said and gestured for them to pass.

"Is life always this easy for you?" she marveled when they reached the upper story. "Just 'Hello, I'm Lord Dashiell' and you get anything you want?"

"Well, sometimes I follow stray ladies to brothels and get beaten up."

She studied the brown bruise on his jaw, and guilt pricked her heart. Then she saw the laughter lurking at the edges of his mouth. The scoundrel enjoyed teasing her. Despite being London's premier rake, at this moment, he didn't seem very different from the boys she and her sisters tormented back at Birmingham. She wrinkled her nose at him and then tossed her head.

Servants dressed in gray livery were carrying trays hoisted high in the air. They streamed into a dining room where a long table was being set with silver and crystal.

Dashiell approached one of the servants. "Do you know where I might find *The Proceedings*?"

The man jerked his head toward a door at the back of the hall. "Thems clerks can 'elp you, sir."

Dashiell led her across the hall and into a paneled parlor with a carved mahogany table running down the center. On its surface were three cut-glass bowls filled with fragrant dried flower petals.

By the far wall, a young man sat with his long legs crossed on a leather sofa. He held the *London Times* before his face.

Vivienne arched a teasing brow at Dashiell. "Go tell him your name, dear cousin," she whispered.

Dashiell stepped forward and cleared his throat. The man lowered his paper, shooting him an annoyed look through the lenses of his glasses.

"I'm Lord Dashiell," he declared in the commanding tone that worked on the guards. "And I would like to see *The Proceedings*."

The clerk rose and bowed. "I'm sorry, my lord, but

our copies are only for the judges." Then he sat again and returned to his reading, clearly unimpressed by Dashiell's peerage or his commanding tone.

Dashiell tugged Vivienne's arm, pulling her into the corridor.

"What are we going to do now?" she cried, feeling bereft after all she had done just to get this far.

"Show the clerk your adorable dimples and tell him, using that sugary voice of yours, that you're desperate for his help."

"What? Oh, you're incorrigible!"

"No, just expedient."

Before she could retort, he gave her a gentle shove back into the room.

"Pardon me," Vivienne said, getting the man's attention. She clasped her hands at her chest. "It's quite important that I see *The Proceedings*." She gave the clerk a sad smile that was just wide enough to make her dimples come out of hiding. As a personal touch, she added a bat of her lashes. "I'm truly desperate. What do you suggest I do?"

The man flushed and his Adam's apple bobbed. He glanced about the room as if to check for other clerks, and then settled back on Vivienne's face. "I'm sure they won't mind if you take a small look."

"Oh, thank you! I just need to locate some cases involving an Adele Jenkinson. It would be between the years of 1815 and 1839."

He nodded. "Why don't you and your…" He looked at Dashiell, who was loitering by the bookshelves.

"Cousin," she supplied, flicking her hand as if Dashiell meant nothing to her.

The clerk's eyes brightened. "Why don't you and your cousin make yourselves comfortable at the table?" He stepped out into the hall.

"Is life always this easy for you?" Dashiell quipped. "Just smile prettily and get anything you want?"

"Of course." She cocked her head and flashed her dimples again. "Make the bad men who pushed my father around go away. Make that terrible woman leave my aunt alone. Make John…" Her throat tightened. She couldn't finish… a faithful husband.

"I'm sorry," he said and squeezed her fingers. They stood silently, touching. He lifted her hand to his lips and lightly kissed her knuckles. "We will make everything better."

She heard the clerk's footsteps against the floor planks in the hall and leapt apart from Dashiell as the clerk pushed the door open with his back.

He held four tomes in his arm which he set on the table. Vivienne took the chair beside the clerk. Dashiell closed the door and walked to the other side of the table.

From the number of cases in each volume, Vivienne despaired that half of England must go to trial every year. Finding Jenkinson would take all day, and she had to sneak back into the Ladies' Flower and Garden Society in thirty minutes. However, the clerk scanned through the pages like some fleet-fingered Apollo of paperwork.

"Ah, here is one," he said after a minute. He slid the book over to Vivienne.

Adele Jenkinson, accused of assault upon a Maxwell Cain of Finsbury.

Maxwell Cain: I be Maxwell Cain of Finsbury. I 'ad finished me dodger and was coming out Taggart's boozing ken that darky and heading back to my crib next to 104 Ironmonger Row, when I saw yon prisoner standing in the plate of meat, calling ANNE WHITCOMB a fusty luggs for prigging her cove.

Judge Bertis: This is a British court of law. I demand you speak proper English. Now what did you say?

Maxwell Cain: Aye, what I said.

Court Reporter: The Prisoner was calling ANNE WHITCOMB names for stealing her lover.

Judge Bertis: And who is this ANNE WHITCOMB? Is she the proprietor of 104 Ironmonger?

Maxwell Cain: No, Govna, MRS. HANNAH STONEGATE. She's the su-pouch.

Court Reporter: Landlady.

Judge Bertis: Just how many women live at this address?

Maxwell Cain: Evlenet. But they be feeles and pals.

Court Reporter: Twelve, but they're sisters and cousins.

Judge Bertis: Yes, of course they are.

Maxwell Cain: So Mrs. STONEGATE comes out and tells yon prisoner to hop the twig. Yon prisoner lugs the su-pouch's strummel real hard. I tries to tip, but the dimber–mort gives me a floorer in the twiddle-dwiddles, and when I was down she wallups me in me lobb. So I—

Judge Bertis: Enough of this low, thievish cant. How many times have you come before this court, Mr. Cain?

Maxwell Cain: Five as a jack-sprat. Earth as a cull.

Court Reporter: Five as a boy and three as a man.

Adele Jenkinson—Acquitted—Aged 20

Vivienne marked the place with her finger and closed the cover to read "Second Session, held April 1827." Vivienne slid the book across the table to Dashiell. "Around the time of the diary entry," she told him.

He leaned back in his chair and pressed his thumb to his temple. He read slowly, his brow creased with concentration as if he were memorizing the words.

"Ah yes, another one," the clerk said. "A most interesting case."

Vivienne took the book and began to read.

ADELE JENKINSON was indicted for stealing a silver rattle of 5 pound value that belonged to Mr. Simon Fox's baby.

Mrs. Mary Fox: I was visiting me husband's family on Tottenham. Me husband's brothers do love to argue. Thunder and crockery, they will argue about the very color of the sky. And such language! Not proper for my baby BELLA's ears. I'm raising her proper, I am. So I took her strolling on Oxford Street.

Judge Bertis: And what day did this occur?

Mrs. Mary Fox: I was just coming to that detail, I was. 'Twas the afternoon of June 7th. I was pushing me BELLA along in her little baby carriage her father made for her. She was jiggling her little rattler—she just adores it. It is silver with pretty red ribbons and comes all the way from her dear grandmama in York. Whenever she cries, and she rarely does, darling thing, I always give her the precious rattle and that quiets her good, it does.

Judge Bertis: Please try to keep to the details pertaining to the crime.

Mrs. Mary Fox: Sorry, sir. Mr. FOX is always saying that I do carry on. So, I was strolling along, happy as a lamb in spring, and she, the prisoner there, comes up and, pretty as you please, rips the rattle from my BELLA's mouth. Well, I would have none of that, thank you very much. I chased her and ran her over proper with me baby carriage. Then, seeing no other ways to restrain her, I sat on her. Two other kind ladies, shocked that a grown woman would steal my precious babe's rattle from her own sweet mouth, sat on her too, all of us calling out for the watch.

Nigel Pickard: I am the inspector of the watch. I did find three women, including MRS.

MARY FOX, sitting on the prisoner and a silver rattle belonging to MR. FOX'S BABY on the prisoner's person.

Judge Bertis: MRS. JENKINSON, this is disgraceful.

Adele Jenkinson: What are you going to do then, Govna? Spank me?

Guilty—Aged 20—Transported 17 years

She checked the cover. The trials were from the fifth session in September of 1827—about the time Adele's backside had been replaced by another's. She gave the book to Dashiell. When he was done reading, he raised his eyes to hers and tapped the page with his index finger.

The clerk searched the books for another ten minutes but found nothing more. Dashiell gave the man two shillings as Vivienne whispered her thanks. Her face had turned pale, and she clutched onto Dashiell's arm.

He led her out to the hall where the servants were still bringing food into the dining room. "What's the matter? Are you ill?" he asked.

"It's all so ugly."

He wanted to draw her to his chest and kiss her worried eyes, caress the tension from her muscles. But all he could do was take her hand and gently rub her palm, his eyes locked on hers.

"Lord Dashiell!" a rich male voice resounded.

They jumped apart.

Teakesbury stood not three feet away, his eyes glittering, his hands resting on the gold mongoose head of his cane. He was all decked out in black robes. A short wig was perched on top of his head. "Oh, bloody hell," Dashiell muttered.

The solicitor's gaze slid from Dashiell to Vivienne, and the back of his jaw pulsed. "Lord Dashiell, you've brought a lady to Old Bailey during a murder trial," he chided. "Really, you have the manners of a yahoo."

Dashiell clenched his teeth. "Now I don't think this has any—"

"Let me apologize for Lord Dashiell's appalling conduct," the solicitor said to her, performing a neat bow. He pressed a hand to his chest. "I'm Robert Teakesbury, solicitor. I say, your eyes are a beautiful pale green"—his smiled turned wry—"like ivy covered in icy snow. Miss Vivienne Taylor, correct?"

Dashiell's fists balled. He reminded himself that punching a solicitor at Old Bailey was never a good course of action.

She glanced between him and Teakesbury, her brows crumpled with suspicion. "H-how do you know me?"

"Dashiell spoke highly of your beauty last evening."

She flashed Dashiell an annoyed look.

"I can say that his description doesn't come close to capturing your radiance." The solicitor linked his arm through hers. "I hope you don't take it amiss if I ask what business brings you to Old Bailey. Surely a gentle young lady such as yourself hasn't come to see a gruesome hanging?"

"I-I just wanted to read about some of my uncle's trials in *The Proceedings*," she answered. "I, um, chanced to meet my aunt's neighbor, Lord Dashiell."

She smiled, trying to hit a light note but sounding very out of tune. "Such a pleasant surprise."

"For God's sake, Dashiell, you should have taken her to my office," Teakesbury admonished. "I have copies of *The Proceedings*. Let us go there now."

"Thank you, but that won't be necessary," she said, politely trying to untangle herself from the man's hold. "I found what I wanted, and now I really should go home."

"Well, let me escort you to your carriage," he said. "There is no reason to go back through the main entrance. I shall take you out another way."

"No, thank you. I walked here."

"You walked!" Teakesbury bellowed. He shot Dashiell a blistering glare as he drew her under the protective black vulturelike wing of his robe. "Come, I shall send you home in the safety of my carriage."

Vivienne tried to step back. "But—"

"I insist," he said, keeping her captive. "It's not safe here for a sensitive young lady." He began to lead her away. She looked over her shoulder at Dashiell, her eyes pleading "help me."

Damn. Dashiell gritted his teeth to keep several profanities from escaping. Yes, Teakesbury was a pompous arse, but if anyone could make quick and quiet work of a miscreant blackmailer like Jenkinson, it was he. Dashiell shrugged, relinquishing Vivienne to the solicitor's power.

Dashiell followed behind as they passed through a narrow corridor leading to the side exit. Teakesbury pushed the door open with his cane, letting her and himself pass, then let go. The door, weighted by a chain, swung back and Dashiell jumped to miss being slammed in the face.

"Good heavens!" she cried, turning and trying to reach Dashiell, but Teakesbury hurried her along.

"Be careful there, old boy," the solicitor said. "You need to watch what you're doing."

Seven

DASHIELL TRAILED VIVIENNE AND TEAKESBURY ON THE way to the man's office on Fleet Street. It was a dark, paneled affair with a high arched ceiling, a cross between a cathedral and a cave. On the back wall, the double doors were closed, concealing his inner office. In the center of the room, clustered around a Delft ceramic fireplace were a round cherrywood table and two leather wingchairs.

Teakesbury slid open one of the pocket doors. "Albert," he called out in a bright voice. A young clerk, presumably Albert, strolled into the room with an awkward gait that looked as if he were constantly on the verge of tripping. He was about eighteen with lanky limbs, a long, square chin, and dark hair that flopped into his eyes. He stopped dead in his tracks, his mouth gaping, staring at Vivienne.

"Albert, would you be so kind as to fetch some tea and my carriage." Teakesbury spoke slowly and with strained politeness. "Remember our discussion about appropriate steep times."

"Yes, sir." Albert shook his head, as if waking, and

ambled to the side door he had entered, muttering to himself, "tea, carriage, remember steep times." When he turned to take one last peek at Vivienne, he slammed into the door jamb. His ears turned red, and he stumbled over his own large feet trying to flee the room.

"I have to be nice to him," Teakesbury explained. "He's the prime minister's nephew." He gestured to one of the chairs. "Won't you make yourself comfortable, Miss Taylor?"

Vivienne sat like a polite hostage, her hands locked together in her lap, pointy boots together. Behind that demure façade, Dashiell knew she was fuming.

Teakesbury pulled up the other chair, leaving Dashiell to loiter about the glass bookshelves lining the walls. The solicitor possessed an eclectic collection of fossils, Roman coins, and fragments of Greek pottery. He prided himself on his oriental manuscripts. One was open, showing two men painted with luminous blue skin sitting before a flowering tree and smoking from a hookah. No doubt, the solicitor had gathered them during his time in India.

"You have a nice collection," she remarked. Dashiell didn't know why but hot jealousy surged through him that she would admire another man's artifacts.

"Do you enjoy antiquities?" Teakesbury asked her. He crossed his legs and leaned his head on his hand, his index finger running up his cheek. Dashiell didn't like the predatory gleam in the man's eye.

"Very much."

"My collection is much bigger than his," Dashiell interjected.

The attorney lifted a brow. "Thank you for that keen observation, but alas it is not size but quality that matters." He turned back to Vivienne. "And I can see Miss Taylor is a lady who prefers quality."

"I say, Teakesbury, that is a fine portrait of *your wife*," Dashiell said, gazing up at a painting of a nondescript blond woman holding a flat-faced, fluffy kitten, gazing at the viewer with soulless, vapid eyes. Mrs. Teakesbury's eyes, that is; the cat's were quite intelligent and very much annoyed.

Teakesbury's smile didn't diminish a fraction. "I commissioned Sir David Wilkie to paint it a few years before he died. You can see his craft, his art, is at its pinnacle—"

"I'll say. He really captured the likeness of that kitty."

"—very different from the amateurish portrait that you unfortunately purchased the other evening."

Dashiell stifled the desire to point out that he would rather buy a thousand ravishing yet flawed Italian Viviennes of five-pound value to decorate his bed chamber than one priceless masterpiece of Teakesbury's bland wife and her cat. Although the feline had its appeal.

"Did you find what you wanted in *The Proceedings*?" Teakesbury asked. "Any note of the Jenkinson woman?"

Vivienne swiveled her head and blasted Dashiell with a hot glare. "How did he know about Mrs. Jenkinson?"

Dashiell tried to sound casual. "I just asked him if he knew her."

"I'm sorry. I don't think I have engaged Mr. Teakesbury as my solicitor."

Teakesbury reached out and rested his hand on

hers. "Dashiell spoke to me because he could trust me. I helped convict his father's murderer. "

She blinked, her face flushing. "I'm sorry."

"A terrible affair," Teakesbury muttered. "I didn't mean to cause you any distress. Dashiell mentioned the other evening that he was looking for Jenkinson in connection with your uncle. Suffice it to say, I assumed that was why you were looking in *The Proceedings*." He leaned forward and lowered his voice. "I assure you that all our conversations will be in utter confidence. You can trust me completely with any matter that may trouble you." He tilted his head. "*Is* something troubling you?"

Vivienne studied the man, then Dashiell. She bit down on the edge of her lip. Before she could speak, the side door opened and Albert returned, holding a tray. He carefully treaded across the room. The cups and pot rattled and threatened to tumble for the entire journey. "Would you like a bit of tea? Would you like a bit of tea?" he muttered over and over. He set the tray on the table and turned to Vivienne.

"W-would you like a bit of me?" he asked. His ears grew blood red and he cried, "Tea! I mean tea. Not me." The poor lad was undone by Vivienne's beauty. Dashiell had a malicious, schoolboy-like urge to brag that he had indeed kissed her luscious lips, and they were every bit as soft and delicious as they appeared.

"Thank you, Albert," Teakesbury said, adopting that false cheery voice again. "Now if you wouldn't mind fetching the carriage."

The enamored clerk lumbered out the door, murmuring "Fetch the carriage. Tea, not me."

The solicitor held up his palm. "Now don't tell me, Miss Taylor. I can always guess how someone will take their tea. People marvel at my talent." He lifted the pot high, letting the air cool the steaming tea as it flowed into a cup. He tossed in two chips of sugar and then added as much milk as he had tea. "Tell me if this is to your liking." He handed it to her.

Vivienne blew across the surface and took a small sip. "Very nice," she conceded.

"I'm never wrong."

He didn't offer Dashiell any tea, nor did he pour himself a cup. He leaned back on the chair cushion. "Dashiell tells me you're engaged. Who is the lucky gentleman?"

"Mr. John Vandergrift."

"John Vandergrift. John Vandergrift. Why is that name so familiar?" He snapped his fingers. "Ah, he is employed by my good friend, Mr. Montag. Tell me more about him."

Vivienne went into a polite description of her fiancé, including his proposal—a trite, down-on-one-knee affair—and the plans for a honeymoon in Scotland.

"Ah yes, I've traveled to Scotland several times," Teakesbury said approvingly. "It is beautiful."

"Really? I've traveled to Scotland several times myself and it was miserable, wet, and filled with Scots every time," Dashiell quipped.

Vivienne's shoulders shook with repressed laughter.

Truly only an unthinking imbecile who had no understanding of her nature would take her to some frigidly cold, damp place like Scotland... where love-making was a quick tryst under mounds of blankets.

She deserved adventure, to be taken to a climate where she didn't have to restrain her passionate nature. He envisioned Greece where the warm night breeze smelling of the sea and olives would waft through the window, rustling her hair. She would be on top of him, the indigo moonlight playing on her bare skin. He would run his thumb over her soft nipples as she whimpered his name, her head thrown back, her thighs pushing him deeper into her.

Dashiell's cock threatened at the image in his head, and he turned around and pretended to be interested in a Viking rune. He wanted to make love to her. Desperately. He would know how to pleasure her. In fact, Dashiell was a master of pleasure and little flirtatious games. He drew ladies in, played upon their weaknesses and physical desire, all the while feeding some dark insecure place in himself. A place he never wanted Vivienne to see.

The front door creaked and Albert lumbered inside. "The carriage is here."

⊱⊰

Teakesbury made a great fuss of installing Vivienne in his brougham. He lifted down the steps himself and held her hand.

She paused. "Mr. Vandergrift was busy today, else he would have helped me. He might be disappointed to learn he couldn't be of use. I do hope you will remember to keep our meeting in confidence."

"Of course," Teakesbury said without missing a beat, his fingers still encasing hers. "I am the soul of discretion."

As the carriage drove away, the man's pleasant expression hardened. "I warned you the other evening to stay away from her."

"I'm helping her with a family matter."

"Dashiell, I wouldn't trust you to help my hound!" he thundered. "Now why is this Jenkinson upsetting her?"

"I'm not at liberty to say."

"Is that so?" Anger flared in Teakesbury's eyes. "Well, I'm going to find out. In the meantime, you leave Vivienne Taylor to her fiancé. She doesn't need you sniffing around like a tomcat."

"It looked like you were doing a bit of sniffing yourself, old boy."

"Lord Dashiell, I am a married man, faithful to my wife. Stop thinking that other men abide by your shabby morals." He began walking away, his cane pounding the pavers. "And don't forget you're speaking at the Imperial Society," he called out. "I have you slated—"

"After Newberry," Dashiell finished. "Yes, you've already reminded me."

❦

Vivienne couldn't run the risk of letting Harold, her aunt's groom, see her exit Teakesbury's carriage. Surely, he would tell her aunt. She needed to stop a block or so away from the London Ladies' Flower and Garden Society and sneak around the back of the building.

She leaned forward in her carriage seat and tapped the glass. The solicitor's driver peered over his hunched shoulder at her.

"I'm not actually going home," she said. "I'm

visiting my former headmistress, Mrs. Highgate. She's infirm with gout and has a terrible wart condition. I forget the address, but she lives near the London Ladies' Flower and Garden Society. Please drive in that direction. I'll recognize her address when I see it."

He nodded his head and grunted.

When Vivienne could see the columns of the Society in the distance, she knocked on the glass again. The groom pulled the reins, and she stepped down before a filthy brown brick tenement building. All the windows were closed and caked with dirt.

Perhaps this wasn't the best address for Mrs. Highgate to reside.

"'Ey now, are you sure this is where ya headmistress lives?" The driver studied her, chewing the inside of his cheek. "You don't seem like the sort."

"Why, um, she is a widow," Vivienne lied in a sunny voice. She looked about, pretending to see nothing amiss. "Very much down on her luck these days. So sad. Good day, then." She opened the door to the building and closed herself in.

The communal hall was narrow and dim and stank with old urine, rodents, and some kind of exotic floral scent—like dried flowers and sugar.

Vivienne kept her ear close to the entrance, listening for the carriage to pull away. A headache that had begun to blossom in the solicitor's office now filled her whole head, like invisible hands trying to squash her brain.

The door to her left cracked open, and a woman with tight, hooded eyes peered out. "I help you?" A thick oriental accent hung on her words.

"No, thank you. I'm just waiting on a friend."

"Ah." The oriental lady nodded and smiled. She opened the door a bit more, letting out a big waft of that warm, sweet scent. "You look so tired," the lady said. "Come, rest. Opium very good. It make you forget."

Raw opium! The substance so vilified by the proper, yet extolled by the artists. Curious, Vivienne strained her eyes to see inside. Within, gold and red fabric fell in swags from the ceiling like a Turkish caravan tent. A well-dressed gentleman lay curled up on a low bed that was draped with purple and yellow sheets. In his mouth, he held a long stick that resembled a flute. White smoke curled about his face. His lids were shut, and his face was relaxed with a gentle smile on his lips as if he were in comforting sleep.

The swirl of smoke was hypnotic. Its sweetness filled her nose, rushing to her head, massaging its taut, aching fibers. Oblivion suddenly appeared so lovely and smelled so delicious.

Then the cold realization hit her head like a hard slap. She was supposed to be sneaking into the London Ladies' Flower and Garden Society and pretending to learn how to irrigate box gardens!

"I must go!" She bolted out the door and back into the bitter, drizzling gray.

She scurried down the walk, then turned and hurried up a narrow pathway that led to the seats in back of the building. She slipped into the last row of the lecture hall and checked the clock hanging on the wall: five minutes to spare. Letting out a quiet sigh, she settled in her chair. At the end of the room, the matronly lecturer held up stems of flowers and other fauna and pronounced their Latin names. "*Lonocera pileata, Digitalis ferruginea.*"

Vivienne pressed her fingers into her temples, trying to ease the pressure in her head. However, after a moment, she felt her neck heat with the sensation of being watched. At the end of the row sat a lady in a turquoise dress that hung like a loose sack over her round form. Perched atop her tower of auburn hair was an old-fashioned leghorn hat decorated with a big fabric geranium. A brown dog that resembled a furry bat peeked his nervous head out from the paisley carpet bag on her lap. The woman smiled and picked up the dog's tiny paw and waved it at Vivienne.

Oh Lord! She had managed to sit near a mad person. Vivienne flashed a polite smile and then pretended to concentrate on the lecture.

"*Leucanthemum vulgare, Buxus sempervirens.*"

Undeterred, the lady in the leghorn hat leaned across the expanse of empty seats separating them and said in a whisper that could be heard several rows up, "Pardon me, do I know you?"

The other attendees turned their heads, their faces scrunched in disapproval.

"I'm sorry, you must be mistaken," Vivienne said, scooting to the side of her chair, away from the lady.

"But your eyes…" She waved her fat fingers over her features. "Yes, I'm quite certain that I know you!" she insisted, impervious to the shushes they were receiving.

"I'm afraid not."

Vivienne rose and hurried outside just as her aunt's

landau lumbered up. Once Harold the groomsman dropped the steps, she ran down the walk and leapt inside the safety of the carriage. She leaned her head against the old cracked leather as the events of the afternoon whirled about her ailing brain. That solicitor had better be as trustworthy as Dashiell claimed. If John found out about—ah! A sharp pain flared in her temples.

❧

Vivienne just wanted to slip through the house undetected, curl up under her covers, and try to make this headache go away before her command evening performance as the perfect fiancée.

But she had no such luck.

"Is that you, my little Vivvie?" her aunt called from the parlor. There was a strange, airy lilt to her words. "Come here."

The moment Vivienne entered the parlor, she felt something was wrong, a foreboding change in the air like the drop in pressure before a storm. Beside her aunt's Bible, a half-empty bottle of *Milner's Coca Tonic Wine* sparkled in the sunlight streaming from the window. What had happened? Had the man in the blue coat returned?

Aunt Gertrude was standing under her husband's portrait, dressed in her customary stiff black, her eyes large and glassy. She hummed "Jesus, Lover of My Soul" in a high, off-key warble. Garth stared at Vivienne from around his mistress's skirt. His face was more wrinkled than ever. He emitted a gurgling whimper as if he were trying to say, "You are in so much trouble."

"W-won't you sit down?" her aunt said, making a wobbly gesture to her chair. "I think we should have a little d-discussion."

Vivienne obeyed like a small apprehensive child being called into her father's library after she had galloped through the house pretending to be a horse, thrusting a broom handle as if it were a jousting stick, and then accidentally tipping over the cupboard, smashing all the family's dishes.

"Did you have a lovely time at the nude lecture?" her aunt asked in a pleasant voice, soothing an errant curl from her cheek.

"What? I—I didn't go to that one. I went to the gardening lecture. Remember?"

"Oh, yes. Mr. Vandergrift would approve. All those quivering pistils and stamens."

"Quivering... Aunt Gertrude, how much coca wine have you imbibed?"

"What my physician recommended, of course. Two spoonfuls. Why do you ask?" Her aunt burped and dabbed her mouth with her finger. "My nerves, you know, are so poorly lately. So poorly. I must ask the apothecary to make something stronger."

"I don't think that's necessary."

"Only the Lord knows how I suffer," her aunt snapped and then released a long breath through her nose, recomposing herself. She pressed her hand to her chest. "I was thinking that soon you will be moving into your husband's bed and—"

"Pardon?"

"I said soon you will be moving into your husband's home. Do listen."

"But you said... never mind." Vivienne reached for her aunt's tonic bottle and discretely shoved it up her sleeve.

"And this will be your last time together with your beloved sisters. I think it would be best if you were with your family before the wedding. I'm selfish to keep you."

Vivienne's heartbeat sped. She couldn't leave now or everything would come crashing down. "No! My father wanted me to be with Mr. Vandergrift. He told me not to leave him alone in London." *Don't let that gentleman even glance at another woman,* he had ordered. Of course, he didn't say anything about early wedding presents. "And I... I just got here."

"I didn't want to upset your father. He was so insistent that you come. I just... simply need my rest. It is all too much for me now."

Vivienne lowered her voice and edged further down her chair. "Is something wrong?" she said slowly. "Something maybe you feel you can't talk about?"

"I-I don't know what you mean."

Vivienne swallowed and continued tiptoeing into dangerous terrain. "Just that you can trust me with anything you need to say." She darkened her voice. "Anything." *Such as your husband was a lascivious profligate.*

The older woman's eyes creased in the corners.

"But perhaps you feel you can't say something, because admitting it might be..." Vivienne paused, trying to choose the correct word: mortifying, horrifying, revolting, disgusting, "...painful like when one is *spanked* or... or *lied to* about being, you know, spanked."

"What are you talking about? You make no sense. Spanking and lying? You're not thinking p-p-properly." Her aunt attempted to wag her finger but only swiped the air. "I shouldn't allow you to attend nude gardening lectures in the future."

Vivienne came to her feet. "I just want you to know that you shouldn't feel you need to keep silent. Because you can trust me with... with whatever you feel you can't trust me with."

Her aunt pressed her palms to her temples. "How you do babble on, hurting my head." She ambled across the carpet and picked up a tiny booklet atop her Bible. She handed it to Vivienne. "Harold gave me this train schedule. He will accompany you home. You may leave on Tuesday after Bible lessons." She lifted the edge of her hem and started to leave the room.

"No!" Vivienne cried, jumping in front of her aunt. "I'm not going home! Not until you tell me what is the matter!"

"I have prayed and prayed to the Lord and this is His decision. I am merely his faithful, suffering servant." She walked from the room, whispering "my poor nerves" as her guardian dog trotted beside her.

Vivienne's lips twitched. She couldn't very well argue with God.

She trudged up the stairs. Her head throbbed and she had to somehow manage to contort her hair into perfect ringlets in the next hour. She just wanted to put on her robe, climb into bed with a book, nibble on biscuits, and pretend that the entire fate of her family didn't rest on her shoulders.

The door to her chamber was cracked, and she

could hear the soft hiccupping sounds of someone crying. In the corner, sitting in the rocking chair, was Miss Banks. Tears poured down her face. Vivienne clutched her belly. She couldn't handle any more drama today.

"Oh, miss. 'Tis been a dreadful day." She rubbed her dribbling nose on her arm. "But don't you worry about a th-thing."

"What has happened?" Vivienne asked, though she didn't want to hear.

"We got our wages today."

Vivienne shook her head. "I don't understand. Isn't that a good thing?"

"The missus tells me to take the s-silver sugar spoon to the pawn shop while you were at your lecture. I only got a pound for it. 'Twas your great-great-grandmother's." She wiped her eyes. "But you needn't be a'frettin' about that. You just enjoy yourself at the opera."

Eight

"What's wrong with you tonight, Vivienne?" John asked. He gripped her hand, pulling her through the crowd milling about the lobby of the opera house. "You seem distracted."

How was Vivienne supposed to answer that question? *My father is inches from ruin, my uncle was a crooked lecher, my aunt is being blackmailed by a detestable madam, Dashiell—that scoundrel whom I kissed behind your back— spilled my problems to a solicitor, and there's the issue of your wedding present at Seven Heavens. And to top it all, I'm supposed to make an endearing impression on the Montags this evening. So yes, I'm distracted.*

Beyond the great closed doors to the theater, the production had already started. The sound of a powerful yet muffled mezzo soprano rang in the air. Vivienne winced. Her head throbbed so fiercely that she was afraid the memory of her first opera would be of her retching all over the shiny polished floor. They were late because John hadn't approved of the gown she had chosen. So he made her change into the silver one she had worn the first night they'd met. She and

Miss Banks worked fast, but still the switch of gowns took thirty minutes. A white lace ruffle ran across her satin silver bodice, exposing the tops of her breasts and hanging off her shoulders. Her white gloves came just shy of her elbows, leaving her upper arms cold beneath the lace. All Vivienne had brought to London was the green cloak. The poor thing was beginning to wear and the earthy fern color would not do against the pale silver gown, so she went without an outer garment. Now her skin was covered with bumps brought out by the cold, damp night.

They hurried up two flights, and the attendant guided them down a dim corridor. As the man opened a door, John leaned in, his musky cologne filling her nose. He whispered, "Make me proud." He gave her a hurried peck on her temple.

The door opened onto an overwhelming panorama of stacks and stacks of theater boxes, each a little scene of finely dressed people in conversation. On the stage, the set of a rustic village nestled among a painted backdrop of craggy hills with a vista of the sea painted behind it. The chorus, dressed as ragged peasants, surrounded an expansive woman in a shimmering rose gown who stood downstage, her arms extended, fingers curled, as if she were baring some soul secret to the enormous theater with her powerful voice.

Then a man clad in formal black and a woman in a midnight blue gown stepped into Vivienne's vision.

"Oh, darling, here she is," said the woman. Despite the age lines on her face, she retained a fragile beauty. Her dark hair, curled in puffs, was streaked with pure white strands. She wore a permanent smile and had a quivering frenetic energy, like a tiny excitable dog.

Meanwhile, the gentleman moved in a slow, unrushed motion. He was tall with wide, imposing shoulders. The skin on his face had begun to sag, softening his features, but his gray eyes were sharp and gazed out from under a heavy mantle of gray brows.

Without an introduction, the lady grasped Vivienne's hands. "Isn't she the most beautiful thing you've ever seen?"

Mr. Montag slapped John's shoulder. "Well done, son."

John made the introductions. Vivienne's muscles eased, and her headache lessened. The Montags weren't the demi-gods she had feared. The evening might not be as bad as she'd originally thought—perhaps even enjoyable.

Her gaze met John's. He smiled, and at that moment she saw something new in his eyes—a tender glow. He loved her. He was proud of her. Her heart felt light and airy, like gossamer. This marriage could work after all. Then she realized he wasn't looking at her, but over her shoulder.

Vivienne whirled around, coming face to face with a young lady wearing a pale silvery blue dress, similar to Vivienne's yet significantly finer in fabric and detail. The girl's green eyes were darker and smaller than Vivienne's, her face thinner, her features more delicate. Dark curls fell from a knot on the top of her head and framed her pale cheeks.

"Oh God," Vivienne whispered, staring at a version of herself. Or was she the version of the other?

The young lady blushed and shyly gazed away.

"Miss Taylor, this is our daughter Elise," Mrs. Montag said, pride warming her voice.

Both ladies curtsied and Elise murmured a greeting too soft to be heard. "Pleased to make your acquaintance," Vivienne replied, managing a reasonably pleasant tone, though her nails dug into her palms.

John stood transfixed, lips parted, staring at Elise, his adoration for her evident to all the opera glasses now turned to the Montags' box. No doubt Vivienne's humiliation was far more entertaining than the production on the stage.

Mrs. Montag squeezed Vivienne's arm, pity in her eyes. Having the Montags feel sorry for her was not the endearing impression she had intended to make.

"Why, I think every gentleman in the opera house must be looking at you," Mrs. Montag said, trying hard. "John, you should be jealous."

"I-I am," he managed.

Several long, embarrassing beats passed in the music before someone spoke again. "Now, why don't you and Elise take the first row and get to know each other," Mrs. Montag suggested. "We love John like a son, so you two will be practically sisters."

"Wonderful," Vivienne said through gritted teeth. Just what she needed, another perfect sister she couldn't live up to.

She and Elise sat next to each other like odd twins: the rich one and the desperate one. Mrs. Montag took the seat on the end, beside her daughter, but Vivienne could still smell her perfume, pungent in her nostrils. John and Mr. Montag hid in the shadows at the back of the box and adopted the deep tones of business conversation.

Vivienne was the first to venture into the dangerous conversational waters. "What a lovely gown," she told Elise.

"Thank you," the other replied, but didn't follow up with a similar comment about Vivienne's dress, which looked almost the same.

So the conversation lapsed back into silence as the chorus started to sing. When they were done, the soprano, now draped in white and clutching a rose, launched into a mournful aria.

Vivienne tried again. "This is my first opera. It's very exciting."

"We come almost every week when we are in town," the other said. "I adore the opera." Her words came out flat, like a bad actress saying her lines.

"How wonderful for you," Vivienne battled on. The seat cushion would make better conversation than this lady. "Which is your favorite?"

Elise shook her head. "I j-just like them all." She said nothing more. Either she was ignorant of the art of conversation, or perhaps it was too taxing on her delicate mind.

Fine, then. Vivienne had tried her best to talk to the lady. She blew out a long breath and lapsed back into the comfort of her headache and the hammering vibrato of the soprano.

Then Elise decided to pipe up.

"I'm engaged as well." Her face brightened like a small child given a toy. "To a viscount."

"Ahh," Vivienne said and waited, thinking this

viscount might have a name or possess some distinguishing feature beyond his title, but obviously he didn't. "Congratulations," she finally said. "That's nice."

Elise snuck a glance over her shoulder at John. "John didn't tell you?"

Vivienne shook her head.

"D-does John ever talk of me?" Elise asked.

Vivienne held her breath. She didn't want to answer this question for what she might hear next. "A few times, yes," she said.

"It's just that he asked me to marry him, b-but Papa said we couldn't because he didn't have a title." She gazed down at her hands and brushed her thumb over a sapphire engagement ring.

"I see," Vivienne replied, trying to sound pleasant through gritted teeth.

"He said he could only love me, so I… I was shocked when I heard he became engaged so quickly after I had to turn him down." She looked at Vivienne with troubled eyes, like an upset puppy's. "I wish that Papa had said yes."

Vivienne stared at the woman-child. Perhaps Elise thought that with her fragile face downcast, with her shy gaze and soft stammering voice—the coveted ethereal grace—she would conceal the true heartless cruelty of her words. Or maybe she was so rich and pampered that she never had to consider the feelings of others.

Vivienne bit down on the inside of her lip so hard, she felt the ooze of salty, warm blood on her tongue. "I… I think I sh-should like to," *fall to my death from this balcony,* "w-watch the opera." She turned her attention to the stage and closed her eyes, pretending to listen to the music, while she suffered her headache in peace.

But then the low rumble of John and Mr. Montag's conversation drifted into her ears.

"Her father owns Taylor Machines," John said.

"Taylor Machines?" Mr. Montag repeated, his tone darkening. "You didn't tell me she was *that* Taylor."

Vivienne's lungs, heart, and several other vital organs stopped.

"What do you mean?" John asked. "Is there something wrong?"

"No, no, no," the elder man said smoothly, as if compensating for a verbal slip, and then lowered his voice. Vivienne strained to hear while keeping her head forward.

"Just that I've heard things," Mr. Montag said carefully. "In passing only, about some creditors and fraud. Probably nothing to it."

Black pain surged in Vivienne's head, and the entirety of her stomach heaved. "I'm going to be sick," she cried. She put her hand over her mouth to try and stem the flow of vomit coming up. She stumbled over her chair and then patted blindly at the door, trying to find the knob.

Someone opened the door and she stumbled into the cool corridor and leaned her head against the wall, taking huge gulping breaths.

Around her, she could hear the others inquiring if she were ill, and if they should call a physician.

John put his hand on her shoulder.

"I'm well," she gasped and turned around. "I'm

well." Behind John stood Mr. Montag, studying her with a knowing look in his eyes. *Oh God.* Vivienne had ruined everything again, and after she had promised her father she would behave.

"John, the poor child doesn't look well," Mrs. Montag cooed. "Why don't you take her home and let her rest?"

"No!" Vivienne protested. "I-I just needed some air. And I w-want to see what happens at the e-end." By God, she was determined to make a good impression if it very well killed her.

She grasped John's arm, pulling him toward the box door when, half-blind from her headache, she slammed into someone rounding the corner.

❧

A large blond woman whirled about laughing before falling on the floor in front of Vivienne, John, and the Montags. Her pale pink gown was hiked up above her knees, exposing her torn stockings.

Mrs. Montag gasped and covered her daughter's eyes with her hands. "Don't look, Elise!" she cried, shoving her daughter back into the box. "It's a bad woman."

The bawd, reeking of gin, gazed up at Vivienne with small, glossy eyes. "I know you," she slurred. "You were with that gentleman and the little doggy."

"I say," Mr. Montag cried.

"You are quite mistaken," Vivienne stammered. "I have never seen you in my life," she lied and yanked on John's arm, trying to drag him to their seats.

"Mama Dellie is right vexed at you for what your gentleman friend did to her place." The woman pushed herself off the floor, coming to her wobbling feet. "That ugly bawd is stirred up like a hot bee. She likin' to sting you," she called back as she weaved toward the lobby.

The corridor turned silent except for the muffled sound of singing.

Vivienne's head felt like it had been jammed into a nutcracker and split open. She gripped John's arm, trying to stay upright. She knew she had to say something for John's sake. This was supposed to be his evening to shine before the Montags, and she had embarrassed him. "I–I truly don't know that w—"

"John, please escort Miss Taylor home," Mr. Montag said with finality that brooked no argument. Then he placed a firm hand on her fiancé's shoulder. "Call in the morning, and we can finish our discussion."

"Come, Vivienne," John said, his mouth tight with disappointment.

Why didn't I leap to my death from the balcony when I had the chance?

❧

John didn't speak again until they were in his carriage, pulling onto the street, then his words ripped into her like bullets. "You say you didn't know that woman, but she seemed to know you. Who was the gentleman she spoke of?"

"I said I don't know her. She is mistaken."

John fell silent for a moment, but his anger was tangible.

"Mr. Montag said there was a question of creditors and fraud with your father's company," he said. "Are you keeping something from my father and me?"

"No!" She stared at her hands, clasped tight in her lap. "The insurance company is fraudulent, not my father. They refused to pay after the fire, despite all the money my father had given them over the years. B-but my father's company is f-fine now. We have n-no debts." Vivienne felt the nausea come back, and she clenched her hands and swallowed hard. She hated to lie, but she had promised her father. "I-I love you," she cried, the words sounding so desperate.

John didn't respond but turned to look out the window. The lamplight cast shadows across his hard cheekbones.

She scooted across the carriage seat and tried to cuddle next to him. "Please don't be angry with me. I'm trying so hard to please you. I'm sorry I didn't tell you about my father's business."

He leaned his elbow against the window and rubbed his forehead. "I just didn't want to hear it from the Montags. If I had known..." His eyes flickered over her face. "How they must look down on me."

Vivienne ran her thumb across a tiny pick in the satin of her dress. "Would you rather marry Miss Montag than me?"

"I'm not going to dignify that with an answer."

"Would you?"

"I asked her, but I was turned down," he said, his voice hard yet brittle. "So it's really not a question, is it?"

"I guess... I guess I just want to know who I'm supposed to be for you."

He exhaled and covered his eyes. "I'm marrying you," he said, as if he were answering an annoying child's question for the thousandth time.

"I'm going to be a perfect wife to you. I am."

"I know. You've told me that."

When the carriage stopped before her aunt's home, he leaned over and gave her cheek a cold, perfunctory peck.

She turned her head and captured his mouth with hers and pressed against him. "You shouldn't," he whispered.

"I want to." At that moment, she would do anything to please him.

She felt his body rise and fall with his uneven breath.

"Behave yourself," he said and slowly extracted himself. "I shall come again on Sunday. You need to go inside." He reached for the door latch and swung down onto the walk.

A few minutes later, she stood alone in the parlor, watching from the window as his carriage drove out of the square.

He wasn't going home; she could feel it. He was going to his *little wedding present* at Seven Heavens. His gift to himself for not getting the lady he wanted, for being saddled with one who embarrassed him and lied to him about her father's debt.

Nine

MISS BANKS TUCKED VIVIENNE DEEP INTO HER COVERS, adding another wool blanket from the clothespress to "make sure you stay warm, love." Then she blew out the lamp and quietly shut the door behind her. Vivienne stared at the dim ceiling and waited for the black nothingness of sleep to relieve her mind, but the horrible scene at the opera was stuck in her head and wouldn't let her rest.

She turned and turned, buried herself under the blankets, covered her head with the pillow, but couldn't block out the anxious thoughts clogging her brain. She couldn't spend the entire night in this helpless state. She had to do something.

She yanked the covers off and stepped barefoot onto the cold floor. She grabbed the tallow candle in a tin holder on the mantel and held it over the coals until the wick caught aflame. Holding the candle, she tiptoed down the stairs.

Her aunt's door was cracked an inch. Vivienne could see Gertrude's sloping form beneath the blankets. Her soft, whistling snores mingled with Garth's wheezing ones as he lay curled at her feet. Vivienne pulled the door shut, careful not to make a noise, continued down the corridor to her uncle's study, and locked herself inside.

"Tell me your secrets, you dirty, lecherous old man," she whispered.

She began her quest at the bookcases. There were five books relating to law, none of which contained a reference to Teakesbury or her uncle. The remainder of his collection were volumes describing the rural villages of England. *Who knows? Maybe his spanking preoccupation carried him beyond the confines of London,* she thought. She moved to the desk, pulling out every drawer, checking for a secret chamber or unaccounted space. Nothing but a few buttons and old folded receipts for coal delivery from 1833.

She stepped back, squeezed her eyes, and took in the old desk's dimensions, trying to think like her father, the engineer. Could there be a secret chamber accessible from the back? She sat on the floor, braced her back against the fabric panels, and pushed the desk's left side with her bare feet. The ugly thing wobbled but grudgingly relented, allowing her to push it out at an angle from the wall. Along the edge, she could see the outlines of the long flat panel. Another secret chamber!

Please, please, please, she whispered, as she wedged her fingernails into the wood and pulled. The flimsy wood fell off and revealed the back of the drawers.

Poorly made piece of rubbish!

"What the hell have you done?" she heard a muffled man's voice say. Cold bumps crawled over her skin. Oh God! She was being haunted by Uncle Jeremiah's ghost for insulting his bureau!

"Why don't you let anyone help you?" said another male ghost.

What? Wait! Vivienne turned and stared at the dusty faux tapestry behind the desk. The fabric panel ran about three feet across, four feet high and five inches from the floor. She leaned in, setting her ear against the cloth.

"I let people *help* me all the time." She recognized Dashiell's rich baritone. "But this is not help."

"When was the last time you had a woman? A week ago? It isn't healthy for you. If you don't get a woman regularly, you start buying more of those old relics and curiosities," Dashiell's grandfather said. "And we ain't got any more room."

Vivienne poked at the dust-caked panel. The fern green fabric gave as if it were stretched over an embroidery hoop. Her finger was positively shaking when she pressed against the adjacent panel. Beneath the cloth, she felt hard wood.

"Bloody hell," she whispered. She curled her fingers around the frame of the hollow panel and tugged.

⁓

Dashiell stared disbelievingly at his grandfather. "I'm not interested in meeting a courtesan you and the boys have found for me." He slicked his hands across his face and into his hair.

"She's not a courtesan but an actress. A good one, too. Has that black hair and blue eyes like Vivienne," the earl said as he preened before the mirror on the commode.

"Firstly, I fail to see how looking like Vivienne has anything to do with one's acting ability. And secondly and finally, Vivienne has green eyes. Green eyes!"

"You can pretend."

"Leave."

His grandfather picked up Dashiell's cologne, pulled out the stopper, and sniffed. "If you're not going to ask that saucy Vivvie to ma—"

"I said leave!" Dashiell grabbed the bottle before his grandfather could fumigate himself and slammed it down on his commode, rattling the various Greek and Egyptian statues there.

"See what I mean? You're frustrated. Now I ain't been to Seven Heavens in a bit, but the boys say Angelica has a new beauty from India. She can bend her back and—"

"Absolutely not!" Dashiell grabbed his grandfather's upper arm and forcibly escorted him into the corridor. "I would recommend that you continue to stay away from that place. You'll just injure yourself if you go and then have to send for me. And I'm not going to explain to the physician what happened." Dashiell slammed the door.

"You're frustrated," he heard his grandfather say from the other side. "You need a woman."

"Good night," Dashiell shouted back, crossed over to his bed, and lay down.

He wasn't frustrated. So it had been three days and eleven hours and approximately forty minutes. Some people spent their entire lives celibate—just none of his relatives.

He picked up his new book on the Norman

invasion of Britain he had bought after leaving Teakesbury's office. He had been reading for three hours, yet only managed to get to page five. His mind kept veering off the lines into some daydream with him clad in chainmail armor and bearing a weighty sword. He would storm the keep of some Saxon castle, fighting off a dozen or more men in blood-letting sword battles, and then race up the winding tower steps to the tower where fair Vivienne waited upon a bed of silken sheets. Then his little fantasy went sordidly downhill as he took her prisoner.

Tap, tap, tap.

"I'm not frustrated," he called out.

Tap, tap, tap.

"I said—"

Wait. That knocking wasn't coming from his door. He turned his head and stared at the mahogany side table littered with his history books and journals.

"Dashiell, can you hear me?" a muffled female voice whispered. "It's me, Vivienne. I'm on the other side of the wall. There's a hole in the brick."

He slid off his mattress and pulled the bedside table from the wall, sending his books crashing to the floor. He knelt and tapped on the dark wooden panel. Beneath his knuckles, he felt her knock answer his.

"Well, blow me," he said. "Wait! Don't go anywhere!"

He hoofed down two stories and through the concaved rooms in the stone cellar. Startled servants leapt up from their various chores which seemed to require an inordinate amount of empty ale glasses. Dashiell curtly nodded and muttered, "As you were," like some sort of military commander, and hurried on.

Hanging on the mews wall, he found what he was looking for: a crowbar.

He returned to his room and locked the door.

"Vivienne, are you still there?" he asked, tapping on the wall panel.

"Yes," she whispered. He could hear a fearful tremble in her voice.

He grabbed his pillow, removed the cover from it, and jammed the crowbar into the empty pillow case. He wedged the crowbar's edge between the panel and the wall and pulled. The panel opened as easily as a welcoming lover.

The brick had been cut out in a square about three feet in dimension, making a frame around Vivienne. A candle at her knees bathed her face with gentle light. Her loose hair flowed down to where he could see her nipples pushing against the fabric of her ivory robe. Below her breasts, set on the brick, was a garnet-colored bottle of wine.

"Oh God," he whispered. Was this some sort of early Christmas present?

But she gazed at him with wide, troubled eyes. "I found this gun hidden in the wall." She gingerly held an old Nock's flintlock pepper-box between her thumb and index finger, as if she were holding the tail of a rodent.

Dashiell took the gun and examined the barrels. The metal glinted in the low lamplight. He couldn't see a scratch. Either the gun had never been used or had been cleaned exceptionally well.

"Do you think my uncle killed someone and Mrs. Jenkinson knows it?" Vivienne asked.

He shook his head. "It doesn't make sense. Why would he feel the need to hide the gun in a wall?"

"But it's evidence of something."

"This isn't an unusual gun. They were very common, and they can't hit anything. A nice American pistol is what I use when I need to inflict some damage."

She tilted her head and studied him. "Are you very dangerous, Dashiell?" she whispered.

"Extremely." He flashed a reckless grin. "I wouldn't play with me."

Yet she did play with him, tease him, taunt him, whether she realized it or not. For her robe gaped, giving him an enticing eyeful of her generous breasts through her sheer muslin nightdress. Her gaze traveled down his shirt where the tails bunched just below his waist. A gentle flush colored her cheeks, and her eyes glowed with a tantalizing mixture of fear and desire. He could see her nipples grow taut under the fabric.

He felt his blood surging to his cock. Virgin or not, this lady better be careful. He needed distraction. Fast. He picked up the wine. "Good God! This is 150-year-old Vinho da Roda."

"A what?"

"A special Madeira from Portugal. They ship it around the world. The heat and motion of the ship temper the wine." He rubbed his finger over the Dutch East India label. "Your uncle might have been a homicidal lecher, but he had excellent taste in wine."

He rose, strode over to his commode, opened the drawer, and pulled out a filigreed silver dagger from

India. He held it to the lamp, letting the light dance on the blade, and then winked at Vivienne. "See, I told you I'm dangerous, love."

She visibly shivered. "What are you doing?"

He didn't answer but put the blade between his lips, for effect, and then snatched up a crystal glass beside his brandy decanter.

Returning to the wall opening, he knelt before the bottle of Vinho da Roda and slid the knife from his mouth. "You might want to back up, love. I could hurt you."

She didn't budge but continued to stare at him with large liquid eyes. He could see the pink edge of her tongue through her parted lips.

He forced himself to focus his attention on the bottle like a Japanese Kendo master. He took a breath and imagined the motion of the knife as it sliced the air and made the perfect cut on the glass. Everything was about the right action at the right time.

Then, in a smooth motion, he pulled the knife back and with a flourish of his wrist, snapped the blade, cleanly taking off the top of the bottle.

"That was beautiful," he said, awed by his own prowess. He checked her response to see if she were duly impressed. She just looked bewildered.

"Uncle Jeremiah didn't imbibe. That could be poison."

"That's a chance I'm going to have to take," he said, as he poured the deep garnet wine into the glass. "Speak well of me when I'm gone."

He whirled the ancient wine, giving it air, then took a sip. The mellow liquid flowed over his tongue, where it blossomed into an ecstasy of ripened grapes, aged wood, and sunlight. "If it is poison, it's worth dying for. Try it."

He gently pressed the glass's edge against her soft lower lip and carefully poured the Portuguese nectar into her mouth. She closed her eyes, her lashes casting shadows on her cheeks. He watched the small contraction of her neck as she swallowed. "Oh, Dashiell," she moaned and seized his hand, forcing him to further tilt the glass.

"Slowly, love, savor it," he said, pulling it from her lips.

"But my day was simply hideous."

"I met you today. Surely I didn't ruin your day."

"You were—are—the best part." She smiled, making those little dimples come out of hiding for a moment. She clamped her fingers on his and made him lift the glass for another long sip. "Meanwhile, my fiancé is in some disreputable place like Seven Heavens with his *wedding present*."

Anger clenched his body. He wanted to eviscerate John Vandergrift in the time-honored English way: slowly remove the man bowels while he was still alive to feel it. "John is a dark cully. You should find someone else."

She leaned through the hole and placed a finger on his lips.

"Hush," she whispered. "You know I can't." Her intimate touch shot through him like a spark of electricity. He wanted to pull her across the wall and take her on the floor, ruining her for John and easing that almost painful throb in his own sex.

She removed the glass from his hand and drank it

down. A bead of red wine rolled from the side of her mouth and down her neck. *Dear God.*

"This is so soothing," she murmured. "I'm beginning to feel so light and good, as if this evening didn't happen."

Her eyes, now glittering, took in his chamber, clearly unaware of his dark thoughts or that her robe gaped, allowing Dashiell a glimpse of her luscious breasts and their pink tips through her thin nightdress. He wanted to cup one in his hand, let his tongue flick—

"Your chamber is filled with naked women," she said, a small giggle trembling on her lips.

"But they're old and missing lots of arms and other appendages," he tried to joke, while shifting to hide his growing ardor. "None of them could compare to you."

"Even with clothes on?" She chuckled, a low and throaty gurgle.

Did she not realize the danger she was in? Another provocative word or touch, and Dashiell would be forced to free those beautiful breasts that taunted him and—

"Wait, there's something else!" She stared into the crevice between the brick and his wood paneling.

She slid her fingers into the crack and then pulled up the paper. When she opened it, the stiff, yellowing pages gave an audible crackle. Inside, he could see a thin stack of other pages.

She held up the top page. "It's a list of names with money and dates. This has to mean something! This could be a list of people who bribed him!"

He took the paper. On it were four neat columns, like a ledger. In the first column were surnames. Beside each name was a series of numbers separated by commas. The column had amounts. None exceeding four pounds—hardly worthy of bribery. In the last column was a date. The first entry was made on 21/2/12 and the final was almost a year later on 22/1/23.

He heard Vivienne gasp. He jerked his head up. Some dark emotion had stricken her eyes. Horror? Fear? He couldn't discern it. She hugged the remaining pages to her chest.

"What is it?"

She released her arms, and the pages spilled onto the floor of his chamber. One floated near his knee. An obscene caricature, the crudely sketched kind he and his young friends passed around at Eton. A buxom expressionless lady was sprawled on a table, her pink dress hiked up and her fleshy limbs high in the air, as a tubby man possessing an absurdly long nose sank his penis between the lady's thighs. His pastel yellow coat was open, and his pantaloons puddled about his ankles.

There were about two dozen of these ribald caricatures and several pages of realistic nude sketches.

Dashiell reached to gather the offensive pictures, but Vivienne clasped his hand, stopping him. Her eyes were large and ripe with raw desire. "Is it… like this?"

"No," he whispered, shaking his head. He reached up and brushed her cheek. "What happens is beautiful, truly."

She set her finger down on a particularly explicit caricature of a woman pleasuring the tubby, long-nosed man with her mouth.

"Do ladies do this to you?"

Oh God. He needed to stop this conversation.

He let out a ragged exhale. "I think you need to go back to—"

"*Do they?*"

He stared at her face, so plaintive, so trusting. He could sink into those liquid eyes. As much as he fought or teased her, he knew he couldn't deny her a single thing. "Yes."

Her gaze drifted to where his shirt pooled over his pelvis and then back to his face. "How does it feel when a lady touches you like that?"

He gritted his teeth. "Please don't look at me all dewy-eyed and irresistible with your robe loose. I'm a rake, Vivienne. I'm no good. Now you need to go to bed and forget about this conversation."

"How does it feel?" she repeated, frustrated. What did she know? Had anyone told her about the relations between a man and woman?

"Do you really want me to tell you?"

She nodded, her mouth parted.

He ran his hand through his hair and then shook his head. *No, Dashiell, send her away*, he thought, but said, "Very well."

He returned his hand to her cheek, rubbing his thumb along the bottom edge of her lips. "It's an acute pleasure. Everything leaves my mind but the feel of the motion of her mouth moving up and down my... um... cock."

He felt her shudder at the word "cock." He wanted to shock her, scare her away. Instead, she pushed against his thumb, letting it sink into her mouth. He felt the ridge of her teeth and the wetness of her tongue as it curled about his finger.

"Vivienne," he murmured and sank his thumb deeper into her. She let out a hum-like cry and tightened her lips around him. He could feel her desire pulling heavily on her body—the same desire that caused his penis to strain against his trousers. This woman should have been bedded long before now. She was dangerous with repressed desire.

Rebelling against the inner voice warning him to stop, he brought his lips to the edge of her ear. Her vanilla and jasmine scent released a drunken, heady sensation a thousand bottles of Vinho da Roda couldn't. "I feel this mounting intensity," he continued, letting his lips graze her ear. "Growing and growing. I want to release myself, let the sensation overcome me, overwhelm me. But I resist and let her pleasure me this way for a while, but ultimately I want her to spread her legs and let me inside her."

Vivienne gasped. Dashiell covered her mouth with his and sank his tongue deep into her mouth, tasting her, plundering her, ravishing her. And ignoring the little voice in his head that warned he was close to losing control.

"I can make you feel the same," he whispered. "There is a sensitive place between your limbs, the smallest bulge, that if I touch you like this…" He flicked his tongue over the center of her top lip. "I can make you tremble and cry out my name as I take you to the peak of the most intense pleasure you've ever known."

Her ragged breath heated his neck. "Show me." She slid through the wall opening and gave herself to him, her mouth feverishly kissing him, her tongue swirling his mouth as her hands ran down his shirt, under his shirt. Her touch felt like warm feathers on his skin. He moaned in her mouth, his back arching. Then those dangerous fingers drifted down, down, finding his erection straining against his trousers. His cock jolted; the blood surged so hard he burned.

She pulled her mouth from his. "I heard you speaking to your grandfather." She spoke low, uninhibited with wine and desire. "I-I didn't understand it all, but…" She kissed his jaw, still tender from Sidney's blow. "Dashiell, do you desire me?"

Say no. You'll only hurt her like the others. You know you will push her away and catch a boat to somewhere. Say no.

He squeezed his eyes shut and let out a cry, like an injured wolf. Using every bit of will he could muster, he lifted her hand off his penis.

Undeterred, she wrapped her fingers around the opening of her robe and slowly pulled the sides back. A deep glow burned in her eyes as she reached for the drawstring at the neck of her nightdress.

"No!" He grabbed her hands, stopping her. If he saw those beautiful bare breasts, he shivered to think what he might do. "Please, Vivienne, don't. You're not thinking clearly. You've had too much to drink."

"Don't you want to see me?"

"I'm a scoundrel, Vivienne. I'll just hurt you, don't you understand? I shouldn't have said anything."

"I dream about you," she continued, her eyes searching his face. "I dream about how you would feel."

"You're a virgin, for God's sake. I can't take that responsibility. I would have to marry you." He combed his hand through his hair. "I'm… I'm incapable of being a good husband. And besides, you're already engaged. Remember Mr. Vandergrift?"

A frigid draft of silence swept through the room.

The terrible realization of what had just happened dawned in her eyes. *How could I have done this?* she thought.

Dashiell muttered a curse, and then his arms were around her again. He was making hushing sounds, trying to comfort her.

"This is my fault," he said. "You didn't know what you were doing. I did. I let everything get out of hand."

She shook her head. She knew enough not to kiss another man, not to let her fingers roam freely over his body. She knew enough to know that she could have destroyed her forthcoming marriage.

"You did nothing that can't be undone," he continued. "John, or whomever you marry, will never know. I'll be silent to my grave. I give you my word."

"More lies." She shook her head. "All I do is lie. Now look at what I have done. I've betrayed my fiancé."

His fingers cupped her chin and lifted her head. "Listen," he growled. "You are innocent. This is nothing. And I can guarantee that John is doing a great deal more than kissing. Do you think he feels any guilt? Of course not."

"But, but I feel so guilty in my soul. I'm not a good lady."

She crawled blindly toward the open panel. Dashiell caught her by the waist.

"Let me go!" Vivienne twisted her body, tearing herself from his arms.

"Wait. Let's just talk."

She scrambled through the hole, spilling onto the floor of Uncle Jeremiah's library.

"We just kissed," he cried. "That was all."

She grabbed the fabric panel and slammed it back in place before Dashiell could wake up her aunt or Miss Banks.

Still, she could hear him call her name. She turned onto her backside and pressed her feet against the massive bureau. The ugly thing resisted, as if Uncle Jeremiah's ghost were there, trying to punish her. She saw the fabric on the panel jiggle. Dashiell was trying to come through. She took a breath and shoved. The old desk slid across the floor into place.

Ten

VIVIENNE COULDN'T SLEEP. GUILT CONSUMED HER body like a raging fever. She tried to pray, but feared even admitting to God what had happened. Through the night, she tossed in her bed, imagining a horrible play with scenes of John telling her that he had spied on her and Dashiell. Not only had she talked to Dashiell as John had instructed her not to do, but she had sneaked into his room and kissed him. And not just a small kiss, but a deep kiss that released a passion in her that John never had, removing all her good sense and making her beg to mingle her wicked parts with Dashiell's.

Inside her heart, what frightened her most was admitting that if Dashiell hadn't stopped her, she would have given herself completely to him, ruining her engagement and sending her father to prison.

Dear Lord, lead me not into temptation again and deliver me from evil and Lord Dashiell. I promise I'll be good.

After Miss Banks helped her dress in the morning, Vivienne trudged downstairs, clutching her Bible.

Her aunt was awake, clad in her usual crisp black, a

steaming teacup in her hand. The coca wine from the day before had obviously worn off. Now she paced back and forth across the parlor floor in an agitated manner, her skirts swishing. Meanwhile, Garth was asleep, curled on a cushion by the fire, making wet, gargling noises.

"What is that vile man doing?" her aunt demanded to know. Vivienne followed the direction of her aunt's glare. Outside, Dashiell leaned against the iron fence, arms crossed, his hat pulled low on his forehead. His hair, spilling over his collar, looked as if a comb had barely grazed its surface. He wore somber deep gray. Under his dark eyes, those blue circles had deepened. Even so, he was more dangerously appealing than ever.

"He's been out there all morning." Aunt Gertrude narrowed her eyes. "He is up to evil, I just know it. I'll wager he is thinking about ways to peek at a lady's drawers and chemise. It is God's will to test my faith that I should live next to the worst sinners in all London. You don't know how many nights I have lain awake, worried that they might corrupt you or your sisters with their wicked ways."

Vivienne's cheeks heated, thinking of the sleepless evening she had just spent, agonizing over her latest bout of wickedness and corruption with Dashiell. "I-I thought I would study the Bible this morning," she declared.

"Do read to me. How my heart warms to hear the Scripture on your lips."

Her aunt took her usual chair where her cane was propped beside the armrest. Miss Banks had left a tray with a pot of tea on the side table. Aunt Gertrude lifted the handle and refilled her cup. She ignored the milk and sugar, but picked up a bottle that read *Dobb's Effervescing Citrate of Caffeine* and added a few drops. She took a sip of tea and then cleared her throat several times, fanning her face.

Vivienne sat on the sofa, turning so she wouldn't have to look at Dashiell. Nonetheless, he remained a dot in her periphery—a tiny fly buzzing about the edge of Isaiah as she read. "*Come now, and let us reason together, saith the Lord: though your sins be as scarlet, they shall be as white as snow; though they be red like crimson, they shall be as wool.*"

If only Vivienne's conscience could be made white again. After last night, she felt her soul was permanently stained as red as Vinho da Roda.

"Aunt Gertrude, I know we are supposed to pray for forgiveness for our sins. Yet, let us say, for example, a man commits a horrible, horrible sin. He regrets it terribly and prays to the Lord for forgiveness, and he assumes the Lord forgives him."

"If he is truly repentant. The Lord knows the true contents of our sinful hearts."

"Oh, she, I mean, he is quite repentant. Yet guilt from his sin still lingers, nibbling at him like a little mouse. He fears the rodent of guilt will never go away, but will eat at him forever." Dining on her conscience long after her marriage to John.

Gertrude pursed her lips together, thinking. "Guilt is a like scar," she philosophized. "It is to remind us of the pain we felt when we fell from the Lord's grace. So the next time the devil tempts us with his fruit," she fisted her hand to her chest, "we will be strong and cast the demon away." Vivienne peeked out the window. The demon in question was now sitting on a stone bench, being eyed by a bevy of hungry pigeons. He lifted his eyes and squinted, as if he could see her through the window.

Miss Banks appeared at the doorway. "Miss Taylor, this letter just arrived for you." She advanced into the room and handed it to Vivienne.

She took the envelope and turned it over. On the back was written "John." Except it wasn't John's economic handwriting, but a fine-penned, elegant hand.

Her fingers shook so badly she could scarce open the letter.

It read, *Garth is desperate for a walk.* Vivienne's face heated. Her head jerked up, meeting Dashiell's gaze.

"Did you receive a letter from your sisters?"

"Oh no, no," Vivienne said, trying to sound casual. "It's just John reminding me that he will attend church with us tomorrow."

"Such a decent, God-fearing man, just like Mr. Bertis. How happy he shall make you."

"Yes," Vivienne said weakly.

"I say, why does that evil man still linger?" her aunt asked. "Just look at him." Her voice lowered as she gripped the head of her cane. "Just look at him. So very handsome, but I swear, he is the devil underneath." She paused and then tilted her head. "Why, I think he is staring at you." She turned to Vivienne.

"I say, the light is awfully bright from the window," Vivienne stammered. "I'm having a hard time reading my Bible. May I close the drapes?"

"Please," her aunt said slowly, suspiciously.

Vivienne rose and strolled to the front window. Dashiell raised the brim of his hat and peered through the glass at her. He waved his hand, beckoning to her. Inside, she tingled as if he were some gravitational force pulling the tide of her blood.

Her hands trembled. *Oh God, give me strength.* She untied the sash and let the curtain fall.

⁂

Dashiell continued to mill about the square, feeling rather ridiculous as nosy neighbors came out and inquired if he were well, then offered him tea and biscuits. "No, thank you. Just enjoying the day and the fresh air," he said. After a while, even the pigeons gave up on him and wandered off in search of other crumb-laden squares.

She never came out, never opened the curtain, never even sent a reply to "John." He could feel her, huddled inside with her Bible, praying that she would never have to speak to him again. A wise decision, since he couldn't trust himself around her anymore. Surely some sort of divine hand had intervened last night and pulled his body from her before he could ruin her.

No, he would have ruined her, broken her heart, and driven her to sobs the way he managed to do to every woman who had warmed his bed.

John may be a blackguard, but the roots of Dashiell's family tree ran straight down to the devil in hell. Vivienne needed saving, but not by him.

It hurt his heart to know he had caused her pain, to feel bad about herself. He just wanted a chance to tell her that she was beautiful and loving and innocent. There was no excuse for his behavior. He knew better, but she didn't. She was absolved. Nothing happened that couldn't be undone.

The temperature was dropping as night came on. The gold and orange tones of sunset fired behind the haze of coal smoke, hovering like a blanket above the chimney pots. Dashiell dug into his waistcoat pocket and fished out his silver pocket watch. Five o'clock. Again he scanned Gertrude's windows, checking for any signs of life, any jiggle or swish of a curtain. The place remained as still and silent as a mausoleum.

He rose, dusted off his clothes, now powdered with dirt the wind had whipped off the pavement, and started toward Hyde Park. He rubbed against the current of shopkeepers, clerks, and laborers crowding the sidewalks and packing the lines of omnibuses, flowing back to the east side of the city.

As he neared the park, he veered off and headed for the heart of Mayfair.

He stopped at a tall white confectionary cake of a house with five stories of bowed balconies overlooking Green Park. A black iron railing ran across the entrance. An old-fashioned torch hung beside the door, illuminating a shiny name plate. There were no initials or names etched on the brass—just a simple pair of angel wings.

He pulled the bell, and the door cracked open. A bald-headed flashman with a thick neck and drooping eyelids gazed down at Dashiell. He had a silver tooth-pick sticking out the side of his lips.

"I've come to see Angelica Fontaine." Dashiell

plucked a pound from his pocket and tossed the coin at the man. He caught it in his large palm, bowed his polished head, and stepped aside to let Dashiell slip through, then quickly shut the door behind him.

The pungent, sweet scent of fresh gardenias and perfume assaulted his nose. A pianoforte trilled an ornamented French Baroque piece, weaving a ribbon of plinking notes through the laughter and chatter.

"Welcome to heaven," came a soft, feminine voice from above.

Dashiell jerked his head up. A petite lady with silken pale skin balanced above him on a tightrope strung across the entrance hall. She was nude but for a tinsel halo and gold bow and arrow. She flashed him an impish smile and dipped her slippered foot to give his cheek a tiny caress. Stationed below her, a trio of gentlemen with pudgy bodies and ruddy complexions that bespoke of easy, country-bumpkin living roared at her little trick.

Beyond the tightrope walker, a gold-painted stairwell zigzagged up the back of the house. Ladies clad in flowing white silk led men across the balconies to the legendary chambers. The names promised adventure: *The Wilds of America*, *Silk Road Splendor*, and *African Safari*.

Dashiell didn't find his pleasure in brothels. Yet tonight he could easily devour two or three of these comely women to sate his hunger. Vivienne was undoing him. He couldn't have her, and he couldn't leave her alone. It was a nasty cycle that needed to end. Tonight.

But first he had to take care of a little business. A small way to apologize to Vivienne.

"Lord Dashiell, I saw you come in."

He spun around. Angelica Fontaine stood behind him in her outlandish heavenly splendor. She must have been watching through a peephole. He wouldn't have missed the madam in her wings of gold-painted ostrich feathers and matching turban. She was a tiny, delicate woman, but her long neck and rigid posture created the illusion of height. Black kohl lined the lids of her hooded, narrow eyes, giving them an oriental slant. Her mouth was a thin, shapeless line over which she had painted generous red lips.

"I feel shunned by you," she said, sauntering toward him. "I entertain princes and dukes, but not the elusive Lord Dashiell." Her tight mouth smiled. "Come, you needn't bother with these common girls."

Wrapping her small, strong fingers around his elbow, the famous madam guided him under the tightrope to the other side of the hall.

"The India parlor, for my more discriminating guests," she said, opening the door to a room paneled in rich, shiny oak inlaid with carvings of leaves and vines. The lulling, warm gold of candlelight reflected on the surface of the etched crystal decanters, chandeliers, and gold-framed mirrors. Languid women draped the furniture, creating a rather artistic composition of bare skin and flowing silk.

"These girls are what I call my reserve," she said. "Are they not the most sublime creatures you have ever seen?"

The women gazed at him from under their lashes, sultry smiles curving their lips. Lovely, yet not one could rival Vivienne. "Yes," he lied, as his grandfather's words echoed in his head: *You can pretend.*

"Best pretty girls in world," declared a hefty man with long whiskers and a husky Russian accent. He squeezed the pocket-sized redhead sitting on his lap. She squealed and wiggled on his thigh.

"Thank you, your Highness." Fontaine curtsied. "The Prince is visiting from Russia," she said in a breezy, casual manner, but then peeked at Dashiell to see if he were duly impressed.

She gestured toward an empty, red brocade sofa. "Please." Scanning the room, she selected four ladies with a slight nod of her head. The beauties slinked over and curled like silky felines about his body.

Fontaine cleared her voice and spread her arms in a grand, dramatic gesture. "Welcome to Seven Heavens," she boomed, as if she were on stage and not three feet away. "You know only good boys go to heaven. Have you been a good boy, Lord Dashiell?"

He winced. All he wanted was some information and a little niggle, not some hackneyed Drury Lane production. "I just want to talk."

"Of course you do, my lord. A little intellectual stimulation can heighten the physical pleasure." She stroked the curls of a dark-eyed, sullen beauty whose chin rested on Dashiell's arm. "Lydia is a poetess. Recite one of your little poems for our guest, darling."

Oh God, no. Dashiell detested poetry. "That won't be necessary."

Tears welled in Lydia's eyes, as if his refusal had mortally wounded her fragile soul.

"Oh, very well," he gave in.

She rose, clasped her hands to her heart, and rolled her eyes heavenward.

Oh rose, thy splendor in bloom hath ceased,
The snows of winter doth increase,
Thy red petals hath fallen upon the white,
As my heart doth bleed at the sight...

And so continued the torrid, romantic comparison of her heart to the withering of a rose in winter and other verses of such banal cliché. Dashiell felt his belly tighten. Wasn't this supposed to be easy?

When Lydia finally bowed her head, signaling the end of the literary butchery, the Russian Prince, who, at most, probably understood a fifth of her words, violently clapped his fat hands. "Pretty girl. Pretty girl."

"Very emotive," Dashiell managed, and then turned back to the madam. "What I meant was might I have a word with you? It's in regard to a private matter."

"First, tell me which lady teases your fancy," she replied.

So, she wasn't going to budge until he put money on the line. The ladies pressed their breasts against him, giving him smoldering eyes and pouty lips. His tense muscles eased under their caressing hands. Oh yes, a little more of this would be the perfect medicine for his taut nerves.

"I can't seem to make up my mind," he teased, making the feather-fingered angels massage a little deeper in his muscles. They tried so hard, he felt terrible having to pick one over another. That didn't seem gentlemanly. And besides, when he would finally mosey out of here in the early morning, he didn't want to be capable of a single damn thought. He wanted every sexual impulse drained from his body.

"What about all four of them for the entire night?" he inquired.

Fontaine's thin lips spread into a satisfied smile. "Girls, make the Egyptian room ready," she ordered. "You should know our guest is an apt student of history."

"Wait." Dashiell held up his palm. He swallowed, feeling suddenly naked and vulnerable. "I also desire, that is... I would like a lady about this tall..." He raised his hand to Vivienne's height. "...with curling black hair down to her breasts and green eyes. Do you have such a creature?"

"I have a similar item with icy blue eyes of winter," she replied, and then cocked her head. "But you only desire a green-eyed girl, do you not?"

He knew from the dangerous, sweet inflection in her voice that his grandfather's words in Rupert's Club had managed to drift down a few blocks and into Fontaine's ear. This woman loved the power of secrets. She must have used them to claw her way across to West London.

"Go, my girls." Fontaine clapped her hands twice. "I'll bring Lord Dashiell up myself." The madam turned and beckoned Dashiell with her finger. "Follow me, if you please."

She led him back to the entrance hall, up the stairs, and to a room on the first floor. At the very end of the corridor, a door opened and a young servant with a pock-ridden face emerged from the servants' stairs holding an armful of folded white linens. "Take those to the Jungle Room," Fontaine told her, nodding toward the series of doors along the balcony. Then she removed a bracelet of keys from her cuff, unlocked the door, and pushed it open.

A blur of white and pink flashed before Dashiell's eyes. A fluffy cockatoo landed on Fontaine's shoulder. Twisting its head, the bird studied Dashiell with one black, round eye. Then it opened its beak, stuck out a stubby red tongue and hissed, bouncing up and down. "Frederick, stop that," she gently admonished, as she soothed its feathers. "Please excuse him. He doesn't like men. I don't know why."

The nervous bird edged across Fontaine's shoulder and put its beak near her ear. "I love you. I love you," he cawed.

"I know you do, my darling," Fontaine cooed to the bird.

Dashiell's eyes scanned the study. It was an odd room. There was no fireplace and only the one, tiny off-centered window. The stagnant air smelled with that rotting sweetness of dying roses. This room, like most of the others in the upper floors, must have been partitioned from the original construction. Paper printed with a pale gold oval pattern covered the walls. Clustered about a round, white marble table were a green cushioned sofa and two matching wingchairs. A dainty writing desk and ladder-back chair were set off to the side. Beside it was another door. About the walls hung paintings and illustrations.

"There you go, my little baby." Fontaine raised her arm and gently nudged Frederick onto his perch. "Please sit down," she said. "I'll be but a minute."

She slipped into the adjacent room, closing the door behind her.

Dashiell studied the art on the walls. He had stopped before a plain charcoal sketch when Fontaine returned without her wings. Relieved of her turban, her hair was midnight black, like Vivienne's, except frizzy with silvery threads running through the coils.

"That's me a thousand years ago," she nodded at the sketch and then tossed her head back in a terse laugh.

Dashiell studied the work. A heavy hand had outlined the contours of the scene and then shaded them with lighter, slanting strokes. A young Fontaine, with her hooded eyes and a slip of a mouth, sat on a window ledge, a rose lying across her palm. In the background, he recognized the obelisk steeple that rose above the tangle of roofs of Finsbury. The bottom of the sketch was concealed behind the frame, but he could make out the scrolling letters "James" rising at an angle from the bottom right.

"Beautiful," he said. "The work of Lawrence James?"

"Yes," she replied, having no emotion in her voice or expression for the man who had left her for a younger woman. She sat in the cushioned chair facing him, set her elbow on the carved wooden armrest, and leaned her temple against her hand. "And now, what do you wish to speak to me about?"

"It's regarding a delicate matter," he said. "Have you heard of an Eliza Cox?"

"Is this a runaway lover of yours?" She cocked a thin, curving brow.

"No woman runs from me."

"They should." She laughed. "You're a no-good

rogue. I can always tell where Dashiell's been by the sound of sobbing married ladies or wagtail actresses."

"They know what they are getting into." Dashiell took the seat across from her, extended his legs out, and stuck his thumbs in his waistband. "Anyway, I'm on a fool's errand to locate this girl. She's the lover of an acquaintance. She's young, maybe fifteen, a bit of a beauty, so I came on the off chance she might have floated your way."

"I'm sorry. I can't help you."

"I have some other names. Maybe you might know where I can find them." He reached inside his coat pocket and pulled out a scrap of paper where he had scribbled the price of a statue of Ishtar. He tossed out a name he had heard circulated in the clubs. "Can you tell me where I can find a Joe Horton?"

"He doesn't have a place. He lives with whomever he's selling. Poor wretches, bruised up and scared. I feel sorry for them." She paused while a thought clouded her eyes. "But what can you do?"

"Well, then Georgina Villiers. What about her?"

She laughed, a throaty, almost malicious sound. "You mean plain Martha Jones before she took up that establishment by Lincoln Inn Fields."

"And, of course, you've always been Angelica Fontaine," he teased. "That tiny trace of Irish in your voice is for show. You're no Mary O'Malley from the dens of Finsbury."

Hot anger flashed across her face. She didn't appreciate fast, unexpected moves. Frederick sensed his owner's edginess and started up with his "I love you" routine.

"I doubt Martha Jones, or whatever she calls herself this week, would have the girl," Fontaine said. "Really, you are looking for a needle in a haystack. There are thousands of women in this city willing to accommodate a paying gentleman." She rose. "And I have the best of them. Now, I believe you are keeping my girls waiting in the Egyptian room."

"I have one more name on my list." He didn't follow her cue to leave but remained in his chair, turning so he could see her face. "What about an Adele Jenkinson?"

Her jugular tensed again. "No," she said after a beat.

"She never brought you a girl to be debuted?"

"Perhaps she came by."

"Do you know where I might find her?"

Her smile stiffened. Annoyance flickered in her eyes. "Lord Dashiell, I don't keep the address of every low madam or pimp in London."

Dashiell paused, searching her expression. Her eyes were tight slits, letting nothing out. He shrugged. "Very well. I'm sorry to have wasted your time."

She bowed her head and performed a low curtsy. "Now, won't you follow me to heaven?"

༄

Dashiell trailed Fontaine's tiny form down the corridor and across the magnificent balcony. Three massive marble statues of barefoot angels that could have been stolen from a cathedral gazed down onto the ground floor where the tightrope walker greeted newcomers.

He mentally reviewed his conversation with Fontaine. He had wanted a little more solid information to chew on. But her reaction intrigued him. She was lying. She knew Jenkinson and chose not to reveal it. Why? Rather than getting closer to any answers for Vivienne, he was finding murkier waters.

"Good evening, Mr. Vandergrift," he heard Fontaine say, knocking Vivienne from his thoughts.

From across the balcony, he recognized the thin mustache and the self-satisfied gleam in the cold, bright eyes of Vivienne's fiancé. A raven-haired limp rag of a girl, no more than sixteen, clung to his arm. Blackness spread from the edges of Dashiell's vision, blocking everything in his periphery. All his thoughts merged into one: kill John.

He tore past Fontaine and grabbed John by his neat cravat. "You have the best lady in London, and you disgrace her by coming here," he hissed through his teeth.

"What?" John clawed at Dashiell's wrists. "Get your hands off me."

"As you wish." Dashiell clamped his fingers around the back of John's neck and then slammed him head first into the shoulder of an angel. John's nose crunched against the hard stone, rivers of blood pouring from his nostrils. The statue rocked on its pedestal, then fell to the floor, cutting a deep gash in the parquet. The stone angel's head broke off and spun on the floor.

"Are you going to pay for that?" Fontaine screeched.

John glared at Dashiell, cupping his hemorrhaging nose. Raw hatred burned like a blue flame in his pale eyes.

"I'm just making you all pretty for your wedding," Dashiell told him.

John's lips tightened around his teeth. He flew at Dashiell with his bloody fist cocked, ready to strike. Dashiell didn't budge, letting John slam the hard bone of his jaw, feeling, almost savoring, the reverberating waves of pain bouncing off the back of his skull.

He heard his own laugh as if it were from someone else's mouth, a growling and predatory sound. His senses slowed. Fontaine's stream of profanity, the shrill gasps of the girls, the trilling piano all became a roaring drone in his ears.

John's fist was flying toward Dashiell's face again. Dashiell felt calm, as if time had elongated. He ducked the blow then sprang up, his knuckles connecting to the ridge of John's cheekbone. The force sent John tumbling backward.

"Goddammit!" Fontaine shouted. "Stop it or I'll have you both removed!"

John, ignoring her order, rushed like a charging ram, crashing into Dashiell's chest. Dashiell felt the banister railing cut into his backbone. The crack of splintering wood echoed in the balconies, and the gilded plaster leaves on the ceiling appeared to be blowing away. He and John were falling through the air, still locked in a combative embrace. The back of his head hit hot metal, and a yellow flame flashed before his face. Glass shattered and a woman's screams pierced the air as he felt his bones smack down on the floor. A bright sun of hurt burst around him, then everything turned black.

"Viv," he murmured.

A few seconds or hours later, the sounds of pounding feet and the shrieks of women roused him.

Throbbing pain radiated from his spinal column. He felt sewn to the floor. He opened his eyes to see two pale blue orbs shining though a haze of gray motion. John. A fist broke through the blur. Dashiell couldn't do anything but take it on the jaw. *This was getting old.*

He drove his knee deep into the scoundrel's gut. John doubled over, grabbed his belly, and let out a low, aching howl. Dashiell balled his fists and swung, hoping to finish off the tenacious cove, but a fat hand caught his fist just before it connected with John's head. Then there were more hands, the square rough kind belonging to men. They were shoved under his armpits, lifting him up. He was hurled at a wall. His cheek smashed against the cold glass of a picture frame. The wall plaster crumbled, and the picture slid down, coming to balance on the toe of his shoe. Dashiell blinked. Behind the cracked glass was a cartoon of a very familiar tubby fop clad in a pastel yellow coat. He was squatting on the ground, using his grotesquely long nose to hike up the hem of a buxom lady's pink gown and ogle the contents underneath.

Dashiell leaned over, picked up the picture, and held it close to his eyes. He focused hard on the pink gown and yellow coat.

"Blow me," he whispered as an idea germinated in his head.

He turned and examined the scene before him, feeling disengaged, as if it too were just a sketched caricature. The flashman and two of the fleshy country bumpkins, previously stationed under the tightrope walker, now had him boxed in, their thick legs spread, fists clasped over their balls. The third bumpkin held the weeping, nude acrobat safe in his fat arms. On the opposite wall, John crouched, blood still dripping from his nose.

Dashiell's gaze drifted up to where Fontaine stood in the splintering gape of the broken banister. Her fingers were wrapped around the handle of a dainty silver muff pistol. She held the gun steady and aimed at his head. The end of the barrel, blackened and scratched, peered at him like a disembodied eye from an Egyptian hieroglyphic. He knew Fontaine wouldn't kill a man in her carefully constructed celestial paradise. She did heaven's dirty business in private.

On the balcony above her, his waiting harem, adorned in Egyptian wigs, peered over the railing with gaping mouths.

His grip tightened around the picture frame. What the hell was he doing here?

"This has been a most memorable evening," he said, turning on his heel and nearly falling. "But I have to go." He steadied himself against the wall and then stumbled toward the door.

❧

Walking back in the cold night, remorse gripped Dashiell. His head hurt too much to think about the situation, or maybe he just didn't want to. He limped along. His back ached, his jaw and cheekbone throbbed, and his muscles were stiffening in the cold air.

At home, he flung open his chamber door and chucked the picture he had taken from Fontaine's onto his bed. He pulled a stone Egyptian frieze of Isis from the wall, turned it over, and slid his fingers into a crack in the stone, fishing out a key.

He unlocked his desk and slid out the pictures Vivienne and he had discovered last evening from under a heavy volume detailing Napoleon's discoveries in Egypt. He took the illustrations over to his bed and laid them out. Two of the sketches were not the caricatures, but realistic studies. A lady lay upon a bed, her head tilted over the mattress's edge, letting her thick, dark curls spill over. A smile curved on her lips as she gazed at the artist from upside down, her breasts rising in peaks from her chest. In her eyes was a tender glow wholly missing from Fontaine's portrait. Dashiell studied the pen strokes. The heavy lines contoured the model's body, but the sheets, the bedpost, were light wisps of parallel lines, all slanting left as they had in Fontaine's portrait. His gaze moved on to the cartoons. A heavy black pen outlined the man's protruding nose and equally protruding appendage. Yet his coat was a series of yellow strokes slanting to the left.

He picked up the inked dark-eyed beauty nestled in her sheets, walked across the room, and held her up to the Italian Vivienne.

"What the hell?" he murmured, as a cold shiver ran over his skin. He snatched the bed cover off his mattress and tossed it over the painting. But that didn't stop the repulsion wiggling like a worm in his gut.

He had an ugly, sinking suspicion that he truly hoped was wrong.

He needed to speak to Vivienne. Unfortunately, she was holed up next door, refusing to acknowledge him. He combed his hand through his hair. He could pry loose the wall panel, crawl through, and sneak up to her room, but if Gertrude caught him, she would drop dead from apoplexy. Or he could stand below her window tossing stones like a pathetic, lovesick adolescent. Neither of these options was practical, and he wasn't going to spend another day loitering around in the park, getting defecated on by pigeons and exchanging polite conversation with snooping neighbors.

Then the realization rose up in his brain like the rising steam from water poured on the burning fires of hell. The next day was Sunday. He knew exactly where Vivienne would be.

Eleven

HER AUNT ROSE FROM THE HARD WOODEN PEW ON THE sixth row in Wesley Congregational Chapel. "I still think it's exceedingly odd that Mr. Vandergrift didn't come."

"Perhaps he is ill," Vivienne replied, as the first notes of "Love Divine, All Loves Excelling" wheezed from the old pipe organ in the balcony above. The song leader stood by his place on the front row and raised his hand. The congregation launched into a joyful noise unto the Lord that resembled a chorus of screeching, lovesick alley cats and cows giving birth.

Vivienne duly mumbled the words to the hymn, but her mind was on John. In truth, she was glad he didn't come to take them to church. She couldn't face him, not yet. Everything was too raw, too close to the surface, like a tiny volcano that could erupt at the wrong word or look and spew forth the burning, destructive truth. And the truth would ruin everything.

She studied the stained glass windows filling the back church wall. Pious biblical men in flowing robes, humbled on their knees, crowded about their Savior's feet. Jesus, clad in white, stood with one hand on his heart, the other with two fingers raised, as if imparting one of his wise parables. The morning light made the window glow with luminous tones of gold and red.

She felt safe here, away from Dashiell. If only she could inhabit this hard wooden pew until her wedding day, eat and sleep and pray like a chaste nun under the watchful blue eyes of Jesus.

Blue eyes. That was peculiar. Jesus must have been easy to spot in Jerusalem. Judas didn't have to kiss Jesus; he could have just said, "Arrest the blue-eyed one."

What are you thinking? Your very soul is in danger and you're worried about artistic representations of Jesus. You really don't have any sense!

The organ pumped and heaved its way through the hymn as the congregation stumbled along at least a measure behind the song leader.

Even before the last flat note died away, the minister, Mr. Charles, all decked out in austere black, rushed up the curving steps of the pulpit, rising like a miniature Mount Sinai.

He opened his massive Bible with a booming thud, silencing the congregation—except for Mrs. Lacey, who sat beside Aunt Gertrude. Happily unaware, she continued chirping out another hymn verse until Aunt Gertrude gave her a sharp elbow in the ribs and issued a loud "Shhh!"

The gaslight dangling on a chain strung from the ceiling reflected on Mr. Charles's bare, round forehead. He took a deep breath, filling himself with the power of the Lord. His jaw started to tremble, causing his flabby jowls to swing back and forth. Slowly, he swept his sharp gaze over the congregation, searching for any signs of new sins committed since the prior Sunday. His eyes halted on Vivienne, and his bushy brows slanted down on his forehead like gray lightning bolts.

Oh God. He knew. He could see past the deceptive armor of her modest, buttoned-up-to-the-collar gown and tight corset and straight into her heart, where her sins were written in bright red blood: she hath lied unto her aunt, she hath willfully disobeyed her betrothed, and doth covet her neighbor. She hath nearly lain with coveted neighbor, and she harboreth sinful thoughts, recalling each wicked detail of the nearly-hath-lain incident.

"Brothers and sisters, we have a visitor amongst the Lord's flock," the minister boomed.

Visitor? But everyone in the congregation knew her. She had been visiting the chapel since she was a little girl. She had had many dinners with Mr. Charles and his wife at their home adjacent to the chapel.

"Good heavens!" her aunt cried.

"What a handsome Methodist," Mrs. Lacey exclaimed. "Now that's how you spread God's love."

What? Vivienne realized that no one was paying attention to her sinful soul, but staring, jaws gaping, at the pew behind her. She turned and let out a shrill squeak.

Dashiell was frozen in an awkward, half-bent position, caught red-handed trying to sneak into church late. He wore a neat dark gray coat with a white rosebud stuck in the lapel. And his hair? All his wild curls were brushed into shiny, neat waves, in the manner of a respectable gentleman.

That wasn't all that was new. He sported a new

purple gash on his cheekbone since she had last seen him up close… if *seen* was the right word for pressing her breasts against him as she fondled his most private parts, begging him to take her to the heights of that exquisite pleasure he spoke of. Her skin heated at the memory.

"What are you doing?" she squealed.

"Come, my brother, don't be afraid," the minister said. "Pray, tell us your name."

Dashiell slowly stood and wiped his hands on his trousers. His forehead glistened with tiny drops of perspiration. He looked like a wounded, pathetic animal hoping the hunter would take another shot and end its misery.

"I'm… I'm…" He pursed his lips together and then nodded his head, resigned. "I'm Lord Dashiell."

The congregation gasped, then grew very, very quiet, as if afraid some seal from Revelations had broken and fiery Armageddon was about to commence.

Vivienne shriveled down in her pew and lowered the edge of her bonnet.

Finally, the minister spoke in a deep, awestruck voice. "The Lord works in mysterious ways. For our brother, Lord Dashiell, surely the most vile sinner in the Babylon of London—"

"Now, wait a minute," the vile sinner protested.

"—has at last found the light of the Savior. Brother, are you casting your sins at the feet of your Lord and begging for His mercy and forgiveness?"

"Well…" Dashiell eyed Vivienne. His neck reddened under his bronze skin. He tugged at his cravat with his finger. "I, um, yes."

"This is a glorious day, is it not, brothers and sisters?" The minister pressed his palms together and rolled his eyes heavenward. "Let us pray, for the wayward sheep has been found. For the most evil of men hath turned from the devil to follow the ways of the righteous."

"But I just came for a visit," Dashiell cried. "You can't expect me to turn Methodist just because—"

"I said, let us pray!" Mr. Charles thundered from his mountaintop pulpit.

Dashiell sat, and the congregation bowed their heads with military precision.

"Dear Lord, today we have witnessed the power of Your saving grace," Mr. Charles began. "You hath seen the dimmest flicker of goodness in Lord Dashiell, a man whose soul many believe was lost to the devil. You in Your mysterious and great ways have brought the lost lamb back to Your fold, just as the girls' orphanage needs a new roof. May he follow the path of goodness for the rest of his days."

As Mr. Charles prayed on, Vivienne couldn't resist the temptation to open her eyes. She peered over the edge of her shoulder. To her surprise, Dashiell had his head bowed and his eyes shut tight, looking quite lost in earnest prayer. Not the notorious heartless rake, but more like a little boy, kneeling before his bed in a nighttime prayer. Her heart swelled. Did he really come with a truly repentant heart? Did he feel the same heavy guilt in his soul as she did? Then he opened his chocolate eyes and stared back at her.

"I need to talk to you," he mouthed.

He dug a folded letter from the inside of his coat.

She watched, mortified, as he reached out and placed it on her shoulder, giving her chin a fast, light caress with his thumb. His touch sent little sparks crackling through her body. She wasn't supposed to feel this way at church. This was very, very bad.

The letter slipped down her bodice and landed in her lap. She peeked at her aunt, who sat stone still, eyes clamped shut, praying with all her might. High on the pulpit, Mr. Charles was in the thick of his fiery entreaty to God. Vivienne lifted the edge of the letter to take a quick peek. Dashiell had written three terse sentences:

L. James made the pictures. When did your aunt marry J? The wall.

Lawrence James made the pictures. That was odd. The man should have no bearing on anything, yet his name seemed to weave through the whole affair.

She glanced over her shoulder again. Dashiell had sunk back into prayer.

She fingered the edge of the letter. She shouldn't see him because she couldn't trust herself. But she wasn't going to get any answers to the blackmail mystery unless she confronted her aunt, although even then she doubted Gertrude would own up to anything.

And she had only two days left.

She closed her eyes. *Lord, what should I do?*

"The prodigal son returned from the land of harlots and sin," Mr. Charles bellowed. "The father saw his son, hungry and ashamed. The Bible says he was filled with compassion and fell on his neck and kissed him."

I'm supposed to kiss Dashiell? That can't be right.

"So sayeth the word of God. Amen," the minister concluded.

Aunt Gertrude's ancient landau lurched out of the church's brick churchyard and onto the street. Vivienne gazed out the back window at the congregation crowded about the church steps. The minister kept a heavy hand clamped on Dashiell's shoulder, lest his prodigal son attempt to make a break for the land of sin and harlots again. Dashiell's lips were spread in a tight, forced smile as Mrs. Lacey and the other ladies from her aunt's Tuesday Bible group swarmed around him like nectar-crazed bees.

"He is quite a handsome man, is he not?" her aunt said slowly, her words dripping with suspicion.

Vivienne whipped her head around. In the opposite seat, her aunt sat ramrod straight in her cascade of black ruffles. Sunlight fell from the window and across her pale face, contracting her pupils to sharp points.

"To some," Vivienne said, trying very hard to sound disinterested.

Her aunt leaned closer, her corset creaking. "I find it exceedingly odd that he attended church, don't you?"

"M-maybe it's as Mr. Charles said—Lord Dashiell has seen the light of the Lord."

"Oh, he has most certainly seen the light of something." She probed Vivienne's face. "Or someone."

A telltale blush rose up Vivienne's neck and over her cheeks.

"Has Lord Dashiell been talking to you?" her aunt asked. "Asking you to do *things*?"

"Things?"

Aunt Gertrude gripped the round head of her cane. "Has he asked you to show him your neat little ankles?"

"My ankles… No!"

"What about your… your *lady parts*?"

"Of course not." *I voluntarily tried to show them to him.*

"Listen to me! Lord Dashiell is a serpent slithering about the tree of knowledge, dangling his fruity bits before you to eat."

"But… but he was praying."

"Praying to crawl inside your pretty, delicate drawers, I wager!" Aunt Gertrude cried, slamming her cane on the floor. The carriage halted with a lurch.

"That's all he wants," her aunt continued, her voice building to a crescendo, her eyes becoming dark and wild. "To touch your lacy chemise, to get a glimpse of your female places, to put his turgid—"

"I think I understand," Vivienne said quickly before her aunt went any further. "Oh, what a lovely day it is outside." She forced a pleasant voice. "Have you ever seen such a lovely day?"

A rotting gig hauling turnips had pulled up beside them. Its disgruntled driver possessed a quashed, ugly face and was spouting an equally ugly stream of profanity at them.

The ladies' door opened, and the loyal elderly Harold peeked inside. "Do you require anything, ma'am?"

Behind him, the swearing driver shoved two stubby fingers into the air, forming the Longbowman Salute. "Dammit, you can't stop in the middle of the street. Move your arse."

Her aunt's body began to tremble. Her nostrils flared with her rapid breath as her brow furrowed. At that moment, she very much resembled her dog. "Just you be quiet, you dirty sinner," she shouted, shaking her cane at the turnip man. "You committer of adultery... you... you coveter of your neighbor's wife. Move your own Satan-filled arse!"

Vivienne gasped. The gig driver turned white. He clicked his tongue and hurried his horse along, away from the scary ladies.

Aunt Gertrude's mouth hung open, shocked by her own words. She released an anguished cry. "The devil has my tongue." She grabbed her black reticule. "I need my pills. Where are they?" She began pulling out handkerchiefs, smelling salts, a tiny notebook, and coins, tossing them on the seat. "I'm so glad Mr. Bertis wasn't alive to hear me. How furious he would be. He was always quick to point out my errors when I strayed."

"Allow me." Vivienne removed her aunt's reticule from her shaking hands and drew out a square tin that read: *Dr. Turner's Serenity Pills for Ladies. Restorative for Sensitive Nerves and other Female Complaints. Tasting of elderberry.* "Take us home," she told Harold.

The servant closed the door, and the carriage shifted as he climbed back on his perch. A shrill whistle pierced the air, and the landau began rolling again. Vivienne restored all the items to her aunt's reticule.

The older woman popped two pills in her mouth and leaned her head back on the carriage cushions. "I'm sorry, my dear," she said. "I worry about you. You're innocent and can't understand the ways of an evil man. He seems so handsome, so beguiling. He makes everything seem like a fun game, but all the while he has designs on your virtue. Tell me you haven't been speaking with Dashiell."

"I have already made a promise to John that I wouldn't." And she had kept her word for almost ten hours before she kissed Dashiell in a dark alley and then tried to show him her lady parts in his bedchamber the following evening. It seemed that all she did now was lie and deceive, desperate to keep her world afloat. Was God trying to see just how much shame he could lay on her before she broke apart? She couldn't help but feel envious of Dashiell—that supposed serpent in the garden, slithering around with his shiny red apples, never burdened with any guilt.

The only course left that didn't require any further lying and sneaking behind walls to meet Dashiell was to confront her aunt about Jenkinson and the blackmail.

Vivienne paused several moments to prepare her words. "You speak of the ways of evil men as if you know. Surely Uncle Jeremiah wasn't such a man."

"How can you even dare think such a thing?" her aunt cried, outraged, as if Vivienne had committed some sacrilegious act. "Your uncle was an honorable, God-fearing man. He didn't commit a single sin in his life. Not a one!"

Maybe this wasn't the best course. Vivienne held her palms up. "I didn't mean—"

"He was a fine man! How—how could you imply—"

"I'm sorry," Vivienne murmured. So much for the truth; back to good old lies and deception. Would God take into consideration extenuating circumstances on Judgment Day?

She took a deep breath. "As my wedding approaches, perhaps you can tell me about your wedding to Uncle

Jeremiah? What gown did you wear? Was Uncle Jeremiah very handsome?"

Aunt Gertrude's eyes lost focus, seeing an old memory. "We were married on the last day in February. My mother gave me a fur-lined coat. But I don't remember what Mr. Bertis was wearing." Her brows knitted, forming lines across the bridge of her nose. "After the minister said we were man and wife, I fainted away."

"You fainted?"

She nodded.

"How old were you?"

"Just a few weeks shy of twenty," she replied. "You were not a month old. Such a tiny thing, you couldn't even hold your head up." She brushed Vivienne's cheek and down her chin, right over the spot that still tingled from Dashiell's touch. "My little Vivvie, you have such a kind heart. I once said you had managed to catch the best bachelor in all England. Yet I think Mr. Vandergrift has caught the best wife. I'm so proud of you. Whenever I look at you, I remember the little baby…" Her voice faded out.

But Vivienne didn't feel proud. If her aunt only knew about Vivienne's lies, Dashiell's kisses, and all those lewd dreams of him that filled her head. If a virtuous wife was above the price of rubies, Vivienne's worth, at the moment, was hovering around the price of dirt.

❦

By the time the carriage pulled into Wickerly Square, Aunt Gertrude's pills had begun working their restorative magic. Meanwhile Vivienne still quietly boiled away in her cauldron of guilt. Outside, nature seemed uncaring of her suffering. It truly was a lovely day. The sun shone, hampered only by an occasional wispy cloud. Delicate green buds had begun to sprout on the trees in the center of the square.

Miss Banks burst out the front door and hurried down the steps to open the carriage. Once Aunt Gertrude and Vivienne were safe on the sidewalk, Harold made that sharp whistle, and the horses started for the alley.

Gertrude watched them leave. "I don't need to keep that old carriage."

"Now, how would you go on getting about, then?" asked Miss Banks. "Those omnibuses full of sinners would tax your sensitive nerves, they would."

"I only leave the house to go to church. Harold could hire a comfortable carriage for me when I need one. It would be cheaper than feeding those horses."

"Oh, come now. Don't talk that a'way." The housekeeper took Aunt Gertrude's arm to assist her into the house. "Harold loves taking them horses around. Like his own children, they are." Miss Banks shot Vivienne a worried glance.

"I think I shall retire to my room before dinner," her aunt declared. "I feel a bit fatigued."

Twelve

Dashiell left Wesley Congregational Chapel twenty minutes after Vivienne. In that short span of time, he'd somehow managed to pledge ten pounds to repair the roof on a girls' orphanage, as well as buy Bibles for an entire village of converts in India who couldn't read anyway.

Returning to Wickerly Square, he gazed up at Vivienne's window. The white curtains were shut tight. He waited a second and fabric rifled as if she had passed by the window.

His heart quickened and he sprinted up the steps to his house. His grandfather opened the door, wearing his banyan that reached to the tops of his bare, scrawny calves. His hair flowed like gray tangled vines down his neck.

"Where the hell have you been?" He looked his grandson up and down, his lips twisting to a horrified grimace. "And what the hell are you wearing? Are you ill?"

"Good God." Dashiell grabbed his grandfather's shoulders and pushed him back inside, then slammed the door. "The neighbors will see you."

The earl put his face an inch from his grandson's. "Did you beat up Vivvie's fiancé at Mrs. Fontaine's last night?"

Dashiell fingered his cravat and shrugged. "Maybe. A little."

"A little? I heard you broke his nose and a few ribs. That you tore up Seven Heavens something awful. What the hell were you thinking?"

"Clearly, I wasn't and that's the problem. I made a mistake. I don't want to talk about it."

The old man shoved Dashiell's chest with the heel of his palm. "Damn right you made a mistake. That John chap is out disgracing Trudie's niece and you didn't have the courtesy to let me and the boys know."

"Well, you tend to injure yourself at Fontaine's, so I doubted you could be of much help. Now please excuse me."

He attempted to step around his grandfather, but the earl gripped Dashiell's shoulder.

"You just stop right there, young man," he said. "You and I are going to have a little talk. I want you to own up that you love little Vivvie."

"Certainly." Dashiell smiled. "If you own up that you love Gertrude."

His grandfather's head jerked back. "I... I don't."

"Well, then, I don't love Vivienne."

The two men stared at each other, waiting for the other to relent.

"This has been an enlightening little talk," Dashiell concluded after a few seconds, turned, and continued up the stairs to his chamber. "We should deny our feelings more often."

He fished his key from behind the frieze of Isis and locked the door. Then he walked over to his bed, pushed the table away from the wall, and removed the panel. On the other side of the hole, he could see the dull back of the green tapestry. He leaned in and whispered, "Vivienne."

No reply.

She'd better not ignore him. By God, he had to go all the way to church to talk to her.

He strode to his commode, picked up his decanter, and poured brandy in a crystal tumbler. The burn on his tongue brought memories of clubs and gaming hells that seemed at odds with a Sunday morning spent at church.

Bloody hell. Was he turning Methodist?

Tossing back his head, he shot down the rest of the dram. He just wanted to sink like a contented toad back to the muddy bottom of his pond of sin and depravation.

He poured another brandy and then lay down on his bed, setting his glass on the table. He resumed his book on the Norman Conquest of England. He read two paragraphs, then settled back into his ongoing fantasy of Vivienne as his little Celtic captive. He took her down to the dungeon of pleasure and—

He heard a scraping sound, and his Celtic prisoner poked her head through the hole. He blinked, jarred by the sight of the cotton gown she had worn to church instead of the sheer, transparent silk of his fantasy. She had removed her bonnet, and her hair, parted in the center, fell in long glossy spirals by her cheeks. She studied him as he reclined on the covers.

A thought darkened her eyes, and she shivered. She quickly stiffened and jutted her chin. "1823," she said. "The year I was born."

Dashiell swung off the bed and kneeled before her. "Look, I'm sorry. I—"

She held her open palm to his face. "I don't want to talk about it. I've been praying very hard for forgiveness, and I'm going to be good for the rest of my life. John will never know."

"Yes," he said slowly, holding onto the *s*. "About John. You see, we had a little—"

"My aunt and uncle were married in 1823," she said. "Isn't that what you wanted to know when you rudely slipped that note to me during prayer, which I'm sure God saw and promptly added to your ever-expanding list of sins? Now what has this to do with Lawrence James?"

"I saw a sketch of James's that had the same technique as the, um…" He cleared his throat. "…*caricatures* we found in the wall."

She hiked one of her lovely, curving brows. "Where did you see this sketch of James's?"

He let out a long breath. No sense in trying to spare her; the truth had to come out. "Seven Heavens."

She sucked in her breath; he could see the mental explosion behind her eyes. "You went from me to Seven Heavens?"

Before he could answer, she grabbed the tapestry-covered panel and flung it back into place.

"Vivienne," he whispered to the fabric backing. "Vivienne."

Nothing.

Dammit.

Then she yanked off the panel and glared at him, angry green sparks in her eyes.

"You don't understand," he said. "I was trying to help you—"

"H-help me!" she cried.

"Shhh." He tried to put his finger on her mouth.

"You're just like John," she said, swatting him away. "You would rather hold a courtesan than me. Why can't I drive you to those 'heights of unbridled passions' and such that they write about in novels? Why can't I be some man's grand passion? You're supposed to be the worst rake in London. You can barely control yourself around women. Do I disgust you that much?"

"First of all, don't insult me," he spat. "I'm not John. Were you a man, I would be getting out my dueling pistols for that odious comparison. And second, I stopped because I—" *love you.* Terror gripped his heart at how easily those three words *I love you* nearly slid off his tongue. All these years, he had fought to contain his affections for Vivienne. Had he finally slipped over the edge? By God, he hadn't... he wouldn't. He ran his fist across his mouth. "...*like* you," he finished. "And I didn't want to ruin you because you know as well as I do that we have no future together. But if it makes you feel any better, at that moment, I had never desired a lady more in my life. An unbridled grand passion, if you want to call it that."

Her lips parted. He could see the wet, pink edge of her tongue. Her breasts rose with her uneven breath. In his mind flashed the memory of her nipples taut under his fingers.

He felt his cock stir. *Bloody hell.* He reached for his glass on the table and swirled the dark amber spirits, but didn't drink. "And I went to talk to Fontaine about Adele Jenkinson. That is all. Remember the whole affair about your aunt being blackmailed?"

That splashed some frigid water on the moment. Her lips drew down in a frown. "Did she say anything about Mrs. Jenkinson?"

"She pretended not to know her."

"How could you tell?"

A wry smirk hiked the side of his mouth. "I'm experienced with lying ladies."

He went on to explain about James's portrait of Fontaine that hung in her parlor and the caricature that Dashiell had smashed into, which matched those he and Vivienne had found in the wall. He further described how the pencil strokes and techniques were similar across all the works. However, he chose to leave out the more pesky details of his visit, including breaking John's nose, destroying Fontaine's place, and having a gun pointed at him.

"Still, why would it matter if Uncle Jeremiah owned caricatures by James?" she asked. "It all goes along with the bad things we already know about him."

"Ah." Dashiell crossed to his desk and slid out the illustrations flattened beneath the book. He sorted through them until he found the pages he wanted. "If we remove the caricatures, we are left with these two realistic sketches." He laid them on the floor before Vivienne. Her cheeks flushed a lovely pale rose as she examined the nude lady lounging upon the bed.

"See how they are not centered on the page,"

Dashiell said. "The covers and bedposts are roughed in with hasty strokes. They're James's originals."

"What would be the difference between having the original versus a reproduction? In the end, he had them."

Dashiell waved the page with the list of names before her face. "Consider these dates. They span from 1821 to 1822. Your uncle didn't reside here then—just your aunt and her family."

"Or these sketches may have no relevance at all," she said slowly. He could see the calculations behind her eyes. "This hole goes two ways. It makes perfect sense for your family to have had these pictures, as well."

"Perfect sense because we here at number seventeen are depraved, shameless rakes." He wagged his index finger. "Except, you see, my family, at least my father and my grandfather, weren't living here. My late cousin Nigel leased the place then."

"Does it matter? I'm not quite sure about these things, but I don't think owning these pictures is worthy of blackmail. It certainly can't be as terrible as that spanking business."

"Unless you knew the person in these sketches," he suggested quietly.

Her lips tightened with annoyance. "What part in this twisted strand of illogic do you see so perfectly that I don't?"

"I may be a worse bedlamite than you, but…" He offered his hand to her. "Come with me."

She didn't budge, her brow creased.

"Just across the room." He pointed to the space under the painting he had concealed with a plaid wool blanket. "Right there. No touching. I promise."

She considered. "Give me a moment."

She propped the panel back in place. He could hear the rustling of her dress, and when she opened the wall again, her skirt was flat, the bustle removed.

She crawled through the hole, ignoring his attempts to help, and marched to the appointed "right there" spot. She waited with a stiff neck, pursed lips, and her arms crossed over her bosom.

"Look at that sketch," he said, handing her the illustration of the lady with the lovely curls lying atop the bed. He walked over to his commode and removed a silver-framed oval mirror. "Now, look in this mirror. Do you see any resemblance?"

"We both have hair and a nose and... um... a bodice." Her brow arched as if to say *why are you wasting my time?*

"Wait. There's more." He exchanged the sketch in her hand for his mirror, letting the page fall on the floor. "Do you remember when I told you that I had bought a Lawrence James painting? Well, this is it." In a smooth motion, he pulled the blanket down and the brazen Italian Vivienne gazed on with her pouting lips and sultry tiger eyes.

"Now study the painting for a moment and then look in the mirror. Look at your mouth and eyebrows and cheekbones." He gave her a gentle mental nudge. "Has anyone ever said you look a bit like your—"

"Aunt Gertrude," she whispered. The mirror slipped from her fingers and thudded on the Persian carpet, a nasty crack cut across its surface.

"I don't know what you're thinking, but it's not right." She pointed to her Italian sister. "This woman is *not* my aunt. That's the Rialto Bridge, for God's sake. In Venice! No one in my family has ever left Great Britain."

"He could have copied the bridge from another painting or illustration. Look at the model." He moved his hand over the painted woman. "See the detail in her face and arms, yet the bridge is in the background, blurred in the lights."

She turned away from him, refusing to consider his hypothesis.

"What if Adele Jenkinson knows about these sketches or that your aunt was a model for Lawrence James?" he continued, speaking to her back.

She spun around. "Do you know how ridiculous you sound?" She flung her arms up. "So what if this painting and these sketches look like me. It's a coincidence. My aunt would never—" She stopped. Her eyes widened. "Oh God. Oh God," she whispered and pressed her hand to her mouth.

He forgot his promise not to touch her and swept a stray tendril from her forehead. "What is it?"

"On the way home from church, Aunt Gertrude said that I didn't understand the ways of an evil man. I assumed she was speaking of you."

He smiled, letting his finger trail down her neck. "Of course."

"She said that such a man makes everything seem like a game while all the time he has designs on your virtue. It struck me as a bit peculiar how she said it, not so much the words, but a familiarity in her voice. As if she had known such a man. Yet when I asked her about Uncle Jeremiah, she flew into a rage about what a wonderful man he was and how he had never sinned in his life." Her eyes found his. "Do you think it is possible—"

"That there may have been a man *before* Jeremiah? Absolutely. I know from experience that genteel ladies are not the sinless creatures that our *favorite* book *The Ethereal Graces of the Delicate Sex* would have us believe."

"If she had affections for someone else, it would explain why she couldn't remember what Jeremiah was wearing at their wedding or why she fainted at the altar. What if she were forced to marry him?"

"I can't think of a better reason why a woman would wed Jeremiah Bertis," he said. "Yet, the material question is: was that earlier man Lawrence James?"

Vivienne took in an audible gulp of air. "You don't think some of those paintings at the Royal Academy could be my aunt?"

He gave Vivienne an even look. "Or more interesting, maybe some of the stolen paintings were of your aunt."

Vivienne shook her head. "I can't ask her about James. I can't admit I know these things."

He gently brushed her curls from her shoulders and massaged her tense muscles. The warmth of her body flowed like a current through his. "Calm down, let's not ask her anything until we have a little more information. First, let me talk to my cousin Katherine— she's Nigel's daughter." He jerked his head toward the west. "She lives by Cavendish Square. She might know something."

"No, no. I shall not allow you to go around asking people about my family. Who knows what you'll say?

I'm already nervous about everything you told Mr. Teakesbury. I insist that you give me your cousin's address, and I'll visit her myself."

"I don't think that's a good idea," he said. "Katherine's a little odd. Besides, you can't leave the square. I'm not sure who is on a tighter leash, you or Garth."

She stepped away from his reach. "When are you going?"

"After you leave."

She paced the room, her brows low and eyes focused on the hem of her gown. She stopped at the commode, picked up a crude stone figure of a jackal depicting Anubis. Rolling it in her palm, she studied the artifact for a moment, and then set it down. "Meet me in the alley in half an hour," she said. "Take me to her address. You can wait outside."

"No."

"But she's *my* aunt!"

He shrugged. "Well, she's *my* cousin."

She glared at him. Then a flicker of an idea lit in her eyes. Her chin began to tremble. She blinked, and little tears spilled onto her cheeks.

"Oh no, no. You just stop that right now."

But she kept the tears coming, letting them pour down like a tiny rain storm. "I'm so worried about Aunt Gertrude."

He ran his hands up his face and through his hair. Women cried to him all the time, trying to get him into their bed, keep him in their bed, or out of someone else's bed. He thought that he had built a strong defense to the weeping woman. Yet Vivienne was destroying him because she knew she could.

"Fine, you can go," he conceded defeat. He glanced at the Huygens and added thirty minutes to the time. "But if you're not there at exactly 2:19, I'm leaving you. I don't care how much you cry."

She sniffed and wiped her nose with the back of her hand. "Thank you," she said, flashing him a weak, wavering smile.

He held out his arm, and she wrapped her fingers around the crook of his elbow, letting him lead her to the passage. As she was crawling on her hands and knees back to her house, he gave her rump a playful swat. She shot him a hot look over her shoulder, those green eyes glittering with outrage.

"Lecher!" she hissed.

"You have twenty-nine minutes," he said and pushed his panel back in place.

He studied the wavy grain of the wood. The smile he wore dwindled. Everything had become too dangerous. He would let Vivienne follow him to Katherine's, but after that, this was his mystery to solve. He may indeed be a lecher, incapable of doing the right thing by any woman, but he wouldn't let Vivienne get hurt. If he couldn't be an upstanding, faithful husband like those dour men lining the pews at church, at least he could be a vigilant guard at the door to Hades, keeping her safe from demons like Jenkinson, Fontaine, and John. Especially John.

❦

Vivienne hiked her skirt and stepped into her bustle. She made a hasty knot over her corset and shoved her dress back in place. Then she locked Uncle Jeremiah's study and slipped the key down her collar, fingering it down her bodice until she could feel the metal inside her corset. She tiptoed down the corridor to her aunt's room. Turning the knob, careful to not make a click, she cracked open the door. The curtains were drawn, but the bright sunlight filtered through the thin white cotton, casting a pale glow in the room. Her aunt rested under several blankets, her body rising and falling with her soft high-pitched snores.

A half-drunk glass of water and a bottle of *Dr. Oliver's Elixir for Tranquil Slumber and Serene Mind* sat on her aunt's bedside table.

Where was Garth?

Aunt Gertrude snored, a gruntlike sound, and rolled over. Vivienne waited. Her aunt's eyes remained shut, and after a moment, she resumed the rhythmic breathing of deep sleep.

Vivienne carefully shut the door and headed downstairs to the kitchen. A tin bathtub filled with water was stationed by the stove, and the floor around it was wet and glistening with bubbles. Paw prints led from the tiny flood across the floor to a cabinet stacked with spice canisters. There, Miss Banks was down on her hands and knees, her expansive drenched backside in the air, her head shoved under the cabinet. "Come here, you blessed ornery dog, and take your Sunday bath."

Vivienne couldn't see Garth, but his gargled yelps rang in the air as if he were being tortured.

Vivienne glanced up at the porcelain clock atop the cupboard. The hands pointed to 1:57.

"Allow me," she said, giving the housekeeper a small poke on her hip.

The housekeeper jumped, banging her head, rattling the canisters. "God and Mary, you scared me!" She popped her face out from under the cabinet. "Garth never wants his bath. Content to live in filth and fleas, he is. Well, not in the mistress's house. See if you can get the furry jackanapes out of there."

Less than half the size of the housekeeper, Vivienne was able to slide further under the cabinet. Garth dripped and growled in the corner, his eyes bulging with fury.

"Just you stop that," Vivienne admonished him, taking his front paws and gently dragging him out as he continued his barking protest. "We have work to do."

Miss Banks tossed a towel on top of him as Vivienne continued to restrain the dog.

"I need to ask you some questions about Aunt Gertrude." Vivienne lowered her voice. "In confidence. Were you employed here when she was married?"

"But a few days, I was. Master Collins, your grandfather, was very ill." Miss Banks vigorously rubbed the squirming, snorting dog. "I was hired to wash all his linens and clothes."

"Could you please tell me what you remember?"

"The physician said he hadn't but a few weeks. The house was to be kept quiet, so we wouldn't excite him none. Your Grandfather Collins sent for his daughters, saying there was going to be a wedding between your aunt and your uncle. Oh, I hate to burden you with this stubborn dog," she said, handing Vivienne the towel. "But do you mind fluffin' him while I get his lavender oil?"

"Of course."

The woman groaned as she pushed off her knee to

stand. "Aye, your mother had just lain in with a tiny thing," she said, opening a drawer in the cupboard, pulling out a black ribbon and bottle that read *Aunt Beatrice's Fragrance for Concealing the Odor of the Gently Bred Hound*. "And your aunt, bless her good heart, was a'staying with her sister to help. Oh, your dear mama was so upset, not only for her father, but because she had to leave that wee precious babe behind."

"I think that was me," Vivienne said. "Did Aunt Gertrude seem happy to marry Uncle Bertis? It's quite important that I know."

Miss Banks leaned down, letting a few drops of oil from the bottle splash onto Garth's back. The scent was so strong that Vivienne sneezed and then held her nose. Garth whimpered, rubbing at his face with his paws, trying to scrape off the acres of lavender fields just doused on his fur.

"Oh, I don't believe in a'gossipin'. No, I don't." The housekeeper's eyes sharpened. "But on the day your aunt was to be married to Mr. Bertis, I was a'coming down the corridor with a basket of sheets when I saw your aunt and your Grandmother Collins. So I stepped into a chamber, but I could still hear them a'talkin'." She shook her head. "I shouldn't a'listened. No, I shouldn't have."

"What did you hear?" Vivienne glanced at the clock. 2:05.

"Aye, your aunt was a'crying, saying she couldn't marry Mr. Bertis—that she hardly knew the man. I remember hearing a pop, like someone being slapped. Then I heard your grandmother say, 'Upon my word, you've driven your father to his early grave.'"

"What?"

Miss Banks recorked the bottle. "But I probably don't remember correctly. My poor mind is a'slippin'."

"I wonder what my grandmother meant."

"No, no, you shouldn't worry yourself about these things," the housekeeper said, sliding a thick black ribbon around Garth's neck. "Or be a'frettin' that your aunt told her mother that she loved another the very day she was set to marry your Uncle Bertis. And then your grandmother, bless her dear departed soul, said that your aunt loved a faithless, low scoundrel."

"Do you happen to know the name of this faithless, low scoundrel?"

Miss Banks shook her head. "You know me, I don't like to gossip. It's not my place to know the personal business of others. And no one I asked would tell me the man's name." She straightened the large bow she had tied around Garth's neck. "Oh, what a handsome dog! Did you ever see such a handsome dog?"

Garth whimpered and hid his face in Vivienne's skirt.

"I have one more question," Vivienne said, scratching the upset hound. "Do I look like Aunt Gertrude when she was my age?"

"Very much in your face and the shape of your eyes and lips," Miss Banks said, brushing her ruddy cheeks with the backs of her fingers. "I remember a'thinking the first time I saw your aunt how beautiful she was. Like a little angel."

Vivienne glanced at the clock. 2:07

"I must ask an important favor. Aunt Gertrude mustn't know."

Thirteen

DASHIELL WAITED IN THE SHADOWS AT THE BACK OF the alley. Leaning against the cool brick wall, he had one ankle crossed over the other, his hat pulled low. He studied his pocket watch. When the long hand edged up to the ten, he snapped the lid shut. He glanced out onto the square. It was empty except for a coal delivery wagon and a black brougham stopped before the neighbor's house. She wasn't coming. Even though he preferred to speak to Katherine alone, disappointment weighted his heart. He slipped the watch into his coat pocket and waited a few more seconds before sauntering down the alley toward Cavendish Square.

"Wait. Don't leave us!"

He spun around to see Vivienne running down the alley, a veiled bonnet and gloves clutched in one hand and Garth's leash in the other. The hound, wearing a huge black bow, scurried along the edge of her gown, curled tongue hanging out.

"You're late." Dashiell tried to sound severe, even as his face lifted with a grin.

She halted, pressed her hand against her chest, and took several deep breaths. "The housekeeper gave my aunt some *Dr. Oliver's Elixir for Tranquil Slumber* to help her sleep," she sputtered, and then began shoving her fingers into her gloves. "If she wakes up before I get back, Miss Banks will tell Aunt Gertrude that I'm walking Garth around the square and then make her go through the linens and household accounts... away from the front windows."

He removed her bonnet from where she held it pressed between her elbow and waist, brushed the curls off her face, and set the bonnet atop her head. Just touching her caused tiny explosions under his skin.

"Did you devise this little subterfuge?" he asked.

"Subterfuge?" She blinked, her eyes blank and lovely. "I don't know what you are talking about. You use such *big* words," she mocked in that sugary voice of hers.

"You frighten me." He knotted the hat's ribbons under her chin. "But you smell nice. Lavender?"

"That's Garth. He had a bath."

Dashiell gazed down at the disgruntled dog. "Sorry, old boy. I'll see if I can find something foul and rotting for you to roll in." Then he returned the conversation to its proper course. "Do you think Miss Banks knows anything about Gertrude's past?"

"We were right. My aunt was forced to marry Uncle Jeremiah. But Miss Banks didn't know the name of the other suitor. She *claims* she doesn't listen to gossip."

"Not listen to gossip? How has your aunt managed to employ the most incompetent help in all of England? Servants are supposed to know everything."

"If that is the case, I'm surprised you haven't scared

off your poor help." She flicked her fingers at Dashiell as if she were shooing pigeons. "Go on ahead. We shouldn't look like we are walking together."

"Protecting my reputation?" he asked.

"Yes, it's been quite damaged by going to church. You need to straighten up and be a good rake again."

He chuckled over his shoulder, catching that devilish gleam in her eyes that endeared her to him, and then she flipped the sheer veil over her face. He strode down the street, checking every few seconds to make sure Vivienne and Garth were still behind him.

Entering the round garden in the center of Cavendish Square, Dashiell waited under a low concealing tree branch for her to catch up.

"Which one is your cousin's?" She lifted her veil and surveyed the houses.

"There." He pointed past the staid brown brick domiciles protected behind iron fences, where the windows were bare of any decoration but for white window curtains, to a home that looked as if it were blooming. Pots, overflowing with ivy, were set just inside the iron gates. Katherine, not content to wait for summer, had fashioned red geraniums out of stiff fabric and stuck the gaudy things among the leaves. Stained-glass balls of aqua, pink, and purple hung from ribbons inside the windows.

As they approached, he could see his cousin had significantly added to her menagerie of plaster frogs and fish decorating the steps.

Garth sniffed Katherine's gate, dug in his tiny paws, and refused to budge. Dashiell had to give the hound credit for possessing a profound sense of self-preservation.

Vivienne picked him up and offered him to Dashiell. "Here, you keep Garth," she said. "I won't be a minute."

He held up his hands, refusing the dog. "Oh no, we're doing this together."

"That might give the wrong impression."

"Pretty hard to do with old Katherine."

"But what about Garth?"

Dashiell banged the brass knocker shaped like an inverted dragonfly with green beaded eyes. On the other side of the door, Katherine's hounds started howling. "Take him with you, of course."

A squawking female voice yelled, "You dogs get away from there." Then his cousin's housekeeper yanked opened the door. She was a wiry, squat woman with thin wrinkled lips, a bony nose, and chapped hands. A nervous straggly dog with a button muzzle and pointy ears like bat wings crawled from under her skirt and began leaping into the air.

"Now you behave," she admonished the tiny thing. "Lord Dashiell's come for a visit. You have to be all proper, see." She performed a terse bob of a curtsy.

"Dashiell is here!" He heard his cousin exclaim from somewhere floors above. "Won't Amelia be thrilled?"

Dashiell didn't know Amelia or why she should be thrilled at his presence. Most women were, of course, just not the ones who hung about his cousin.

The housekeeper pulled the leaping dog away. Behind her were Katherine's four other hounds. All too big for a row house. One looked like an Italian greyhound, and the rest were sad, mixed-breed mutts his cousin had collected off the streets. All female, of course.

Katherine hurried down the stairs. She wore her auburn hair in a towering bun with one of the red flowers from the pots outside attached to the top. She was a pudgy woman with a generous extra chin, fat arms, and tiny feet. She wore a ruffled lavender dress that was better suited for a young girl and not a lady in her late thirties. Despite her size, she moved with surprising grace, bouncing like an excited child down the stairs.

When she saw Vivienne, she stopped and clasped her hands atop her expansive bosom. "You!" she cried.

Vivienne raised a nervous brow at Dashiell.

"Good afternoon, Cousin Katherine," he said and bowed. "May I present Miss Vivienne Taylor. She is Mrs. Bertis's niece. Remember your old neighbor, Gertrude Collins?"

"Ah!" She clapped her hands. "That is why she looked so familiar. We attended a lecture together at the London Ladies' Flower and Garden Society. I've been thinking about you since that moment."

"Have you?" Vivienne asked and started to edge back to the door. Dashiell held her arm tight and flashed her a *don't say I didn't warn you* look.

"Why, yes," her cousin said. "It's quite vexing when you can't place a face. Yet…" She squeezed her eyes and peered at Vivienne. Some thought formed on her lips, but vanished as her gaze drifted to Garth cradled in Vivienne's arms. "What a lovely little baby! I just love babies. May I hold him?"

Vivienne's eyes widened with alarm. Dashiell tried not to laugh. Slowly, she offered up the poor hound, who whimpered and wiggled in her arms, petrified.

Katherine crushed the poor shivering pug to her chest and rubbed the wrinkled skin between his ears. "You're a cuddly thing, yes you are," she cooed. "Why don't you play with the girls? They just love company." She set Garth on the floor and immediately the other hounds leaped at him. The pug, frightened out of his little dog wits, shot like a bullet down the hall with the other dogs bounding in pursuit.

"Now remember, girls, he's your guest," Katherine called after them.

The housekeeper scrambled after the pack. "Stay out of the garden, and don't be upsetting my mint."

Cousin Katherine studied Dashiell with bright eyes. "So what happened to your face? No doubt you became embroiled in a brutish fight with some other savage man." She shifted her attention back to Vivienne. "Men are so tribal. Not as civilized as women." She linked her arm around Vivienne's elbow. "Wouldn't you agree?"

"I… I guess that would depend upon your definition of civilized," Vivienne stammered. "Do you mean merely refined manners or the general context of building and sustaining a culture and society?"

"Why, you're just as clever as Amelia," Katherine responded and then nodded her head toward Dashiell. "You don't like him, do you?"

Vivienne's cheeks flushed with color. "We are just… *acquaintances*."

"Good. Dashiell's horrible. Just horrible. I only tolerate him because he is sometimes mildly amusing. You're not one of those silly ladies who is attracted to rakes, are you?"

"I hope not."

"My friend Amelia Stone is visiting. A brilliant, brilliant writer and fellow member of the Society for Educated Ladies in the Fields of Literature, Science, and History. We meet here every Thursday. You should come."

"I would love to," Dashiell answered.

"Don't you dare attend that meeting, Dashiell," Katherine barked. "I invited Miss Taylor, who I can tell is excessively intelligent despite her association with you." She patted Vivienne's arm and began to lead her up the stairs. "Anyway, Amelia is writing an article about women who are attracted to terrible men, such as Dashiell. She believes women possess wild, dark natures that male-dominated society has sought to stifle. She says some women express these stunted desires upon rakish men." She glanced over her shoulder at her cousin. "Well, don't just loiter about down there, Dashiell."

"Yes, do hurry up. We're waiting on you," Vivienne admonished in her sweet voice, pursing her lips to repress her laughter. *Saucy minx.*

"Are you going to express your stunted desires on me?" he asked.

"Miss Taylor is not amused by your sad attempts at flirtation," his cousin retorted.

Vivienne wrinkled her nose at him.

They entered a parlor that was painted a dark magenta. The walls were filled with paintings of dogs. Over the fireplace hung a portrait of Katherine's mother. She couldn't have been more than thirty-five at the time of the sitting, but already her beautiful face looked harsh and tired.

A round table stood in the center of the room. On its surface were two stacks of books, a figurine of a frog on a lily pad, and a magnifying glass. A sofa and three chairs were scattered about; all bore the telltale marks of canine paws and teeth. The forest green upholstery was tattered, and the horsehair stuffing poked out in spots.

In the corner, behind a fire screen, a thin young lady with an ashen complexion rose from where she sat at a tiny writing desk. Her dark eyebrows looked like slashes rising up from the rims of her spectacles. Intense brown eyes burned behind the lenses.

"Look, Amelia," Katherine said to the woman. "My cousin has come to visit."

Dashiell bowed. The serious woman acknowledged him with a slight nod. He suspected a full curtsy might demonstrate some kind of symbolic surrender to male-dominated society.

"He has brought a lovely acquaintance named Miss Taylor," Katherine said, bringing Vivienne forward.

The writer's neck flushed a bright crimson. "H-hello," she stammered and began to fiddle with the frame of her spectacles.

Good God, is there anyone in the world who isn't attracted to Vivienne?

Katherine chattered on. "As I said, Dashiell, Amelia is writing an article on the perverse attraction of rakes. I've run out of horrible things to say about you," she said pleasantly, seeing no insult in her words. "Perhaps you can answer her questions."

"Just make it up," he said. "The ladies will only desire me more." He winked at Vivienne.

She rolled her eyes heavenward and then smiled kindly at Amelia, innocent of her effect on the besotted lady. "I would love to read your article when you are finished."

Amelia opened her mouth but couldn't even speak. Just a high humming sound came out.

"Oh, we must have tea!" Katherine exclaimed. She scrambled to the servants' bell by the door and yanked on the string. The clanking of the bell bellowed through the entire house. When the poor housekeeper didn't bend the rules of nature and appear in two seconds, Katherine poked her head out into the corridor and hollered, "We need tea and tea cakes. My special cakes."

She turned, reached up, and adjusted the flower in her hair which had started to slope to the left. "Miss Taylor, you may sit beside me on the sofa."

Left to fend for himself, Dashiell pulled up the shredded, cushioned chair next to Amelia's desk, but she gave him a scorching unwelcoming glare, so he chose the equally shredded chair closer to the door.

"So, to what do I owe the honor of this visit?" Katherine asked Vivienne.

Vivienne took a breath and ran her tongue over her upper lip. He could tell she was about to dive into one of her intricate lies. "Well, you see, I'm doing a survey on the history of Wickerly Square—"

"Did Cousin Nigel and your family have any connection with Lawrence James?" Dashiell said bluntly.

"Oh," Katherine said. She became very still. "You want to know about Lawrence James?"

"Yes," Vivienne answered.

His cousin turned crimson and began to tremble like an overheated steam engine.

"Is there something the matter?" Vivienne asked, giving Dashiell a worried look.

"Lawrence James," Katherine repeated, then let out a high, agonizing cry. "I can't," she wailed, then burst into tears and fled the room.

Vivienne, Amelia, and Dashiell exchanged shocked glances. After several seconds, Amelia rose to go after her, but Katherine had returned and stood in the doorway. She blotted her wet face with a handkerchief embroidered with violets.

"I can carry this shameful secret no longer!" she cried, holding her head high, as if addressing an audience at Drury Lane. "I must tell the truth. Come, support me, sisters." She held out her arms and Vivienne and Amelia rushed forward, each taking a hand. "That man, that destroyer of feminine goodness, the exploiter and violator of women is... is... my brother."

Vivienne's gaze flew to Dashiell's. He rubbed the bridge of his nose. He should have known he shared blood with that roguish degenerate. Solving the little mystery had just escalated from protecting Vivienne to a family matter. And his family had more matters than anyone else's in Britain except perhaps Henry VIII's. They tainted anyone who came in contact with them.

"Come, sisters," Katherine said. "Take me to the sofa and let me purge my soul of this horrid story."

With Vivienne and Amelia sitting on either side of her, Katherine sniffled, straightened her shoulders, and began. "One wintry morn, when I was five, I was playing at my mother's feet in the parlor. The house-keeper came to tell Mother that a common woman and a young boy waited at our door and refused to be turned away. My mother being the most charitable of souls—a living saint, I tell you—asked that they be brought inside by the fire." Katherine's eyes became unfocused as she gazed inward at her memories. "The woman was a sad, haggard prostitute. She was dying of the *disease,* but I didn't understand such things then. Holding her frail hand was a boy. Eleven years old, she told us. He was short for his age, quiet, and possessed large solemn eyes—like my father's." She clutched Vivienne's arm. "The woman said she had heard that my mother was kind and compassionate."

Dashiell looked down at his hands, still swollen from pounding John. Katherine was right, her mother was a saint. He just had snatches of memories of her, for he was very young at the time she had come to visit. He remembered the warm, cozy feel of her bosom when she embraced him. No one had hugged him before and he clung to her, refusing to let go. She laughed, a gentle musical sound, and said he was a special boy.

"The dying woman got on her knees before Mother and pleaded for her to provide for her child." Katherine blotted her eyes with her handkerchief. "Mother couldn't have any more children and she always wanted a son, so she took Lawrence in. Father was furious when he learned what she had done and called her such terrible names, for he never acknowl-edged Lawrence. So to shield the boy from my father's wrath, she took the meager funds she had inherited from an aunt and sent Lawrence off to school. Mother wrote him every day, so proud of her 'son,' as she now called him. He sent her beautiful pictures and wrote how he had amazed the art masters with his talent." Katherine's face hardened. "But he was a deceitful demon in disguise, I tell you."

"All men are lowly swine," Amelia said, the ugly sneer on her lips coloring her words.

"That's not true." Dashiell had to stand up for the few decent members of his sex.

"Be quiet, Dashiell!" Katherine cried. "You know that deep down, beyond your deceptively charming façade, you're no better than my father or your own."

He felt Vivienne staring at him, but he couldn't meet her eyes. He couldn't deny his cousin's words. Perhaps it was best that Vivienne came after all. Maybe now she could better understand why he kept himself from getting too close to her.

Katherine stood, crossed to the mantel, and studied the portrait of her mother. "When Lawrence was but sixteen, he was sent down from school. It seems he'd had intimate relations with the local curate's daughter. Lawrence denied it. Of course my mother, enamored of her handsome, brilliant son, believed him. She begged my father not to put the boy on the street. Father contracted a chill and his will was weakening, so Mother got her way, but not until after Father ranted cruelly against her."

Dashiell could hear the barks and yelps of dogs from outside the door. The housekeeper entered, holding a tray high above her head, safe from the hounds jumping at her feet.

She lowered the tray onto the table and picked up the tail feathers of a teapot shaped like a hen. She poured steaming tea into yellow chick cups. There were two silver platters, one with plain hard biscuits, which she set on the floor for the hounds and muttered, "Here you go, you beggars."

On the other platter were little mound-shaped tea cakes topped with one plump dot of pink icing. Vivienne's face colored and her gaze latched onto Dashiell's face. *Do these look like what I think they look like?* Dashiell's chest shook with silent laugher as he reached for one of the obscene confections.

"My special cakes," Katherine said proudly, returning to the sofa. "The Society just adores them."

"So do I," Dashiell said with a straight face. He licked off the frosted top and smiled, enjoying seeing Vivienne squirm in her tight dress.

Poor Garth peered around the doorframe. His round eyes were tense and frightened, his smashed face trembling, his ribbon torn off. He looked at Vivienne, who was sitting next to Katherine and all the other dogs, and decided he was safer under Dashiell's feet. "Are the bitches bothering you, old boy?" Dashiell asked as he scratched the dog's neck.

Vivienne took a dainty sip of tea and then cleared her throat, pretending not to hear him. "So you said Lawrence moved into your home. Do you remember what year that was?"

"Oh, I'm terrible with dates," Katherine said, flicking her hand back. "Maybe 1821 or '22. Alfred Willet, the artist, was terribly popular around that time. He painted scenes of horses and hunts and other such boring things. My mother met him through her friends, and she showed him some of Lawrence's work. He was most impressed and agreed to become Lawrence's mentor."

Katherine took a big bite of a cake and washed it down with tea. She dabbed the edges of her mouth with a linen and continued. "Then one afternoon, she and I had gone shopping at the drapers when we ran into Mr. Willet crossing Bond Street. When Mother inquired as to how Lawrence was coming along under his tutorage, he replied that she should speak to her husband. Then Mr. Willet ever so rudely walked away without uttering another word."

"What had happened?" Amelia asked.

"Oh, sister, when we came home, my father was sitting in the living room in his nightshirt, for the physician insisted he had to keep to his bed. In Father's hand was a small stack of pages. 'Mr. Willet sent me the most interesting illustrations,' he said, and then threw them at her. When they settled on the floor, my mother screamed and begged me to turn away. But it was too late. I saw *them*." She clutched her bosom. "My heart aches as I recall the sadness in Mother's eyes. Even now, decades later, I can scarcely speak of it." Katherine pressed the pad of her thumb against her lips.

Vivienne reacted quickly. "Had he drawn pictures of an impolite nature?"

Well done, old girl, thought Dashiell.

"Terrible, horrid, *disgusting* caricatures," Katherine cried. "Degrading to the beautiful feminine form. 'Aren't you proud of your *son*?' Father asked in a nasty mocking way. 'But this is just the beginning.'

He went on to say that Lawrence had done something far worse. Mother made me go to my room, so I didn't learn any more details. But several hours later, I heard someone banging on the door. I looked out my window and saw Lawrence waiting on the step below. The butler and a footman set a trunk on the steps and said Lawrence wasn't welcome in our home any longer."

"Did you see him after that?" Vivienne asked.

Katherine shook her head. "We left for Spain two weeks later. Mother never mentioned him again. But I think he truly and finally broke her heart. She became like a quiet shadow and nothing I could do would cheer her." She unpinned the flower from her hair and held it in her palm. "My mother's favorite flowers were geraniums. I suppose with all my work with the Society, I'm just trying to rectify the travesties wreaked upon my mother's soul by Father and Lawrence James."

❧

Outside his cousin's home, Dashiell examined the sky. Over the rooftops on the left side of the square, heavy clouds had rolled in for the evening. The air was colder and heavy with moisture. Vivienne clutched the traumatized Garth close to her body, her lips drawn in an anxious frown. She looked different from the cheery lady who had appeared at his door several days ago. Her eyes had lost their jovial light.

Dashiell straightened the bow on her bonnet and gave her chin a tiny caress with his thumb. "I'm sorry. I didn't know."

Her eyes searched his face. "You tell me you are a cad and a scoundrel," she said quietly. "There is much about your life that I don't know about or understand, but surely you are not as vile as Lawrence James."

He wanted to say no, but he also wanted to keep Vivienne safe from more hurt. And that's all that Dashiell was to women: hurt.

"Yes, I am," he said, and the words came out like a hard, desperate growl. He felt her body shiver, and she cast her gaze down.

"What am I going to say to my aunt? I thought this blackmail was about my uncle, but now it seems my aunt's life wasn't as simple as I thought. Yet in my heart, I feel no contempt, just compassion." Vivienne raised her eyes to his. "I understand how she felt. How easy it is to go astray."

Guilt pricked his heart. He should have told her to leave that night of the Vinho da Roda when she gazed up from those caricatures with hot, repressed desire in her eyes. Instead he'd kissed her, playing little love-making games of which she was too innocent to know the rules. He suspected the same games had been played on her aunt's young trusting heart. "Don't tell her anything."

"But I have to ask her about James and the black-mail. I don't see another way. I've run out of time. She is making me go home on Tuesday afternoon."

"What?" A panic seized his body at the thought that she wouldn't be there anymore. He knew he would have to let her go, that it was best that they were separated. He just thought he would have more time to prepare himself. "Why didn't you tell me?"

"I just didn't think it mattered to you."

"You were supposed to tell me everything."

She gave him a tiny remorseful smile. "I've broken our sacred Bazulo vow. I'm sorry."

"You should be," he said, meaning to tease her, but instead he sounded angry and frustrated. "Is John going with you?"

She shook her head.

He turned away from her, needing a moment to rein in his emotions. He tugged at his cravat as he stretched his neck from side to side and then he kicked a loose paver. As much as it pained him to know he wouldn't see her, touch her, or talk to her, he knew she would be safe in Birmingham, away from John, while he took care of the dirty business here in London.

"What's the matter, Dashiell?" she asked softly.

He spun around. She had set Garth down and now had her arms crossed about herself. A breeze blowing through the square reddened her nose and cheeks and lifted the edge of her bonnet. He cupped her chin in his palm. "I'm going to take care of everything. I just need you to trust me."

"You just admitted to being a scoundrel, and yet you ask me to trust you?"

He didn't like the way she looked at him with those fragile, anxious eyes. They cut straight through his clothes, skin, a couple of ribs, clear to his heart. Despite the daylight and the impropriety, he drew her to him.

"I promise I'm going to protect you and your aunt," he whispered. "You needn't worry about a thing."

Of course, he had no idea how he was going to quiet Jenkinson, but he suspected it would cost him a great deal of money. "I just have one request." He released Vivienne, and then bent slightly until they were eye to eye. "I just want you to stay away from John. I'm not going into detail, but I assure you he is just as vile as James."

"Or you?"

He winced.

"I know," she said gently, then averted her gaze. "But I don't have the luxury of a choice anymore."

"Yes, you do. Let me lend you money."

"I could never repay you and I would be beholden to you for the rest of my life. How would I explain it to my father? No, I must marry John." She sighed and stepped around him and started walking back to Wickerly Square.

He watched her. Her head hung low, her shoulders fallen, but she kept her spine straight. The posture of a lady struggling to be strong. At that moment, he was determined to be her hero. He was going to find a way to get money to her father if he had to build his own damn railroad. He was going to deliver her safe and sound to an upstanding, kind husband worthy of her devotion. Then he could slink back to his old, dissolute life with a clean conscience.

A carriage rattled beside him. Dashiell felt a prickly heat on his skin, as if someone were watching him. He turned to see a man inside a passing black brougham staring at him. Their eyes locked for a split second, and then the carriage turned down the opposite street and disappeared into the traffic.

❦

Vivienne and Garth entered the alley running behind Wickerly Square. She peered up at her aunt's house rising above the back mews walls. All the curtains were shut tight on the windows, and no smoke billowed from the chimney pots. She didn't want to go back inside. She wanted to run away, but she couldn't think where. She couldn't go home, and she couldn't go to John. All she could see in her mind was the comforting darkness of being held in Dashiell's arms, and the memory of floating on the heady sensation caused by the contours of his hard body against hers. She turned to check if he was still behind her, but she didn't see him. She waited a moment, hoping he would appear. When he didn't, she felt a deep sadness in her heart that she might not see him again.

Tears brimmed in her eyes. Finding out about her aunt's liaison on top of Vivienne's usual worries had left her emotionally distraught. She didn't think she could handle any more. And now she was forced to go inside her aunt's home and pretend she knew nothing. She waited a second more for Dashiell, then gave Garth's leash a small tug. "Come," she said and turned to go home.

Dashiell was leaning on the wall before her, his arms crossed, studying her from below the rim of his hat.

"How did you get ahead of me?" Her voice was breathy with relief.

"I'm full of surprises, love." He pulled off his glove and gently ran his fingertip under her eyes, brushing her tears away. "Don't cry. You know how it hurts me."

"I'm so overwrought. Too much has happened."

"I know," he whispered and then took her elbow and led her to an arbor of sorts made by a neighbor's unclipped ivy hanging over the wall.

His fingers tightened around her arm. "Listen, if that Willie chap comes by tomorrow, be sure to let me know."

"How?"

"Leave a note at—oh wait—dammit!" he spat, took off his hat, and ran his hands through his hair. "I forgot that I have to be at the Imperial Society for History tomorrow. The meetings last several eternities, and I'm supposed to speak on Roman bridge construction."

Vivienne smiled, happy for a moment to think about something other than her aunt and blackmail. "Such as the time Caesar built the bridge across the Rhine to intimidate the Gauls. That's one of my favorite stories from history."

"Are you trying to make me fall madly, obsessively, and completely in love with you?"

As I am with you? she thought. "I wish I could go. I would wager you are a fascinating lecturer."

"I will give you the abbreviated version tomorrow night. Can you meet me at the wall around 10:30 in the evening? Your aunt should be in bed by then."

"I'll try." Though she knew she would build her own bridge over the deep, cold waters of the Rhine to be there.

She gazed at his face. The bruise on his jaw had turned a deep yellow with a brown center, and the new one on his cheekbone was a feathery purple on the edges. "You said you would take care of things. Please be careful. I don't want you to get hurt anymore." She rose to her tiptoes and gingerly kissed his wounded jaw, feeling the rasp of his masculine skin.

"Dangerous," he murmured. His arms encircled her waist and drew her against him as he pressed his lips on hers. She didn't have enough strength to fight in that brutal battle between how she should behave and the wild urges of her body. She surrendered to the warmth and peace he gave her, closed her eyes, and opened her mouth to let him inside her.

The rattle of a coal service cart turning into the alley, a door being shut, Garth snorting about her feet—all seemed to be far in the distance. She tightened her hold on his biceps, her lips and tongue frantically moving against his.

His body stiffened, and he grasped her shoulders and gently pushed her against the wall. His chest heaved with his ragged breath, and his eyes glowed like burning cinders. "Woman, I warned you that I was as depraved as Lawrence James."

She put her hand behind his neck and tried to pull him down to her hungry lips, but he covered her mouth with his hand. "Please go home," he said quietly.

She didn't move. Her world would be cold and overwhelming without him. She never wanted to leave him; he thrilled her, made her laugh, and talked to her. He never got frustrated with her like her father or condescended to her like her fiancé. She wished she was marrying him instead of John. He filled her mind and heart, making her so full she would have no desire to stray from Dashiell as she had from John.

That heavy cross of guilt fell back on her conscience.

"I'm horrible for kissing you," she said. "I prayed that I would be good. Obviously I can't."

He reached to touch her, but his fingers stopped a few inches from her face, and then he dropped his arm to his side. His features screwed up as if he were in pain. "You're not the only one struggling," he said and lightly brushed against her shoulder as he walked away.

Tears blurred Vivienne's eyes. She wiped them away with the sleeve of her gown, feeling ashamed for sinning with Dashiell again. For heaven's sake, she had prayed for the last forty-eight hours to be forgiven for their previous wicked kiss. Now she had to start all over again; no doubt God was losing patience with His hopeless little lamb.

"Let's go home." She picked up Garth, whimpering at her hem, and hugged him.

Fourteen

The Imperial Society for History, Cartography, Exploration, and Related Matters kept rooms on Piccadilly Street. The building had been constructed not ten years ago, but the great hall had been modeled after its medieval ancestors. Heavy oak paneling and murals of William the Conqueror and Henry V in battle decorated the walls. Three rather barbaric-looking iron chandeliers hung down on chains from the ceiling.

Dashiell arrived in the late morning and sat in the back of the room. He was the last of seven lecturers. He shifted about in his wooden seat, restless, his eyes trained on the great clock rising over the stage. Hours passed and speakers came and went from the podium, their words flowing through his ears, making no impression on his brain. He thought only of Vivienne. The way her lashes had fanned her cheeks and the parting of her lips as she rose to kiss him under the ivy. How she wrinkled her adorable nose when she teased him at Katherine's house.

He would solve her blackmail problem and free

her from John. His eyes scanned the audience of gentlemen slumped back in their chairs, arms crossed, faces blank, as they listened to the speaker. One of them had to make a fine husband for her, provided he understood that if he made Vivienne shed one tiny tear, Dashiell would scuttle his nob.

He wondered how his life would be in the coming years. No doubt, he would continue drifting around the world and women's beds in his usual detached fashion, whereas Vivienne would be married and have a family. He tried to imagine her as a mother. With her high spirits and curiosity, her children would adore her. He felt a primal surge of anger that she wouldn't have his children. In his heart, she was his and always would be, no matter whom she married. This was the best way he could love her.

❧

At dinner, Aunt Gertrude dangled pieces of roasted hare from her fingers and played the "Who's Mama's favorite doggie?" game. Garth would stand on his hind legs like a circus dog to reach the meat.

Meanwhile, Vivienne, who had barely slept for worrying, stared at her pea soup, her eyelids slowly closing, her head drooping. *Don't fall asleep!* she admonished herself, jerking herself upright. She took a gulp of tea and then another, hoping it would give her enough energy to stay awake until Dashiell returned.

"My dear, are you getting ill?" her aunt asked, concerned.

"Probably. I don't think I should leave tomorrow."

Her aunt would have none of it. "Go lie down after

supper. I shall have Banks bring you *Dr. Oliver's Elixir for Tranquil Slumber*. That should help you. I know you want to be with your family."

No, I want to be with Dashiell. But she knew tonight was the last time they could ever be together. She wondered if he would try to kiss her and if she should let him, for fear that one little kiss would lead to a great many bigger and more dangerous seductive acts that she had no will to resist.

The thud of the front door closing echoed in the room. Garth came down to all fours, raised his head to sniff the air, and released a low growl.

Miss Banks slipped into the dining room. "I'm sorry to disturb you," she said. "But Mr. Vandergrift is a'waitin' in the parlor. Now, don't you ladies be a'frettin', but he seems quite upset."

Vivienne's spoon slipped from her fingers, hit the side of the soup bowl, and fell on the floor. Garth sprinted under the housekeeper's skirt and out of the room.

"Good heavens," said her aunt. "We shall be there directly." She looked at her niece. "I wonder what could be the matter?"

He could have found out about the blackmail or your husband's spanking or your paintings on exhibition at the Royal Academy or my father's debts or that I fondled Dashiell. Any or all of those. "I don't know," Vivienne stammered.

Vivienne clutched her aunt's arm as they entered the parlor. Garth had trapped John by the mantel. The dog was hunched on his front paws, his curly tail high, barking at the man's shoes. Vivienne gasped. A white bandage covered John's nose, and a purple bruise swelled around his left eye which glared at her like blue flames. "Get this stupid hound away from me!" he ordered.

"Mr. Vandergrift!" her aunt cried, shocked. "Come here, you naughty hound." She tried to bend, but her corset was too tight.

Vivienne knelt down and grabbed the dog by its collar. Garth dug his paws into the carpet, straining against his captor, intent on getting at the man.

"Miss Taylor," John said coldly, straightening his cravat. "Tell me, do you have relations with Lord Dashiell?"

"What!" her aunt cried. "How can you say such a thing? My little Vivvie promised me that she would have nothing to do with that scoundrel."

"And I recall that you made the same promise to me," he said to Vivienne, a dark, knowing tone slithering under his words. "Have you kept your word?"

All eyes turned to Vivienne; even Garth quieted and studied her.

"Yes," she whispered, the lie searing her throat.

"I'm sorry, I didn't hear you," he said. "You could repeat your answer."

"Yes!" she cried.

"Really, you are acting like a jealous youth, Mr. Vandergrift," her aunt said. "Vivienne adores you. She would never disobey you."

"Ahh." He wagged a finger. "Miss Taylor, did I ask you explicitly not to leave the square?"

"Yes." She could feel herself being reeled into his trap.

"Then can you tell me where you were yesterday afternoon?" he said slowly. Vivienne opened her mouth but couldn't form any words. Inside, her mind screamed. *You've done it. You've ruined your family. They are going to lose everything. Those men are going to hurt your papa. Because of you!*

"Why, she was here yesterday," her aunt stated, ignorant of the truth. "We went to church together and then Vivienne stayed home, no doubt reading the nice book you gave her."

"And… and I helped bathe Garth," Vivienne added weakly.

"Sir, you are upsetting yourself for no reason," her aunt assured him.

"Really?" he said. "Well, I asked Mr. Montag to inquire into her father's company. This morning, he showed me the actual documents from Mr. Taylor's creditors detailing the extent of his debt." The edge of his teeth glinted beneath his tight lips. "Twenty thousand pounds." He paused, letting the number hang heavy in the air. "I was humiliated before Mr. Montag."

The floor appeared to tilt, like a boat riding a wave. Vivienne gripped Garth's collar, trying to keep herself upright.

"W-what?" Her aunt dropped her cane and pressed her hand to her mouth as she staggered to the side table by her chair. "My nerves. Where is the Milner's tonic?" She fumbled through her bottles, knocking some onto the floor.

"How long did you think you could hold such a sum from me?" John thundered at Vivienne. "Until after our wedding day when I was trapped?"

"We just need one or two orders," Vivienne explained. "Enough to make a few hundred pounds for payment."

"Indeed, sir, I can speak for Mr. Taylor," her aunt said, taking a large gulp of something in a green bottle. "He will honor his debts. But surely, there has been a misunderstanding. Surely."

He shook his head. "I'm afraid her father's financial problems are not all that concerns me." His spoke in an eerily cool voice, his left eye glittering from its bruised socket. "I had my manservant follow you yesterday afternoon when you were supposedly at home."

Vivienne's hard swallow was audible.

"He claims that you brazenly embraced Lord Dashiell in Cavendish Square. Can you deny this?"

"Sir, you are quite mistaken," Aunt Gertrude cried. "My Vivvie is a virtuous lady. How dare you—"

"My man even described your pug dog, ma'am."

"No!" her aunt gasped. "Not my Garth." Aunt Gertrude slumped into her chair. The dog pulled from Vivienne's grasp and rushed to his mistress's side, whimpering and pawing at her dress.

"Y-you d-don't understand," Vivienne choked, hot tears running down her face.

"I don't?" John asked. "Well then, please enlighten me as to why you knowingly lied and disobeyed me."

"I… I…" How could she explain about Lawrence James and the paintings? "I can't." Vivienne broke down into sobs, her whole body convulsing. "I just can't."

John began to walk around her like a predator after its wounded prey. "Miss Taylor, I admit I was attracted to your beauty in a moment of personal weakness. It wasn't until a few days into our engagement that I became aware of your severe deficiencies in character. Even then I tried to guide you in the proper course."

"I'll be good," Vivienne pleaded through her tears. "I promise. Just let me try again."

"I have given you too many chances already. But you cannot be worked on. In your heart, you are a deceitful young lady. Headstrong, ignorant, and foolish. It pains me to say these words in the presence of your aunt, but I must retract my offer of marriage."

"No!" She reached blindly for him, for though her eyes were open, she couldn't see. Her hands fell through empty air. "Don't do this!"

John bowed before Aunt Gertrude. "I'm sorry to cause you such distress."

"Pray to the Lord, Mr. Vandergrift," her aunt implored him, her hands clasped together. "*For if ye forgive men their t-trespasses, your heavenly Father will also f-forgive…*" Her voice faltered under her guest's blistering glare.

"My humblest apologies, but I cannot," he said. "It is Vivienne who should pray to the Lord for forgiveness. I shall take my leave." He strode to the hall without even giving Vivienne a glance.

She couldn't let him go, knowing she had destroyed her entire family. She chased after him, swinging the parlor door shut behind her. She grabbed his arm. "I'm sorry. I'll be a good wife. Give me another chance. I beg you."

She could hear Garth sniffing about the doorframe and growling.

"No," he said, trying to free himself, but she held on.

"But you kissed me. You said you loved me." She searched his face, looking for any tenderness, any soft emotion she could latch onto.

"Miss Taylor, please have some dignity." He yanked away, causing Vivienne to lose her balance and fall to her knees on the hard floor planks.

She couldn't go home and tell her father what happened. "I'll do anything." She gazed up his trousers to where his sex bulged and rested her hand on his thigh and inched closer. "Anything."

He studied her face. His flat pale eyes now glittered. "Do you think giving yourself to me will sway my decision?" He touched her face, letting his thumb circle her cheek.

She latched onto his hand and kissed his fingers. "Anything," she whispered again.

He leaned down until his lips touched her ear. "I couldn't keep company with a common whore, much less marry her," he snarled.

He may as well have kicked her in the heart. Rage burned through her. "Then you're a liar," she hissed. "I know what you are and where you've been. I know about that little 'wedding present' you keep at Seven Heavens."

"I don't know what you are talking about." He reached for his hat and tugged the brim over his forehead. "Good day, Miss Taylor. I sincerely regret making your acquaintance," he said, stepping around her as if she were rubbish in the street.

"No, I regret making *your* acquaintance," she spat, rising to her feet. "I'm tired of putting up with your tedious conversation. I'm tired of pretending to find your infantile observations interesting. I'm tired of trying to make myself love you. You are an arrogant ignoramus. I assure you that only a lady whose father is in debt would stand for your hypocrisy and lies, you pompous, conceited arse!" She began to turn away but another thought seized her, and she whirled back around. "And one more thing. Mrs. Smith-Figgle's book *The Ethereal Graces of the Delicate Witless Ninnies* is vapid and insipid, just like your *perfect* Elise Montag." She fled to the staircase, opening the parlor door as she passed. "Go to him, Garth."

The last she saw was a barking blur of black and tan streak across the entrance hall as she raced upstairs and locked herself in Uncle Jeremiah's study.

Tears flowed down her face as she pulled the old desk back with her hands, shocked at her own strength. She yanked away the fabric panel and knocked on Dashiell's wall. Nothing.

"Oh, Dashiell," she whispered. "Please come home. I need you."

❦

Newberry spoke well over his allotted time, so Dashiell didn't get to the podium until just after five. He lectured for an hour while using wooden slats, rocks, thread, and glue to illustrate how Caesar's army built a bridge over the Rhine. Then he answered questions. One gentleman asked what happened to Dashiell's face, which caused a nervous ripple of laughter. An elderly member said his nephew was coming to town and wanted to know what clubs young bucks frequented these days. Another asked the name of Dashiell's tailor. The men were still raising their hands as the servants were bringing in the tables for dinner.

As Dashiell was wrapping up his artifacts, and the servants were setting out the silver and pouring glasses of wine, he spied Teakesbury slipping through the massive double doors at the back of the hall. He made a beeline for Dashiell, his cane tucked under his arm.

"You look terrible," Teakesbury said as a greeting. "You shouldn't be out in public with that contusion."

"You don't think it adds to my roguish appeal?"

"Perhaps to the low sorts you consort with." He leaned in and lowered his voice, twiddling the edge of his mustache with a fat finger. "I've heard Fontaine is furious about what you did to her place. Not like you to go to brothels."

Dashiell shrugged. "Maybe I'm turning over a new leaf."

Teakesbury tapped the table with his knuckles. "Or maybe you went to talk to Fontaine."

Dashiell stopped in the middle of wrapping up a Roman pump lever and studied the solicitor's face. The bemused twinkle in Teakesbury's eyes had sharpened to something rather hard and predatory.

"What's this to do with you?" Dashiell asked. "Have you finally connected her to the stolen paintings?"

"No. In fact, I wanted to ask you about the paintings."

"Well, hell, you got me." Dashiell held up his palms. "I stole them."

"I don't think you are very funny." He jerked his head toward the corridor. "Meet me outside."

Dashiell sighed. "Just give me a minute."

He finished packing up his precious ancient children and made sure they were safely installed in his carriage and sent home. Then he found Teakesbury waiting in the corridor, leaning on his cane to examine the portraits of past presidents of the Imperial Society. The scent of beef and brown sauce wafted from the great hall. In the next room, Dashiell could hear the muffled chatter of men and the ring of cutlery.

Teakesbury began to speak, keeping his gaze fixed on the third honorable president. "I was contacted by the police today. Two stolen paintings floated up at a pawnshop near the Strand."

Dashiell's heartbeat quickened, thinking of Gertrude. "Did they ask the owner who brought in the paintings?"

"The shop owner said a large man who called himself Stephen. Probably a made-up story. You can't crack those reptiles down there."

"It doesn't make sense to take the masterpieces to a pawn broker."

"These weren't the masterpieces," he said. "Not all the paintings stolen were. Anyway, one painting recovered was a poor rendition of Ariadne being comforted by Dionysus."

"Are we merely discussing art criticism, or do you have a point?"

He tilted his head and gazed at Dashiell with a bright eye. "The lady had blond hair and a turned-up nose."

Young Adele Jenkinson, Dashiell thought. "Tell me what you know about the robbery."

"Mrs. James and her servant took her son to the park in the afternoons, which is when the thieves came in through the alley and broke into the gallery. They must have been watching her abode for some time to know her schedule. The curator and I had been getting the paintings ready to transport to the Royal Academy, so it was an easy snatch."

"And Mrs. James didn't witness any of it."

Teakesbury looked down to where a beetle scuttled across the wood planks near his feet. He smashed the insect with the butt of his cane. "Mrs. James came home and found a massive oak cabinet had been shoved before the door to the stairwell, no doubt to block any entrance from the family quarters during the theft. The back gallery door was unlocked and the wood around its frame splintered. James's paintings and sketches were scattered about the gallery floor, indicating the thieves were after something specific.

"Sketches?" Dashiell's mind sharpened. "Were any of those stolen as well?"

Teakesbury shrugged. "We can only assume."

"And the neighbors?"

"The street is crammed with shops, so they wouldn't have taken notice of anyone different milling about. However, the police think more than one person was involved because of the size and weight of the cabinet that had been moved to block the door."

"A really large, strong man could have moved it, perhaps?"

"It's all just speculation."

"What about in the park, anything out of the ordinary?"

Teakesbury shrugged. "Mrs. James paid a small man who danced for her son."

From inside the hall, he could hear the clank of a spoon being beat against a glass and the president asking everyone to be seated. Dashiell fished out his pocket watch. 8:03.

"Damn," Dashiell muttered and then turned to the solicitor. "Don't leave without talking to me."

The two men sat beside each other at the table. For the next two hours, they spoke politely with the other men at the table of expeditions to Egypt and Italy and the difficulty of finding competent local guides.

Dashiell's gut clenched with anxiety. He could feel that something terrible was about to happen. He needed to get to those masterpieces before the police and hush up any unsavory business. He could weather scandal, but Vivienne and her family could not. He was glad she was getting the hell home and wished she could take her aunt with her.

After the dishes of boiled apple pudding in vanilla cream had been cleared away, the men leaned back in their chairs, making discreet belches and stretching their legs as servants brought around boxes of cigars. Dashiell rose and slapped Teakesbury on the shoulder. "I'm leaving. I'd appreciate it if you walked me out."

Teakesbury held up the newly lit cigar between his fingers. "I'm busy."

"I said, I would appreciate it if you walked me out."

"You have the manners of a Hottentot, Dashiell." The solicitor stubbed out his cigar in the ashtray in the center of the table.

In the cloakroom, Dashiell sent for their coats and turned to Teakesbury, speaking in a low tone. "I want you to introduce me to James's widow."

"Why?"

"I'm not at liberty to say at present."

"Well then, I'm not at liberty to let you talk with my client."

Two footmen emerged from a back room. One held the gentlemen's coats over his arm, and the other carried their hats. Dashiell held out his arm as the footman slid on his coat and straightened the shoulders. "Then I'll find her address myself and call on her," he said, letting a dangerous smile curve his mouth. "Just me and her, a lonely widow. All alone. I'm so damn charming, anything could happen."

"Don't you touch my client!" Teakesbury snatched his coat from the footman, as his face reddened with anger. "Three o'clock tomorrow. I'm not free until then."

Dashiell combed his hair with his fingers and set his hat on his head. "Until tomorrow."

He bowed and sauntered out of the room until he was out of Teakesbury's sight. Then he quickened his step and hurried outside. He checked his watch under the gaslight. 10:41. Dammit. Rather than try to walk back, he hailed a passing hack.

"Wickerly Square," he told the driver and tossed him up a coin. "And make haste, man."

Fifteen

PLEASE, PLEASE COME HOME EARLY, VIVIENNE PLEADED as she knocked on Dashiell's panel for what must have been the fiftieth time.

At nine-thirty, Miss Banks had tapped on the door of Jeremiah's study. Vivienne slipped into the corridor and quickly shut the door behind her. The rims of the housekeeper's eyes were reddened and she held a bottle of *Dr. Oliver's Elixir for Tranquil Slumber and Serene Mind*. "The mistress is asleep," she had whispered. "Let me help you get ready for bed."

In Vivienne's bedchamber, the housekeeper untied Vivienne's corset. "Now don't you be a'frettin' that you've hurt your aunt something terrible," she said, yanking at the laces. "You're a'goin' home to your sisters, leaving the plague in blue at your aunt's doorstep. But don't you a'worry that your father and aunt will end up in the poor house, and Harold and me are on the street. You're young and need to enjoy yerself."

She left the room, leaving the elixir on the commode.

Vivienne pulled off her chemise, tossed a nightdress

over her shoulders, and tied the drawstring at the neck. She grabbed her robe from the chair and scurried to Uncle Bertis's study and waited, curled on the floor and clutching her stomach. For hours, her head swirled with the terrible scenario of those men beating her father, molesting her and her sisters, and her father living in the cramped, grimy rooms in debtor's prison—all because of her. By the time the pendulum clock read eleven o'clock, the fireless room had grown cold with the fall of night. She drew her knees under the hem of her robe to cover her cold toes.

"Please Dashiell," she whispered. "Don't forget me. I'm so scared."

She heard the door open on the other side of the wall, and Dashiell's rich baritone say, "No, no, that will be all. Just put everything in my library. I'll sort it in the morning."

A door shut.

Vivienne bolted up. She reached to knock on Dashiell's panel, but he had pulled it off before her hand connected with the wood.

Just seeing his warm chocolate eyes made her burst into sobs. She threw herself over the divide and into his arms. His feel, his cardamom scent, his heartbeat soothed her taut nerves.

"Oh God, Vivienne. What happened?" He ran his hand up and down her back. "You're shaking all over."

She couldn't talk. Her throat was sore and tight. She buried her face in the darkness of his chest, not wanting to ever leave again.

But he gently grasped her shoulders and pulled her away, until he could see her face. "Talk to me."

She looked down, unable to meet his gaze. "John found out about my father... and... and us. He doesn't want to marry me anymore. H-he c-called me a... a whore."

His fingers tightened, hurting her arm. "Goddamn, I should have killed him," he growled.

"W-what am I going to tell my f-father?"

He put his hands on her cheeks and tilted her head up, forcing her to look at him. "Hush."

"But—"

His kiss halted her words. She didn't try to fight, just drifted in the soothing feel of his touch. His tongue caressed her mouth. She tangled her fingers into his curls and deepened their kiss. Holding him silenced all the chaotic thoughts in her head. Her mouth slid from his lips to the edge of his jaw, feeling its hardness and rasp, then she moved lower into the hot concave of his neck. She could smell the residual scent of musky cologne. She kissed his pulse, letting her tongue taste the slight saltiness of his skin. He moaned. "Oh, sweet lady."

Her fingers flowed down, beneath his coat, and rested against his chest. His muscles were hard and flexed under her touch. She could hear the rush of his breath by her ear. She didn't want to think about or consider tomorrow. She didn't want to leave this room or Dashiell ever again. She wished she could hide here for the rest of her life.

She wished she could marry him.

"Dashiell," she whispered, because saying his name was like some magic spell that soothed her worries.

He slid back the edge of her nightdress, exposing

the skin of her shoulder. Bending his head, he took a small nibble, letting his tongue play along her collarbone, sending hot shivers over her skin. His lips dipped lower, down her chest. Was he going to kiss her breasts? The prospect caused a heavy, wet heat in her feminine core. She caught her breath, but he stopped and started up her neck.

"We are going to kiss, that's all," he said. "I'm just comforting you. Understand?"

She wanted more than comfort. She wanted him. What had he said? If he ruined her, he would have to marry her.

She pulled back her robe and reached for the drawstring of her nightdress.

"No," he whispered, but he was too late. She had already slid the gown down. She stared at his eyes, as he studied her bared breasts.

He let out a heavy, ragged exhale. "Why are you torturing me?"

"Touch me," she murmured.

He seized her arms. His mouth took her nipple. She gasped as tremors of pleasure flowed through her body as his tongue flicked on the tip. She had never felt a sensation so sweet and intense. She held her breath and arched her back, pushing herself deeper into his mouth, craving his touch. Some urge, some raw instinct she didn't understand made her press her feminine folds against him, like a kneading cat, trying to relieve the deep throb inside her.

His mouth released her breast. "Dear God, we need to stop. You're making me excited. I'm not going to be able to control myself."

Her hand drifted down to where his sex pushed against his trousers.

"Let me see you," she whispered, kissing his neck. She was tired of the mystery, tired of Lavinia's stories, Mrs. Hudson's cucumbers, and all those stunted desires Amelia supposedly wrote about.

"Please, no," he cried through clenched jaw and scooted back from her touch. Anger filled her. She wouldn't be pushed away and left to incinerate in her own desire.

"Let me," she said.

His chest fell with a long sigh. He closed his eyes and opened his arms by his side, surrendering to her.

She leaned closer, suddenly nervous and apprehensive. She unbuttoned his waistcoat and massaged his belly muscles with her hand. But her eyes kept drifting to his member, swollen beneath his clothes. Slowly, her fingers dipped at his trouser waistband, finding the buttons. His body stiffened, and he sucked a breath as the flap fell down. His penis rose up.

"You're beautiful," she whispered. Her hand hovered just over him, but not touching. "But how can a lady possibly get that... in... It's so big."

"I adore you," he said, taking her mouth for another deep kiss. But she had to stop and marvel at his sex again.

She wanted to touch him, but didn't know how. All she knew was what she had seen in those caricatures. The thing he said other ladies did that pleased him. And she wanted to please him. So she leaned down and took the tip into her mouth.

"Good God, Viv!"

His skin felt so soft, yet he was as hard as a stone. Not knowing what else to do, she kissed his cock, like she would his mouth, running her tongue along him. He shuddered.

"I shouldn't let you do this," he cried. "You need to stop." His fingers tightened about her curls. For a moment, she thought he would pull her away. Had she done something wrong? But instead, he slowly eased himself deeper into her mouth and then withdrew. He did this again and again. She followed his rhythm. She could hear him catch his breath and let out quiet moans. Her heart swelled knowing she was pleasing him.

Still, she wanted more, she wanted to take him to a place where he couldn't control himself. She didn't want to hear him say *no* ever again. *Yes, Vivienne, I love you. Yes, Vivienne, I want to be with you forever. Yes, Vivienne, I'll marry you.*

She gazed up at him. "Tell me that I make you happy."

His face tightened as if in pain. "Oh, love," he said and ran his finger down her cheek and then caressed her lips with his thumb. "Do you truly want to pleasure me?"

She nodded, taking his fingertip into her mouth.

"Come here," he said. He stood up and tossed his shirttail over his cock, stepped out of his shoes, and held out his hand to her. When she rose, he swept his arm under her knees, lifting her into his arms.

Was he going to love her as a husband loves a wife? She wasn't afraid at all. In fact, she had never felt so certain about anything in her life. Looking back, to the first time she saw him when she was still just a girl, she somehow knew she wanted to be his before she could even understand what that meant.

Then he laid her upon his bed. She sank into the mattress. He untied her robe and spread the sides like wings from her body. His gaze drifted from her face, slowly down to her breasts. She loved how he studied her, how her body heated and shivered under his intense gaze.

He buttoned back his trousers and then reached for his cravat and undid the knot. "You pleasure me when you wrinkle your nose and laugh." He slid the cravat off his neck and let it fall on the floor. "You pleasure me when we walk side-by-side talking about nothing." He removed his coat and waistcoat. "You pleasure me just by being near me." He leaned down, one knee on the bed, and brushed her lips with his. She ran her hands under his shirt, lifting the fabric until she could see the contours of his taut muscles around his belly and the rise of his chest. He yanked the shirt over his head, revealing his strong shoulders and arms.

She put her hand behind his neck. "You're so handsome," she said, drawing him to her for a languid, deep kiss. His lips drifted down her neck and to the breast he had neglected before. He teased the hard tip with his tongue, making her writhe under his touch. She clutched his biceps, wanting to pull him onto her, feel him on her—inside her. Do something to sate this hunger.

He lifted his head. A devilish twinkle lit his eyes, as if he were playing, knowing full well the need he elicited in her body. He slid his hand up the inside of her thigh, bunching her night dress around her waist.

He looked down at her most private place. The back of his jaw tensed, and he let out a low sigh. Suddenly, she felt shy and vulnerable.

"Are you going to do those things from… from James's caricatures?" she asked.

He curled the side of his mouth. "Maybe a few of the more gentle pleasures." Then he grew serious again. "But I won't penetrate you. I won't ruin you. What happens tonight will be our little secret. I'm just going to help relieve you of this tension."

He drew up one of her knees, opening her wider. Vivienne released a deep breath, feeling nervous and excited to be so intimately known.

"You're exquisite," he said quietly, then ran his finger between her folds. Her gaze flew to his face. A slow smile spread over his lips as he began circling that small peak between her thighs.

Her muscles tensed, and she opened her mouth, but couldn't make a sound but the tiniest whimper as an intense pleasure wracked her body.

"Just don't fight the feeling," he advised, moving his finger faster.

Tremors shook her body, and she arched her back, pushing herself against him. "It's so sweet."

He continued working his magic. She could scarce keep her breath as pleasure mounted in her like compressed steam. Her legs began to shake, even as the rest of her body became rigid.

He leaned down and gently sucked her nipple and then flicked his tongue across its tip. She released a high, soft cry as tiny spasms broke over her body. She wanted more, something she couldn't articulate, his scent, his feel, all of him. She reached up and grabbed his shoulders, toppling him on top of her.

"I want to feel you," she gasped.

"Dear God, you're undoing me."

She felt his cock, straining against his trousers, and began to rub her mound against it, wrapping her legs around his. He moved with her, matching her rhythm, urging her to go faster.

"Tell me to stop," he hissed, his voice hoarse and thick. "Say 'no, Dashiell.'"

Her nails dug into his arm. Her knees trembled as her heels pressed into the mattress. "Yes! Yes! Yes!"

"Dammit, woman, I can't control myself."

She felt him pull away. "Don't!"

He was back again, but this time his trousers were pulled down, just the bare skin of his sex rubbing her peak. His breath was hard against her cheek. She could feel the power of his body pushing against her. She writhed beneath him, her desire stoked and desperate for some release. She was almost there. Almost... Her mind went silent as pleasure like waves crested through her. She clutched him, sliding her swollen lady parts against his hard cock, milking the sensation.

Vivienne's climax resonated to his core. He could hear the thoughts in his head, warning him not to do what he was about to do. But some primal beast had taken over. He couldn't stop himself.

He covered her mouth with his, her fingers threaded his hair. His penis was so hard, it hurt. He thrust, feeling her virgin barrier resist and then slowly give.

She stiffened and her body rose up. For several seconds, she was still. He was terrified that he had hurt her. Then her lips curled into a smile, and she released a long, soft moan, relaxing around him. "At last," she sighed.

He clenched his teeth. *Yes, at last.* All those years of pent-up yearning, now flowing forth like a wild, foaming river. He tried to restrain himself to a slow pace, but couldn't. She was so tight, so amazing, and so beautiful in her wantonness. He thrust and thrust, ravenous.

What the hell are you doing? He had just taken her virtue. And not the way it should have been done. Not slow and gentle, but desperate and fevered.

"I'm sorry, I'm sorry," he cried in her ear.

"But it's sublime." She shifted under him, raising her knees higher, allowing him deeper inside of her. Her thighs moved with his rhythm, racing him, teasing him. She kept her eyes, darkened and glossy with desire, fixed on his face and her lips parted, tiny soft whimpers escaping from her throat. Everything was happening too fast. He couldn't rein himself in. She might come again, but there was nothing he could do to help her along. He was too close to the edge of orgasm.

She cried out his name as her nails dug into his biceps. Her back arched, her legs started to tremble as she bucked wildly against him. The mattress was creaking, the bed posts slamming against the wall.

From some dark corner in his mind, a tiny, rational voice called "Pull out" just as she climaxed, her vagina contracting around his cock. The pleasure was too intense. He squeezed his eyes shut, blocking that panicked voice of reason screaming for him to withdraw. White light flared in his head as he released his seed, his being, into her womb.

For a moment, neither spoke. A quiet awe filled the bed. Then slowly he came to rest on her body, now damp and languid from lovemaking.

She wrapped her arms about him. "I love you."

A sweet, complete peace radiated from her touch that melted his heart. He pulled her tighter, feeling raw and afraid. His soul was naked, all his defenses breached.

He couldn't muster the playful or teasing post-coital words he usually told his lovers. Vivienne was innocent and trusting. She didn't understand that what had just happened was different for him. He hadn't loved her correctly. Not as he supposed a man should make love to a virgin, gently and carefully. He was wild and unrestrained.

"Tell me you love me too," she whispered.

The perspiration on his skin grew cool. He bolted up. "What the hell have I done?" he cried.

She squeezed his arm. "What's the matter?" she asked. Her voice was still drowsy and soft. Her eyes were so tender, so trusting. She shouldn't look at him that way. He wished he were a decent man who could hold her and tell her nothing was wrong. But everything was wrong. A shameful urge came over him, telling him to flee.

He reached for the waist of his trousers, which were crumpled around his knees. He hadn't even taken the time to pull his trousers off, he was so mad with passion.

"You needn't worry," she said soothingly. "I will marry you."

Something in her inflection, beneath the softness,

sounded almost scheming. He felt as if he were being choked and reached to tug at his cravat, but he wasn't wearing one.

"What did you say?"

"I will marry you. You said if you ruined me, we would have to marry."

For a moment, all he could do was stare. "Is this what you wanted?" he finally asked, in a tight voice. "To marry me?"

She smiled, a beautiful grin, a gentle light coming to her eyes. "I've always wanted to marry you."

He felt like he had just had taken a hard blow in the gut. "Did you…seduce me?"

Her lips trembled. "W-what?"

"John jilted you, so you came running to me?"

"No!" She rose up to her knees on his bed. Her nightdress, bunched about her waist, slid down, exposing her belly. "It—it just happened. Perhaps I thought you might marry me, but—"

"Was that when your mouth was on my cock or when you were begging me to ravish you?"

Vivienne gasped.

He couldn't believe he had said those words. What the hell was wrong with him? He was out of control. "I'm sorry… I didn't mean it. It's just, dammit, Vivienne, I all but told you I couldn't marry you."

"No. You said you weren't capable of making a good husband, but now—"

"You aren't so picky."

Her face crumpled as if she were about to cry. "I think you would make an excellent husband and… and father."

Husband? Children? "I have to get away from here."
He swung around, looking for his coat and cravat
tossed on the floor.

She pressed her hands to her belly. "But I might
have a child now. Isn't that what we've done?"

He pinched the bridge of his nose. "Oh God. You
don't know anything, do you?"

Of course, no one had instructed her on the feminine
arts. She hardly knew how babies were created, much
less how to prevent one. Still, a scary thrill ran through
him at the idea of Vivienne having his children. In his
head, he pictured her holding a newborn to her breast,
like a beautiful Madonna. Then a black rage filled him.
Images of his own mother replaced the Madonna. And
inside he felt hollow and terrified like that little boy left
alone in the darkness of his enormous chamber with
instructions from whatever nurse just to let him cry.

"A woman rarely becomes pregnant after her first
experience," he said, trying very hard to believe the
old myth his mates tossed around at Cambridge.

"Oh," she said, sounding bereft, her head drooping.
He didn't know if she were disappointed that she might
not have a child or that her marriage trap had failed.

"I need to think," he said. He grabbed his shirt off
the floor and yanked it over his head.

"But—"

"I can't breathe!" he shouted.

"What is happening?" she cried.

"For God's sake, don't look at me like that. I'm a
little upset at the moment. J-just put your clothes back
on." He wrapped his cravat around his neck and made
a weak knot with his shaking hands.

"But I'm compromised. You have to marry me."

"Not necessarily," he said absently. *Where the hell are my shoes?* He had to get out of here so he could breathe again. "Just… just get some sleep, and we'll discuss our situation tomorrow."

"*Situation?*" Vivienne echoed. They were a *situation*. She had experienced the loveliest moment of her life, and she'd thought he felt the same.

She remembered the prediction his angry red-headed lover had made not a week ago: *You're not different. Soon this bounder will break your heart and bring you to tears, like he did all the other ladies.*

"You don't love me," she whispered.

Her limbs felt weak, her face trembled, and hot tears poured from her eyes. But she wouldn't sob hysterically, or throw ancient vases, or hurl insults at him. At least she would be unique in that respect. She clutched her falling nightdress about her, grabbed the robe from where it had fallen on the floor, and ran for the passage. She hoped he might move to stop her or call her name. Once in the study, she waited a moment, giving him a last chance. Nothing. She jammed the panel back into place. With a mighty push, she shoved the bureau back and then kicked its side, again and again.

Foolish girl. You made John leave you and then you gave away your virtue to the worst rake in London. And now your family is going to starve because of you.

⁓

Dashiell shot back a glass of brandy and then poured another. He stared at the crumpled bed cover. Hot tears burned in his eyes.

"Damn me," he shouted and threw the tumbler so hard the glass exploded when it hit the fireplace, spraying the floor with tiny shards. This time he had gone too far.

He shoved his feet in his shoes and did what he always feared he would if Vivienne got too close... he fled.

Sixteen

TWO HOURS OR SO LATER, DASHIELL WAS DRUNK IN A grimy timbered tavern off Soho Square with his new best lads Lionel, a reed-like, nasal-voiced young man who had just lost his fiancée to a bank clerk, and Gilbert, a big mountain of a bartender.

"I've known her all my life," Dashiell told them with a wave of his hand, splashing the drink he was holding. "She was my little sister, and she grew into this beautiful lady. Stunning. Ravishing. Helen of Troy couldn't rival her. And her mind. The female Aristotle, I tell you." He gulped from his glass and then set it and his head on the bar. "She wasn't supposed to grow up, dammit, and become dangerous. I'm a loggerhead, a coxcomb, a lout. I can't help myself. I didn't want to hurt her, but I did. I did."

"You want another drink, my good fellow?" Gilbert asked.

Dashiell raised himself and looked at Lionel. "You know what I want? I want you to punch me." He pointed to the side of his chin without a bruise. "Right there. Give me a good hook."

"Really?" Lionel slurred. "You want me to hit you?"

"Go ahead, I deserve it," Dashiell assured him. "I'm a low, cowardly cully. A fatheaded, faithless blackguard."

"If you insist." Lionel pulled back his thin fist and drunkenly gazed at it for a moment, as if he didn't recognize his own hand, and then let it fly. He missed Dashiell entirely, stumbled, and then fell into the husky gentleman next to them, seemingly embracing him.

The man flashed them a dark eye. "Sorry, old chap," Lionel said, straightening himself. He slinked back. "I never was a fighter," he cried. "Lost every fisticuffs at Eton. A regular dandyprat, I am. That's why my fiancée left me for that bank clerk."

"Now, now, just have another drink," Dashiell said, patting him on the back.

Gilbert set another glass down before each man, including himself, and poured. "So what's your problem, old boy?" he said to Dashiell "Why did you have to hurt her?"

Dashiell stared at the flames from the coal fire dancing on the amber brandy. In his drunken mind, he was reeling back through time to the little boy, clutching his history book to his chest, calling out for his mama who wasn't there. To the same little boy, writing letters to his mama, begging her to come home. To all the still stone goddesses in his house, beauties who couldn't hurt him or leave him. The words fell from his mouth. "My mama abandoned me. She didn't love me."

Lionel banged his fist on the wood. "My fiancée abandoned me for a bank... wait a minute, did you say your mama? Why are we talking about your mother?"

Gilbert started to sniff, his big shoulders heaving. "My mother said I was one child too many and sent me to an orphanage."

"That's so sad!" Lionel hunched over and began weeping into his brandy.

Meanwhile, a slew of memories began falling on Dashiell: his mother fighting with his father, her tears, the tears of the actresses and courtesans Dashiell had hurt, Vivienne's tears, the beautiful light in her eyes as she rested on his chest after they made love, the young girl hanging from a tree asking him what "whore-monger" meant, her mischievous grin and the way she wrinkled her nose, the day his father sat Dashiell down and explained that his mama wasn't coming back, the night his father lay bleeding from a lover's bullet, Vivienne whispering "I love you."

His body started to quiver, and he felt as if he would come out of his skin. He leaped onto the bar. "Ladies and gentleman, I would like to talk about marriage and mating customs," he declared. "Let's start with China, where I shall soon be traveling."

An hour later, Dashiell had finished two more drinks and moved on to lecturing about the harems of the Ottoman Empire, despite the fact that the patrons were booing him, a few even throwing utensils at him, and his now not-so-best-lad Gilbert had threatened to call the watch. "Unknown to many in the west, harems have a rigid hierarchical structure," Dashiell slurred and then stopped, recognizing the wild gray hair and hat of his grandfather coming through the tavern door.

"What the hell?" he said, approaching his grandson.

"One of the boys told me I was supposed to come get you. That you were embarrassing yourself."

"Actually, I was just leaving," Dashiell said.

"Damnation, son," the earl said as he helped his grandson off the bar. He tossed an arm over Dashiell's shoulder as if he were injured and began to guide him to the door. The entire tavern broke into applause.

Outside, the night air felt dense and wet with unfallen rain. In the narrow gap between high roof-tops on either side of the street, Dashiell could see the dark gray clouds blanketing the night sky. Low fog flowed in from the alleyways. He supported himself against a lamppost and swallowed hard to keep the contents of his stomach down.

"Let's get a hack and take you home," the earl suggested.

Dashiell panicked. He couldn't go back to his room, where Vivienne's scent still lingered on the sheets. Not yet. He shook his head. "I can't go home."

"Why?"

"I don't want to talk about it."

"But—"

"I said I don't want to talk about it!" He shouted so violently he lost his balance and had to grab his grandfather's shoulder.

From one of the windows above them, a gravelly male voice yelled, "Then shut your damned 'ole!"

"I just want to walk." Dashiell pushed off the post and concentrated on the ground, trying to walk an unwavering straight line. After a block, he gripped his belly, feeling the brandy wash up in the back of this throat. "I need to sit," he muttered. Up ahead, he saw the open iron gates of Wesley Congregational. He just needed to make it a few more steps.

"What are you doing?" his grandfather asked as Dashiell stumbled into the brick courtyard. The earl waited at the gate, as if he might get struck by lightning or suffer some other horrible kind of Biblical death upon entering the church grounds. "You can't go in there."

Dashiell staggered over to the steps and slumped down on the cold brick.

His grandfather cautiously tiptoed across the yard. "Tell me, what's the matter?"

Dashiell opened his palms and closed them again. "I bedded Vivienne."

"You did *what* to Vivienne?" his grandfather shouted, his voice echoing in the courtyard. His right hand lashed out like a whip and popped Dashiell's bruised chin.

"Bloody hell!" Dashiell spat through his clenched teeth. In the tall narrow house connected to the church grounds, he saw the spark of a match and then the brightening glow of a lamp being lit behind a sheer curtain on a third floor window.

"What's going on out there?" Mr. Charles stuck his head out his window.

"Hell's fire," Dashiell hissed to himself, then cleared his voice and tried to speak in a polite sober tone. "Nothing, we're leaving," he said, trying not to slur. "A th-thousand pardons."

"Brother Lord Dashiell, is that you?"

"Dammit. Dammit. Dammit." Dashiell cursed under his breath. "Why, yes. Just out for a night stroll."

"Wait there, I'll join you."

"Oh, that won't be necessary."

"I couldn't sleep anyway. I'll be just a minute." He shut the window before Dashiell could protest again.

Dashiell leaned back and propped his elbows on the upper steps. "I think this could be the worst night of my life."

"Are you going to marry her?" his grandfather asked.

Dashiell studied the faint outline of the gibbous moon, obscured by drifts of clouds. "I don't know," he said quietly.

The hard edge of his grandfather's knuckles slammed Dashiell's jawbone.

"Will you stop that?" Dashiell yelled, cradling his face.

The door to the minister's home opened, and Mr. Charles padded out, holding a lantern and wearing a black night robe and bright knit slippers. "Good evening, gentlemen."

Dashiell and his grandfather mumbled their greetings, keeping their eyes averted and focused on the bricks at their feet.

"Is something wrong?" the minister asked.

"Yes," the earl said. "Dashiell deflowered Vivi... er, someone he shouldn't have."

Dashiell bolted up from his step and staggered dizzily for a moment before his head cleared. "Now, now, you just stop that!" He pointed to his grandfather. "This scoundrel, this cur, this... this Caligula thinks he has the moral rectitude to judge me." Dashiell lurched forward and shoved his chest into his grandfather's, causing the old man to stumble backward. "You're a bloody d-degenerate."

"Careful now." Mr. Charles inserted his arms between the men. "I'll have no fighting or swearing in the Lord's presence. Do you understand?"

Dashiell slumped back down on the step. He felt light-headed, and his body rocked on some drunken current.

"Does this have to do with Miss Vivienne Taylor, Sister Gertrude Bertis's niece? I thought I overhead her name before I came out to meet you."

Dashiell couldn't answer the minister. He let out a long breath through his nose. He should have said no, but he couldn't. He was desperate for counsel that his grandfather couldn't give him. But he feared Mr. Charles would launch into a miniature sermon, condemning Dashiell and Vivienne's sin and saying that they deserved to languish in the furnaces of hell. Instead, the minister sat beside Dashiell.

"Are you going to marry her?"

"I d–don't know," Dashiell replied, burying his head in the darkness of his palms.

"Do you love her?"

Dashiell's throat throbbed. His head ached, his heart ached. Yet he said nothing. For several seconds, the men stood in silence, except for the crunch and rattle of passing carriages and the low calls of the nightingales in the trees that grew out of the pavers on either side of the chapel.

Dashiell felt the minister's reassuring hand on the back of his neck. "You want to marry her, don't you?" he said softly. "You want to return home every day and see her smiling, so happy to be reunited with you. Or come to her bedside as she lies exhausted yet beaming, proud of the little newborn she nourishes at her breast. Or to simply sit with her in the evening and recount your day, what book you read, or who you met on the street. You want her to know every aspect of you."

Dashiell wiped his eyes. God, he was so drunk he was weeping like a little boy. "Yes," he tried to say, but the words got mangled in his throat. "But I—"

"You want to be the good husband, the faithful husband, the loving husband. But you're afraid you'll disappoint her… and yourself, as you have been disappointed before. You're afraid that in your heart, you are unworthy."

"Yes," Dashiell choked.

"And you're right."

Dashiell bit his lip. What he always knew was now confirmed by a man of faith. The little light of hope he harbored was snuffed out. He just wanted to slink back to some grimy gaming club, drink himself to death, and then slip quietly into hell.

"Look at me, Brother Lord Dashiell," the minister ordered.

Dashiell lifted his eyes, too far gone to be ashamed of his tears.

"But this love you have for Miss Taylor is worthy," Mr. Charles said. "It is far more noble than yourself. This love offers salvation for you, but only if you give it a place to grow. Stop being afraid, stop running away. These fears are mere shadows. Put your faith in that hope for love, trust that it will give you strength and help you be the man you want to be."

"I love her," Dashiell cried, the words repressed for years now tumbling from him. "I love her. I love her."

"I know you do," the minister said quietly. He rose, stretched his arms over his head, and yawned. "Now you boys go home, get some sleep, and sober up. Then ask Miss Taylor properly. If you bring around a special license tomorrow, I'll marry you."

※

Dashiell and his grandfather walked back to Wickerly Square. The clouds had thickened, blocking the moon. The streetlights, blanketed in fog, burned in big glowing orbs.

"I guess I could move back to Berkeley Square," his grandfather suggested. "Seeing how you're going to need a nursery."

"Don't do that. You'll want to be near Gertrude."

The earl lapsed into silence.

"I'll figure out accommodations and what not after I make Vivienne and me officially husband and wife," Dashiell said, the word *wife* warming his heart.

He would make up for leaving her like he had done. For his terrible words. He would explain that he was scared because he loved her so much.

In his bedchamber, he collapsed onto his bed and pulled up the wool blanket. His muscles felt loose and heavy against the mattress. He turned his head and buried his nose in the down of his pillow, where her scent still lingered. His mind started to ease, and he closed his eyes, sinking into a dream where he and Vivienne were walking hand-in-hand at the

Acropolis when the waning sunlight bathed the old ruins in gold light.

"I love you," she said, her voice low and soft.

"I love you too," he whispered in his dream. "My beautiful wife."

Seventeen

THE STARK MORNING LIGHT CREPT THROUGH THE crack between the closed curtains. Vivienne lay on her side in bed, the scent of Dashiell lingering on her body. The coals had burned to black ash several hours before and now the room was cold, but she didn't move to lift the covers that were wrinkled at her feet. Her brain felt thick and numb.

Obviously, their sacred Bazulo vow didn't extend to lifelong commitment after succumbing to unbridled passion and having one party beg the other to take her virtue.

In a few hours, she would board that train bound for Birmingham where she would have to tell her father what had happened. "Hallo, dear Papa! I fell in love with England's worst rake, Lord Dashiell, and John caught me in his embrace, so I got jilted. Then I went crying to Dashiell and tried to trap him into marriage, but he left me too. And I still love him. I can't stop this ache in my heart, like a knife sliced it open and the bleeding won't stop. But I guess my feelings really don't matter, because now you're going to debtor's prison."

And getting tossed from the ladies' seminary ended any glorious dreams of becoming a governess. She was useless. A bad seed.

She turned and gazed at the bottle of *Dr. Oliver's Elixir for Tranquil Slumber and Serene Mind* that Miss Banks had left the previous evening. The sunlight illuminated the brown glass, making it glow like a garnet. At the very bottom of the label it read "Opium, Alcohol, Foxglove, Valerian, Henbane, and Dr. Oliver's secret ingredients. A mere drop brings hours of blissful stupor."

"Opium very good," the oriental lady had said. "It make you forget."

And Vivienne knew that if she had enough opium she would forget… forever. She would never have to see Dashiell again or remember how perfect she felt in his arms, never have to go home and tell her father what had happened.

She reached for the bottle.

There was a tap at the door.

"Yes," Vivienne said, shoving the medicine back. Miss Banks entered, holding a tray with a steaming tea cup and plate of toast.

"Oh, Saint Mary, you do look a fright," she exclaimed, rattling the dishes.

"I—I didn't sleep," Vivienne said. "I was… was worried about Aunt Gertrude." Lies just rolled off her tongue so easily now. There was no hope for her. She was beyond redemption.

"Oh, now, don't you be a'worryin' that you've got to go home and tell your dear father that you were a'sinnin' with Lord Dashiell and now your poor papa is going to prison." She shoved the teacup under Vivienne's nose. "Have a bit of nice tea. I made it special for you. Added a drop or two of the mistress's *Dobb's Effervescing Citrate of Caffeine*."

Vivienne sipped the liquid and released a series of violent coughs.

"Very good, miss. Now, let's get you dressed. The mistress wants you to come down so the ladies can pray for your soul," the housekeeper said in her cheery lilt.

Vivienne slid off her covers and wobbled as her feet hit the floor. Her leg muscles were sore and goosy.

Miss Banks fussed with Vivienne's corset and petticoats. She dressed her in the plain green crepe dress Vivienne had worn the day she arrived to London so full of those proverbial good intentions. She was going to be the perfect, loving wife. She was going to save her family and her father would adore her. For once, she was going to be the favorite daughter.

Now she was on the road to hell.

"Oh, miss, what will become of us?" the housekeeper said. "We'll be out in the street, beggin' for our keep. I just know it. Those vermin won't stop until they good and destroy the missus. But don't you fret about us. No, no, you go home to your father and sisters. The Lord will take care of us just like he did Job," Miss Banks said, reaching for Vivienne's hair and wrenching it into a tight bun.

Through the window, Vivienne could hear the muffled rattle of carriages arriving for the Bible lesson.

"Oh, there are the ladies now, and my scones are still in the oven." Miss Banks hurried out.

Vivienne crossed the room, drew open the curtains, and narrowed her eyes in the light. Below, a line of black, boxy town carriages stopped before her aunt's home. Footmen held open the doors and helped down ladies in lacy black caps.

She couldn't do it. She couldn't face those righteous women with her sins still fresh on her skin.

On the bedside table, the bottle of elixir glinted in the sunlight.

It make you forget.

She snatched up the medicine and unscrewed the cap. The floral odor of opium and Dr. Oliver's secret ingredients tickled her nose.

Come rest, the oriental woman had said.

Yes, rest. Sweet, sweet rest.

Vivienne tilted the bottle. The liquid touched her tongue.

Then she saw a speck of blue in her periphery. She turned to look out the window. Coming into the square, swinging his shoulders with his jaunty carefree gait, was the man in the blue coat. In his hand, he held an envelope.

"That little rat!" she hissed. He was going to interrupt her aunt's Bible lessons with his ugly demands!

A vicious rage tore through her. An idea formed in her head—so vile, the thought sent a shiver through her. Below the haze of tiredness clotting her brain, she knew that perhaps this plan wasn't a good idea. That she needed to sleep and then she could think more clearly. But time for that luxury had run out... just as Dashiell had.

I will save my family! I will if it's the only thing I can do.

She would be like Cleopatra, except without fatal cobra bites, using her beauty and wiles to save her beloved Egypt. She would be like Joan of Arc, except without execution and French sainthood, raising an army to defeat the English. She would be like Queen Elizabeth, except without virginity, fending off the Spanish armada and leading her country to prosperity.

Vivienne dropped the bottle, letting the contents leak onto the carpet, ran to the clothespress, pulled out her boots, and jammed her feet inside. She tossed her green cloak over her shoulders, grabbed her reticule, and then flew out of her chamber and down the stairs.

Mrs. Lacey waited in the entrance hall, holding a pair of opera glasses with an aqua porcelain handle.

"I'm ready for Lord Baswiche today," she said and held the lenses to her face, magnifying her eyes into two blue orbs. She gazed up at Vivienne. "Good heavens, look at you! Did I miss the wedding?" Her elfin features softened. "Isn't the first time wonderful? I remember Mr. Lacey and I had left the church and were walking to my grandmother's house for dinner, but he just couldn't wait to have me." She broke into giggles. "I tried to explain to the watch outside Hyde Park that we were newlyweds. But they arrested Mr. Lacey anyway."

"I'm sorry, but there will be no wedding," Vivienne said and sailed out the door.

Willie was coming around the line of carriages when she planted herself in front of him. He jerked to a stop and blinked. "You!" he exclaimed.

Vivienne didn't reply. In a fast motion, she seized his envelope.

"You're not supposin' to 'ave that!" He swiped at her hand, but she whirled around, turning her back to him.

She ripped open the envelope and plucked out the contents. She unfolded a single sheet of thin paper. On the page was a clumsy tracing of a nude woman, sitting on a chair with one knee drawn up. Her face was turned at a quarter angle, gazing out a sunlit window.

Above her, written in misshaped letters was "*No julry this time.*"

Willie watched her face, a sneerlike smile hovering on his mouth. "Pretty, ain't it?" He reached for the paper, but she crumpled the sketch in her hand. "'Ey, give me that back."

She ignored him and started walking.

He jumped after her, grabbing her elbow. "What do you think you're playing at? You—"

She yanked her arm away from his grasp. "I'm going to give your mother her payment."

"'Ow's that?"

"Me. I'm giving her me."

❧

Dashiell opened his eyes. The pale light of morning flowed in from his window. *He was going to marry Vivienne.* The very thought that hours before had petrified him, driving him into the night, now caused a quiet peace in his heart, like the unruffled water on a lake at daybreak.

He nestled deeper into his blanket, wanting to linger in this tranquility a few moments longer. Soon, he had drifted back to sleep, and the sweet dreams of his future life with his beloved Vivienne.

❧

Vivienne stood outside Jenkinson's brothel. The bright sound of children's laughter rang in the air as they explored the pockets of the drunks sprawled unconscious about the pavement. Mothers clustered about the doorsteps, holding their crying babies and looking at Vivienne with tired eyes.

"Tell Mrs. Jenkinson to meet me outside," Vivienne told Willie.

He scratched the side of his nose. "She won't like it," he said as he turned to go inside his home.

Vivienne scanned the rotting building. The window that had been broken during her last visit was now boarded up with rough scraps of wood. Her life had come to this sad place, when just a week before she was deciding on which gown to wear to her wedding. She felt tears come back. She blinked them away and steeled her spine. She couldn't feel sorry for herself when she had done herself in. She grimaced to think that she had tried to trap Dashiell into marriage, even if it was one of the sweetest moments of her life.

The brothel door opened, and Jenkinson stepped out, hugging a tatty gray wool shawl about her shoulders. Her tanned face was rough and slightly swollen as if she had just woken up. Suspicion tensed her eyes. "Wot the 'ell are you doing back 'ere?" she demanded.

Vivienne's heart beat like a trapped moth. "I'm Gertrude Bertis's niece. My… my aunt hasn't any more money. You won't get any more from her. She is dying," Vivienne lied. Hot dizziness filled her head, and she had to pause before she could continue.

"I'm... I'm offering m-myself for you to sell to Mrs. Fontaine on the condition that you give me all the sketches."

"Well, aren't you the dutiful niece? A right li'l martyr, you are." Jenkinson squeezed her eyes and looked hard at Vivienne. "Where's your gentleman friend?"

"I don't know." Vivienne swayed on her feet. For a moment, she thought she might collapse on the street.

Jenkinson's mouth cracked into a knowing smirk. "Got wot he wanted and left, did he?"

Vivienne couldn't answer; her heart hurt to hear Jenkinson so bluntly sum up the situation. She gazed down at the dirt trapped in the cracks in the pavers, wishing she could seep through them and disappear. "Do we have a bargain or not?" she snapped.

Jenkinson considered for a moment, her tongue licking the corner of her mouth. "Sidney!" she yelled over her shoulder.

The giant peered out from an open window at the top of the brothel. He was shirtless. Red sores and sprigs of coarse black hair covered his massive chest and belly. "What?" he grunted in his deep voice.

"Get dressed and bring them sketches of Gertrude, you damned useless bugger," she screamed, waking several of the sleeping drunks. "We're going on a li'l stroll."

Sidney grunted again and disappeared into the dark interior.

"And you"—Jenkinson grasped one of Vivienne's locks that had escaped its pins. She wound the curl tightly around her finger—"you better not be lyin' to me this time." She pulled Vivienne's hair, tilting her head toward her own. "'Cause if you are, your aunt might find her pretty li'l niece floating in the Thames. You understand?"

Sidney ambled out, wearing an eggplant-colored coat that he couldn't button over his belly. He wore no waistcoat, and his shirt hung sloppily about the waist of his trousers. Greasy spikes of hair poked out from under his hat. Jenkinson snatched away the folded pages he held in his fat paw.

"Is that all of them?" Vivienne said, looking at the sketches. There only appeared to be five. She expected more for all the misery Jenkinson had caused her aunt.

"Did I need any more?" The madam shrugged. "A respectable lady will pay a great deal to save her honor. But I didn't want her ugly jewelry anymore. It don't bring nothin'." She let the pages fall from her hand and float down to the muddy street.

Vivienne knelt and grabbed them before the wind could blow the papers away.

Eighteen

WITH SIDNEY'S HAND CLAMPED AROUND HER UPPER arm like a human shackle and Jenkinson holding Vivienne's opposite elbow with her thin rough fingers, they started toward Mayfair.

Overhead, the sky was pale blue with stripes of coal smoke. The sun edged over the rooftops, warming the air. Yet Vivienne shivered as if she were naked in the snow. She kept her head up, refusing to listen to the scary thoughts circling in her head. She was Joan of Arc going to battle.

"You look as scared as when they put me on the boat to Australia," Jenkinson said. "That's wot your uncle done to me."

"Is that why you went after my aunt? Because you thought you could get some degree of revenge on Jeremiah Bertis?"

"He was one of them types who likes peculiar things. Then 'e don't pays me, but puts me away for seventeen years in Australia. I was going to make 'im bleed whether he were dead or not." Jenkinson laughed, a hoarse phlegmatic sound.

They led Vivienne to the back of a tall row house stacked with rounded balconies. All the windows were curtained. A scrawny woman in her mid-forties with concave pock-scarred cheeks answered the door; her tired eyes took in Vivienne. "The mistress will want to see this one."

Sidney kept his fat hand tight on Vivienne's wrist as they followed the woman through a dining room. The table was covered with an ivory cloth and set with white china and silver platters. As she passed, Jenkinson nonchalantly lifted the butter plate and shoved it into her dress, then continued on as if nothing were amiss. They were taken to a huge, airy hall. Three balconies were stacked like cake layers. A grand chandelier rested on a blanket while a thin, short man hung new crystals on the edges. Above them, three men hoisted a massive stone angel, heaving breaths and wiping sweat from their brows, while two other workers sat on their haunches, hammering new balustrades into the railing.

In the center of the room, a thin woman supervised their work. Black hair frizzed about her forehead and she wore a brown lace gown. Her mouth was pursed in a thin line. Perched on her shoulder was a large white bird with pink feather-tips. "Move it three inches to the left," she ordered.

This must be Fontaine.

"You heard her, boys!" one of the workers said.

The men lifted the angel, their straining grunts echoing in the high ceiling.

"No, no, you've gone too far," Fontaine cried and flung up her arms. "I said three inches, not three feet. Come back."

"Stay behind me," Jenkinson told Vivienne and then tried to get the woman's attention by clearing her throat, which led to a small coughing fit.

Fontaine's head whipped around. Her eyes were shiny, black and hard as onyx.

"Annie," Jenkinson choked out between phlegm.

The woman didn't say a word, but cocked a thin brow to convey her annoyance. The bird on her shoulder spread its wings and stuck out its stubby tongue.

"I mean, Mrs. Fontaine," Jenkinson corrected herself. She stepped forward, wringing her hands, her shoulders hunched. "I—I brought you a girl."

"I thought I told you never to come here," the woman snapped.

Sidney shoved Vivienne forward. She stumbled, colliding with Jenkinson, and then righting herself before Fontaine. Vivienne stared at the black boot points peeking below the madam's skirts. "Joan of Arc," she whispered, trying to muster her courage. "Save your family."

But as her eyes rose up the small woman's body, the tiny bit of pluck she possessed petered away. Despite Fontaine's diminutive size, she emitted a power so strong and terrifying that Joan would have turned her army around, Cleopatra would have fled to the nether reaches with Marc Antony, and Queen Elizabeth would have converted to Catholicism.

The hammering and grunting stopped, all eyes fixing on Vivienne. Her head turned woozy and tears blurred her eyes.

"Oh my," Fontaine said, a quiver snaking through her voice. Her tiny, strong fingers latched onto

Vivienne's chin. The large bird began bobbing and squawking, "I love you. I love you."

The famed madam put a hushing hand on the creature. "Do you, my dear?" She drew a handkerchief from her cuff and wiped the tears from Vivienne's cheeks. "Look at those green eyes," she whispered. "Just like his. Tell me, what's your name, beautiful child?"

"V... Vivienne Taylor."

Fontaine released an audible breath.

"Old Gertrude's 'er aunt!" The nubs of Jenkinson's teeth glinted under her sneer. "Didn't I do right by you? Didn't I?"

A slow smile cracked the madam's lips. "Oh, yes." She held the *s* like a long sigh.

"And she's genteel." Jenkinson jammed her finger into Vivienne's back. "See, say something genteel-like."

Without thinking, the words from *The Ethereal Graces of the Delicate Sex* bubbled up.

The softly murmured word, the downcast gaze, and gentle blush of rose. These qualities are the perfection of the proper female. A lady's true nature is to please her helpmate. Her beauty must appease his sight, her gentle words must calm his woes, her shy smile must convey the pleasure of his presence.

The men broke into applause.

"See! See!" Jenkinson said. "She's already been trained proper. Them rich gents will pay a pretty penny for her."

Fontaine beckoned with her hand. "Come into the

parlor. And Adele, tell your ape to go help the men with that damned angel."

Jenkinson jerked her head. "You 'eard 'er," she said to Sidney.

Vivienne followed Fontaine into a room paneled in shiny carved oak. The thick mirrors strewn about the walls reflected the glowing embers in the grate, bathing the parlor in warm gold light.

Fontaine spun on her heel, coming face-to-face with Vivienne. The bird on her shoulder cocked its head, regarding Vivienne with one eye.

"What happened to your fiancé, Mr. Vandergrift?" Fontaine asked.

Vivienne's breath caught. How did this madam know about the engagement? Had John been talking about her in a brothel? Her skin heated with shame, but she forced her head high. "He left me."

"You are a beautiful creature," Fontaine said. "Surely you can find another husband in no time."

Vivienne swallowed, her throat burning.

"You have disgraced yourself, haven't you?" the madam asked.

When Vivienne couldn't answer, Fontaine laughed, a silky, purring sound. "Why do I sense Lord Dashiell's handiwork?"

Tears filled Vivienne's eyes again.

Jenkinson jabbed her. "Stop your sobbin'."

"Don't you dare talk to my sweet, sweet cherub that way!" Fontaine cried. She ran her hand along Vivienne's cheek and cooed, "It's all so perfect."

Vivienne saw nothing perfect in her situation, unless the madam meant perfectly humiliating, desperate, embarrassing, or heart-breaking. "My family is in terrible trouble," she said. "They're going to take my papa to debtor's prison. I must make money."

"And you will, you will. Your papa will be so proud." There was a curious, rather malicious arch under Fontaine's words. "Come, Frederick," she said, extending her arm. The bird hopped down to her wrist. "There you go, my lovely baby," she said, gently shooing him onto the wood railing on the back of the sofa. Then her voice went cold. "I'll give you twenty percent for her," she told Jenkinson.

"Twenty percent!" Jenkinson cried, outraged. "That's wot you gives everyone. Now, I could 'ave kept 'er meself, but I'm sharing 'er because we're business partners."

"Business partners?" Fontaine laughed. She tilted her head and stared at Jenkinson, her eyes sparkling. "Isn't it a coincidence that you brought Judge Bertis's niece to me. I wonder how she came to your door. I hope you haven't done anything unlawful?"

"Wot do you mean?" Jenkinson paled under her tan, turning her skin an ugly burnished yellow. "I know you 'ated Gertrude. I did this for you. You told me about them sketches."

"What sketches?" Fontaine asked. "I don't remember anything about sketches."

Jenkinson's eyes widened. "But... but you told me—"

"Have you been pestering poor Mrs. Bertis?" Fontaine asked.

"Poor Mrs. Bertis?" Jenkinson echoed. "You never liked her. I bring her pretty niece, and you behaves like the rest of them Mayfair folk, pretending your 'ands ain't dirty. Nows you give me thirty percent tonight, or I'll just take 'er 'ome!"

Vivienne felt dizzy. Was there more to this blackmail than just Jenkinson? The game was turning, and she wasn't sure what was happening. Had she made a terrible mistake? Well, of course she had... trusting Dashiell with her heart. And body. But how did her aunt know these women?

"Very well," Fontaine said and waved her hand as if the money meant nothing. "You can come back tonight and wait in the kitchen for your share."

Jenkinson bobbed a curtsy. "We've always done right by each other, well, except for that one time. But no need to mention that anymore. Mebbe when I get my business going good, we can be like we used to be before Lawrence James. Just Annie and Adele."

Fontaine flashed an impatient smile and cleared her throat, a humming purr. "Good-bye," she said sweetly and then held up a finger. "And leave the glass angel figurine where it belongs, on the side table."

"Oh, I forgot to put it back," Jenkinson said, her face turning red. She dug deep into her dress. "'ere it is. Heh-heh. I thought it was such a pretty little bauble," she said, setting it down.

After the door had closed, Fontaine rolled her eyes. "That evil woman sets me on edge. Don't listen to her. She was a liar from the egg. I'm so thankful that I've gotten you away from her. Now, let me see you." She crossed to the sofa where her bird waited and patted the cushion for Vivienne to sit. Vivienne obeyed, feeling naked even though she was fully clothed.

"Don't be nervous," the madam said and untied

the ribbon to Vivienne's bonnet, pulling it away. "So beautiful."

Frederick leaped down and pecked the edge of the hat.

An enigmatic smile lit Fontaine's face, revealing her small, white, square teeth. "I will make you the most prized courtesan in England... no, in all of Europe. You will be the mistress of royalty." She grasped Vivienne's hand. "Now come!"

Fontaine broke into a jog, as if she were an excited little girl, pulling Vivienne along. She flung open the parlor door. Frederick flapped over their heads and landed on the railing on the second balcony.

"Boys, we're going to have a special auction tonight. One like we've never had before."

She released Vivienne's hand and waved her fingers before her face, as if she were conjuring something. "She will be a masterpiece. I see a stage with a huge frame draped with white silk... and... and stars. Get velvet. Yards and yards of midnight blue velvet and nail it to a backdrop. Then you will glue little twinkling beads on it."

Fontaine flounced the edge of her skirt like a Spanish dancer. "And on the center of the stage will be a sofa. More velvet. She will lie upon it, dressed in white silk and with wings, of course. And the girls." The madam hurried to the stairs and clutched the banister. "They will stand on each step and sing." She began to hum, swaying to her own music. "'She is a gem beyond compare,'" she sang. "'A beauty fair, a face so... so...'"

"Rare?" a man suggested.

"Quiet!" Fontaine shouted, her hands fanning about her ears as if the man's utterance had hurt her delicate eardrums. "*I* see it, *I* sing it," she said with quiet menace. "And *you* just keep quiet and build it."

She turned and stared at Vivienne; her eyes seemed to pulse. Vivienne backed up. *Oh, Lord, what have I gotten myself into?*

"And they will lead you down and… no!" she screamed. Vivienne and the men jumped.

The madam rushed to the chandelier resting on the floor and began to circle it, gazing up to where a rope had been fed through a pulley in the ceiling. "She will float. I see a moon. Silver and crescent. Yes, you must build a swing to hold the moon." Fontaine closed her eyes and opened her palms, as if she were receiving a divine revelation. "And she will descend from the heavens like an angel. And it will be perfect," she declared, and then turned silent for a moment, as if to revel in her vision.

Vivienne had her own vision of descending from the heavens and falling mercifully on her head. An ugly splat of silk and feathers. However, her death could hardly help her father.

"Get to work," Fontaine said quietly, her lids still shut. Then she popped them open and stared straight at Vivienne. "Come with me."

Vivienne hesitated, looking over her shoulder at the door. She had the urge to run, perhaps fulfill her childhood fantasy of dressing like a sailor and boarding a merchant ship bound for the Orient. But she knew her father didn't have the luxury of running from his creditors. They would hunt him down and lock him in debtor's prison because of her. "Joan of Arc, Queen Elizabeth, Cleopatra," she whispered. "Joan of Arc, Queen Elizabeth, Cleopatra... and Dashiell." Her belly clenched as the full weight of her decision fell on her. She wanted Dashiell. She wanted to wake in his arms and have him tell her this was all a nightmare. That he had never left. Her tears came again but she wiped them away and followed Fontaine, her head high and stiff. Dashiell may run away, but she wouldn't.

❦

Fontaine led her up the stairs to the first floor. The madam stopped at a door at the end of the hall and pulled out of her cuff a silver bracelet with three keys. She unlocked the door and held it open for Vivienne. Vivienne stepped into a stuffy, windowless parlor.

"Come, Frederick," the madam called. The bird swooped inside and flew into its cage that hung down from a chain on the interior wall.

"Sit down." Fontaine gestured to a sofa as she crossed to a writing desk where an ornate red glass lamp stood. She pulled out a matchbox from a side drawer, removed the shade of the lamp, and lit the wick.

"How do you know so much about my aunt and me?"

"I actually knew your father very well. Intimately, in fact."

"What! My father is a decent man. He would never... he doesn't even come to London."

"You poor, poor child." Fontaine shook her head. "You don't know who you are, do you?"

"I'm... I'm Vivienne Taylor," she said, suddenly

feeling that was the wrong answer. "I think. How can I not know myself? Is this a philosophical question?"

Fontaine laughed. "Wait here. I have something to show you."

She opened the door beside the writing desk. Vivienne caught a glimpse of a carved mahogany bed. A beam of sunlight fell across the white bedspread and onto a thick flax rug. Then Fontaine swung the door shut. Vivienne heard a cork pop and the *glump* of liquid being tilted in a bottle or flask. There was the muffled sound of scraping and something being shifted. In his cage, Frederick swung around on a bar. "I love you," he called out.

A minute later, Fontaine returned holding a scroll. She tossed it on the sofa cushion beside Vivienne. "I think you will find these sketches rather familiar."

Vivienne unrolled the paper to reveal hasty sketches of her own face at different angles. In one, she looked to be about twelve and sitting in a tree like the one outside Dashiell's home, reading a heavy book, her brows drawn down in frustration. In another, she squatted with a piece of chalk, drawing on a sidewalk. She remembered that chalk picture; it was of Dashiell and her finding a hidden tomb of a Pharaoh. In the center of the page, she sat on the bench outside Gertrude's home, pigeons about her feet. Something in the soft lines and the gentle smile on her face gave an impression of tenderness.

"What… what are these? How did you get them?"

"They are the work of Lawrence James."

"James?" Vivienne shook her head. "I don't understand. I've never met the man."

"Ah, but he knew you," Fontaine said. "He followed you his whole life. He was always saying what a lovely girl you were." She paused. "He was so proud of his daughter."

"What? How dare you! My mother loved my father. She was a saint. She is dead and—"

"Dead?" The madam hiked a brow. "Oh, no, no. Your mother Gertrude Bertis is very much alive and she is no saint, despite what she would have you believe."

Heat rushed to Vivienne's head. "No."

"Twenty-three years ago, Lawrence impregnated Gertrude Collins. Lawrence was turned out of his house, and Gertrude sent away with her married sister, Cassandra, to the country. When Gertrude came back to London, she didn't have a baby, but her sister did. I'll let you draw your own conclusions."

"No, you are wrong!" Vivienne screamed at her. "You must be!"

"Am I, Vivienne?" The madam regarded Vivienne for a moment, her eyes black and impenetrable. "Did you always feel like you didn't belong in your own family? That you were never good enough for them or like them?" She stepped closer and the planks under the carpet creaked. "Lawrence would see you walking around the square at Gertrude's for hours after the judge had punished you. You looked so forlorn. He wanted to steal you away." She gave a small cough as if something were blocking her throat. "He loved you."

"No," Vivienne murmured, shaking her head.

"Surely you know about the masterpieces of his that were stolen. Well, two of them were of a beautiful girl with black hair and green eyes. You, my dear. You were his masterpiece."

Vivienne paused, letting the words sink in. "H-how did you know Lawrence James?"

Fontaine crossed to Frederick's cage and poked her finger inside. The bird attached himself to it and declared his usual sentiment.

"Let me guess, you fancied yourself in love with Dashiell," Fontaine said. "So you threw yourself at him, thinking you were different from the other women he's had, but then, like the others, he left you. A story that grows wearisome from being told too many times."

Vivienne's anger flared. She was tired of being toyed with. "You didn't answer my question."

"Yes, I did." She turned. "It's the same way I knew Lawrence, except over the course of twenty years."

Fontaine's eyes focused on the empty cushion beside Vivienne, as if she were talking to an invisible person. "I recognized his talent," she said and beat into her chest with her balled hand. "I supported him, I whispered his name in the ears of men to show his work, I fed him, I clothed him, I made him famous. I listened to him go on and on about his love for Gertrude. And do you know what he gave to me?" She was almost screaming, her eyes turning dark and glossy.

Vivienne was too terrified to speak. She could only shake her head. She was surprised James managed to stay with this woman an hour, much less twenty years.

"Nothing!" Fontaine cried. "He left me for one of my girls. A mere baby. He married her. He gave her all his work. It was mi—" Fontaine stopped herself.

It was mine, Vivienne finished in her head.

The madam let out a ragged breath. "Now, you needn't worry about anything," she said with a forced sweet tone, clearly changing the subject. "If you listen to me, you'll have plenty of money to send to your father. He will be indebted to you."

⁂

Dashiell cursed and rubbed his head, which still ached dully from the previous evening's indulgence. How could he have slept so long? Poor Vivienne was probably beside herself.

He knelt on the floor of his library, staring at the family jewelry and the other antique treasures in his safe, searching for an engagement ring. He held a ruby and diamond ring to the lamplight. Something wasn't right about it. It was too staid, too normal, not exotic or mysterious enough for Vivienne. Nonetheless, he set it in the box by his knee and dug deeper in the vault, pulling out his great-grandmother's sapphire and diamond rings, a gold pendant of unknown origin, two Egyptian amulets, a Celtic brooch, a Roman beaded bracelet, and an emerald necklace. He dropped them in the box alongside the ruby ring. He would give them all to her when he proposed—no, pleaded—for her hand.

"You look handsome, son," he heard his grandfather say. He stood just inside the doorway, a somber expression on his face. He wore a black suit with a striped gray and white waistcoat. His hair looked different. It wasn't tangled wildly about his head as usual. "I'm proud of you... well, proud that you're getting married, not that you deflowered Vivienne and then cried about it to that minister. I thought that was a bit excessive."

"Let's just leave that all in the past and not mention it again."

"Pardon, my lords," Rivers said. He stood in the corridor outside the door. "Mrs. Bertis is here."

"Oh, hell," Dashiell blurted. "I'm going to get a righteous earful."

"Don't worry, son. I don't recall Adam and Eve having a wedding before they made those sons of theirs. They were just walking about the garden naked and feeling no shame."

Dashiell looked at him askew. "Been reading the Bible, have you?"

"I figure since Trudie and I are going to be in-laws, we ought to have something we can talk about over the dinner table."

"Tell her we'll be down directly," Dashiell told the butler.

Rivers cleared his voice. "She's in your bedchamber, my lord."

"What in hell!" Dashiell dashed from the room, his grandfather jogging behind him.

They found Gertrude pacing about his room, using her cane to open the clothespress and tap the drawers. The panel on the wall was removed and the bedside table overturned. Garth was sniffing about the Persian carpet, not far from a round wet spot.

"I wager you thought you were clever," she hissed. "Well, I guessed your dirty secret." Dashiell looked at Gertrude with her expansive bosom and figure roped in by her tight corset and then the hole in the wall. How did she manage it? On the other hand, Gertrude's tubby housekeeper seemed subject to the laws of nature and couldn't do more than poke her head through.

Dashiell's eyes flicked to the Italian Gertrude, formerly Vivienne, hanging on his wall, relieved to find it still concealed behind a blanket.

"Where is she?" Gertrude demanded, waving her staff in the air. "You will not corrupt her. You will not tease her, tempt her, make her show you her... her *nether regions*." She whacked his statue of naked Aphrodite with her cane, knocking off the grapes the goddess dangled from her fingers.

"Stop!" Dashiell cried.

"My little Vivvie!" she cried, unconcerned for the damage she had wrought on antiquity. "Where are you? I've come to rescue you from this Babylon, from this temple of Baal."

Dashiell took a deep breath and launched into his rehearsed speech. "Mrs. Bertis, I want you to know that I adore your niece. And—Ow! Put that cane down." He rubbed his calf where she had struck him.

"Be quiet, you foot soldier of Satan," Gertrude spat and lifted the edge of his bed covers to peer beneath the bed. "Produce her immediately. You will not keep her in your shameful den of flesh."

"She's not here," Dashiell said.

"What do you mean, she's not here?"

He paused and then answered slowly, "She's not physically present in my Babylon, my temple of Baal, my den of flesh. Is something wrong?"

"I don't believe you!" Gertrude shrieked. "You have her. I know you do. Ever since she's been here, you've wanted to see her neat little ankles, her lacy drawers. You dream of her lacy drawers, don't you?"

"That may be true," Dashiell said, worry beginning to settle in his chest. "But she's not here. Is she missing?"

"No, she's not missing," Gertrude answered. "I've… I've merely misplaced her." The woman's nostrils contracted with quick sharp sniffs and her lips quivered. "She's supposed to go home today to her papa. The ladies from the church have been searching about the square for nearly an hour." Tears sprang into her eyes. "My poor child." She pressed her palm to her face. "Banks, I need my medicine."

"Don't you be a'worryin', but I'm a bit stuck." Miss Banks took a large breath and yanked herself free, tumbling back into her home.

"Now Trudie, don't you upset yourself." His grandfather took Gertrude's arm. "You don't need any of those tonics or elixirs. What you need is a good man to take care of you." He led her to the mattress, sitting her down on the edge. The woman was too upset to fight. "You just rest here and let my grandson find her. I'm sure she is a bit distraught after he bedded—"

"I don't think we need to discuss that at the present," Dashiell said and gave his grandfather a swat with the back of his hand.

"I must find her." Gertrude picked up Dashiell's bed cover and blotted her eyes. "My little Vivvie is lost."

"When was the last time you saw her?" Dashiell asked.

"Last evening when Mr. Vandergrift came to call,"

she replied. "How that man deceived me. He's the very devil, I tell you. All men are wolves in sheeps' clothes." She sniffed and raised her head. "Except for Mr. Bertis. What a fine ram he was," she said in reverent tones.

"No, he wasn't," the earl said. "He was the worst wolf of the lot, leaving his wonderful wife at home to wither while he went raking about the town."

"Raking?" Her jaw dropped with her sharp intake of breath. "How dare you! Mr. Bertis would never touch a woman. He... he never touched me," she wailed.

"He was a lecherous spanker. A regular Pontius Pilate on the bench. And it's high time you knew it. You ought to give my grandson and me more respect. We ain't like the others. We're the Lord's sheep in wolf's clothes."

Gertrude's brows furrowed in confusion upon hearing the word "Lord" uttered from the earl's lips and no bolt of lightning coming down to strike him dead.

"Have you... have you felt the Savior's redeeming grace?"

A beautiful light entered her eyes, like the one in her portrait on his wall. "I'm feeling something," the earl replied.

"Oh, hello, there you are," a sweet elderly female voice said. A woman with pure white hair and an elfish smile poked her head through the panel. "Why, isn't this convenient? Mind if I come in and look about? I've always wanted to see a real rake's bedchamber."

Gertrude straightened her back, resuming her usual stoic countenance. "Have you found her, Mrs. Lacey?"

The woman teetered in, her bright eyes taking in

all the wall hangings and furnishings. "It's downright savage," she said. "I'll have to tell Mr. Lacey." Her gaze settled on Gertrude. "A young man arrived with a letter. The ladies thought it might be about little Vivienne, so I said I would bring it to you."

Dashiell snatched the envelope from the lady's fingers and studied the address written in a fast, flowing hand that could have been Vivienne's. He flipped the letter over. On the back was a silvery seal with angel wings pressed into the wax. The wings on the doorplate at Seven Heavens. His heart quickened.

He ripped the seal and pulled out the letter.

"That is mine!" Gertrude barked. "Give it here!"

He ignored her as his eyes scanned the lines.

Dearest Aunt Gertrude,

I regret that I must leave without saying good-bye. Please do not worry about me and know that I am well. Take comfort in the assurance that the situations which have caused you great distress have been resolved. I will always hold the love you gave me in my heart and hope that I can amend for the pain I have brought upon you and my family.

"Oh God, she's sold herself!" he cried before he could stop himself.

"What?" Gertrude struggled to rise to her feet. "Give me that letter."

Dashiell crumpled the missive and shoved it inside his coat pocket. "Vivienne is in trouble. I need you to stay here." He started for the door.

"Where is she?" Gertrude demanded. "What do you know?"

"I know that I love your niece," he said. "I know that she is the most precious person in the world to me. And that I'm a fat-headed coxcomb of a sinner." Then he turned on his heel and rushed into the corridor, down the stairs, and out into the street.

Nineteen

DASHIELL SPRINTED THROUGH THE CITY TO GREEN Park, all the while cursing himself.

Why the hell did you leave your bed? You could have made love through the night, in between resting in each other's arms, envisioning your future together. Instead you ran away like a frightened little boy afraid of the scary monster hiding in the clothespress. But now he was truly terrified. He and Vivienne may not have a future at all, except a brief kiss before they strung him up outside Newgate for killing Fontaine.

The paths were congested, so he veered onto the wet grass, ignoring the shocked stares of the passersby. By the time he reached Fontaine's brothel, his shirt was soaked with his sweat and his heart was flying like a racehorse. He said a brief prayer. *Dear God, if You keep Vivienne safe, I promise I will walk the path of the righteous for the rest of my life. I won't look at any other ladies or satisfy that itch to stray, get drunk, and embarrass myself in pubs, or spend all my money on old rubbish. I'll be a proper, loyal husband.*

Unless I have to murder Fontaine. In which case, I will go to hell in peace.

He slammed the brass knocker. A bald-headed flashman cracked opened the door. "Lord Dashiell." He grinned around the silver toothpick in his mouth. "Mrs. Fontaine says you're not welcome—"

Dashiell rammed the wood with his shoulder, pushed the flashman back, and rushed inside. "Vivienne!" he wailed up the stacks of balconies. "I've come for you, love."

Three muscled men gripped a rope, hoisting a massive chandelier to the ceiling. They stopped mid-heave and stared at him. As did the two workers sitting on the floor painting a silver crescent and the three more on ladders, hammering on what looked to be a large frame. Overhead, about half a dozen ladies hung about the balcony railing, yawning. Not yet dressed for the day, their hair was loose, and they wore sheer blue robes edged with ruffles.

The flashman clamped down on Dashiell's shoulder. "Now, Mrs. Fontaine don't want any trouble."

"Well, she dived head first into it when she crossed me, old boy," Dashiell spat. He recognized the poetess from the other evening. "I'm looking for a young lady who might have come here," Dashiell told her. "She has black hair, green eyes." He flattened his palm at his shoulder. "About this tall."

The poetess pressed her hands to her chest. Her lids fluttering, she began to speak.

> *Her soul in pain, she did wander*
> *Into these woods of hearts asunder*
> *To forget the girl she was before*
> *Her childish dreams are nevermore.*

"Does that mean yes?" Dashiell asked.

The flashman gave a snort of a laugh. "She's with the mistress."

"The poor thing is distraught," a low female voice added. Dashiell spun. Fontaine stood in the middle of the parlor doorway; her arms were raised, resting on the threshold. On her shoulder, that damned pink bird had his wings spread, tongue out, hissing. "It seems a callous scoundrel used her and left her to cry." Fontaine shook her head, clicking her tongue. "Who would do such a horrid thing?"

"You want I should get rid of him?" the flashman asked, tightening his grip on Dashiell.

"In a moment," Fontaine said, stepping into the hall. She tilted her head and studied Dashiell. "First I shall enjoy myself."

"How much do you want for her?" Dashiell spat through his clenched jaw.

"Oh, I'm letting the market decide." Fontaine flicked her wrist toward the ceiling. "A Lawrence James masterpiece in flesh and blood should surely fetch an enormous sum."

"What are you talking about?"

She tossed back her head, laughing deep in her throat. "Vivienne is a very valuable young lady," she purred. "You and Mr. Vandergrift should have been more careful. But now she is with someone who knows her true worth."

Dashiell's hands curled into fists. He had never hit a female in his life, but wanted to land Fontaine a facer. Then another. And another, until that smug smile was erased from her pasty face.

"Dashiell?" The sound of Vivienne's voice sent a hot shiver over his body. She stood just inside the parlor, wearing the same type of robe as the other ladies. She clasped her arms about her, as if she were cold. Her large, fearful eyes sliced into his heart.

"Forgive me!" Dashiell started to rush for her, but the flashman's arm slid around his neck, locking and squeezing him like a python.

"I'm a totty-headed numbskull," Dashiell managed, clawing at the man's hairy forearm. "I've come to take you away. I swear I'll do nothing but make you happy for the rest of your life. I'll take care of your family, any cousins, nieces, and nephews, and… and… pets. Just come home."

She didn't move, but continued to gaze at him as if he were a stranger.

"Say something, my love," he pleaded. "Please. Talk to me."

Fontaine laughed. "You're a little late, my lord. You should learn to treat your ladies better." She strolled to Vivienne and linked their arms together. The bird leaned toward Vivienne and cooed, "I love you."

"Go back and rest, dear," Fontaine told her. "I'll take care of horrid Lord Dashiell for you."

But Vivienne didn't budge, keeping her eyes latched on Dashiell. "Why did you leave me?" she asked him.

"Because I was a scared little boy who—you see, my mother abandoned me when I was a small child and I'm not sure what that has to do with my problems, but I'm just afraid to be vulnerable and—"

"Enough, Lord Dashiell," Fontaine said. "Nobody cares. Men, you may get rid of him now."

Dashiell jammed his heel back, hitting the flashman's shin. The man groaned, and Dashiell spun from his hold, to find himself staring down his nose at the poised hammers, wrenches, wet paintbrushes, and balled fists of the workers. Two men had abandoned the chandelier, leaving one poor chap to dangle from the rope to keep it from crashing down.

Dashiell held up his palms. "I'll give you fifty-five pounds," he told Fontaine. "And I'll walk out with Vivienne."

"Fifty-five pounds?" Fontaine echoed. "Is that all you have?" She broke into laughter, the workers joining in.

"I can give you an early Persian tablet," Dashiell said, mentally cursing himself. He had spent his entire life collecting useless baubles. "Two Egyptian mummies, Roman coins, some Greek statues, er, bits of mosaics—"

The madam gestured about her. "Does this look like the British Museum to you?" Again the men thought she was hilarious. Even that amorous bird was shaking his feathers. "What would I do with a mummy?"

She released Vivienne's arm and sashayed toward him. "You insult my sweet little cherub. Some of the wealthiest merchants in London are coming here tonight to preview her. Very important men who are willing to expend far, far more than fifty-five pounds." She stopped just a foot from his face. He could smell the sweet brandy on her breath. "No, my lord, the bidding starts at one hundred for a night. If a man wants to take her as his mistress, well, the talks begin in the thousands. As you know, Vivienne has a family to take care of and a mere fifty-five will hardly do."

"I'll get the money," Dashiell promised. "Whatever amount. You have my word."

"Your word?" Fontaine's neck jerked back with a chortle. "Your word means nothing to me or any lady in London." Her bemused smile tightened to a snarl. "Now get out," she growled and turned back to Vivienne. "Dearest, come away. Don't let Lord Dashiell upset you."

"Goddammit, woman!" he shouted. He felt the restraining hands of the flashman and the cold blunt edge of the wrench pressed under his ear and a hammer not three inches from his nose. "I know about those paintings," he blurted, hearing the desperation in his own voice. He would say anything to keep Vivienne from leaving his sight.

Fontaine looked over her shoulder at him. "And what paintings do you mean?"

"Your ex-lover's—the ones you stole," he said, reaching for anything he could use.

The madam spun slowly around. "I don't know what you are talking about. However, if—"

"You're lying," Dashiell goaded.

"—you find the paintings," she continued, "perhaps we can make an arrangement: Vivienne for the paint-ings." She lifted the edge of her lip. "Oh, never mind, I don't want the blasted things. I'll keep Vivienne—his precious little daughter."

"What?"

Vivienne clutched her robe and stared at the floor. "She said that—that I was the bastard child of my Aunt

Gertrude and Lawrence James. And I was given to my mother to raise."

"Bloody hell," Dashiell whispered. Years of memories, broken fragments, flashed through his mind, suddenly falling into place.

Fontaine tilted her head, triumph bright in her eyes.

"And you think by humiliating Vivienne, you'll get back at James for casting you aside," Dashiell spat. "You're a cold whore."

"How dare you come to my place and disrespect me after what you did to Vivienne!" Fontaine hissed. "You humiliated her, not I. I'm trying to help."

"Oh, now you're Saint Fontaine!" Dashiell spat.

"Go back to your easy actresses and courtesans, your Eastern harems, your oriental concubines," Fontaine said. "I'm sure you'll quickly forget about Vivienne just as you did all the others." She hiked a brow. "Men, Lord Dashiell desires to leave. Show him to the door."

The flashman shoved Dashiell toward the door. Dashiell pretended to cooperate for two steps, then spun around, snatching the hammer that had previously been pressed into his jaw and slamming it into the flashman's oncoming fist. The crunch of bone and a howl echoed in the room. One of the workers flew at Dashiell to tackle him. Again, Dashiell pivoted, knocking the man's shoulder, sending him sailing in another direction as Dashiell raced for the stairs, slashing his hammer before him like the Nordic god, Thor.

The other workers gave chase, except for the poor bloke still hanging by the chandelier rope. Dashiell dashed across the first floor balcony, the ladies screaming and jumping out of his way. He leaped onto the railing and pushed off into the air.

"No," he heard Fontaine scream as he grabbed the chandelier chain, his feet crunching down on the gaslights. The rope slipped from the poor chap's grasp, and the massive creation descended to the floor with Dashiell riding atop.

The room exploded with bright, shattering crystals. Fontaine's girls were screaming, and the pink bird began flying in circles above the wreckage, squawking.

But inside Dashiell's mind all was silent except for one thought: *Get Vivienne.*

He turned to find himself once again staring at the eye of Fontaine's pistol. She clutched it in her right hand, her left gripping Vivienne's arm.

"Get out!" the madam screamed. "You bloody scoundrel."

"Not without Vivienne."

She jerked the barrel toward the door. "I said, get out!"

"Do you think I'm afraid of your gun? Woman, I've had a kris, zhanmadao, blunderbuss, basilisk, scimitar, and 24-barrel Belgian mariette pointed at me. Go ahead, shoot. I want to see you try."

Fontaine's nostrils were dilated, and her lips trembled as she considered. She slowly moved the gun and pressed it against Vivienne's temple. A collective intake of breath resounded around the room. "Care to see me try?" she asked.

"Dear God," Vivienne cried. "Dashiell!"

At that moment, any previous ideas he had about

fear and helplessness fled away, seeing the pistol pressed against Vivienne's head. Nothing mattered anymore, just the metal against that beautiful skin he had kissed. Her eyes, large and pleading, seeking his.

"Just put the gun down," he begged. "Vivienne has done nothing. Go ahead and shoot me if it will make you feel better, but let her go."

"If you really care about her, you will leave," Fontaine retorted.

Dashiell held up his hands and slowly unfurled his palms. "You win, Fontaine. Just… just put the damn gun down."

"Walk calmly out of here," she said.

He obeyed and began edging to the entrance, keeping his gaze locked on Vivienne's.

"Let me come back tonight," he said. "Let me try to win her. Please."

"You have some nerve, wrecking my place—not once but twice—and then begging to come back. No, you've lost Vivienne forever." She looked at the flashman. "I never want to see him again."

The flashman rammed his uninjured fist into Dashiell's gut and another man opened the door.

Vivienne cried out. Fontaine pressed the gun barrel against her temple.

Dashiell doubled over and spat on the floor. "I love you," he choked, clutching his belly. "I love you." The flashman hunched his large shoulders and rammed Dashiell, pushing him over the entranceway.

"The Bazulo vow!" he cried and then hit the iron railing. The flashman slammed the door shut.

❧

The hall was quiet. Vivienne could feel everyone's stares on her skin, as well as the cold barrel on her forehead.

"Clean this mess up," Fontaine ordered. "Hang Dashiell! That man will not alter my plans. I have made promises to some of the most influential men in the city. Put some damn candelabras out. And take whatever crystals aren't broken and hang them on the backdrop as stars."

The madam removed the gun from Vivienne's head and replaced it in some secret pocket in her skirts.

"I didn't mean to scare you, my little sweet cherub," she said, her voice turning saccharine. "You have to understand I did that for your own good. I know you have feelings for him, but he's a faithless liar. He only wants one thing, and when he tires of it, he wanders off again." She caressed Vivienne's cheek. "No, no, my dear, I have very wealthy and powerful gentleman who are dying to meet you. Men who could take good care of you and your family, unlike Dashiell."

Vivienne only uttered a dull, stupid "Oh." But inside, her mind was coming back to life as if she were surfacing from being deep under water. In this mire of lies and secrets, one thing became very clear: Dashiell hadn't deceived her when everyone else had. He told her he was bad when her uncle, her aunt, John, her father, almost everyone she knew lied, claiming they were virtuous and good, making her feel unworthy. Dashiell left her just as he had warned her he would. But he came back like he had promised in the Bazulo vow years ago.

She had seen the terror and fear in his deep

chocolate eyes. Yes, he was a rogue, a scoundrel—but he was no coward, no liar. He truly loved her.

Vivienne studied Fontaine's severe face containing those small agate eyes. At that moment, she wanted nothing more than to see the madam swinging from a rope.

What would Cleopatra, Joan of Arc, or Queen Elizabeth do to exact revenge on a hideous brothel owner?

Vivienne's gaze drifted up to the floor with Fontaine's parlor. Just where were those stolen masterpieces?

∞

Fontaine escorted Vivienne back to the Jungle Room where she had previously changed into the robe. The walls were deep green and lined with mirrors painted with trees, vines, and wild jungle cats.

"Rest, my cherub," the madam told her. "Dream of the money you will make tonight. I'll come back to have you dressed in a few hours. I have a wonderful costume planned. You'll adore it." Fontaine closed the door. Vivienne heard the lock turn.

She crossed to the bed, where beneath the netting, her reticule and gloves waited. Her cloak, dress, and gown had been removed. She opened her reticule and dumped the contents on the leopard fur covers. She took the sketches of her aunt she had gotten from Jenkinson over to the grate and watched as the flames flared up and consumed them. Then, returning to bed, she picked through her candies, nail file, farthings, and notebook until she found what she wanted: four hair pins. She was going to need a strong lock pick.

Twenty

DASHIELL'S MIND WAS A RAGING TANGLE OF THOUGHTS as he sprinted to Teakesbury's office. He tried to force himself to think of ways to get Vivienne free, but he wasn't rational; everything circled back to killing Fontaine in the most primeval ways.

Teakesbury's dull-witted clerk, Albert, opened the door and inquired if he needed assistance. Dashiell stormed past him, heading to the solicitor's office.

He found the man at his desk, reading glasses perched on his nose, a notebook open before him. Across from him, in leather wing chairs, sat an elderly couple.

"And for my young nephew," the woman was saying, "I would like to bequeath my grandmother's doilies. I'm sure a young man would appreciate those."

"Teakesbury, you've got to help me," Dashiell cut in. "I need to have that damned abbess arrested, or I will bloody well commit murder."

The woman gasped as her husband bolted from his chair. "There is a lady present! Watch your language, you... you miscreant!"

Behind Dashiell's back, Albert was jumping about,

waving his large hands, trying to get his attention. "Er, excuse me, my lord. If you please, Mr. Teakesbury is engaged at the moment."

"Yes, with me," Dashiell spat.

The solicitor tossed down his glasses, ran his hands down his face, and then rose. "Please wait in the parlor, my lord," he said in a pleasant voice that could sharpen flint. "I will see you momentarily." He took the doorknob and began to shut the door.

Dashiell stuck out his hand. "But I've got to kill someone."

"Momentarily," the solicitor hissed, giving the door a hard shove, sending Dashiell back into the parlor.

Albert stood, staring at him. "Would you like a bit of tea?" he asked.

Tea? Dashiell wanted poison. Something that he could slip into Fontaine's glass. "How about some hemlock or belladonna?"

"W-we only have oolong or pekoe."

"Never mind."

Dashiell began to pace about Teakesbury's glass cabinets, trying to connect lines. Jenkinson blackmailed Vivienne's aunt. Fontaine knew Vivienne's aunt was actually her mother. Both women knew Gertrude Bertis was James's lover. He kept arranging the pieces in his head. Could Fontaine have been instrumental in the theft? He pressed the heels of his palms into his temples. "Think, damn you!" he muttered. But he couldn't. His eyes kept drifting to the Roman javelin on Teakesbury's shelf. He imagined throwing it, a swift smooth flight into Fontaine's throat, and if that didn't do her in, a deep jab of the well-preserved gladius could finish the job nicely.

Fifteen minutes of this mental torture passed. Where was Teakesbury? "To hell with this," he spat. "Can you give me Mrs. James's address?" he asked Albert. "I desire to speak to her. It's pressing."

Before the clerk could answer, there was a knock at the front door. Albert walked in his clumsy gait over and opened it. A courier handed the clerk a letter. "Urgent from Miss Whitcomb," he said and ran off.

Clearly, Miss Whitcomb's burning problem trumped Dashiell's, because Albert broke into a jog, muttering "Whitcomb urgent." He dashed into his employer's office.

Dashiell gave Teakesbury a few more seconds and then stalked toward the door, giving up on the man. He would find Mrs. James's address himself, but first he wanted to get his .34 pocket Paterson revolver—a clever little invention designed by an American named Samuel Colt that Dashiell had won in a card game with a member of the Texas legislation in London.

"My lord, why do you care to commit murder?"

Dashiell turned. Teakesbury stood alone in his parlor, his hands stacked on the top of his mongoose cane.

"I need to speak to Mrs. James," Dashiell said. "Vivienne's in trouble. Fontaine has her."

"Good God. How did that happen?"

"There's no point in going into that. I, well, acted like a scoundrel. But—"

"Dashiell, can't you keep your instrument in your trousers?"

"—I think Vivienne probably tried to settle things with Jenkinson and ended up at Fontaine's. She's getting debuted tonight."

Teakesbury released a low breath and shook his head. "Let me go over and speak with her."

"Be careful. The woman is mad! She held a gun at Vivienne's head to get me to leave."

"She *what*?" He spiked his cane on the floor. "I'll talk to her and make her see reason."

"I don't want her to see reason. I want her to see the hanging rope. Give me Mrs. James's address," Dashiell said, grabbing the man's arm.

"Why?" The solicitor brushed Dashiell off as if he were a piece of lint on his coat. "What has she to do with anything?"

"I want the exact details of the robbery. I'm going to put Fontaine in prison. I don't think Jenkinson acted alone. She hasn't the brains. Mrs. James might tell me more on the subject."

"Listen to me, you want revenge on Fontaine so badly you're drawing connections where there are none. And even if we did have a damn shred of evidence, she is one of the most powerful people in the city. She's not going to crumble in a few hours. Have some sense."

"Very well, I'll just murder her."

"Stop that talk! What you need now is money."

Dashiell balled his fists in the air. "You don't understand, she's not going to let me win. She's full of bitterness and wants to watch me suffer because she sees me as Lawrence James." He slicked his hand down his face. "I'm scared I can't save Vivienne."

"I am going to do everything in my power to help you," he said. "Albert! Bring my coat and hat." He pointed at Dashiell. "Get some money and meet me at Seven Heavens."

"I don't have enough."

"Then find a moneylender!" Teakesbury thundered. "For once, use your brains instead of your tallywag, my good man."

❧

Dashiell sat back in a hackney on the way to his man of business and stared out the window. His muscles were taut. His fingers drummed his kneecap. He felt like a bug trapped in Fontaine's web, her spidery fangs about to sink into him. Teakesbury had better come through for him. Because if another man touched a hair on Vivienne's head, Dashiell would make what the Romans did at Carthage look like child's play.

Outside, the stately buildings of the west side of London gave way to the tarnished, narrow domiciles of older London to the east. The afternoon sun glinted over the rooftops, seeming to set the towers of St. Paul's Cathedral ablaze. Dashiell closed his eyes. Behind his lids, the image of the great dome and towers still burned.

A thought like a clean sword blade pierced his mind: young Fontaine's image in front of the obelisk steeple in Finsbury, the court case in *The Proceedings* against Adele Jenkinson involving an Anne Whitcomb also in Finsbury, a Miss Whitcomb sending an urgent letter to Teakesbury.

Dashiell pounded on the roof. "Stop! Stop!" He swung open the door before the carriage had halted.

"Swing north to Finsbury," he shouted to the driver.

"I thought we were going to—"

"Forget that. I need to go to…" Dashiell ran his

bottom lip under his teeth as he tried to summon up the details of the case. But his mind was a jumbled wreck: *were Angelica Fontaine and Anne Whitcomb one and the same, was Teakesbury a damned crooked lecher, get Vivienne, kill Fontaine and maybe Teakesbury.*

Then the address arose from some recess in his addled memory. "Ironmonger Row 104! Hurry."

The carriage turned into the neighborhood of Finsbury. The streets were cast in cold shadows. Ironmonger Row was a series of row houses. Long paned windows stretched across the ground floors with the name of the shop or pub painted above. The address in question was a narrow brick domicile. On the ground floor, shuttered windows flanked the door and a torn awning shaded the entrance. Above, two women conversed by an open window, displaying their scrawny arms and almost bare breasts to the men passing below.

He tapped for the carriage to stop. When it did, he stepped down. "How long have you been driving a hack in London?" he asked the driver.

"'Bout twenty years, sir."

Dashiell nodded toward the women. "Has this residence always been a brothel?"

"As long as I can recall. Though it ain't exactly a bordello. It's a boarding house. Bawds rent rooms there." A knowing smile spread his dry, cracked lips. "You want I should leave you here?"

"Yes." Dashiell threw the man a thruppence. "Just circle the block and pick me up again."

The man cocked a bushy incredulous brow. "Might you need more time, sir?"

"Oh no, it will only take me a minute," Dashiell assured him.

The driver shook his head and clicked the reins.

"Ain't you 'andsome!" one of the women called out. "Want to come up for a li'l company—a little sumpin' sumpin'?" Her companion flashed a saucy smile and leaned over the sill, exposing more of her bosom.

"No, thank you," Dashiell replied. "I'm just observing the beautiful view." He reached into his pocket and tossed up a shilling. "But thank you for your kind offer."

"Bless ya, sir! Bless ya!" the women cried.

Dashiell gazed up at the windows of 104. They were long and arched, like the ones in Fontaine's portrait. He pivoted and looked south. The obelisk steeple rose over the rooftops, just as he recalled from the sketch on Fontaine's wall. He pressed his thumb to the bridge of his nose. *Think, Dashiell, think.* Inside his brain, a creaking, rusted door slowly opened.

"That lying blackguard," Dashiell spat and took off in a sprint to catch the hackney cab.

"Enjoy yourself, sir?" the driver asked.

"Take me back to Teakesbury's office. Now."

❧

Dashiell tapped on the solicitor's door. Through the heavy glass, he could see the wavy distorted form of Albert approaching.

The clerk opened the door. "My lord, Mr. Teakesbury is not back. Would you care for a bit of tea?"

"I need to leave a message for one of his clients."

Dashiell lowered his voice. "Your employer believes she could help me with a private matter."

"Of course."

"Her name is Anne Whit… Whitfield… Whitacre."

"Whitcomb?" Albert suggested.

Dashiell snapped his fingers. "That's it, my good man, Anne Whitcomb. Are you certain she's a client?"

"Yes, my lord, she's always sending Mr. Teakesbury letters."

"Would you mind retrieving her address for me?"

Albert disappeared to the back of the office, muttering "retrieve address." Dashiell didn't wait for him to return. He headed down the walk, his mind reeling with what he had just learned. The street was jammed with people, yet he felt very alone. Vivienne was trapped, Fontaine wouldn't let him near the brothel, and he couldn't trust that treacherous rogue, Robert Teakesbury.

There was only one man who could help him.

❧

"Just don't make a scene," Dashiell warned his grandfather. Overhead, a jewel orange striped the sky in the gloaming. The tall narrow building blocked the last of the light, casting the tiny lane behind Seven Heavens into darkness. The screeching meows of two amorous cats echoed through the alley.

"Go through the front door without saying a single word," Dashiell continued as he straightened the man's cravat in a desperate attempt to make the earl look inconspicuous. "If anyone asks about me, tell them I've been disowned and you aren't speaking to me anymore. Then when no one is looking, nonchalantly walk to the back of the house and open a window or a door for me."

"Son, I've snuck in and out of more places than you could shake your cock at. And I didn't have to have someone open a window or door. This is embarrassing."

"I really don't need your commentary at the moment," Dashiell hissed through his teeth. "Did the boys fetch someone from Scotland Yard?"

"Now don't you worry. The boys are all concerned, seeing how you have to get your fiancée out of the bawdy house. We'll save Trudie's niece."

The earl turned to leave. Dashiell's blood rushed as the panic he had been struggling to keep pushed down surged forth. He grabbed his grandfather's arm. "There's something you need to know. Vivienne isn't Gertrude's niece, she's her daughter."

"What?"

"Vivienne is the daughter of Gertrude and Lawrence James. It was hushed up. The picture in my room that looks like Vivienne, some of the paintings at the Royal Academy—"

"The nude ones!"

"They are of young Gertrude."

His grandfather's lips parted as he gazed heaven-ward, his eyes glowing with a beautiful light. "She's my soul mate. I knew the day I first spied her. I could see below the drab and truly scary surface to the naked seductress within. Had I known! Oh, son, I've been hiding my love all these years."

"And you're going to have to keep hiding it unless you save her daughter."

He raised his arm and called out, "Trudie, I'll save her for you!" like a battle cry and broke into a trot down the alley, his hair streaming behind him.

"It's not the bloody crusades," Dashiell hissed after him. "And don't make a scene." But his grandfather had already rounded the corner.

Dashiell ran his palm, now reeking of the earl's cologne, across his face. What was he doing bringing his grandfather here? This was a stupid, hopeless idea, born of desperation.

He rested his hand on his Paterson. If all else failed, he would shoot five .34-caliber bullets into Fontaine with ease. And he would swing from a rope, knowing Vivienne was free.

❧

"Now, put on the halo," Fontaine commanded a gawky female servant.

Vivienne stood barefoot in the jungle room, staring at the mirrored walls where painted tigers peered from the brush. A servant set the large halo, a great circle of jutting rays, on Vivienne's head, securing it by jamming pins in her scalp. Fontaine and Vivienne both wore great feathered wings stretching from their shoulders. But while Fontaine's feathers were the same gold color as her dress, Vivienne's were pristine white. They matched her silk robe, which was also trimmed in feathers and opened in the front, exposing a feathery corset that pushed up her breasts. Her hair had been tortured with a hot round iron to land in perfect curls around her shoulders. White powder had been applied to her pale skin and her lips stained a vivid red. The servant had drawn tiny black circles under Vivienne's lashes. Vivienne wanted to grab the kohl and extend the lines off the edges of her eyes like an ancient Egyptian lady's.

I am Cleopatra, she told herself.

No, you're not, a voice echoed in her head. *You're a very odd angel bird.*

Through the door, Vivienne could hear the low rumble of men's chatter and the strings of a small chamber ensemble rising from the hall. "Are there many people here?" she asked. It felt as if a red hot butterfly was flitting around her insides. She glanced to the bed where she had hastily concealed her lock pick that she had been fashioning all afternoon.

"By the time you float down, there won't be any room for them to move." The madam smiled. "Remember, when you get off the swing, you take a few tiny steps on your toes—always on your toes, men love when ladies walk on their toes, it gives the body a better line—and then lie across the sofa, elegantly, as if you were silk." She flourished her hand before her, batting away the bed netting hanging from the bed posters. "Drape yourself." Fontaine demonstrated the technique on the mattress, causing Vivienne's throat to catch. The madam was not half an inch from the tiny bulge of Vivienne's pick.

"You're a beautiful painting to be gazed upon," the madam continued. She leaned forward, her elbow practically on the pick. She raised a brow, pursing her thin mouth into a coy smile. "Then you open your robe a little to taunt the men. Maybe glance at them, demurely, teasingly, from below your luscious lashes. Are you paying attention?" Fontaine demanded.

"Taunt," Vivienne squeaked as Fontaine eased closer to her pick. "Tease."

"Then I'll cue the girls to stop singing and begin the auction." Fontaine slid onto the pick and then flinched, touching her side. "Ouch. What the hell is under here?"

"I'm so scared!" Vivienne cried. "I can't go on!" She covered her face and pretended to weep.

"Your cosmetics!" Fontaine shrieked, and both she and the servant leaped forward, pulling Vivienne's hands away.

"You may leave," the madam barked at the servant, and the girl skittered out.

Fontaine cupped Vivienne's chin in her palm. "Now listen, it will be like it was with Dashiell, only much better, because instead of heartbreak, you'll get money," she said in a voice that strained to sound comforting. "You simply begin by telling the gentleman a few compliments—men are very simple creatures, really. Then you just lie there, thinking of all the pounds you'll give your father and how grateful he'll be that you saved him from prison." She crossed to the door. "Now practice walking on your toes and draping yourself, but don't upset your face or hair. I'll come get you when I'm ready."

"When will that be?"

"Half an hour. We need to open a few more bottles of wine to get our clients in the proper mood." Fontaine slipped out of the room.

Vivienne heard the lock click, rushed across the chamber, and pulled back the covers.

"Oh, bloody hell."

Her little pick was mangled. For a moment, she thought she really would break down into tears.

Would this tiny obstacle stop Queen Elizabeth?

She bent it back in shape, muttering to herself that she doubted Queen Elizabeth ever found herself captive in a brothel.

Vivienne crossed to the door and carefully slid the pick into the keyhole. She paused for a moment, closed her eyes, and remembered Dashiell holding her to his chest, his arm wrapped protectively around her shoulder. *Please work, please work!* She turned the pick and the lock popped with no resistance.

She squatted down and inched to the balcony. She peered over the railing, wishing she'd had the good sense to remove the enormous halo with its beams of light shooting out from her head. In the matter of a few hours, workers had managed to make Fontaine's vision manifest, sans the chandelier Dashiell destroyed.

A stage had been constructed behind a massive picture frame. Nestled about ferns and candelabras was a velvet sofa which Vivienne assumed she was to tiptoe to and drape upon. A lady clad only in angel wings like Vivienne's soared above the crowd in a swing decorated with a large crescent moon. On each of the stairs leading from the ground floor were more ladies wearing wings and holding candles in their hands. A sea of men in dark evening clothes thronged the hall, but she couldn't see Fontaine's gold splendor anymore.

That burning butterfly in her stomach fluttered its wings at the thought of any man touching her the way Dashiell had, putting his part in… *Stop thinking about that!*

Just then, a man with wild gray hair turned and looked up, his glittery, wild eyes catching hers. Lord Baswiche! His bushy brows raised in recognition, and he began pointing wildly at himself and mouthing something. She panicked and rushed down the corridor, away from the balcony. Dashiell had better have sent his grandfather to bid on her for him; otherwise the idea of the earl wandering in on his own free will was disgusting in so many aspects.

She pushed the thought to the nether reaches of her mind where waited the mounds of other scary thoughts she refused to think about, else she would become overwhelmed and paralyzed. "Joan of Arc, Queen Elizabeth, Cleopatra," she whispered.

When she reached the end of the corridor, her heart was pounding.

She inserted the pick into Fontaine's door, her fingers shaking and slick with perspiration. The lock clicked and turned as easily as the way her body had risen to Dashiell's touch. She slipped inside and quietly shut the door behind her.

"I love you," Frederick called from the corner and began jumping excitedly about his cage.

"Shhh!" she hissed and hurried across the room into Fontaine's chamber, closing herself in. Through the wall, she could still hear Frederick squawking his admiration.

In the corner, a coal fire flickered in an iron grate. She picked up a length of rolled newspaper from a basket, held it over the flame until it caught, and then lit a red glass lamp. An oak vanity with an oval mirror stood opposite the bed. Lace was draped from the sides of the mirror. Porcelain figurines of ladies, cosmetic jars, nail files, and perfume bottles were scattered about the surface.

A few feet from the fireplace was another door. Its lock resisted when she tried to turn the knob. She used her pick again to reveal a closet. On the rod hung garish dresses decorated with excessive amounts of feathers, beads, tassels, ribbons, and fake flowers. A coal slipped on the fire, and flames roared up. The light flashed on the mirrored wall at the back of the tiny room. On the right side, hat boxes without lids were stacked on shelves. She pulled out one and peeked inside to find it filled with wigs—blonde, red, and black. Others contained gemmed masks, red silk sashes, and leather whips coiled like snakes. Why would Fontaine keep such things in her closet? She slid out the bottom box, praying the sketches or paintings were inside. Glass glinted in the lamplight. She reached inside and held up a sculpture of a man's... cucumber! She gasped and dropped it in its container. The ringing of breaking glass echoed around the room.

"I love you!" Frederick called from the other room.

Where are those sketches?

Vivienne felt around the closet floor, feeling nothing but ladies' boots and cold planks. She backed into the bedchamber and began pulling out drawers, digging through stockings, chemises, corsets, petti-coats. Nothing. Nothing. Nothing.

Hang it!

The evil woman was impenetrable. Desperate, Vivienne knelt and tried to peer under the bed, but her ridiculous wings got in the way. Then she heard a heavy footfall, and Frederick began hissing. She shot across the room, into the closet, and pulled the knob behind her. She turned, getting her wings and halo tangled in the gowns, and snatched one of the leather whips.

Her breath was roaring through her nostrils. The chamber lock clicked and then footsteps thudded on the carpet, approaching the closet. The knob turned, and the door creaked open. She threw her arm forward, and the whip slashed the air, popping the intruder's upper arm.

Dashiell blinked and jerked his head back. "Did… did you just whip me?"

For a moment, she was too stunned to speak, and then she raised the whip again. "Yes!" she cried and slashed, this time harder than before. "And that's for leaving me!"

He shielded his face with his arm. "Ouch! Where did you learn to use that?"

"I didn't get any sleep. I cried the entire night. I almost killed myself. And now I'm here." She snapped the leather. "Say you're sorry. Say it!"

"I'm sorry. I'm sorry as hell. Just… just don't hurt me."

She dropped the whip and flung her arms around his neck. "I love you."

He lifted her from the floor as she opened her mouth and let his tongue inside to taste her. His musky scent, tinged with perspiration, filled her nose. She kissed him frantically, pressed herself against him, unable to get close enough because of her stupid wings. She wished she could burrow beneath his skin and hide herself inside him.

"I didn't mean those terrible words I said." His

usual smooth baritone was brittle and shaken. His lips brushed hers. "I was scared out of my mind. Can you ever come close to forgiving me?"

"You'll have to take me with you to Egypt and Greece and—"

"Arabia, Africa, India, Siam. I'll take you wherever you want to go. I'll—"

Her kiss halted his words. Dashiell had been out of his mind, almost homicidal, for the entire day. And now, even as he held Vivienne in a vile madam's chamber, she brought peace to his mind. He closed his eyes and slid his tongue along hers, his hand running up and down her arm. "I'm never letting you get away from me again."

Vivienne pulled back. "How did you find me?"

"My grandfather saw you and snuck me in." He chuckled softly, smoothing a curl from her face. "I know you are as reckless and dangerous as I am, so I figured you were heading to Fontaine's chamber to find something to hold against her."

"She has pictures of me sketched by Lawrence James." She shook her head, her eyes crinkling at the corners. "He knew me, loved me. All my life I was trying to please a man who wasn't my father and to my real father I was a masterpiece, but he never acknowledged me or helped raise me."

"I'll take care of all of this. I just need to make sure you're safe first."

"Everyone is connected," she continued as if he hadn't spoken. "I came here thinking that Jenkinson had been behind the blackmail. But now I'm not so sure. This is much bigger than I thought."

"Here's another little surprise for you." He related what he had learned thanks to Teakesbury's incompetent clerk.

"It would have been very beneficial if those elusive masterpieces had floated up," Vivienne said. "Fontaine is the central figure connecting everyone, yet we can't pin her down. We need to get her, Jenkinson, and Teakesbury in a room and then press each to betray the other." She rubbed her lips together. "Is Teakesbury here?"

"No, no, I don't like what you're contemplating," he said, wagging a finger. "Now you're coming with me. Scotland Yard will figure it out later once you're safe." He seized her hands.

"No, they won't. No one is going to get near Fontaine. I bet that hall is filled with politicians, magistrates, and peers, and not a one of them is going to say a word against her."

"I don't care, you're leaving."

"Those stolen paintings were of me. I've been stolen!"

"And now I'm stealing you too." He started to pull her to the door. She yanked free.

"No! I'm going to—" She stopped. Her tight, angry expression suddenly eased. "You're right," she said slowly, coolly. "But I really can't leave in these wings and halo." Her voice was bell-like and sweet. Then she did that adorable little wrinkle of her nose. "They would get in the way. Let me take them off?"

She untied her sash, and her robe and wings fell to the floor with a thud, revealing her lacy, feather-adorned corset that pushed up her breasts to beautiful, delicious mounds. The outline of her shapely legs and thighs were visible beneath the long, gossamer chemise as if she had nothing on at all. Dashiell's higher reasoning faculties went silent, like a noisy fly suddenly swatted flat. The only thought lighting his brain was "I want."

Vivienne ran her fingertip over her bodice, a coy, taunting, teasing smile on her lips as she gazed at him from under her beautiful lashes. "I'll change in the closet. Give me a moment."

She tiptoed into the closet, flipping her hair to glance over her shoulder at him, casting him another seductive look, before closing the door behind her.

He stood dazed for a moment. *I want. I want.*

A dim ray of rationality broke through his desire. "Wait a minute, you're trying to seduce me again. What are you doing in there?"

She didn't answer, but there was a great deal of bumping and thudding in the closet and then he heard her utter "Stupid halo." A few seconds later, the door opened. She stood on the threshold sporting a red wig and a lavender dress with embroidered green vines connecting roses made of bright red beads. The bodice gaped and sagged as if she had missed more than a couple of buttons, and the feathers from her corset poked out the top. Poised in her hand was another whip, ready to lash out at him.

"Vivienne, whatever you're thinking—that is, if you *are* thinking—my answer is no. We're leaving."

"Fontaine is coming for me in the Jungle Room," she said, edging toward the door. "I just have to get Teakesbury and Jenkinson there."

"You're insane." He lunged at her.

She snapped the whip, popping his arm.

"Ow! Vivienne!"

"I'm so sorry," she cried. "I love you more than anyone in the world. Truly. But I have to find myself." She turned and fled the room.

He dashed after her. "You stop right now."

Her hand flashed by Frederick's cage. And then he was blinded by white and pink feathers flying in his face. He crossed his arms, shielding himself. The bird kept swooping at him.

"Damnation!" He captured the bird by its feet. Frederick flapped his great wings and hissed at him.

"Now, just calm down." Dashiell became very still and stared at the bird the way he had seen snake charmers do with cobras in India. "Good bird." He slowly reached out and rubbed the side of the bird's head with his finger. Frederick opened his beak and shot out his blunt tongue. "Good bird," he said soothingly. The bird quieted, swiveled his head, and studied Dashiell with one eye.

Dashiell looked about; the room was empty except for the bird and him. What the hell was he going to do now? If he stalked into the hall, he would be spotted in a matter of seconds. He did some quick arithmetic as he scratched the bird. There was him, his grandfather, and the boys. Seven or so men against about seventy-five. Historically, those were never favorable odds without rifles, arrows, cannons, or trebuchets.

The only thing he knew was that Fontaine was coming to get Vivienne in the Jungle Room. He slowly turned. The edge of Vivienne's discarded wings and robe peeked through the doorway. A scary idea germinated in his head, one that only a desperate man, who had lost all reservation about humiliating himself, would ponder.

"I must be mad," he whispered.

"I love you," Frederick cooed.

Twenty-one

A FEW MINUTES LATER, DASHIELL PEERED OUT OF Fontaine's door into the corridor. The sound of ladies singing drifted down the hall. "She is a gem beyond compare, a beauty so rare, a face so fair."

He wrapped the white feathered robe tighter about his body and then pulled a strand of long black hair from Frederick's mouth. "I told you to stop eating my wig," he scolded the bird, perched on his shoulder.

Dashiell stepped into the hall. His wings and halo got caught in the doorframe, sending tiny white feathers flying. "Dammit," he muttered.

He turned, edged out of the room, and tiptoed on his bare feet down the passage as he mentally counted off his more manly deeds: *drank with a legion of elite French Zouaves in Algeria, got in a sword fight with a band of Barbary pirates, and entertained a sultan's harem in Bursa.*

A gent with a vacant, inebriated expression weaved toward him. "Hallo there, beautiful lady. Haven't seen you before."

Dashiell grabbed a strand of long hair from Frederick's beak and spread it across his mouth, letting out a girlish giggle. "I'm new," he said in a cracking falsetto. "Can you tell me where the Jungle Room is?"

"It's the one in the middle of the balcony." The man staggered backward and flung his hand toward a door. Dangling just below the balcony railing was a strange contraption: a swing hanging by ropes twined with ribbon and supporting a huge crescent moon.

The drunk's eyes glittered. "Want a wild night in the jungle, pretty thing?" He curled his fingers and swiped the air. "Reorw," he hissed and broke into a dirty chuckle. Dashiell giggled again and then swung his fist, slamming the man's jaw, sending him sailing into the wall. The bird began bobbing up and down and hissing on Dashiell's shoulder.

The inebriate slid onto the floor, rubbing his chin, a stupid grin on his face. "Oh, you're that type. There's another chamber for that."

Dashiell straightened his halo and stepped over the man. He proceeded down the corridor, glancing quickly over the balcony, before slipping into the Jungle Room. He stepped beside the door to conceal himself. There he waited, listening, his hand on his Paterson and Frederick eating his wig. The head of a tiger gazed at him from where its skin had been made into a rug. On the mirrors, other felines peered at him with green and yellow painted eyes.

Outside, the singing stopped. He could make out a female voice raised as if in greeting. The doorknob shook and then turned. "It's unlocked," he heard a female voice say. Two white-winged figures entered. He slammed the door shut behind them and pointed his gun.

"Where are Vivienne and Fontaine?" he demanded.

The two young women screamed and grabbed onto each other.

"M-Mrs. Fontaine g-gave us the key and said we were s-supposed to escort her to the swing."

Dashiell groaned. "Oh, bloody hell."

He stalked out onto the balcony. Below, the madam stood on the stage, addressing the audience. And there, on the front row with a cigar sticking out from the edge of his smiling mouth, was Dashiell's second least favorite person behind the madam: Robert Teakesbury. But Vivienne was nowhere in sight.

"She is a masterpiece of love." Fontaine's voice resounded as if she were performing at Covent Garden. "A Lawrence James portrait in real life. A prize for the discriminating connoisseur of the erot—"

"I love you!" Frederick squawked and swooped from Dashiell's shoulder, flying in a large spiral down to the picture frame where he perched himself.

Fontaine's head jerked up, her gaze latching onto Dashiell.

Without thinking, he jammed his gun through his robe and into his trousers and leaped over the railing onto the moon swing. He heard a grunt from the men hoisting the ropes above, and one side of the swing fell. He held on, sliding down the rope and landing on the stage with a graceful thud. "Hallo, lads, here I am: your masterpiece of love."

Dashiell righted his halo and began drawing little circles around his would-be breasts with his index fingers.

The audience went silent, faces paralyzed. Fontaine's mouth flapped open. A lone voice rang out. "Damn, son. I thought we weren't supposed to make a scene."

"Dashiell!" Fontaine screamed and leaped at him, her fingernails out like claws. He sashayed aside, letting the madam career past him. He shot his grandfather a hot "come here now" look and jerked his head toward the side of the stage.

"I am the Aphrodite of Mayfair, Venus rising from the Thames." Dashiell swayed his hips like an Arabian dancer as he edged across the platform toward his grandfather. "A goddess above all goddesses."

Laughter rippled across the crowd and the men began clapping in time to the gyration of his pelvis.

His grandfather reached the stage first. "Dash, you're scaring me."

Dashiell flourished his arms in cascading waves as he leaned down. "Vivienne's here," he said to the earl. "Find her and get her out."

Fontaine caught up with him, grabbing his arm. "Get off my stage." Her lips were pursed in a rock-hard smile, trying to appear calm and in control, but her eyes were like daggers.

Dashiell seized her and spun her like a top, as he watched the earl disappear through the throng.

Fontaine ripped her hand free. "What do you think you are doing?"

Dashiell didn't answer, but dragged his fanned fingers before his eyes while undulating his groin. "Between my limbs await the erotic mysteries of India," he told the men. "The secret perfumed garden of Arabia."

Whooping cheers rang out.

"What have you done with Vivienne?" Fontaine spat in his ear.

Dashiell quivered his arse at the audience while slowly raising his arms until the back of his hands met between his wings. He tried to bend his back and toss his long wig hair like the dancers he had seen in the Ottoman palaces, but he lost his balance, falling backward onto his wings and sending his halo rolling across the floor. The audience howled.

Dashiell curled onto his side. His wig had spun on his head and now covered his eyes with long black locks. He blew them aside. "So, fellows, who wants a night of sublime, exotic delight? Start your bidding."

❧

In the back of Vivienne's mind, a tiny unformed thought nagged her like an itch on her back that she couldn't reach. She had missed something. What? She tried to ignore the niggle as she searched through the sculleries again.

Where is Jenkinson? The madam must not have come for her money. But that made no sense. Jenkinson could have been run over by a train, leaving vultures to peck out her innards, and she would claw her way out of hell to get her money.

Vivienne checked the clock hanging above a cupboard of white plates. Fontaine would arrive in her room in three minutes.

The servants cast her curious looks. They stood about a massive table, their knives slamming the wood as they cut up geese and lamb legs.

"I think we have another insane one on our hands," said a weary old woman, carrying a pan laden with raw turbot. She opened the door of a great oven set back in an alcove and shoved the fish inside.

An explosion went off in Vivienne head. "Bloody hell," she whispered and spun around, flying down the servants' corridor and up the back stairs to Fontaine's room.

Men's loud laughter and hands clapping in rhythm echoed through the passage. Were they getting ready for her grand entrance? Well, they could keep waiting because she wasn't going to be any man's mistress, paramour, concubine, or whatever—except Dashiell's, provided she could get them out of the brothel alive.

Fontaine's parlor was open. Vivienne crept inside and closed the door behind her. "Dashiell," she whispered, but got no reply.

The room was empty, pink and white feathers strewn about the rug. She passed into Fontaine's bedroom. Dashiell's coat, cravat, and shoes had been tossed on the bed. The closet door was wide open. Her halo, wings, and robe were missing.

"What in the world?" she whispered, but then snapped herself back to attention. She had a mission and less than a minute to complete it.

She began ripping the dresses from their hangers, exposing the paned mirrored wall at the back of the closet. She quickly scanned the surface, seeing no lock anywhere. She snatched the lamp from the commode and held it to the mirror. On the second mirrored pane from the left, she found was she was looking for: tiny fingerprints.

She paused a moment to think. How would her father—well, the man she knew as her father—engineer a secret door? She pushed on the frame beside the prints. The wood gave and then she drew it back until she heard a soft click. "May you enjoy Newgate, Fontaine," she whispered and carefully slid two columns of panels back, revealing a small black safe. On the top, James's sketches were stacked. Unless the masterpieces were miniatures, she doubted they could fit in the safe.

"No, no, no!" She banged the heel of her palm against her forehead. "They have to be in here."

She kicked aside the shoes, wigs, and whips on the floor, until she could squeeze herself against the corner of the closet. She peered into the small room. A large trunk stood on its side against the inner wall.

⤳

"I am well-versed in oriental languages of pleasure," Dashiell said, moving his arms like cascading waves as he slid his neck from side to side. Frederick had his claws dug into his wig, pulling out long strands while ignoring his owner's terse commands to get away from that molly lobcock.

Teakesbury had pushed through the horde, stationing himself by the side of the huge picture frame, not three feet from Dashiell. "Stop this ridiculous act." His lips were pulled back, baring his teeth. "You are disgracing yourself. I'm trying to help you."

Like hell you are.

"Three farthings for the evening!" a man shouted.

The flashman, using his enormous shoulders, shoved through the men crushing the stage. "Get him out of here!" Fontaine commanded him. The hulk of a man hunched down, flexed the muscle of the hand that wasn't bandaged, and rushed at Dashiell like a charging bull.

"Oh, damn." Dashiell leaped for the rope swing and cast himself into the air, swooping around the man. "Come fly with me to the heights of grand passion," he told his audience and then slammed into the stairwell. Fontaine's clients applauded.

Dashiell grabbed the rail and jammed his foot between two balustrades. "Hello, lovely," he said, winking to one of the angel girls holding a candle. She shrieked and rushed into the arms of the woman a few steps above. "I make them all scream," he assured the men.

Along the back wall, he saw his grandfather was wandering, turning his head about as if he were lost.

What the hell is he doing in here! Vivienne wouldn't come into the hall. He wanted to throttle his grandfather—and, for that matter, Vivienne—once he saved her hide, provided he wasn't being carted away to Newgate for murder, or Bedlam for this bit of madness.

"A half-groat," a man called out.

"Stop encouraging him!" Fontaine said.

"Just a half-groat!" Dashiell cried in outrage. "For this luscious body?" He trailed his hand down his chest to his balls. "Come now, you don't grasp the sheer enormity of my love. Sixpence, at least."

"A shilling!"

"One pound for you to get down, immediately," Teakesbury spat.

The flashman was now pushing clients aside as he made for the stairs. Dashiell took to the air again.

"Let go of that rope!" Fontaine screamed at the workmen on the top balcony. Suddenly, Dashiell was falling. He seized the top of the picture frame and, for a second, hung suspended.

A terrible crack resounded and then the ripping of fabric. "Oh, hell." The flimsy structure fell apart where it had been poorly nailed together at the edges. Dashiell landed feet-first on the sofa. He waved his arms frantically to keep his balance, but tumbled over the back, toppling the sofa.

He opened his eyes, but all he saw was black, or perhaps the wig was blocking his vision. The audience's howling laughter sounded like an oncoming train in his ear.

Save Vivienne!

He struggled to his feet. His left wing dropped to the floor. "I'm a fallen angel, boys," he stammered and staggered backward, hitting the velvet background. Little crystal stars twinkled and jingled around him.

"Two pounds," a guest said.

"Three pounds," upped another.

"I love you."

"Frederick, come here immediately!" Fontaine ordered. The bird circled onto the madam's shoulder. "Your little show is over, Lord Dashiell. It's all been very amusing, but it's time for your closing act, and I assure you that you will never be able to cross my threshold again."

"Four pounds!" a man bellowed.

Fontaine and the flashman were closing in on Dashiell; he was trapped against the midnight sky façade. He'd always hoped that once in his life he would do something truly heroic: pistols in both hands, a powerful steed between his legs, reins in his teeth as he flew across an Indian plain, firing at a gang of Thugs, or quietly slitting the throat of a notorious

Turkish assassin with a yatagan in some dark alley. He never imagined that his most noble deed would happen while wearing a dress and dancing seductively before drunken men. But he would sacrifice his pride and life to set Vivienne free. He reached into his robe for his revolver.

"A thousand pounds to take her as my mistress," a female voice called out.

A shiver ran down his spine. *Vivienne!*

Silence thundered through the hall. Everyone spun around to the direction of the woman's voice. The crowd edged back, and there standing among them in a tawdry red wig and an ill-fitting lavender gown with gaudy bead roses was Vivienne. In her hands, she gripped a painting of herself.

"Son, I found her!" his grandfather called out. "She was wearing a wig."

Twenty-two

WHERE DID HIS BRILLIANT LADY FIND THE MASTERPIECE?

"My love," Dashiell began in a strained voice, holding up his hand. "Let's just talk about this in private." With the masterpiece in Vivienne's possession, Fontaine couldn't do a thing to her. He just had to edge his love to the door and out the building.

"Of course," she cried, using those frightening sugary tones. "It's so improper to discuss the details of such an arrangement in public." Her gaze landed on the solicitor. "Mr. Teakesbury, would you be so kind as to represent my interests?"

"Aren't you clever?" Fontaine hissed. The muscles around her jaw twitched.

Vivienne tilted her head. "Thank you," she replied tartly. "Oh, and Mama Dellie, I searched everywhere for you, and here you are lurking in the corner. You have been so helpful in this whole affair. Would you care to join us, as I believe you had a stake in this deal?"

"My sweetness, I would prefer it if we just walked out of here." Dashiell gave Vivienne a hot *don't even think about what you're thinking about* look. "Right now."

"Come, let us all meet in the parlor," Vivienne said pleasantly, as if he'd said nothing at all, but then she glanced over her shoulder, gazing at him from under her lovely lashes. "You too, my little butter biscuit."

He'd worked so hard to save her and now he might have to kill her.

"Wait, where's the masterpiece of flesh?" a man shouted. "I didn't come here to see some molly in a dress."

Fontaine's lips tightened. "Girls, talk to the gentlemen. There will be no auction this evening."

Fontaine ignored the cries of protest and stepped down from the stage, her face stony and drawn.

Dashiell followed the party toward the parlor. Outside the door, he snatched his grandfather's elbow. "I need a Scotland Yard officer!"

"The boys are working on it."

"God dammit." He slipped his hand through his silken robe and felt the hard heel of his gun. "If anything happens to me tonight, give all my antiquities to Vivienne. Except for the erotic Roman ones. You can keep those."

❦

"Joan of Arc, Cleopatra, Queen Elizabeth," Vivienne whispered, waiting for them to assemble in the parlor. Her body was shaking, but she didn't feel scared, only angry, and not a consuming boiling rage either, but a quickening of her mind, ready for anything.

Teakesbury strolled in, paused for a moment to take in his surroundings, and then chose to sit on a sofa. He reached into his coat, fished out a cigar, and lit it on a lamp on the side table. Behind the haze of smoke, his features were relaxed, and a bemused smile adorned his face as if he were watching a theatrical production. Jenkinson followed behind the solicitor, her lips pursed, her frame slightly bent, and her fists balled, ready to fight.

Meanwhile, Dashiell stalked up to Vivienne, his silken robe flowing about him, his remaining wing flopping behind his arm, and laid a strong possessive hand on her shoulder. He leaned close, his lips near her ear. "I swear, I love you with all my being, but if we make it out of here alive, I might throttle you."

Vivienne clung to the "I love you with all my being" part, letting those words strengthen her resolve and discarding the less than helpful ones.

Fontaine was the last to enter. She closed the door behind her, her small eyes hot and nostrils pinched. Frederick edged back and forth on her shoulder. "For God's sake, take those ridiculous wigs off," she muttered as she crossed to the mantel, her gold wings creating a draft in her wake.

"Gladly." Dashiell ripped his off and tossed it onto the sofa opposite the one assumed by Teakesbury. The bird flew down and began plucking the black strands.

"I've grown rather fond of mine," Vivienne said coolly, refusing to be cowed by the woman. "Queen Elizabeth had red hair."

"I don't care if Queen Elizabeth had fern green hair," Fontaine spat. "Just give me the painting, and you can have this ridiculous, faithless coxcomb of yours. But when he leaves you—and he will—don't you dare come crying about your sad papa and debtor's prison again."

"Very good then, let us go, my dear," Dashiell said, tugging Vivienne's arm.

But Vivienne wasn't leaving yet. In her hands, she held a portrait of herself painted by her father whom she had never known. Her identity, her life, everything she thought she knew about herself was wrapped up in this theft and blackmail. For the last twenty years, she had been unwittingly floating along on lies and secrets. Now she wanted the truth.

She didn't budge an inch, even when Dashiell hissed under his breath. "Vivienne, dear, give her the painting and let me get you out of here."

"Wot do you mean, letting 'er go," Jenkinson cried. "Where's my money?"

"For God's sake, just shut your mouth, Adele!" Fontaine exploded.

"Ah, you must be Mrs. Jenkinson." Teakesbury sucked from his cigar, then released a curling stream of smoke. "You live in St. Giles with your son Willie and a massive lover named Sidney."

"Aye, so wot of it?" Jenkinson retorted, as she plucked a porcelain peacock from the mantel and shoved it down the front of her dress.

"And I would advise you to be careful," Teakesbury said. "You wouldn't want to go back to Australia, would you?"

"How do you know about me and Australia?"

"I'm Robert Teakesbury, solicitor," he replied, as smooth as satin, but Vivienne noticed how tightly his hand gripped his cane. Between his whitened knuckles glittered the tiny glass eyes of a golden creature. He was playing at something, but she couldn't figure out what.

"I've had my clerks watch you," he continued. "You stole sketches and paintings from my client, Mrs. Lawrence James."

"Wot? I didn't steal nothing." She yanked the peacock from her gown. "And I—I was just looking at this. Pretty like."

"Come now." Teakesbury gave Dashiell a patronizing, knowing smile as if they were privy to a private joke. "We spoke about Jenkinson just yesterday."

"I don't remember," Dashiell said slowly, though Vivienne knew how his steel trap of a mind worked and wagered he remembered every detail of that conversation. "Remind me."

The solicitor complied. "Scotland Yard determined that the Lawrence James robbery was carried out by a strong person or persons, capable of moving about an enormous cabinet. Meanwhile, as Mrs. James walked her child in the park, she was entertained, or should I say detained, by a little man in a blue coat. A few days later, a painting of young Mrs. Jenkinson here surfaced in a pawn shop near the Strand."

"I didn't steal nothing!" Adele spat.

"Mr. Teakesbury, you are so clever," Vivienne said, flashing him the dimpled smile that Dashiell had once instructed her to use in order to get what she wanted. She watched the solicitor shift in his seat under her spell.

She stepped forward, but Dashiell immediately

reined her back to him. "Oh, stop." She giggled and jerked herself free. "I just want to see Mr. Teakesbury's sweet little cane. Do keep this, my dearest." She thrust the painting at Dashiell and then crossed to the sofa. She put her hand on top of Mr. Teakesbury's and watched his Adam's apple lift, the bemused glow on his face faltering for a moment.

"Isn't this simply darling!" she cried and drew the cane from the solicitor's grasp. She waved the creature's face at Dashiell. "It's an Indian mongoose. Such a precious creature."

She grinned at Teakesbury again, dimples in full force, refusing to acknowledge Dashiell's scowl and the way he jerked his head toward the door.

"I adore how they eat mean old scorpions and venomous cobras." Vivienne wrinkled her nose. "I think it's a shame that Cleopatra didn't have one." The man reached for his stick, but she kept it in her hand, turning to Jenkinson. "So, Mr. Teakesbury, you're saying that Mrs. Jenkinson stole the masterpieces, but that doesn't explain how they ended up in the secret room behind Mrs. Fontaine's closet."

The wealthy madam's eyes narrowed, the heat of her hatred burrowing into Vivienne's skin.

"What?" Dashiell asked.

"There's a secret latch on the mirrored wall in Mrs. Fontaine's closet, my sugar cake," Vivienne explained to him. "I found it after you left, else I would have told you."

His mouth opened, his face assuming a slack-jawed look. "I—I love you. I'm taking you to the Valley of the Kings. We're going to find some tombs."

The bird looked up from dining on its wig. "I love you," it repeated.

"Damn you, Frederick, be quiet!" its owner yelled.

Head low, the shamed bird edged to the other side of the sofa, emitted a low sad "I love you" and then flew over to land on Dashiell's shoulder.

"Hey there, lad," Dashiell said, scratching the side of Frederick's face. "I know how you feel about me."

"I believe we were trying to ascertain how Mrs. Fontaine ended up with the masterpieces," Vivienne said.

Fontaine didn't answer, but kept her eyes fixed on Vivienne, except for a flicker in Teakesbury's direction. When she finally spoke, her words came out haughty and cold. "Adele brought the paintings to me. She knew I would pay to keep them safe. And naturally, someone in my position can't simply go to Scotland Yard."

"Well, that explains everything perfectly," Vivienne said. "Clearly, Mrs. Jenkinson has spent the last fifteen years in Australia studying art and readily knew which pieces were the most valuable, stole them, and then sold them to you."

"Huh?" Jenkinson said. "I ain't studied no art!"

"Are you suggesting that I asked Adele to steal those paintings?" Fontaine laughed, slow and measured, from deep in her throat. She approached the other madam.

Although a good three inches taller than Fontaine, Jenkinson cowered, slumping her shoulders.

"Adele, answer very, very carefully." Fontaine enunciated each syllable with crystalline precision. "Did I tell you about the painting in Lord Dashiell's hands? Did I ask you to steal it?"

"No. I didn't steal nothin'! I didn't know nothin' about no masterpieces."

Fontaine's lips curled in triumph.

"But you told her about the sketches of my aunt." Vivienne wagged the mongoose before Fontaine's face. "And you knew Mrs. Jenkinson desperately wanted revenge on my uncle. And you knew she would be willing to steal to get it. Why shouldn't she conveniently pick up a painting or two after she had gone to all the trouble of breaking in?" She shook her head. "It's just I find it exceedingly odd that she would know to take the most valuable pieces."

"I didn't take no masterpieces!" Jenkinson spat. Her mouth hung open, exposing the stubs of her black teeth. "Just some paintings lying about. One of me that Lawrence did when I was pretty. And I was pretty. Prettier than you." She pointed her finger at Vivienne and then at the painting in Dashiell's possession. "But I didn't take that there painting. I never saw it before today."

"She's a lying thief," Teakesbury said, tapping the glowing red end of his cigar on the rim of a pewter bowl. "I deal with these low sorts every day. Lord Dashiell, your Miss Taylor shouldn't be exposed to this degradation any longer. You take her along and let me handle the situation. And, miss, do return my cane."

Vivienne didn't comply, but pressed the mongoose to her bosom. She arched a brow at Dashiell. "Well, I actually believe Jenkinson when she says she didn't take no masterpieces."

Dashiell hiked a corresponding brow, their gazes latched together.

"Because they weren't there to take," Dashiell whispered as the revelation dawned in his brain. *My God, Vivvie's brilliant!* He continued, the words rolling out, "Teakesbury had already put them in a safe place that only his client Angelica Fontaine would find. Presumably, her closet."

Teakesbury broke into laughter, clutching his belly.

"Wot?" Jenkinson spat.

"You were set up," Vivienne explained to the simpleton madam. "They knew you were going to steal those sketches and whatever paintings were about. The whole time, you were being manipulated to take the blame for a greater theft."

Jenkinson whipped around to Fontaine. "You took the best paintings for yourself and didn't leave me nothin' but rubbish." She released a low growl and snatched up the porcelain peacock again, jamming it into her dress. "You did me wrong every time, Annie."

Tears of mirth streamed down Teakesbury's face. He pulled a handkerchief from his pocket and wiped his brow. "I say, Dashiell, you've found a truly remarkable girl, but I have no ties with Angelica Fontaine beyond coming here tonight on your behalf."

"Such carefully chosen words, sir," Vivienne countered. "You said, 'I have no ties with Angelica Fontaine,'" she repeated, slightly puckering her beautiful lips that Dashiell wanted to kiss. "Adele, answer very, very carefully: is Angelica Fontaine Annie's real name?"

The lowly madam tossed her head in a derisive snort as she shoved a beaded box from a side table into her now bursting bodice. "It's plain Anne Whitcomb.

She ain't French. She was always putting on airs she don't 'ave. Her ma was an Irish laundress and whore."

"And, according to your clerk, Albert," Dashiell told Teakesbury, "Anne Whitcomb is very much your client."

Teakesbury turned silent. He reached for his cane but it wasn't there.

"You said Fontaine holds secrets on all the officials in London," Dashiell reminded him. "Why do I suspect she has been whispering them in your ears all these years? She gets to move without impunity into Mayfair, and you move from being a lowly solicitor fresh from India to one of the most powerful solicitors in the city."

"You all are going to Newgate," Vivienne said.

"My little cherub, you are swimming in waters over your head." Fontaine squeezed her kohl-lined eyes to mere slits. "I suggest you back down now, or I will make your life hell on earth."

Dashiell watched as a dead calm washed over Vivienne's features, but her eyes were glittery wild things.

"You had to make everyone suffer because James scorned you," she said, gripping the head of Teakesbury's cane to her chest. "You had to steal from James's widow because James left you for her. You knew Mrs. Jenkinson would use those sketches to hurt my aunt, but you didn't care. You hated my aunt because James loved her and not you."

"You watch yourself," Fontaine hissed. Dashiell slipped his hand inside his robe, extracting his revolver and concealing it behind the portrait of Vivienne. He edged to the left, to get a clear shot of the madam.

"And you were going to disgrace me, because James

was proud of me." Vivienne's voice began breaking up. "Because I am…" She choked, tears swelling in her eyes. "Because I am a masterpiece, and you are nothing. Nothing!" she screamed like her lungs were coming out.

"Don't you dare speak to me that way! *You* are nothing, not me!" Fontaine swiped the air. "I made all this by myself."

"You made this on the backs of other women," Vivienne retorted. "And I'm taking it all away."

"Just you try." Fontaine's hand swept toward the folds at the side of her skirt.

"Vivienne!" Dashiell shouted as a gleam of light flashed in his eye. He dropped the painting, revealing his aimed gun. A few feet away, Vivienne held a long shiny blade that extended from the mongoose's neck under Fontaine's chin. The remainder of the sword cane had fallen on the carpet. Fontaine hadn't had time to fully retrieve her muff pistol. The ivory heel protruded from her dress, the barrel aimed at her own leg.

"Hand me the gun," Vivienne ordered her.

She's amazing!

Fontaine kept her fingers around the trigger.

"Joan of Arc found her sword on the altar in the church of Saint Catherine," Vivienne said. "She swore she would never use it to kill anyone."

"You are the most peculiar, irritating girl ever," Fontaine spat. "What are you trying to say?"

"I'm not Joan of Arc." Vivienne pressed the blade into Fontaine's skin, and a drop of blood rolled down the shiny steel. "Hand me the gun."

Fontaine released the weapon, letting it thud on the rug.

The room was silent except for the rise of chatter from the adjoining room.

Keeping her blade trained on the madam, Vivienne kicked the pistol and then reached down, lifting it. "Dashiell, my butter biscuit, um... now what do we do?"

"One moment." He backed to the door, switching his aim between Teakesbury and Mrs. Jenkinson, who had stopped mid-theft, clutching a statue of a boy with grapes. He cracked the parlor door and called out, "Grandfather!"

The earl hurried in, his palms up. "Son, the boys couldn't round up an officer that Fontaine ain't got something on."

The powerful madam released a purring laugh.

"What!" Dashiell shouted, his mind already doing the calculations: two guns, a sword, seventy men, and ten feet to the door.

"Well, the boys' spirits were awfully low, seeing how they couldn't help you," his grandfather continued. "So they stopped into the club for a dram and found him."

"Him?"

A handsome young man with a prominent forehead and sporting a tiny mustache and whiskers strolled into the parlor.

"Prince Albert!" Vivienne gasped and curtsied, all the while keeping her sword pointed at Fontaine.

"Lord Dashiell, I heard that you were in quite a predicament," the prince said. His gaze raked Dashiell up and down. "I say, nice dress."

The prince sent his footman for the Chief Magistrate. Vivienne was willing to wait for the man to arrive, but Dashiell was beside himself to get her out of the brothel. He ripped off his robe and remaining wing, then gave the painting, sword cane, and Fontaine's pistol to the prince. Using his own gun, he corralled Teakesbury, Fontaine, and Jenkinson onto a sofa and handed the weapon to his grandfather, instructing him to stand guard. The revolver dangled from the earl's fingers in the general direction of the suspects, as his grandfather was more interested in making friends with the hissing Frederick. "Be a nice birdie, be a nice birdie. I always wanted a birdie."

Vivienne curtsied to the Prince and Dashiell gave his farewells to the others. "I'll see everyone in court." He swung Vivienne up into his arms. "Hang on, my love," he whispered. Her muscles were quavering and jellylike, and a cold perspiration broke over her skin. They were free. She pressed her lips into the warm skin under his ear, ignoring the shocked stares they received as Dashiell, coatless and shoeless, carried a woman in a red wig and garish gown out of the brothel and into the street.

Under a streetlamp, his carriage waited. His groom and a footman, lounging on the carriage perch, threw down their cards and tankards of whatever they were drinking and leaped to the ground.

The groom opened the door and then yanked down the steps. "Do you still want me to go to—"

"Yes," Dashiell said.

Vivienne stepped inside and slid onto the cushion.

Dashiell leaned across her lap, his shoulder brushing against her breasts as he yanked down the window blind. He grabbed a brown wool blanket from the floor. While he was tucking it about her neck, she stole a kiss. He groaned as he pulled the wig from her head and buried his face in her falling hair.

"Don't leave me tonight," she whispered.

His mouth sought hers. She savored the taste of him, his scent, his feel, everything she thought she had lost.

"I'm never leaving you again," he said. "I'm going to be a human burr, stuck to you wherever you go. Just try to stay away from bawdy houses in the future."

The carriage lurched forward.

"Are you taking me to a flat?" she murmured, imagining their bodies entwined on a soft bed. Knowing again that amazing sensation of him moving inside of her, and then drifting off into lovely sleep in his arms, leaving this dreadful day far behind.

"A flat?" He chuckled softly in her ear and then nibbled its edge.

She became nervous. Didn't men keep their mistresses in rented rooms? For a woman who'd almost sold herself into prostitution and spent an entire day in a brothel, she really should know these things.

"Well, you're my mistress, remember?" she joked to cover her uncertainty. "Isn't that where I should put you?"

His lips brushed the side of her jaw. "Don't you worry, my dear, I have the perfect love nest for us." His mouth covered hers again.

An anxious thought pricked her conscience and she pulled back, taking his face between her hands.

His eyes were wild and glassy, and his hoarse breath warmed her face. "Are you truly going to take care of my family?" she asked.

"Your sisters, your father, your aunt, your mother, any yet unknown half-siblings, whoever and whatever."

She gazed down. "It's all so ugly, isn't it?"

"Hush now." He brushed a lock of hair from her face and threaded it behind her ear. "Maybe to the more proper and dull-minded, but not to me. I come from a deep, colorful line of scoundrels, rakes, and blackguards. My family tree is a wonder of the forest. It grows in directions no other flora does."

She laughed as she ran her hand down his face, gingerly brushing her fingers over his bruised jaw.

"I love the sound of your laughter," he said, his lips caressing her eyelids, her cheeks, her chin. "I love your brilliant mind. I love the fanciful way you see the world. I love your courage. I love you. You're perfect."

She shivered. "Say it again." She moved closer until her lips barely touched his.

"You're perfect."

"No, the 'I love you' part."

"I love you."

She closed her eyes and released herself to his kiss. The chatter of pedestrians, the neighing of horses, and the rattle of the wheels sounded miles away as they held each other. Lost in a lull of Dashiell's embrace, she didn't know how much time had passed when the carriage stopped.

"We're here," Dashiell murmured. "Our little love nest."

She gave him a shy smile. "Is it bad of me to say

that I can't wait to touch you? To feel that amazing, quivering release when you caress me *down there*, to see the beautiful light in your eyes when you're moving inside me."

He raised a quizzical brow. "I don't know if they allow that here."

The groom opened the door, and in the dim gaslight, Vivienne could make out the brick and stained glass arched windows of Wesley Congregational Chapel.

"What? No!" She pushed against Dashiell's biceps. "I can't go in here. You're mad."

"Mr. Charles is waiting for you." Dashiell gestured to the minister who was hurrying across the courtyard, dressed in a dark evening robe. A brass lantern dangled from his hand.

"You told him!" Her face heated.

"I had your aunt send him a letter." He kissed her fingers. "Everyone was worried about you."

The minister, whom Vivienne had known since she was a tiny girl, gazed over Dashiell's shoulder. She was ashamed that he should see her this way. The edges of his eyes were crinkled with sympathy. "Come, my poor child," he said. "We have a warm chamber prepared for you."

"I'm sorry, Mr. Charles," she cried. "But I don't think I should stay here. So much has happened—"

"Nonsense, you need to rest," he insisted, beckoning her out of the carriage. "You're going to have a very busy day tomorrow."

Dashiell drew her close, pretending to arrange the blanket about her. In truth, he wanted to feel her again, one last time, before he carried her inside the church.

"First, I must have a word with her, alone," he told Mr. Charles. "In the chapel."

Dashiell lifted her in his arms again and trailed the minister up the steps. Inside, the chapel was dim except for the glow of the minister's lantern. Dashiell set her on the front pew and draped the blanket over her shoulders.

"Brother Lord Dashiell, I expect you know your duty," Mr. Charles said, as he placed the lantern below the altar. Its flame cast an orb of light that reflected off the gold and rich mahogany on the apse and stained glass windows. "I'll check back in a few minutes to make sure you do." He nipped through a side door to his connected home.

Then they were alone. Dashiell was nervous. He didn't know what to say. He had been too busy running about town, getting beaten up, sneaking into a brothel, and wearing women's clothes to think of the actual words of his proposal beyond "I'm a jingle-brained scoundrel. For the love of God, marry me."

He took a deep breath and did the customary thing: dropping to one knee, taking his beloved's hand. "My beautiful Miss Taylor, I have loved you since I first saw you." That sounded rather peculiar. "Well, not in the same way that I do now. My love was more innocent then, now it's… never mind, I'm digressing. I know I'm not worthy of your affection, but if you would take mercy on me and consent to be my wife, I would—"

"No."

He leaned in. "That's not the right answer, love."

"We can't get married. It is wrong. I'm not respect-able anymore. Can't I just be your mistress?"

He flung up his arms. "By God, Vivienne, I was ready to kill someone to get you free. I nearly got shot... again. I danced before all those men. And now you won't marry me! This is a direct violation of our Bazulo vow."

She jumped to her feet. "There is no Bazulo tribe in Africa. You made it all up."

"I did not," he said rising to meet her. "The third paragraph near the bottom of the eleventh page in very fine print states: If one member of the sacred vow is disgraced in the eyes of society, the other must marry said disgraced member."

She arched a brow and considered him. "Well then, I don't think I was disgraced. It's a matter of semantics."

"I was certainly disgraced. Didn't you see that angel ensemble I wore? And my exotic dance?"

Vivienne started to giggle, her back shaking.

"I've fallen from society because of you, and you must do the honorable thing by me and then hide me away in Egypt or Greece or Arabia or Africa."

"Stop being silly."

"I'm not being silly." He captured her hands in his and rubbed her knuckles with his thumbs. "This is an earnest question: Do you want to travel the world together, hand in hand, husband and wife?"

She nibbled the corner of her lip. He could see the debate behind her eyes.

"Tell me the truth," he gently prompted.

"It's all I've ever wanted," she admitted, her eyes glistening.

"Then say, 'Dashiell, you're marrying me. I'm dragging you around to all corners of the globe. We're going to have a passel of children who are just like us: wild and unruly. And we'll adore them. We won't keep any secrets from each other. And we'll be completely loyal, trusting, and in love with each other until death do us part. And death had better not come a'knockin' for a long, long time.'"

Tears now streamed down her face. "Marry me" was all she could manage before he swept her into his arms.

❧

Vivienne flashed Dashiell a mischievous smile as she gazed at the members of the Wesley Congregational filing into the church pews for the wedding.

"You aren't nervous, my darling?" he asked.

"Of course not," she said. "Are you?"

"Yes! This could be a terrible mistake."

"Now, you shouldn't worry about a thing," Mrs. Lacey said from the pew behind them. "I've heard reformed rakes make the best husbands. You wouldn't believe it, but my Walter was rather rumbustious in his day." She giggled, causing her white curls to dance. "Still is when I put on my—"

"Thank you," Vivienne said, keeping a straight face while Dashiell's lips trembled with silent laughter. They turned around to face the altar.

He leaned in. "I plan on getting rather rumbustious in our bedchamber tonight," he whispered in her ear, sending a tingling through her body.

Still, she gave him a sharp rib. "We are in a church!"

The clouds outside the massive stained glass windows drifted apart, and beautiful sunlight illuminated the chapel. Mr. Charles raised his prayer book and began to speak, his jowls quivering. "Dearly beloved, we are gathered together here in the sight of God and in the face of this congregation to join together this man and this woman in holy matrimony. A man whose sins were so numerous that many believed his soiled and sullied soul irrevocably lost to Satan. But through the miracle of God's love, the faith of an honorable woman, and the financing of the construction of the library wing, he hath found redemption."

Vivienne watched as her mother, the bride, gazed demurely into her fiancé's face, a lovely blush coloring her cheeks and a gentle smile lifting her lips. She no longer took her tonics and elixirs, finding true love to be the miracle cure for her pesky nerves. Her adored Lord Baswiche stood beside her, his jaw slack, his eyes shining with amour.

"They look like smitten adolescents," Vivienne whispered to her husband.

"That's because my grandfather's mind stopped maturing at age fifteen," Dashiell quipped.

"I remember not a year ago, we were standing before that very altar looking just as in love," she sighed, thinking back to that beautiful morning when Dashiell slid a Roman ring on her finger, how Vivienne had called her aunt "Mother" for the first time, and her mother called her "Daughter," the tears they shared, and then that evening when Dashiell showed her some of the many ways they could love each other: on the bed, across the desk, in the chair, against the wall, with silk ribbons and feathers.

"We've been married a year!" he murmured and winked. "It seems like an eternity."

She wrinkled her nose at him.

"And I relished every moment of that eternity, my love," he assured her.

"One year," Vivienne whispered, turning the ancient ring on her finger. The world she had left behind twelve months ago for Greece, Egypt, Africa, and Arabia had radically changed. Dashiell sold some stock to lend money to her father. Her father in turn received a huge order from a railroad that rivaled Mr. Montag's and paid Dashiell back, including some extra money that he claimed was Vivienne's dowry. The case of art theft never came to the courts. Mrs. Fontaine and Mr. Teakesbury accepted minimal sentences, their careers destroyed. Meanwhile, poor and powerless Mrs. Jenkinson was transported back to Australia. Vivienne understood that John, through mismanagement of funds, had lost his position and fled to Canada.

Now Vivienne and Dashiell were back in London and could scarce move through the house for all the crates of antiquities they had shipped home. In the evenings, they would gather in her mother's parlor where her mother would read to the earl from Songs of Solomon. "Let him kiss me with the kisses of his mouth, for their love is better than wine," and then the two would titter, causing Dashiell to make terrible faces at Vivienne and cough into his balled hand as if he might vomit.

Mr. Charles continued to thunder from the altar.

"I require and charge you both, as ye will answer at the dreadful Day of Judgment, when the secrets of all hearts shall be disclosed, that if either of you know any impediment why ye may not be lawfully joined together in matrimony, ye do now confess it."

Dashiell started to raise his hand to tease Vivienne. She clamped onto it, lacing her fingers through his and keeping them by her side. His touch always elicited a warm, melting sensation inside her.

"What about a sojourn to South America, love?" he whispered. "Leave the sickening love birds alone?"

"I'm afraid I might be otherwise engaged." She glanced coyly at him from the corner of her eyes.

When he arched a suspicious brow, she slid his palm over her belly. He blinked as the realization fell on him.

"You wanted a passel of wild and unruly children," she reminded him quietly.

"Yes, but… it's too soon." His eyes started to dart about as he grabbed his cravat. "I can't breathe. I can't think. I have… have to get away."

Members of the congregation turned to look as her husband tried to edge down the aisle, but Vivienne held him tight.

"I'll make a terrible father!"

Mr. Charles's head jerked up from his prayer book. "Brother Lord Dashiell, do you know of an impediment? I beg you to confess."

"Now, son, we talked about this," his grandfather said. "Trudie has already forgiven me for that—"

"He doesn't have an impediment," Vivienne quickly interjected. "I mean, none to their marriage."

She drew her husband back. "Calm down," she whispered in a soothing voice. His reaction didn't alarm her. After a year, she intimately knew the ebb and flow of his personality—the initial panic, followed by a shaky resignation, then whole-hearted exuberance. "You'll be a wonderful papa," she assured him. "It says so in the Bazulo vow in the third paragraph of the seventh page."

At the altar, Mr. Charles united the right hands of the groom and bride. "Those whom God hath joined together, let no man put asunder."

Acknowledgments

A heartfelt thank you goes to my critique partner and best writing friend, Catherine Scott/Catriona Iams. She holds my hand in the scary writing places and articulates my characters' struggles and desires, lighting the way through the hard scenes. Her wisdom and understanding of craft infuse these passages. I also would like to thank sage teacher and writer, David Fulmer, for believing in my work, teaching me the craft, and pushing me to become a better writer. I have so much gratitude for the brilliant Laura Valeri who sees to the heart of the literary problem. I sincerely thank Nancy Mayer for her generosity and patience in answering my numerous British history questions. To my wonderful agent, Paige Wheeler, for her professionalism and faith in my work. To my editor, Deb Werksman, whose guidance and vision for *Wicked Little Secrets* sent the story to greater heights than I could have achieved alone. And finally to Tina Whittle, who always has my back, Abigail Carlton, for the "fruity bits" and "nether regions," as well as Virginia Hall, Kevin Moreau, and Liz Fichera. It's been a wild, crazy journey.

About the Author

Susanna Ives started writing when she left her job as a multimedia training developer to stay home with her family. Now she keeps busy driving her children to various classes, writing books, and maintaining websites. She often follows her husband on business trips around Europe and blogs about the misadventures of touring with children. She lives in Atlanta.